DOUBLE ALCHEMY: CLIMAX

Susan Mac Nicol

A BLINDING LIGHT

It begins with a Book of Shadows discovered by a London coven. The grimoire is as dangerous as it is rare, which is why it evokes modern-day warlock Quinn Fairmont's desire. He collects objects of great power and beauty—like his lover, Cade Mairston.

Against all odds he and Cade found each other, but their perils have just begun. First is the ex-lover who once held Quinn in thrall. And, someone has been killing warlocks. Could it be one of their own kind? There are those too who would challenge Quinn's power in their quest to overthrow him as Grand Master. Or is the danger something darker, something invoked inadvertently, rising from the shadows, building from the very inside of a man until it brings an end with a quick flash of light? Of the truth, the surface has only been scratched. Now Quinn and Cade must go deeper and find both answers and an end. They must learn what lurks in the hearts of men…and whether it seeks to love or destroy.

DOUBLE ALCHEMY: CLIMAX

Susan Mac Nicol

www.BOROUGHSPUBLISHINGGROUP.com

DOUBLE ALCHEMY: CLIMAX
Copyright © 2014 Susan Elaine Mac Nicol

Digital edition created by Maureen Cutajar
www.gopublished.com

ISBN 978-1941260463

To all those people out there who believe in fairies. And witches and wizards. And trolls, goblins, Warlocks, the Loch Ness Monster, vampires, werewolves and the Yeti. Because without them passing down stories and spinning yarns about creatures that may or may not exist we wouldn't have the wealth of legend and out-of-this-world beings that make our lives so damned interesting. So, thanks to you all for being believers. Keep up the good work so we have something to pass down to future generations.

ACKNOWLEDGMENTS

As always, to my family who may roll their eyes when I wax lyrical about writing, gay man sex and the use of various implements and practices that shall not be named. They may not understand my obsession with this genre but they support it.

And again a huge thanks to my publisher, Boroughs Publishing Group, for their support through some rocky times I've had in the past year, their unfailing optimism that I am going to make it big and the gorgeous covers and inspirational blurbs that they create for me. I couldn't ask for anyone better to be in the proverbial writing marriage bed with.

And to my wonderful online friends once again, the ones who support, nurture, cheer, tease, advise and are downright bloody rude sometimes yet always manage to cheer me up and encourage me to keep going. Thank you; you have no idea just how much each and every one of you are appreciated in my life.

CONTENTS

DOUBLE ALCHEMY: CLIMAX

Prologue

Dead bodies were always bad form at coven meetings, and this one was no exception. Laura Claybourne looked helplessly at the body crumpled on the ground then stared around at the other members of her coven. Their fear and shock had rendered them mute.

Laura, a.k.a. High Priestess Misty Ravenbrook of the Ravenbrook Coven, was out of her depth. She'd never had someone die on her watch before, let alone so malevolently. Hells bells, she was going to have some explaining to do to the Praetorium.

Chapter 1

Quinn Fairmont, Warlock and current Grand Master of the Warlock Consortium, scowled deeply as he perused the report from his right-hand-man Percy Ballantyne. Apparently, some idiot witches had chanted something from an unknown Book of Shadows and in the process, killed one of their own. Quinn's frown grew even fiercer as he read further.

"Bloody hell," he muttered to himself. "When will these damn people learn you can't just go about chanting things when you don't know what they mean? Found someone else's Book of Shadows indeed. Honestly, they need their arses kicked." His frown turned to a slight grin. "I'll bet Valensia is one unhappy bitch right now and that woman's psycho at the best of times."

Valensia had been Quinn's last-ever female lover—and they bore an intense dislike of each other as a result of some rather sly trickery on Valensia's part. Quinn was not likely to ever forgive her for it.

You find it amusing that the witch is upset. I confess the idea brings me some measure of comfort as well.

Taliesin, Quinn's magyckal alter ego, a powerful sixth-century sorcerer, muttered in his head. The two men were intricately linked in time and body and shared memories, thoughts and emotions.

Quinn chuckled. Surprisingly, his Withinner had never liked the seductive Valensia, and Taliesin generally thought *any* woman, or man, was fair game.

"Will you never tell me the story behind your dislike, old friend?" Quinn said in amusement, as Taliesin stirred. "I'd love to find out why the great Sir Bonkalot can't bear this particular woman. I'd have thought she'd be a welcome addition as a string to your ever-upright bow."

The reason should not concern you. I simply cannot bear the wanton hussy.

"I sense jealousy there," Quinn murmured as he closed the file. "Better be careful or I'll start thinking you have some human emotions in you after all."

As the ultimate Warlock leader of the Consortium, Quinn prided himself on having one of the most extensive and knowledgeable networks of magyckal happenings, stories, mishaps and reported dangers and sightings. He had a varied network of people, Fey and human alike, feeding him information. Urgent matters were escalated directly to him, and magyck gone wrong and causing another's death was always high on Quinn's list of monitored activities.

He wondered, with his book acquisitor's keen curiosity, whose Book of Shadows it was that had been found. It must have been a very powerful person indeed to be able to cause an event such as the recent one and he'd really like to get his hands on it. His predatory propensity for collecting ancient and archaic texts came to the fore and for a minute, he wanted the book so badly, he would have been prepared to do anything within reason. But he definitely wasn't prepared to ask Valensia for it. That would be a disaster for them both.

Perhaps I can find another way to get it off her, via a third party—or maybe even steal the bloody thing.

He was pondering how he might manage this when he heard a noise at the front door and a soft murmuring as someone greeted the cat, Marco Polo. Quinn looked at his watch in surprise. Three p.m. He'd lost track of the time. Something he was good at doing when he worked. He smiled widely. His boyfriend, Cade, was home early, although it *was* Christmas Eve. He'd probably been given the afternoon off from the Institute of Anthropological Studies where he worked.

Quinn sighed, standing up and stretching his six-foot frame to get the kinks out of it. He'd been sitting at his desk for the better part of the day, and he had a burning need for some activity. He wondered to himself with a sly smile whether Cade was in the mood for some as well. He went onto the first floor landing to meet him. All thoughts of any lovemaking activity vanished when he saw his lover walking up the staircase.

Cade's face was pale and drawn, eyes deep sunken and red. His normally confident stride and demeanour had been replaced by something else entirely. Cade smiled at him faintly but Quinn knew something was wrong.

"God, what's wrong?" He moved to his lover swiftly, enveloping him in his arms at the top of the stairs. Cade leaned gratefully into Quinn's warm embrace, his soft dark hair tickling Quinn's face and his taut body pressing against his in an uncommon gesture of pure need.

"We had a tragedy at the Institute today." Cade worked as both a researcher and lecturer at the Institute for Archaeological Studies in Golders Green. He was a much-lauded member of the team there with his willing nature and expertise. "Do you remember me telling you about Graham?"

Quinn nodded, remembering the story of Graham Knox, one of Cade's associates, who'd lost his wife and son in a motor accident just over two weeks ago. Cade had been at the funeral.

"He killed himself this morning at his office in the Institute. He shot himself."

Quinn heard the catch in his lover's voice. Cade had been very fond of Graham, counting him as a friend as well as a colleague. Quinn had met him a few times at various office functions.

Quinn was horrified. "That's terrible. Was it because of the death of his family?"

Cade nodded and Quinn hugged him tighter, wishing he could take his obvious grief away. "He left a note saying he was sorry, but he couldn't face life without Kim and Eddie, especially with it being Christmas Eve. He said he couldn't face Christmas alone. I can't believe he's gone, Quinn."

Cade's voice was flat. Quinn knew he'd suffered tragedy in his life before and this latest death seemed to have hit him hard.

Quinn held him tight, feeling helpless in the face of his pain. "Why didn't you call me, you muppet? I'd have come and fetched you earlier from work," he murmured softly as he rubbed Cade's back in soft, soothing strokes.

Cade shrugged. "It was a total circus at the Institute and Ambrose really needed my help to keep things under control. Once everything was sorted, Ambrose told me to get home for the holiday and be with you."

Professor Ambrose Tickler Brown was Cade's boss at the Institute, an older man who thought the world of Cade and treated him like a son. Quinn held Cade closer, his arms encircling him protectively.

"Come on, let's go downstairs and sit in the lounge. I'll make you tea if you like. I'll try not to let it stew too long, I promise."

That elicited a small smile from Cade. Quinn's cooking and culinary skills were definitely below par. Quinn had never seen the point when there were plenty of eating establishments and takeaway outlets in the area that pandered to his every whim. His tea making tended to err on the side of pure tar as he constantly forgot to remove the bag, being easily distracted and getting caught up in anything else that took his fancy. Often were the times Cade had come looking for him only to find a cup of cold stewed tea and no Quinn as he disappeared to his study or the basement.

Cade's arms reluctantly uncurled from Quinn's waist and he followed him down the winding staircase to the ground floor of the house they shared in Hampstead Heath.

Quinn disappeared into the kitchen and left Cade on the couch staring at the lights on the five-foot Christmas tree in the bay window. Five minutes later he sat beside Cade as his boyfriend's hands cupped his tea, the contents of which Quinn thought looked fairly passable. Quinn stroked a wayward lock of hair off Cade's forehead. "So, tell me exactly what happened," he asked quietly. "I imagine the police came?"

Cade nodded. "Graham was in his office early this morning, and about ten o'clock his secretary heard this almighty bang, went rushing in and found him dead in his chair across his desk. He'd blown a hole right through the side of his head." He winced. "Needless to say, Greta, his PA, was hysterical, the whole place was in an uproar, and Ambrose managed to seal off the room before everyone went rushing in. He's very good that way, quiet and calm and just takes control. He handled the whole thing when the police arrived."

"I'm really sorry," Quinn said softly. "I know you thought a lot of him."

Cade's body shuddered in his arms. "It's the way of things, isn't it? We live, we die and we leave people behind who love us." Cade idly traced the seam of Quinn's chinos. "I'm just glad you've had no more near-death experiences. I don't think I could cope with another one."

Quinn chuckled. "I was contemplating having one earlier, actually."

Perhaps a little story would take Cade's mind off the tragedy.

Cade looked at him in puzzlement, his grey eyes worried.

Quinn grinned. "I got wind of a book that I really want." His eyes gleamed avariciously. "But it's with someone I really don't want to see, so it will be a definite battle of wills, possibly even to the death, to get it off her."

Cade glanced up at him, his curiosity overriding his grief. "Her? Who is this formidable lady who has my Warlock quivering in his boots? Or should I say his Ralph Lauren footwear?" He raised a suggestive eyebrow.

Quinn felt a little uncomfortable in that he'd opened his mouth to something he didn't really want to get into too much detail about, especially with Cade; his past relationship with Valensia. He glossed over his comment with a careless shrug.

"Oh, just a really difficult woman I know—knew," he amended hastily, cursing his slip. "Don't worry, I'll make a plan to get it one way or another."

Cade glanced at him from under furrowed brows. "I know you, mister. There's something you don't want to tell me about this woman." His eyes narrowed in suspicion and Quinn groaned inwardly.

Shit, here comes the third degree. I'm a stupid bastard, why didn't I keep my mouth shut?

"Is she a past girlfriend or something? You have that furtive look in your eye."

Quinn cursed Cade's unrelenting knack of noticing his tells. He sighed as Cade regarded him intensely.

"Yes and no," he said, his answer sounding feeble even to his own ears.

Cade sat back. "How can it be both? From the way you're acting, either she was and you bonked her, or she wasn't and you bonked her anyway."

"God, you have such a subtle way of putting things," Quinn muttered.

"Who the hell *is* this woman?" Cade asked.

Quinn drew a deep breath, knowing Cade the Inquisitive wouldn't let it go. "Valensia is her name."

Cade frowned. "Valensia who? Would I know her?"

Quinn shook his head. "Just Valensia. She, erm, doesn't have another name. I certainly doubt you'd know her," he remarked drily.

Cade glared at him. "Don't be silly. Everyone has a bloody surname."

"Not if they're the self-professed Queen of the Witches, they don't," muttered Quinn, knowing even as he said the words how ridiculous they sounded. Cade's mouth dropped open and Quinn had to smile at the complete look of disbelief on his face.

"The Queen of Witches? You *are* joking?"

Quinn shook his head in amusement. "No, Valensia is one of the most powerful witches in Britain. Through a fairly complicated and probably totally underhanded process, knowing her, she managed to become Regina—Queen—and has been ever since."

"And you relationship with her was what? My sexy Warlock King and this Queen of the Witches. Exactly what did you get up to?" Cade asked silkily.

Quinn felt himself flush. "We had a relationship, which turned out to be pretty one sided and very short lived."

"Go on." Cade's grey eyes regarded him appraisingly. "Tell me more." Cade was well aware that Quinn used to swing both ways. It had only been in the last six years he'd been man-exclusive.

"God, you're like a bloody pit bull!" Quinn said in frustration. "It was many years ago, I'd just turned thirty and Valensia was this young twenty-one-year-old woman. The sparks flew, and one thing led to another and to put it in your words, we bonked." He glared at him. "There, happy now?"

Hell. My ploy to take Cade's mind off things has turned into an inquisition for me instead.

"I don't see what's so one sided about that? It sounds pretty mutual to me. Even though I would have thought twenty-one was a little young for you at age thirty. Why did you split up?" Cade looked at him. Quinn flushed redder than before.

Cade gazed at him, his face quizzical. "You seem very embarrassed about something, baby. Your face keeps lighting up like a beacon. That's pretty unusual for you." He leaned forward and touched Quinn's leg, his hand travelling up toward his thigh teasingly. The tragedy of today seemed a little forgotten as they sparred.

"Valensia is half witch, half Fey," Quinn said between gritted teeth. "She had the same sort of attraction for me that you had. Once we'd gotten the first—urges—out of the way, we tried a proper relationship. It lasted six months and then," he hesitated, seeing Cade's silver eyes fixed on his face intently, "I told her I couldn't do it anymore. I realised that I was more into men and I had to be honest with her." He sighed. "She was also possessive and hard, and yes, too young for me. When I broke it off, she took it very personally. She wouldn't let me leave her house. She performed some sort of magyck that took me some time to break— three days in fact—and in the meantime I was imprisoned in her bedroom, on tap for whenever she fancied a bit. It was degrading and downright bloody exhausting." He scowled fiercely. "But she knew how to enhance her Fey side all right, with magyck, and it was fucking horrible being turned on and off like a bloody light switch!"

Cade's shoulders shook silently, his face hidden from view in Quinn's neck as he tried to contain his laughter.

"I'm glad you find it so funny, Cade," Quinn said smoothly, his eyes narrowing.

Cade chortled loudly as he lifted his face. Quinn saw mirthful tears in his boyfriend's eyes and he scowled as Cade shook his head in amusement. "God, the thought of you being some witch's sex slave is just too bloody precious! What a terrible ordeal for any man to have to endure!"

Quinn reached over lazily and pulled Cade toward him roughly, as his mouth found his. He was glad he'd made him laugh, even if it was at his expense. For a short time Cade had forgotten about Graham. Quinn kissed him thoroughly, his mouth demanding and hot, his hands already creeping inside Cade's button-down shirt and touching his midriff.

He heard Cade's low moan as his tongue sucked his and Cade's warm hands slid up over Quinn's broad shoulders and then entwined themselves into his hair. The sensation in Quinn's groin intensified as Cade's skilled hands moved down and untucked his shirt from his jeans then slid lazily over his stomach. For a moment both men were lost in the kiss and the feel of each other's skin. Finally Quinn removed his mouth from Cade's and they regarded each other, both breathing deeply.

Cade eyed him lasciviously. "Well, that made me feel a lot better. I can see why Valensia kept you locked up. I might try that trick myself with you, locking you in the bedroom."

Quinn reached down, trailing his fingers along the jawline stubble that was Cade's five o'clock shadow. "I don't think I'd mind that at all," he drawled. "Especially if you tie me up like last time. I liked that part. I liked tying you up too, so we'll definitely do that again sometime soon."

Cade snorted. "Last time we did that, we could hardly walk the next day. But it was fun." He leaned in and kissed him again, nibbling his bottom lip.

As Quinn reached for him again, Cade stood up swiftly with a laugh. "Hold your horses, stud, and those naughty thoughts. I really need to go pee. Perhaps you can open a bottle of wine and we can sit and enjoy each other a little." He smiled sadly. "I know

Graham's gone but we're still here and it's Christmas Eve. We need to forget all the bad stuff for a while."

He disappeared to the bathroom. Quinn needed no urging. He went over to the wine rack, drew out a bottle of red wine and proceeded to open it, pouring it into large wine glasses. He heard a plaintive "meow" below him and turned to see Marco Polo rubbing himself against his legs.

"Marco, where have you been all day then? I don't think I've seen you at all today."

He took the two glasses of wine over to the centre table, placing them down and picking up the remote control. With a few button presses, the curtains closed around the room, the lights dimmed and with another flick, the Bluetooth system switched on, linked to Quinn's mobile phone. The mellow tones of one of his favourite artists, Ben Howard, filled the room with sound. He looked around in satisfaction, happy that he'd set the right mood for a bit of 'enjoyment' with Cade. It all looked fairly festive and he'd rather be nowhere else than here with him now.

It might seem shallow, the two of them enjoying themselves when Graham and his family were dead, but Quinn was realistic. He knew better than most that the past couldn't be undone, that neither of them could change anything and that life itself needed to be celebrated. Especially on Christmas Eve. Quinn might not believe in the religion of the event but he knew Cade liked the tradition.

Quinn had just sat down and taken a sip of his wine when he felt a tickle in his nose. He looked down and swore. His nose was bleeding again, small drops that dripped onto his favourite Ralph Lauren work shirt. Nosebleeds appeared to have become an occupational hazard since he'd undergone Unity with his Withinner, had a hex put on him by a witch and undergone a major battle with an uber-Warlock. It was something he was learning to live with but his laundry pile seemed to be getting higher and higher each day.

He stood, making his way over to the kitchen and as he stood up, his vision blurred and a familiar nausea rose in his chest. Gagging, he barely made it to the ground floor bathroom before vomiting up what was left of the steak and ale pie he'd had earlier on. He hugged the toilet bowl, his head spinning and his spirits plummeting as he realised what was happening.

Somewhere in the city, a Warlock was dying.

Cade stood anxiously watching Quinn sitting on the closed toilet, his face pale, his head back, trying to stem the flow of blood from his nose. It hadn't abated since Cade had come down and found him being sick in the bathroom. The facecloth had once again been run under cold water and placed across the bridge of his nose.

"Are you feeling any better?" he asked quietly. Quinn suffered terribly when one of his own died and the resulting aftermath left him drained for days afterward.

Quinn nodded. "The sick feeling's gone. It's just this bloody nosebleed. I'm getting sick of this," he said fiercely, closing his eyes, his brow furrowed.

Cade laid a hand on his shoulder. "Do you think it's Jeremy Payton who's killed someone?" Jeremy Payton was the Witchfinder General, a psychopathic fifteen-year-old boy that Quinn had been tracking for the past two months. He was a real danger to Quinn's world. Jeremy had escaped the last battle Quinn had fought with him by literally disappearing into thin air.

Quinn sighed tiredly. "I don't know. Perhaps, but it could just be a simple death, if there is such a thing, by which I mean one not involving the Witchfinder. It was a violent death, I could sense it. But until we find out who died, we have no bloody idea. Perhaps

Percy can help when he calls." He frowned. "He's normally called by now. I wonder what's keeping him."

His words triggered a wash of dread in Cade. "Quinn, you don't think—"

Quinn forestalled him, shaking his head. "No, it won't be Percy that's died. If it was I'd feel much worse, believe me." His tone was grim. "Percy and I have shared blood, sweat and tears and I'd definitely know if something happened to him."

He reached up and removed the washcloth, lifting his head upright and gazing at Cade with shiny, black eyes. Cade gasped in awe. Quinn's pupils were so large the iris could hardly be seen, like someone in a vampire movie when their eyes became completely obsidian. It was an incredible sight, sexy but disturbing. Cade chided himself for having that thought even as he saw his lover suffering in front of him.

"What is it? You have a really strange look on your face." Quinn was looking at him with a worried expression.

"Your eyes, they've gone almost completely black again, like they did when I found you in the kitchen that time being hexed. You look demonic."

Quinn looked in the mirror and sighed. "I haven't seen this much reaction since the last incident in the kitchen. It makes everything look different for me, as if it's all lit up, like auras. It's been a lot more prevalent since the Unity with Taliesin."

He stood up, a little shaky, and threw the washcloth into the basin. "Don't worry, they'll go back to normal within a while. I'm not possessed or anything," He smiled tiredly. "Well, I am but it's only Taliesin. I promise my head won't go spinning around in the middle of the night."

He chuckled at Cade's apprehensive expression.

"I promise you I'm fine. I need to get upstairs and call Percy, see what's happening." Quinn shook his head as if trying to clear his thoughts and made his way out of the bathroom.

Cade picked up the blood-sodden washcloth, rinsed it out and popped it in the laundry hamper. He followed Quinn up the stairs, looking at his watch. Eight o'clock. He supposed that sexy get together they'd been planning on the couch was now a thing of the past. In truth, all he now wanted to do was get into bed and hope this day would never be revisited. God, what with friends shooting themselves and Quinn having a turn, it was turning out to be a really eventful evening. Probably best to just get into bed and read if he could concentrate. Quinn certainly wouldn't be coming to bed anytime soon. Once he got in his study talking to Percy, Cade would be lucky to see him before midnight.

Chapter 2

Quinn frowned as Percy's phone went to voice mail for the third time. He'd been calling every half an hour and still no word from his Marshall. That was very unlike him. The first tingling of dread caressed the back of Quinn's neck like the slow stroke of a lover. He'd even tried getting hold of Magnus, his other senior Marshall, as the two of them were often together, but Magnus's phone simply rang with no message. Quinn regarded his phone in frustration as he looked at his computer screen, the winking cursor seeming to mock him as it stayed put in place. Even his instant messaging service was having no success connecting to his team. He rubbed his eyes in exhaustion and took off his glasses to look at his watch. It was midnight so there was nothing much more he could do now—he might as well go to bed.

Quinn yawned, locking his computer screen, and stood up, stretching his tired limbs. As he looked out of the study window into the darkness outside, he saw a faint shadow by the lamppost directly across the street. Although he saw no one physical, he distinctly felt the presence of someone standing there. He blinked his eyes and rubbed them again. The shadow was still there and he got the eerie impression it was looking directly at him. It was very tall and thin. Quinn stood completely still, his eyes narrowed as he watched for any signs of movement. A car slowly drove past, obscuring his vision for a moment and when it finally passed, the shadow was gone. Quinn watched steadfastly for a few minutes until he was satisfied that there was definitely nothing in the surrounding area, before making his way to bed to curl up next to a warm and softly snoring Cade.

Quinn's phone rang at close to two a.m., just as he'd managed to fall into an uneasy sleep. Cade mumbled beside him and Quinn quickly picked up his phone, switching it to silent. He swung his legs out of bed, sitting naked on the side.

"Percy, where the fuck have you been? I've been calling you all night," he hissed angrily. "All I want is someone on my bloody team to tell me what the hell is going on!"

"I'm sorry. We had a young warlock who could make things disappear. He has no idea how he does it but this time it was me." Percy's voice was wry, his tone apologetic. "He has some strange new power with the ability to send people into some sort of limbo land. I had the devil of a time getting out of there and getting the others out as well."

"Has he been taken into custody until you can find out how the hell he does it? I don't want the silly blighter doing it to all and sundry. That would just be bad for us as a whole. We don't need any more bloody exposure." Quinn's voice was grim.

Percy sighed. "Yes, he's at one of the Consortium centres. They'll test him, see what's causing it. If we can repeat it it'll make a great parlour trick. Anyway, that's by the by. You'll want to know if we know anything about the Warlock death."

"That's exactly what I want to know."

"Nothing's surfaced yet. We're working on it."

"Well, step up the efforts. If someone's lying dead out there somewhere we owe it to them to find them and let their family know. Not to mention find out how they died and who did it. Has there been anything yet on Jeremy Payton?" Quinn rolled his shoulder as he sat, feeling the tenseness in it.

"No. It's as quiet as a nun. I'm not sure this death is the Witchfinder though. It just doesn't feel like him."

Quinn nodded. "I think the same. Keep me informed and let me know the minute you know anything. Oh, and in a couple of days I'm going down to visit that witch Misty Ravenbrook from the coven that had the death. I need to understand what the hell happened there. A Book of Shadows doing the rounds killing people is definitely something we need to look into."

"Not to mention that you wouldn't mind getting your greedy paws on it," Percy remarked in amusement. "I know you too well, Quinn."

Quinn scowled. "Yes, well, that's not fucking likely to happen if Valensia has it. But we need to figure out for ourselves what happened."

"I agree; it's a dangerous affair." Percy yawned. "God, I need some sleep after today. Quinn, go back to sleep, I'm sorry I woke you up so late. We'll catch up tomorrow then?" Percy rang off.

Quinn sat in quiet contemplation for a minute until the bed shifted and a warm form come up behind up and begin to massage his shoulders. He groaned in satisfaction. "God, that feels good. I'm sorry I woke you."

"It's okay, I'm getting used to it." Cade's warm breath brushed his ear and the quick darting of his tongue inside it made Quinn shiver. He groaned in pleasure as goose bumps formed on his bare skin. Cade's strong hands dug into his shoulder muscles, getting to the rigid muscles beneath and Quinn winced as he unknotted them.

"You could do this for a living, you know that? Anyone would love to be man- handled by you and those hands of yours." He grinned as Cade's warm breath ghosted against his back, and he smelt the warm male fragrance of him in his nostrils.

"Are you pimping me out like a damn rent boy?" Cade whispered in his ear. "Because I have to say you might not like it when I take it seriously and find someone else with a good, strong body, and a large—""

His boyfriend's words were cut off as Quinn growled deep in his throat and turned round swiftly to take his mouth in a passionate kiss, his lips pressing against Cade's, feeling his lips part and a wet, needy tongue slip into his mouth. He pushed Cade back on the bed, seeing desire for him in his eyes, hearing his breathing grow quicker as he covered his lover's strong body with his. He loved the warm strength of Cade's stomach against his, and the strong legs that scissored between his, twining like snakes against his heated skin. He gasped as Cade's hands slid down his backside, stroking his buttocks as Cade pressed himself against Quinn urgently.

"God, you always feel so good," Cade groaned. "I love your body, you know that? Every single muscle, every bit of skin, every warm place no one else can feel but me."

They kissed, tossing about on the bed amongst the rumpled sheets, hands touching skin wherever they could find it, warm, soft strokes leading to more urgent movements as passions grew more intense. Quinn slid his fingers down Cade's shaft, hearing his moan of pleasure as he stroked him firmly, already slick and warm along his cock. Cade twisted beneath him as Quinn rubbed his own needy dick against his strongly muscled thigh. His groin tingled with heat and lust.

Cade moaned. "Don't stop, just keep going. Your fingers are so good at doing this. You make me so fucking horny."

His soft pants of passion echoed in Quinn's ear and it made him want to immerse himself inside Cade, slide into that velvety passage that was his and his alone. Quinn knew Cade's body well, knew just when to increase and decrease the pressure enough to drive him crazy with want. He brought Cade to the edge of orgasm then stopped. Quinn loved his moans of frustration as he teased him, his fingers knowing exactly when to cease their movements and start again, leaving him moaning deeply in his ear.

"You're killing me, you bastard," Cade gasped. "Please finish it."

"I'll finish when I'm ready," Quinn whispered, his tongue darting in Cade's ear. But he knew he couldn't keep it up much longer anyway. He needed to get inside Cade, find his own release. Quinn took pity on the body writhing beneath him and increased the pressure on Cade's cock, feeling his body tense beneath his, revelling in the moaning in his ear. Cade came with a shout, warm fluid coating Quinn's hands. His hand tightened on Quinn's hips as Cade shuddered in release beneath him. Quinn rose smiling above his sweaty lover, mouth biting down on Cade's shoulder, eliciting a hiss of both pain and pleasure.

"Forget any foreplay," Cade hissed. "Just want to feel you inside me, I can take it. Hell, I think my arsehole has an automatic release valve when it comes to your cock."

Quinn suppressed a laugh as he thrust into Cade. His mouth found his, greedy and insistent, his tongue making love to the other in its passion. Not for the first time, Quinn marvelled at how this man made him feel, as if he was the only thing that mattered, Cade's all-encompassing possession of him something to be cherished. Cade was heat and passion, velvet and steel, and Quinn gasped as he climaxed, that feeling of extreme pressure and unbearably intense heat flooding though his groin, his hips, up his spine. He exploded in a rush of heat and wetness that made him cry out. Cade held his shuddering body tight to his, his hands keeping Quinn inside him until he was totally spent and breathless on top of him. Quinn grinned against Cade's sweaty neck. "I thought you were trying to sleep. Not that I'm complaining of course. I needed that after tonight. You too, from the feel of you." He rolled off to lie beside him.

Cade chuckled quietly. "I always need that where you're concerned. And I have to say I'm pretty turned on by those black eyes of yours. I find it very sexy."

"I'll have to try and do it more often then," Quinn murmured softly, rolling off Cade's warm body, his eyes half closed. "The bugger is I don't know what causes it or how to induce it. I remember it happened once when I was in school; I was about ten years old. The teacher even called the school preacher because she thought I was possessed by something. It took Daniel all his influence to convince them it was some sort of genetic family trait." He grinned in the darkness. "It was great, though, because I convinced all my friends I was some sort of anti-Christ and they towed the line for a long time after that. I got free lunches and some of their pocket money."

Cade laughed quietly. "God, you were quite a bully and a conman, weren't you? Little Quinn Fairmont, devil incarnate. I can really see that."

Quinn snorted. "I was a little bit of a terror. Daniel and Moira really had their hands full with me. It made for very interesting times, I can tell you." He turned over his side and Cade spooned himself against him, arms around his waist. Neither of them worried about wet spots or mess, content to wash sheets regularly and be damned.

Quinn reached up and placed his hand on his. "Good night," he mumbled, already half asleep.

Cade nodded sleepily. "Night. Try not to have any bad dreams tonight. Think of fluffy bunnies and naked men or Santa Claus in your mind."

"Only naked man I want to think of is you. Bunnies can actually be quite terrifying if you know what I know about them, and Santa Claus gives me the creeps so I'll stick with just you in a sexy elf costume."

Cade kissed Quinn's shoulder gently as he fell asleep.

Cade awoke before Quinn the next morning and slipped quietly out of bed, leaving him still sleeping. Quinn was swaddled in blankets with just the top of his tousled blond head showing. Christmas Day to Cade was something special. Not for any religious reason. He remembered the times he'd spent with first his dad and then Sally before they were taken from him. Christmas had always been a family event, full of great food, laughter and watching reruns of bad programmes on television. Quinn didn't do Christmas. He'd been fairly apathetic about it in the run up to the festive season, saying it was just an excuse for commercialism to rear its capitalist head. He hadn't talked about it much, seeming fairly reticent about the whole prospect, although Cade knew he'd bought Christmas presents for him and Daniel and work friends. They were all scattered under the tree, beautifully wrapped, and he just knew Quinn hadn't done the wrapping. Cade had painstakingly wrapped each of his presents himself, a job he took both pride and a certain satisfaction in. His presents to friends had already been duly distributed, apart from Quinn's, which lay under the tree.

Cade had bought him a new suede jacket as his old one had been ruined in his fight with Andrew de Vere. Burning energy bursts were definitely not recommended for items of clothing. As far as he knew, Quinn planned on giving his presents out as people popped in to say hello. He wasn't a particularly forward planner when it came to this sort of thing—birthdays and other seasonal occasions seemed to pass right by him.

Cade had to admit that Quinn had very much remembered his birthday on the seventeenth of November, though, planning both a late dinner, a moonlight trot around the Heath in a horse and carriage and a very inventive lovemaking session when they finally got home.

Quinn's birthday present had been a beautiful leather satchel with his initials on it, with a Mont Blanc pen and pencil set similarly engraved. Cade hadn't been sure about the whole 'man bag' idea, but now he didn't know what he'd do without it.

This year, Cade had managed to convince Quinn that the least he could do was enjoy a Christmas dinner together at a rather upmarket local restaurant. Other than that, neither of them had any other plans for Christmas Day other than perhaps curling up together in front of a warm and crackling fire and perhaps getting merry on gluhwein and red wine. The sexual calisthenics Cade planned were also most definitely on the docket. He made coffee for them both, taking it back to bed. When he walked back into the bedroom, Quinn was sitting up against the headboard, covers over his waist, talking on his mobile.

Quinn waved to Cade as he came in and pointed at his phone. "Percy," he mouthed. "I won't be a minute, I promise."

Quinn had a feeling Cade wouldn't approve of business calls on Christmas morning, King of the Warlocks or not. Silver eyes regarded him with censure as Cade shook his head at him in mock disapproval. He placed their coffees on his bedside table and crawled back under the covers. Cade reached over under the blanket and caressed Quinn's hip, his hand slowly travelling down to Quinn's groin and Quinn grinned, reaching down a hand and holding Cade's in a firm grip away from his nether regions.

"Behave, you man slut," he whispered as he held the phone away from his mouth. He watched with some apprehension as Cade blithely ignored him and disappeared under the covers. Quinn tried frantically to stop that hot, wet mouth going where he thought it was going and twisted around with acrobatic flair, trying in vain to listen to his Marshall on the mobile.

"Send me all the details you can about that Book of Shadows. Use your contacts to try and see if there's any inscription or anything that will help me identify—fuck! "

His words broke off suddenly as his efforts to prohibit Cade from his intentions were unsuccessful. Below the blanket, Cade took him in his mouth, causing extremely sensitive sensations and Quinn almost dropped the phone as his hips curved upward, his eyes closing in sheer satisfaction.

"Percy, I'm going to have to call you back. Something's come up," he said in a strangled voice and disconnected the mobile, leaning back against the headboard as Cade's lips and tongue became even more active. "Cade, as much as I love what you're doing, I wish you'd let me finish my bloody conversations…"

His voice trailed off once again as Cade's hands stroked him softly in that sensitive place in between his legs, midway to groin and his backside, and he groaned loudly. His hands crept under the covers and buried themselves in Cade's hair, twisting the strands between his fingers as he held Cade's head in place, not wanting him to do anything other than what he was doing now.

"Hell, that feels incredible, just keep going…"

Cade's lips tightened around him. For the next few minutes, Quinn gasped at the sensations he was causing with his warm, wet mouth and busy tongue. His groin finally exploded in a series of mini eruptions as he came in Cade's mouth, feeling his lover licking up every drop. Finally Quinn lay spent, his eyes closed in sheer bliss as Cade crawled up from the covers with a smile, licking his lips.

"Merry Christmas," he murmured, kissing him deeply, and Quinn tasted his own semen on his mouth. He pulled Cade to him, his tongue entwining with his as he lay across him. Finally they came up for air and Cade snuggled into his shoulder. "I thought I'd give you an early present."

"You could have waited for me to put the phone down," Quinn murmured, his eyes twinkling. "I'm sure Percy knew exactly what had come up from the chuckle he gave just before I put the phone down. I'll never live it down with him."

He leered at Cade. "Do you want me to return the favour? I'm more than happy to reciprocate."

Cade's eyes darkened into smoky pools of grey filled with desire. "I wouldn't say no…"

Quinn looked at him and grinned. "I think I would be remiss if I didn't give you what you've just given me."

Cade sighed in contentment as Quinn disappeared under the covers. Later they lay cuddled together, both satiated and ready for a shower.

"I can get used to this Christmas morning tradition of giving presents in bed." Quinn drawled lazily as his hands threaded through Cade's hair. Cade loved the feel of those warm hands running through it. "What else have you got planned for today?"

"Just you, me, lunch, then a roaring fire, watching old movies on TV and drinking a lot of gluhwein." Cade chuckled as he stroked Quinn's stomach idly, running his fingers along a jagged scar. "It's freezing outside. The weather forecast says it might snow and if it does, I definitely plan on making snow angels with you in the garden."

Quinn smiled at him. "That isn't a euphemism for something, is it? You do mean make snow angels? I have no desire to be ravaged in the garden at minus one degree. All my bits will freeze and fall off."

Cade laughed. "No, I promise I won't ravish you in the snow. In front of the fire later, definitely. That's a given."

Quinn kissed the top of his head. "I look forward to that bit, then." Quinn sat up and swung his legs out of bed, as he stood up and stretched. "Shower time." He padded through to the bathroom as Cade watched the taut muscles of his backside admiringly.

Cade lay back in bed with a satisfied sigh, watching as Marco Polo jumped up onto the bed. "Surely Christmas Day couldn't get any better, Marco. A good man, early-morning sex and a whole day together in front of a real fire. Sheer bliss, kitty, sheer bliss."

His face darkened as he remembered the people who wouldn't be enjoying any Christmas this year or any other. Cade felt a deep sense of sadness when he thought of Graham and his family. The only consolation he had was that he hoped that somewhere, somehow, they were all together again.

Chapter 3

Christmas had come and gone and the New Year was now just a distant memory. Both Cade and Quinn were back to work harder than ever, their paths crossing morning and evenings. Quinn's responsibilities kept him even busier than before. With Graham's death, Cade had found himself taking on extra responsibilities and he was now teaching more classes. Their life together had grown into some sort of pattern and their few months living together had started to feel comfortable. Quinn loved coming home to Cade's welcoming embrace and warm body.

Quinn's best friend and business partner, Jomo Onyango, was back at work with QuinnCo. After the events of last year, when Jomo had been attacked and badly injured in Quinn's house, Quinn had convinced his friend to work from his own home when he could. It worked well as Jomo's girlfriend, Ulinda, had moved in with him. Jomo now worked one day a week with Quinn from Quinn's home and the rest of their time together was spent on Skype communicating where necessary. Quinn had more time to do his Warlock business in private as he became more and more involved at the Consortium. He definitely missed his friend's company and wise words but deep down inside, he knew it was the only way to keep him safer. He had Cade to worry about now as well.

Quinn was currently seated at a large, round table in a dimly lit but very sumptuous hall, surrounded by some of his Marshalls at the Annual Consortium Dinner in the middle of rural Kent. The hall was set within a dome of magyck to prevent outside influences. It was a necessary evil, a get-together of some of the most powerful Warlocks in the country, even the world.

As Grand Master, Quinn was honour bound to be there. He didn't really feel like it tonight. He'd had a fairly rough day visiting and commiserating with a family about the death of their son, the Warlock who'd died on Christmas Eve, which had caused Quinn's recent reaction. Russell Pinkerton had been hit by a truck on the M25, his car dragged under the vehicle for the best part of a mile. There had been very little to identify and healing by his Withinner had been out of the question. The young twenty-five-year-old teaching assistant had stood no chance.

These dinners generally lapsed into talk about the Witchhunters Alliance, the best way to fight it and of course the most discussed topic in hand currently: the hunt for the Witchfinder General and Quinn's failure to find him after having him so closely in his sights. Quinn's current nemesis, James Barton Sinclair, sat opposite him at the table, his rheumy green eyes in his florid face, his wine glass empty again as he gestured arrogantly to a passing waiter to fill it up for what Quinn thought was about the tenth time.

Barton Sinclair looked at him with a sceptical expression. "So, Quinn, I understand you told everyone that the Warlock you killed—again—had two Withinners? I must confess I find that a tad difficult to believe. I've never even heard of such a thing. Are you sure you weren't mistaken?"

Quinn regarded James thoughtfully. "I saw them both leave his body. I can assure you I wasn't seeing double."

"But you were hurt? Everyone knows the mind can play tricks on itself when the body is weak."

Quinn toyed with his whisky glass, his bad temper level increasing exponentially with every flick of Barton Sinclair's fleshy pink tongue on his lips as he licked off wine with hedonistic enjoyment. "Yes, I was hurt. But I know what I saw." He raised his eyes, meeting Barton Sinclair's with an unflinching icy topaz gaze.

The other man shrugged. "Perhaps but I have to say I still think something else was at play. Perhaps a trick of the light, or a desire to find an excuse so one can say one *was* actually fighting against all odds." He smiled, the gesture not reaching his eyes. "I imagine you count yourself lucky that you did win that battle. The alternative—losing—would have been quite a humbling experience for a Fairmont." His voice was sneering.

The man is a buffoon. Can you not simply stick a knife in his ribs one night and toss his fat carcass into a river? If you invoke me, I will do it for you. No one can arrest me for his demise.

Taliesin was definitely not happy with the turn of events and Quinn held down a chuckle at his Withinner's words.

Old friend, as much as that holds a great attraction for me, I'm afraid it's not quite the way to go. He'll get his comeuppance one day, I promise you.

Percy Ballantyne, Quinn's right-hand man in the Consortium, shifted at Quinn's side and his face darkened at James's words. He looked at Quinn with a frown and Quinn shook his head almost imperceptibly at him as Quinn regarded the West Country Marshall with a flinty stare.

Time for payback.

"James, sometimes I believe you think you are beyond all the necessary niceties to make sure someone stays on your side. I have to say it sounds like a fairly short-sighted approach." Quinn looked down into his whisky glass. He was going to enjoy this next bit. "I understood from Percy that you'd put in an application for some funds from QuinnCo to re-build your current home after a bad storm and a landslide? Normally I wouldn't countenance such a thing but as your house also doubles as a centre for bullied youngsters and a community meeting place, I was fairly disposed to grant you the quarter million pounds you said you needed. But it appears my generosity might have been too—how shall I say this—quickly predisposed toward a positive outcome."

He glanced mildly at Barton Sinclair, whose face had paled at Quinn's words. Quinn knew Barton Sinclair was in dire need of those funds and the Grand Master leaned forward, his face hard.

"Whilst you and I can agree to disagree on matters of Warlock concern, such as how we would both manage the Alliance, without it affecting anything else that may be connected, the one thing I won't tolerate are personal slurs or inferences that I manufactured a story to protect my own skin. I tend to get rather tetchy about things like that."

The others around the table hid their grins at Quinn's words. Barton Sinclair was not a man well liked by anyone and Quinn hid a small smile of his own as the other man scowled fiercely and tried to regain his composure.

"That wasn't what I meant at all. I'm sorry if I said something to offend you. I assure you it was not intentional." The man's bluster and attempt at digging himself out of a hole he'd created gave Quinn a sense of distaste.

He nodded. "Glad to hear it. I'll let you know the decision about the grant next week when I get back into the office." He leaned back and sipped his whisky, the ire he'd felt dissipating slowly. Percy winked at him and Quinn grinned.

But Barton Sinclair wasn't ready to give up to easily. "I imagine I can ask about the progress of the Witchfinder General hunt without being…misconstrued?" His tone was sarcastic.

Quinn waved his glass at him. "Go ahead. I'm sure Percy can fill you in on what's been going on."

Percy leaned forward. "Since August until now, we've had thousands of people, Fey and humans alike, keeping an eye out for Jeremy Payton. He's gone to ground so deeply we haven't been able to find him. We get leads and follow them up but I think I can safely say not one of them has been an actual sighting or magyckal happening to do with the Witchfinder. It's as if he's disappeared into the ether. There have also been no specific Warlock murders attributed to him either. At least on that side it's a positive thing. Based on Quinn's last assessment of him, when he was on de Vere's yacht, there was definitely something different about Jeremy Payton and his powers. For a man to simply dissolve like he did, that means very powerful magyck."

Barton Sinclair leaned back comfortably in his seat, regarding everyone around the table with mock surprise. "Well, that's another thing. This so-called *increase* in his powers, how do we think that could have come about? Has anyone formulated any theory on it?"

His tone was gloating. The hairs on Quinn's neck stood up as once again the thick-skinned Barton Sinclair made it sound as if Quinn was exaggerating or worse, lying about his encounter with Jeremy and Andrew de Vere. Percy smoothly forestalled anything Quinn was about to do, something Quinn was fairly glad about as he wasn't sure just how he would have managed his rising temper.

"We *do* actually have a theory, Barton Sinclair," Percy said bitingly. Quinn was a little nonplussed by Percy's comment. If there was a theory, he hadn't heard it from his Marshall himself yet.

Percy continued as he cast an exasperated look in Barton Sinclair's direction. "The people doing the research say the only way that a Witchfinder General could gain powers of that nature is by channelling the actual Witchfinder General himself."

Barton Sinclair spluttered as his wine spat out of his mouth, spattering the man next to him with red droplets. The unfortunate recipient of the contents of Barton Sinclair's mouth glared at him fiercely. James Barton Sinclair ignored him.

"That's the biggest load of poppycock I've ever heard!" His broad West Country voice echoed out across the room, causing people to turn and stare curiously at their table. Quinn sighed in exasperation at the attention they were getting as Barton Sinclair continued his tirade. He was perturbed at Percy's words too and more than a little irate that this was the first time he was hearing them. Taliesin stirred inside, his faint mutterings making no sense and it was distracting.

Sorcerer, shut the hell up. I'm trying to bloody concentrate!

"Have your teams nothing better to do than come up with half-baked ideas like that?" Barton Sinclair expostulated angrily. "I've never heard such a load of cock and bull in my life. Channelling the actual Matthew Hopkins who's been dead close on five centuries? That's the best anyone can come up with?"

Quinn sat forward, his eyes glinting, his hands clenched on the white tablecloth in front of him. "I can assure you, if that's what Percy's telling you, it's probably the best idea we have. I have complete faith in him and his team." Percy looked at him a little worriedly, and Quinn saw the unspoken guilt in his eyes. His Marshall knew he was in trouble for blurting out something he hadn't told Quinn about in advance and something Quinn was now putting his head on a block for.

"The idea is not as fantastical as you may believe. There have been numerous stories based on factual research about the reincarnation of Matthew Hopkins throughout the centuries: Neville Chalminster's 'Rise of the Demon' written in 1932, and Lucas Brevier's 'Witchfinder Reinstated' from the late 1960s. They were both highly regarded Warlock historians and occultists and they both had some quite clear evidence that it might not be as farfetched as we think."

Percy nodded in relief at Quinn's quick comeback, leading Quinn to thank the stars that his passion for book collecting led him to be a constant researcher in both paranormal and supernatural oddities.

"So the idea may not be as absurd as you think. Percy and his team are still investigating and I'm sure that when he has more to share, he will do so." He glared at Percy and Percy nodded, looking chagrined.

Later, out of earshot of anyone else, Quinn rounded on Percy, his face thunderous. "Fucking hell, Percy, don't ever do that to me again! How could you have come out with something like that without at least telling me first? That bloody tosser Barton Sinclair could have had me by the short and curlies."

Percy sighed, his face mutinous. "He was just being such a prick. I couldn't let him talk to you the way he was doing. He's such an arsehole, with that supercilious tone. It just slipped out. I was going to tell you after the dinner."

Quinn shook his head in frustration. "I appreciate the sentiment, but I think I can handle that jackass myself. Now tell me about this theory you have."

The two men were sitting in a small, private room in the conference facility, enjoying coffee and in Percy's case, a cigar. He puffed away in enjoyment as Quinn watched him, amused. "I will never understand your predilection to those bloody things. How can you take all those poisons into your body?"

Percy shook his head sagely. "If you have to ask a man why he smokes a cigar, then there's nothing more about it that I can explain to you." He chuckled and leaned back in his armchair. "There's an ancient text circa 1890 about a possible reincarnation of the Witchfinder General into a Warlock called Montague Druitt. He was a barrister, reputed to be a sexual deviant of some sort and also implicated in the Jack the Ripper murders. There is a lot of speculation, and the details are not clear, but it appears that he found an old Book of Shadows and tried out some of the spells in there and accidentally conjured up the spirit of Hopkins." He frowned. "Why does this story sound so familiar? Anyway, no one really knows what happened, but for a while it appeared that Druitt was able to do things he'd never done before. Unfortunately he was found floating in a river when he was thirty-one years old, his pockets weighted down with stones. It was never determined whether it was a suicide or someone decided to get rid of him."

Quinn listened in fascination. "We have this ancient text? I can't say I've heard of it before. I'll have to take a look at it." He felt the usual stirrings of greed to possess this manuscript. Taliesin sounded excited when he spoke.

I have seen it. It is as your Marshall has said. Druitt was a very complex character, his ending fairly strange.

Percy nodded. "Yes, it's in the Reponosium, along with other documents that seem to bear out the fact that something evil had occurred with Druitt. Some think he was killed for being a witch—hence the pocket full of stones and the whole drowning thing."

The back of Quinn's neck tingled and he leaned forward, his face alight with a sudden clarity. "The reason you feel the story is familiar is because we heard one very like it only a few weeks ago. The Book of Shadows found in Suffolk by that coven, where one of their witches was killed, the one Valensia now has. What if there's a connection? Perhaps that spell book was responsible for whatever is making Jeremy Payton stronger. If they can do one spell, they might have done another one before."

Percy's face was stunned with the implication. "You're right." He looked at Quinn a little guiltily. "I've not managed to find out much about it yet. Valensia is really keeping it under wraps and with the way she is, no one really wants to ask her about it." He coughed slightly. "Now, if it was you asking—"

Quinn shook his head vehemently. "No fucking way, I'm not going anywhere near that woman. You know what she did to me last time. That woman has no idea what the word 'no' means."

Percy barely kept the smirk off his face and Quinn glared at him. Taliesin sniggered deep inside, a laugh mixed with some other emotion Quinn was unsure of.

"Yes, I'm aware of the horrible fate worse than death that you experienced as her sex toy." Percy chuckled at the narrowed eyes and fierce frown of his Grand Master. "But she'll talk to you and perhaps this time you can be forewarned, so you don't get...*imprisoned*...again."

Quinn still shook his head. "No bloody way, not unless it's a last resort. And I mean last. In fact, that High Priestess who was there at the time the witch died... I'll go see her first, see if she can tell me anything more than she already has. Perhaps there might be a clue there we can follow up. They may have performed some spell before this one and I might be able to see if there's any connection."

Percy nodded. "I'll do that. But you know that one day you'll have to find a way to get that book from her. There's no way around it."

"Yes, well, that's a maybe. I still think we should get someone to steal it."

His Marshall sighed. "No one will go near her. I can't find a talented thief brave enough to take on Valensia's wrath. You know you're the only one who can convince her to hand it over."

"But at what bloody cost?" Quinn muttered. "Death by sex? My sanity? Losing Cade? It's not an option. Let's see what the coven leader has to say first before you even think of prostituting me for the cause." He chuckled grimly. "God, I hope to hell Cade never hears me saying something like that. He'd give me such a boxing that my ears would ring for a week."

Percy laughed softly. "That he would." He looked at Quinn slyly. "Talking of Cade, it's probably about time you made your way home. I'm sure something might come up again if you got home early enough."

Quinn flushed as he glowered at Percy, who kept a straight face.

"You think you're so bloody funny, don't you?" Quinn said, grinning slightly. "Just because you don't get enough at home, don't begrudge me mine."

Percy shrugged his shoulders. "After nearly ten years, my wife and I still have great sex. Just not with each other." He smiled wickedly. Having heard this comment from his friend before, Quinn was never quite sure whether Percy was joking or not.

Ten minutes later he was home, having invoked his Withinner to make the journey, but feeling a little green with the time travel. The house was dark, with only the dim wall sconces giving off a glow as he walked up the spiral staircase to the bedroom. It was past midnight and he was sure Cade would be sleeping. He tried to be quiet as he undressed then went into the bathroom to brush his teeth. He slid into bed and pulled the covers up over his waist as he turned over his side to face him.

Cade was still breathing steadily as he slept on his side turned away from Quinn. He reached out a hand, softly brushing Cade's hair with his fingers, hearing his low, sleepy mutter. He leaned in and kissed the back of his head.

"Good night, baby," he whispered before he too settled into sleep.

Chapter 4

Cade's strong arms powered through the pond. As it was early January, the water was freezing and there were only a few swimmers hardy enough to take the plunge. Cade was oblivious to them as he swam through the murky water, his attention fully focused on reaching his goal: a bobbing buoy in the middle of the pond surrounded by ducks. Cade's breathing was even as his strong legs propelled him forward in the water.

This was his release, to swim, out of the insidious grip of everyday life with its complications and emotions. The water offered a solace seldom felt, a place to forget everything and simply concentrate on the physical activity of staying afloat. It was his haven.

He reached the buoy and touched it, feeling a surge of triumph that he'd made it. He wiped water from his eyes and turned to wave at the shore where Quinn sat watching him. He refused to get into the water at these temperatures, saying drily Cade had an advantage with his Feyness and there was no way Quinn was risking frostbite with his extremities. He'd drawled lazily that would do neither of them any good for their sex life, a sentiment Cade had to agree with.

He bobbed around in the middle of the pond for a while, gazing around in pleasure at the trees and the foliage that surrounded the water, the tranquility and other worldliness of the area adding to its attraction. Then he sighed and took a few deep breaths, preparing for the swim back. Something brushed his foot and he moved it swiftly. He hoped it wasn't a pike. The other fish he could put up with, but pike with their sharp teeth scared the hell out of him. He kicked out, feeling movement below him. The water was dark and he saw nothing. Cade turned and started his swim back. He'd only gone a few strides when something brushed against his side. Startled, he reached a hand into the water and shooed whatever it was away. It came back, insistently, stroking his side and Cade shivered. It felt too large to be a fish. Cade stopped swimming and held himself in place treading water. He saw ripples around him as the thing circled.

"Bugger off, you poxy fish," he muttered, "Go back home and leave me be. Haven't you got a dinner plate you need to be on?"

As he swam back to shore, the presence followed him at a distance. Cade's strokes grew stronger as he tried to out-swim it, but it kept up easily, simply increasing its pace. He'd never felt anything like this before. If he'd been in the sea, he'd have thought it was a dolphin or similar, as the waves the thing was now causing got larger.

He gave a muffled salty curse as something grabbed his foot, a hand pulling him, softly, insistently, down into the water. He tried not to panic. His arms flailed above the water in an effort to resist whatever was dragging him into the murky depths, but finally, he was fully submerged in the dark brown depths of the lake. He tried to calm his beating heart and hold his breath. As his eyes grew accustomed to the murk, he saw a faint outline below, something definitely un-fishlike. It looked human and now terror rose in his aching chest. His lungs were burning. His hands and arms swept violently around his body as he tried to free himself. As he did, he heard faint hissing in the water, whispers that assailed his water-submerged ears, sounds that made no sense.

"Ella dimis zimus. Ella dimis zimus."

Cade was truly panicking now, not only at the fact that he'd been underwater a while but that his lungs weren't as overtaxed as they had been. His chest seemed lighter and he had an overwhelming urge to breathe the water in. Something resonated in his being, a little voice telling him to let go. It freaked him out because he knew if he did that, he would die. Instead he closed his eyes and made a last-ditch effort to break free and reach the surface. He would never know where the words came from, or even what they meant, but he heard himself shouting them in the water.

"*Asé nomo de figo, asé nomo de figo*!" As he repeated it for the second time, he was released and shot up toward the surface, taking a deep and heaving breath as he reached air.

*****

Sitting on the bank, with his coat around his shoulders, Quinn wondered, not for the first time, how this man of his managed to find the stamina to swim in the freezing depths of the heath pond. He shivered. He knew Cade loved the water, but short of someone throwing Quinn in kicking and screaming like a girl, nothing would induce him to join him. He watched Cade reach the buoy and turn and wave, then saw him begin the swim back. Quinn frowned now as he looked out across the expanse of water. Cade seemed to have disappeared. Quinn supposed he might have thought swimming under the water was the way to go, but he didn't think the murky colour was quite conducive to that. He watched anxiously for a sign of him. Cade was a formidable swimmer with his Sprite heritage, but he still worried.

He heaved a sigh of relief when he saw a figure break out of the water and start the swim back. He stood up, noting the pace at which Cade was swimming. "Christ, talk about a swimming world speed record. What's the damn hurry, Cade?"

Feeling a prickle of unease, he went down to the water's edge to greet him as he got near the shore. Cade reached and gripped the metal stairs on the dock, his strong arms catapulting him out of the water. Quinn had to admire how Cade looked wet, the water droplets on his body beckoning him to lick them off. He tried to focus instead on a face which was dark with both anger and a touch of fear. Cade's chest rose and fell as he struggled for breath after the frantic swim.

Quinn frowned. "Is everything all right?"

"No, it's not bloody well all right. Something in that lake tried to pull me down into the water." Cade picked up his towel and dried his hair fiercely, wiping his face and dropping it, sodden, to the ground. He picked up his sweatpants and tee shirt and started to pull them on over his wet Speedo jammer. Cade insisted on wearing them when he swam, saying it gave him more movement. In Quinn's opinion, it had another purpose. His lover looked great in the tight costume and managed to fill it rather nicely.

"Perhaps it was a piece of pond weed or a fish?" he asked sympathetically.

Cade turned and glared at him. "It was not a weed or a fish. It swam beside me for a while then grabbed my foot and literally pulled me down under."

Quinn's spine tingled. "Why would someone want to pull you under? Do you think it was someone pulling a prank? Another swimmer, perhaps?"

Cade gazed at him, his breathing slowing down and his eyes meeting Quinn's. "I heard voices down there. Whatever it was whispered something, I don't have a bloody clue what they meant. It sounded like 'elli dimi zimmi' or something like that." Cade gazed at him in confusion. "I heard their voices and all of a sudden I said something back, something I can't remember. Whatever I said made them let go and I was able to get to the surface." He reached out a hand and gripped Quinn's arm. "What the hell was all that about?"

Quinn hitched a breath, thinking that what he'd feared had happened. Another Sprite had made contact with Cade.

Cade regarded him sombrely and his eyes narrowed. "You know what this is, don't you? Tell me please, what the hell just happened to me?"

Quinn sat down on the bank, and motioned for Cade to sit next to him. "You're freezing and you really need to get warmer. Here, put on your coat." He picked up Cade's heavy jacket and passed it over. Cade shrugged into it, his body still shivering.

"The heath is probably one of the most active areas for Sprites." he said quietly. "I think one of your own kind just tried to send you an invitation."

Cade gazed at him open mouthed. "A Sprite?"

Quinn nodded. "These lakes are known to have a high population of your kind. These waters are old and there's a lot of magyck in them."

"They bloody well tried to drown me!" Cade exclaimed indignantly.

Quinn chuckled softly. "You wouldn't have actually drowned, and you certainly wouldn't have died. If you use the power given to you and another Sprite shows you how, you can breathe underwater." He let his words sink in, seeing Cade's look of incredulity, and he smiled as he reached over and chucked his chin gently. "Close your mouth. You don't want to catch flies."

Cade shut his mouth obediently as he looked at him with eyes that were disbelieving. "I can learn to breathe underwater? I don't have gills, though—do I?" He scowled. "And why haven't you told me that before?"

He looked so horrified at the thought Quinn laughed out loud. "You're thinking like a human, not a Sprite. You don't need gills. It's magyck. It lies within you and its part of your inheritance from your mother." He sighed. "I was worried someday one of them might try something like this. It was only a matter of time but it's sooner than I'd expected. I'm sorry I didn't warn you about this, but I honestly thought it wouldn't happen for a while." He shook his head. "The other Sprite sensed you and probably thought you'd be fine. It had no way of knowing you were a Sprite virgin." He smiled faintly and leaned over to move a strand of wet hair off Cade's face. "You're shivering. Come on. It'll be dark soon and you need to get you home and all warmed up." He grinned. "We can try that body heat thing everyone talks about. Just bare skin, me and you, and that should make you toastier."

He stood up, pulling Cade to his feet as his boyfriend shook his head in amusement. "Is that all you think about, getting naked and having sex?"

Quinn raised his eyebrows suggestively. "Is there anything else worth doing?"

Cade chuckled, his earlier distress seeming to dissipate now that he had an explanation as to what had happened.

"Well, it just opens the door to me once again asking you to tell me more about what being a Sprite is all about. I know we've talked about it recently but I still get the feeling you're not telling me everything." He leaned forward and ran a cold hand down Quinn's cheek. "Instead you distract me with your body and promises of raunchy sex. And while I love that idea and may find myself so distracted, it's not going to work on me forever, Quinn." His face grew more serious. "Especially if it's going to lead to finding myself in situations like this one."

His voice was slightly challenging and Quinn sighed inwardly. He knew his lover was right and that he would still face some issues in the pond though if he insisted on swimming there. The words Cade had said he'd heard whispered were probably some form of bastardised Greek. Quinn thought it was probably "Join us" that had been chanted. He'd no idea what Cade would have said back but somewhere in the recess of his mind he'd dredged up something from his birthright and managed to stave them off. Quinn felt a distinct sense of disquiet. His Fey man was growing up and he wasn't sure he liked the idea. Taliesin, however, did.

Quinn, Cade deserves his place with them as both a Sprite and a Healer of note. You have to encourage and teach him. So he can learn something of their world. He will never leave you, you know that.

But Quinn didn't know that for sure.

Taliesin, I'm not having this conversation. Let me be. You've made your views known. And you know mine. I'll tell him what he needs to know for now.

Quinn scowled and Cade looked at him worriedly. "Everything okay?"

"Fine, just thinking about what you said. I promised you I'd tell you more so maybe tonight we can sit and have a drink and you can ply me with your questions." Quinn felt a frisson of unease but quelled it. "*Then* we can have raunchy sex." He leered at Cade.

Cade chuckled sexily and leaned forward to kiss him, a long, lingering kiss that made Quinn's groin ache and his heart beat quicker. "You and your one-track mind. Come on, mister, let's get home. You've got me all excited about thinking what questions I need to ask now. And the sex of course. Always the sex." He strode off ahead of him, his long legs power walking, and Quinn hurried to catch up with him.

He put his arm around Cade's waist as his lover leaned into him. Quinn smelled the dampness in his hair and the faint scent of lingering aftershave. Quinn's resolve quickened. He loved the feel of this man in his arms and he was damned if he was going to let anyone or anything take Cade away from him.

Chapter 5

Quinn switched off the engine, leaned back in the seat of his car and took a deep breath. It had been quite a drive from Hampstead Heath to Long Melford. The traffic had been a bitch and he was not in the best of moods. In hindsight he should have used Taliesin to get there but he'd fancied the drive. It let him think and gather his thoughts. He was about to talk to the leader of the Ravenbrook Coven, Misty Ravenbrook, a.k.a. Laura Claybourne in real life, and find out about the events leading up to a young girl's death earlier that week. He took a deep sigh and unravelled himself from the car. Quinn walked up to the front door of the library where Misty worked and raised his hand. Before he could even knock, the door opened. A short, slim woman in her late twenties or so smiled at him hesitantly.

"Mr. Fairmont? I'm Misty Ravenbrook. Won't you please come in?"

Quinn stepped into the quiet and dimly lit room and nodded at her. "High Priestess, I'm pleased to meet you. It's good to be able to put a face to the name after so many telephone conversations." He smiled at her and noticed she seemed pleased at his deference and use of her formal Wiccan address. It bode well for the meeting, he thought.

She smiled back at him tentatively. "Please, come in and take a seat. I'm afraid we only have office chairs. They're not very comfortable, but I'm sure you'll be fine."

"Believe me, I've sat on worse."

He removed his beige suede jacket, lowered his frame onto the chair she'd indicated and stretched long legs out in front of him as he observed her closely. She observed him back, her eyes lingering on his body as she looked him up and down.

Quinn raised a sardonic eyebrow. "Do I have something on my face?"

Her face reddened at his quizzical yet amused tone. He was used to people looking at him as if they were trying to spot the real Quinn Fairmont. That, and sometimes the look of desire he saw in their eyes. Quinn knew he was an attractive man but there was only one man he wanted to look at him as if he could gobble him all up. He was currently at home with his cat and probably muttering about his forthcoming dissertation.

"I'm sorry I'm staring," she stammered. "It's just I've heard so much about you that it's a pleasure to see you in person, even under the circumstances."

"I'm sure my reputation has been somewhat exaggerated, High Priestess," Quinn said drily. "Contrary to popular belief, I don't have a toad squatting on my shoulder as a familiar, I don't breathe fire and I most certainly don't shape shift." He grinned.

Misty blushed. "I wasn't sure how you'd be getting here," she burbled on.

He raised an eyebrow questioningly. "You thought perhaps I'd simply appear like a genie in a lamp?" He chuckled softly at her consternation and embarrassment. "Don't worry, it's a common misconception that I travel everywhere by using my Withinner. Time travel tends to make me feel ill, actually, so when I get the chance to take my Jag for a long drive, I take it."

He sat back in his chair, his long arms loosely folded across his chest and his affable nature disappeared in an instant.

Time for answers.

"So, you know why I'm here. I need you to tell me everything you can about that Book of Shadows your fellow witch found and what you actually did with it, leading up to the time that one of your own was killed."

His voice was commanding and from the paling of her face, he knew it had the desired effect. The woman had little choice but to tell him the whole story.

She sat back, her hands folded in her lap to stop their trembling. "One of our coven members, Nightwolf Shadow, came across an old book in a small occult bookshop in Glastonbury. He liked the look of the book so he bought it. He said it looked to him like someone's Book of Shadows and it had some interesting spells in it."

Quinn leaned forward, his eyes focused on her face.

Misty cleared her throat. "Last summer, on the Solstice, we decided to try one of the spells in the book. It seemed to be a rejuvenation spell and we thought we'd try it on a dead geranium…"

Her voice trailed off. Quinn felt a surge of anger. He uncrossed his arms and leaned forward aggressively.

"You tried this spell on a plant? Did you *know* what the whole spell was about?" He heard the sarcasm in his voice and tried to quell his rising temper.

Misty swallowed again. "I knew most of the chant; there were a few words we thought we knew, but we weren't a hundred percent sure." She looked at him hopefully. "The geranium came back to life and even shed a few blossoms. It died shortly after, though."

"And did you try this spell on anything else?" Quinn asked smoothly.

Misty nodded. "One of the coven's budgies died and we tried to reanimate it, but the spell didn't work at all. Nothing at all happened."

Quinn shook his head in disbelief but didn't say anything. "And the second spell—where Melody Bright died? How did that all come about?"

Misty's eyes glimmered with tears. "She had a really bad case of eczema, her body was rife with weeping sores and patchy skin. There was a healing spell in the book we thought we'd try. But instead it let something out. Something dark came out of the book and suffocated her. I killed her." Her voice was now a whisper and despite his frustration Quinn felt a twinge of sympathy at the desolation in Misty's eyes. He sat back and shook his head, passing his hands over his eyes tiredly.

"You chanted something when you had no idea what it all meant and got one of your own killed in the process. When will you witches learn these spells aren't toys to be trifled with at your bloody coven meetings?"

Misty's face flushed as she stared at him angrily. "Mr. Fairmont, I can assure you I'm not a novice. I do admit I cocked up with this last spell and got one of my coven members killed in the most horrific way imaginable." Her voice caught. "But I've been doing this a long time. I go back three generations as a witch and I'm proud of it. This is the first death I've ever been involved in and I can assure you, I dislike it every bit as much as you do. I was responsible for her death, for God's sake! Do you know what that's like?"

Quinn's heart rate increased and he clenched his fists.

Oh yes, I know exactly how that feels, High Priestess.

He ignored her question as he stood up and paced around the room. Finally he stopped and sat back down again. Misty had remained sitting, staring down at the floor as he strode around like a caged lion.

When Quinn spoke again, he tried to be gentle. "I'm sorry if you feel I denigrate your abilities, Misty. I truly don't mean to. I understand witches better than you think. My mother was one, as was my aunt, the woman who raised me when my parents died. So I'm well aware of you all and your abilities and I have the greatest of respect for them. It's just this blatant disregard for the dangers of doing something when you don't know what it's all about that drives me crazy—witch or Warlock."

Quinn sighed and continued. "You didn't kill her. Whatever was in the book killed her. Remnants of something dark, something evil. It is a unique circumstance though. That could never have been envisaged, High Priestess. Not the cleverest thing you could all have done, though."

Misty nodded wordlessly.

Quinn sat forward. "What happened then?"

She swallowed. "I told the others to go home, so at least they would be spared Valensia's wrath then I called the Praetorium." The Praetorium was the Witches' organisation similar to the Warlocks' Consortium, a high council that sat in consultation and managed their affairs.

He turned to face her. "I assume Valensia summonsed you to account. Tell me how that went."

Misty's face paled at the memory of her meeting with the Regina. "I did and it was a most unpleasant experience, I can assure you. Do you know Valensia at all?"

He nodded curtly.

Better than you can imagine.

"Well, then you know that she is extremely temperamental and rather sadistic. My meeting with her was extremely painful and I was lucky to get out of the Praetorium in one piece. As it is, she gave me this as a punishment."

Misty lifted the swathe of long brown hair that covered the back of the neck. Quinn winced at the sight of the small ugly puckered scar on the back of her neck.

"She used her athame to cut me as a warning not to do something so stupid again." Misty dropped her hair. "I can assure you after the pain I experienced getting this, I won't."

"I'm sorry about that," Quinn said softly. "She can be very—mercurial—in her moods and not someone to get on the wrong side of." He hesitated. "I imagine she wanted the Book of Shadows herself?"

Misty nodded. "Yes. I had to hand it over when I went to see her. It's in her chambers, I imagine. She's keeping a close eye on it."

Quinn mouth twitched at that news.

Not what I wanted to hear. I'd rather you still had the damn thing.

"Tell me about the book," he said quietly. "Describe it in as much detail as you can."

"It was a book about A5 size. It looked like leather, very old and faded. There were some old stains on the front cover, possibly water, I don't know. The writing was old, done in some sort of red ink, dragon's ink, I think, and the handwriting was very flowing. I thought it was a woman's Book of Shadows." Misty frowned. "There was a strange symbol on the very first page."

Quinn gazed at her intently. "Could you draw this symbol?" he asked, his eyes watchful. Misty nodded. He rummaged around inside his leather jacket, pulling out a pen and a small spiral bound notebook. "Draw it," he demanded.

She placed the book on the table as she sketched. He watched as she drew a wheel with eight segments, which represented the eight sabbats of the witches' year, along with two symbols, looking like an M and a sideways V together, in curly writing. He frowned as he looked over her shoulder, at the slightly blurry figures on the piece of paper.

I should have brought my damn glasses with me.

"They look like runes. I know the Year of the Wheel symbol but I'm not sure about the single marks. Do you have any idea what they are or what they mean?"

Misty shook her head. "All I know is this was drawn on the inside of the book. I have no idea what the two separate initials mean."

Quinn looked at her sharply. "You feel they may be initials? Perhaps belonging to the witch who created and owned this book?"

Misty shrugged. "I suppose they could be. I don't have a clue who could it be; the seventeenth century is out of my comfort zone."

Quinn frowned. "How do you know the book was created in the seventeenth century? It could have been anyone's."

Misty looked at him, her gaze clear. "I felt it strongly after the second spell we did, before I handed it over to Valensia. I touched the book just after Melody died. It burnt me and there was a foul smell. The one thing I sensed when I touched it was fear, distrust and hatred. I smelled the sweat and the blood on that book. It reeked of Witch Trials. I think the book belonged to someone who was perhaps persecuted in that time."

Quinn's stomach lurched and he turned to look out of the side window into the darkness beyond. "That's an incredibly useful piece of information, thank you. It'll help me with what I'm working on." He turned to look at her again. "The witch that died, what happened to her body?"

Misty looked down at the floor. "Valensia ordered it to be burnt. The *thing* that went into Melody, that darkness, no one knew what it was. The Regina didn't want to risk it getting out, so they burned the body to cinders in a sealed crematorium and left it there. The bones and mortal remains of poor Melody were never given a decent burial. I had the other coven members do a release chant. I hope it gave the poor woman some peace."

Quinn nodded but his mind was elsewhere. "What went into Melody was probably old residue from the casting of any original magyck or intense emotions. They tend to have a fairly malevolent presence when they're stirred up. As the book was already in the circle with you, the salt protection wouldn't have worked to keep it out like it would normally."

He felt a twinge in his shoulder and he rolled it from side to side. He noticed Misty's concerned eyes on him.

"Old injury making itself known," he murmured as he stretched. "You've told me everything you can think of about this book?" he asked. "I hope you've left nothing out. It's very important I know everything."

Misty nodded. "I've told you everything I know, Grand Master. There's nothing else."

He nodded. "Very well. Thank you, High Priestess. I know this must have been difficult for you. It's never easy when one of your own dies, and I know Valensia can be quite an unpleasant handful. You were lucky not to get out any worse off. She has a vile temper."

"You sound as if you know her well?" Misty asked curiously.

Quinn snorted. "It was a long time ago and I doubt she's got any better with age or maturity." He picked up his jacket and shrugged his arms into it, picking up the notebook and his pen and putting them into his jacket pocket.

"Thank you for the meeting; I appreciate it. If you think of anything else, contact me. This is my number. Call me anytime."

"This is more than just a witch's death, isn't it?" Misty murmured quietly. "For you to be here, visiting me and giving me your number personally—this is bigger than we thought, isn't it?"

Quinn thought she was very perceptive. "It may well be. Obviously our meeting is strictly between us. I'd prefer that even Valensia didn't know about it. I'm sorry if that puts you on the spot, but it's why I insisted on driving down here to meet you late at night. I don't want this getting out to anyone."

"You have my word," Misty said quietly. "And if you need anything from me again, you know where to find me."

He smiled at her. He nodded as he opened the door and stepped outside. "Stay safe and look after yourself."

He disappeared into the dimly lit car park and walked toward his car, unlocking it, the beep of the central locking echoing in the still night air. He started the car.

That had been a very interesting conversation and one that had been worth the journey. Something was definitely wrong with that Book of Shadows and Quinn had every intention of getting the book from the Praetorium. He grinned wolfishly.

It might take a cunning plan, Valensia, but that damned book will *be mine.*

Chapter 6

Driving home, Quinn was disturbed at the news the witch had given him. He thought for sure now that there was a definite connection between Jeremy's increase in powers the time they had fought and the chanting of that first spell by the coven at the Summer Solstice. He also trusted Misty's instincts. He'd researched her before their meeting and he probably knew more about her than she did. Her family had indeed been well respected and influential and she was no fly by night. A little reckless, perhaps, but that was a flaw he understood well.

He frowned, remembering the scar on the back of her neck. Valensia certainly hadn't tempered her mean streak and Misty's words definitely meant Quinn would have to meet with the Regina and face the music. He desperately needed to see that book, if not get it into his possession. He wasn't going to be a big girl's blouse and ask Percy to go with him for backup—he'd never live it down——but he would certainly fortify himself against Valensia's wiles as much as he could. His Withinner stirred inside him.

Quinn. That book is the answer to everything we seek. We have to do this even though neither of us wishes to. I will see what I can find out about those initials. Perhaps we may get lucky.

"Old friend, you do realise we're going into the lioness's den? Valensia will relish this opportunity to get one over on me." He chuckled drily, realising what he'd just said. "Literally, as well as figuratively. How the hell I'm going to tell Cade about this one, I have no idea."

Quinn changed gears expertly as he watched the road ahead, busy and congested despite the lateness of the hour. He'd probably get home just before midnight at this rate. But it was worth it to spend time in his car, a quiet solitude where he could think and plan and enjoy the simple mechanics of driving, something he'd always been partial to. When he got home the house was in darkness and he crept into bed quietly. For a while he lay there, listening to Cade's steady breathing and wondering how to break the news to him that he needed to see an old flame who was still intent on jumping his bones regardless of any relationship he might be in—and was not averse to using magyck to do so. Quinn could have kept it from Cade, he supposed, but if anything happened and he found out he hadn't told him, he had the feeling he'd lose his lover. No, best to come clean and hope he took it well.

******

"Fuck, Quinn, how can you even think of going to see that bloody woman after what she did to you?" Cade looked at Quinn in disbelief as he waved his hands around excitedly. Quinn sat at the dining room table, sighing heavily as he fiddled with the cutlery. They'd just finished a late dinner and were enjoying a glass of wine before going up to bed.

"The woman kept you as her sex slave for three days, and now you need to go see her so she can maybe do the same? Can't someone else go and see this crazy bitch?"

Cade had forgotten how amusing he'd found Quinn's original story, faced now with the fact that it could happen again.

Over my dead fucking body! Cade paced the room in agitation. He'd never felt this possessive of anyone else Before Quinn—or as he preferred to think of it, "BQ"

Quinn sighed again. "Valensia won't even think of speaking to anyone else about this matter. Unfortunately for me, she still feels she has a claim on me. We didn't part on particularly good terms as you could imagine. The woman is a bloody menace but I need her."

Cade scowled fiercely. "Really?" His temper flared at those words.

Quinn amended his statement hastily. "Not like that, you muppet. I need to get her to give me the book."

"Well then, I need to come with you and make sure she doesn't touch you and that she knows who you belong to." Cade blatantly ignored Quinn's raised eyebrow at the fact that he "belonged" to someone as he continued his tirade. "I'm fed up having bloody witches thinking they can do what they want with you. Just like Mary-Sophie when she took on more Fey blood and tried to get you to hump her."

Quinn leaned forward, his elbows on the table, one hand propping up his chin, his eyes glinting. "Firstly, there is no way in hell that you're coming with me. I don't need a bloody bodyguard and if I did, it most definitely would not be you. I'd end up with a major girl fight on my hands. Secondly, whilst I love the fact that I 'belong' to you"—his voice was silky and Cade sensed the slight ire in it—"this is not the time for emotions to get in the way of what needs to be done. I have to get that book in order to save lives and that means I go alone."

Cade glared at him. "Mr. 'The End Justifies the Means'? Does that mean if she wants you to screw her before she gives you the book, you would? If that was what it took?"

A wave of anger flooded his chest as well as the feeling of pure fear that that was indeed what Quinn would do.

Quinn regarded him angrily, his jaw tensing. "I have no intention of prostituting myself, not even for the book. I don't know how you can think I would."

Cade shook his head. "You've looked at me in the eye and told me a bare-faced lie before without flinching."

Quinn's eyes narrowed.

Cade continued mercilessly. "The night you went to see Andrew de Vere and Jeremy on the yacht. You told me Percy and Magnus would be with every step of the way. But they weren't, were they, Quinn? Once again, it was just you, alone. And look how that turned out."

Quinn remained silent and Cade knew he had no comeback on that because it was true. Quinn stood up, his arms rigid at his side as he turned to look out of the picture window at the misty heath beyond. "I know what I said at the time but I didn't want you worrying." His voice was harsh. "Forgive me if I tried to spare you the gory details."

Cade's heart sank at his tone. He knew Quinn was currently stressed with everything going on and he probably wasn't helping matters. "I do understand you trying to protect me. It's what you do. But who protects you?"

Quinn turned to face him, his eyes softening at Cade's worried face. "I've been protecting myself since I was seven years old, longer even. And I have Taliesin, don't forget. He's no fan of Valensia either, for some reason I haven't quite gotten to the bottom of yet, and we're more prepared than we were last time. Last time I couldn't even invoke him so I could disappear. This time will be different."

A look of relief crossed Quinn's face at something his Withinner had probably said. He reached out his arms to Cade and pulled him into them, wrapping his arms around his waist. Cade encircled Quinn's neck with his arms and laid his forehead against his. Quinn smelt of cinnamon and musk, a result of his shower gel. It was addictive and Cade breathed it in, loving the fragrance of Quinn.

Quinn sighed. "I promise you I will not let that woman take advantage of me again. Taliesin agrees." He grinned slightly. "I'd rather commit *hara-kiri* than let her get her claws into me. I know most men think it would be a noble thing to be shagged to death by a beautiful woman but I'm not one of them. I'd rather come home to you and let you do that."

Cade reached up, taking Quinn's chin in his hands and kissing him ardently. When he released him, he stared into his eyes intensely.

"You make sure you do, or I'll be hunting the two of you down. *Hara-kiri* will be the least of your worries if that happens." He grinned and Quinn's body and face relaxed as he grinned back.

"Deal." Quinn moved his hands away from Cade's waist and looked at him mischievously. "Talking of shagging to death, it's time we went to bed. I have to be up early in the morning to meet Valensia and I'd like to get some shuteye before I go. So if we get up there now, you'll have time to show me that new Kama Sutra position you've been researching." He saw Cade raise his eyebrows. "Yes, I've seen you reading all about it on the internet. You really should switch on private browsing, Cade."

He disappeared up the stairway with a wicked chuckle as Cade followed him, his face flushing. The bloody man was infuriating in ferreting out secrets and had an uncanny knack of always being a step ahead of him. The slinking form of Marco Polo sidled up the stairs, no doubt in the hope he might be able to acquire a comfortable spot on the bed.

"No chance of that, kitty. With what I plan on doing to that man, there'll be no room for you and you may find yourself getting squashed." Cade snorted. "I'll give him something to think about tomorrow when he meets that old flame of his." His voice sounded jealous, even to his own ears. "He'll be so worn out, he won't have the strength to do anything else."

Cade reached the top of the stairs and pushed open the bedroom door with a definite sense of purpose.

Chapter 7

The following morning, aching everywhere and definitely needing more sleep than he'd gotten the night before, Quinn drove up to the Praetorium for his meeting with Valensia. He felt a little like a boy going on his first prom date—apprehensive and hoping he was well prepared enough to meet what lay ahead. He had no condoms in his wallet but he did have a veritable plethora of spells, chants and protective magyck surrounding him and Taliesin. It was almost enough to publish their own Book of Shadows on 'How to avoid being targeted by a sex-crazy witch.'

Cade had been fairly quiet this morning when Quinn had left and he knew Cade had visions of him being seduced and constantly used as a living vibrator, but he'd assured him he would allow no such thing. Quinn had insisted on meeting Valensia at a public place and was going nowhere near her private home in Chelsea.

The witch on reception nodded at him warmly as he walked across the marbled floor of the grand Praetorium and leaned on the shiny wooden counter.

"Mr. Fairmont, the Regina is expecting you. She asked if you'd take a seat for a minute as she'd like to collect you personally."

I'll bet she bloody does!

Quinn nodded and sat down in one of the deep armchairs scattered around the entrance hall. He observed the comings and goings in the reception area, a vast network of people entering the hall, being escorted up the long, curved, gleaming wooden staircases to the second floor, where most of the Praetorium staff held their meetings, strategy sessions and anything else. Witches, Feys of varying description, Warlocks—Quinn saw them all, some of the Warlocks looking distinctly uncomfortable upon seeing their Grand Master sitting waiting. They looked around anxiously to ensure someone was coming to fetch him. Quinn watched in slight amusement as one of them approached the woman on reception and quietly asked her if she knew she had the Grand Master of the Consortium waiting like a common person. The witch smiled and said she did indeed know and that the Regina was on her way. The man scowled, looking at Quinn with a raised eyebrow. Quinn inclined his head graciously in thanks at the man's intervention. The man shook his head in disgust at the Regina's tardiness and moved on with a mutter.

The hall had been noisy, the sounds of people talking, debating and even arguing. When there was a sudden lull, Quinn knew that Valensia was coming down the staircase. He watched her as she glided down the stairs, one hand laid languidly on the banister. She'd always been an exceptionally beautiful woman and the maturity that surrounded her made her even more so. Valensia was tall, about Quinn's height, with an hourglass shape and a tiny waist currently clinched in with an ornate gold belt, held by a buckle shaped like a pentagram. Her dress swirled around her like burgundy fog, swathes of darkened silk that clung to her form and highlighted all her considerable attributes.

Her hair was long, past her waist, jet black and lustrous. As she moved toward Quinn, her deep blue eyes regarded him in sheer avarice. He already felt the pull of her half-Fey blood even though he'd taken Mirrabar blood and various other herbs and potions to counter the effect. Quinn felt the familiar stirrings in his groin and the dryness in his mouth and he stood up, wanting to take any action that may relax him.

His Withinner stirred in greed inside him and he cursed silently.

Taliesin, you need to control yourself too. I can't have you going off half cocked—or fully cocked, as it may be. Remember our agreement and our plan. Don't fucking fail me on this one or I'll come in and rip your bloody heart out.

Taliesin sighed. *She is even more alluring than I remember. She is perfect.*

Quinn regarded Valensia mildly even as he cursed his Withinner.

Fuck perfect! Get a bloody grip! I thought you didn't fancy her?

"Quinn, you look wonderful as always. Have you been working out more? Those shoulders certainly look as if they grown a few inches since we were together last. You've become even dishier with that extra maturity. Being with men obviously agrees with you."

Her voice was slightly spiteful, low, seductive, sounding like black velvet would if it could speak. She'd never forgiven Quinn for breaking it off with her and making a life solely as a gay man. She'd be twenty-eight now and looked years younger. Her hand reached out and softly caressed his arm, causing a tingle to run up from his wrist to his shoulder. He remembered the last time a witch had done that. Mary Hawthorn had planted a hex on him that way and getting rid of it had nearly killed him.

He'd trusted Mary. With Valensia he was impervious to such things. *He'd* grown up too. His magyck was a lot stronger than it had been seven years ago when he'd first met her.

"I gym. I could say the same for you, Valensia. You look wonderful."

She chuckled. "And here we stand exchanging pleasantries like civilised people. Wonders will never cease." She turned and motioned for him to follow him. "Follow me, handsome. We have a lot to talk about. It'll be more private in my suite upstairs."

Quinn followed her as she shimmied up the stairs, the perfect globes of her backside tautening as she walked. Quinn couldn't resist. He watched them all the way up the stairs, cursing himself for doing so but unable to help himself. He'd known there would still be some attraction, the spells and chants couldn't deplete it altogether, but he still resented it. He thanked the stars Cade wasn't there to see his roaming eyes at work. The man would have a conniption.

They reached Valensia's "suite," a palatial accommodation of office and living room with a very large leather sofa in the one half of the room, a large Flokati rug on the floor and a fire burning in the hearth. Quinn immediately became uncomfortable. This looked far too inviting for a business meeting. Valensia sat down behind a solid six-foot-wide teak desk and planted her long legs with their elegantly booted feet up on the desk. She leaned back in her chair, raising her arms above her head in a faux stretch so her breasts tightened against the silk of her outfit, the dress unbuttoned almost down to her midriff. The dress slid silkily off her long legs, leaving a bare expanse of tanned, perfect leg that seemed to lead up to her navel. Quinn swallowed, seeing the tanned skin and curves of her breasts underneath and her nipples through the fabric. He tried to remain expressionless as he raised his eyes to her mocking ones. Taliesin appeared to have the same control problem.

Breathe, my friend. Remember Cade at home. I will try help but I must confess I am struggling too. We have to help each other.

Quinn scowled. *I know I'm into guys and so does she but my dick seems to have a mind of its bloody own, what with the Fey attraction.*

Taliesin snorted in silent amusement. He sounded breathless and Quinn wondered grimly what the hell his Withinner was doing in his time. The images conjured up in his mind made him shiver with distaste and he tried hard to cast them out before he went too far with them.

Valensia eyed him up and down. "So, I know why you're here. You want my Book of Shadows. God, the only thing that could ever hold your attention—other than someone with a penis—was a book. I was never sure which one actually would win out if you had to choose."

He ignored her barbed comment and nodded. "Spot on as usual. It's not that I *want* the book. It's that I *need* the book. It holds some valuable information that the Consortium needs so we can stop the Witchfinder general from killing any more of us. The battle is coming. I can feel it. It's building up, and when it starts, it's going to be like nothing we've ever seen unless we find out why this human vessel, Jeremy Payton, is so much more powerful. And why he's currently so quiet. That doesn't bode well."

"What makes you think I don't want the same thing? I have people here who are more than capable of figuring out the book's secrets themselves if I want them to." Her voice hardened.

Quinn shrugged his shoulders. "Without being derogatory, you know that the Consortium and its resources are infinitely more powerful than the Praetorium and its witches. You can't argue that fact. A Warlock's power with a Withinner is seven times that of a witch. You know that we're the right ones to take a look at the book and deal with the Witchfinder. Obviously we would need your help. I wouldn't consider a plan that didn't have an alliance of both of our kind on one side."

She apprised him mockingly. "You Warlocks, always so macho and manly." Her face grew darker. "I have to say I liked that attitude when you were inside me, Quinn. I don't like it when you're sitting in front of me trying to convince me to do the right thing according to you."

Her beautiful face broke into a scowl and she took her feet off the desk and stood up. "I've taken a look at the book myself and although it definitely is someone's Book of Shadows, the spells in it appear fairly harmless. That stupid High Priestess of the Ravenbrook Coven couldn't shed any more light on it."

Quinn was relieved that Misty hadn't said anything to Valensia about her feelings about the book originating in the seventeenth century. He watched as Valensia prowled the room like a panther, her feline strides angry.

"I can assure you I wasn't being chauvinistic." Quinn remarked mildly. "You know me well enough to know that's not how I think. But we have the Reponosium too and our research facility is far better than yours. I only want to look at the book and you can have it back when we're done with it."

Privately he thought there was no hope in hell that she'd be getting that book back and he knew she knew that too. It was a game waiting to be played.

"Darling Quinn. If I was disposed to give you this book, what would my reward be?" she purred as she walked over to him and stroked his cheek gently, her long fingernails trailing across his skin causing a reaction that was all too familiar.

Quinn thought of Cade and he looked up at the witch, his eyes narrowed and his voice steely. "That might have worked once but it won't work again. This time we talk like adults, not like two sex-starved teenagers who can't get enough of each other. Last time you tricked me and it won't happen again."

She laughed softly as she sat down on his lap, winding her arms around his neck and leaning in toward him. He smelled her perfume, her arousal and felt heat rising off her body. He also felt the traitorous stirrings below and his heart beat faster as his hormonal body reacted to her closeness and the magyck she held inside in her blood.

Quinn, in God's name, remove her! I can hardly think myself.

Taliesin sounded extremely agitated, his voice replicating the turmoil Quinn felt in his own body.

Valensia's lips brushed his hair. "Are you sure about that? Because your body is definitely saying 'take me.'"

"That's just my body, but my mind is saying something different. I've actually got my own man at home and honestly, he's the only one I need now."

As Valensia looked at him, her face abruptly twisted with displeasure. "Yes, I've heard about him," she snarled. "A damn Water Sprite, Quinn? How much fun can that be for you?"

"I can assure you he's more than enough," Quinn said quietly. "I love him; that's what makes the difference. You should try it sometime."

She reached out a hand and slapped his face then raked her nails down his cheek, leaving long blood trails. He welcomed the pain. It distracted him from her sex appeal and her pheromones seeping into his nostrils, which were making him feel extremely horny even with all the magyck protecting him. He had to hold out. The protection spells and all the extra effort he'd taken were definitely working. If he hadn't cast them, he'd be shagging her senseless right now, consequences be damned.

"Don't you fucking mock me, Quinn Fairmont!" He wasn't sure but he thought he heard a quiver in her voice. "I was in love, remember? Then you left me, you bastard. To pursue life having sex with men instead of me."

She stood up, moving over to the window, gazing down at the busy London street below. He watched her warily as he stood up to stretch his legs and try to get rid of the extreme turbulence in his lower body.

"Let's not rehash all of that. It was seven years ago and you were never in love with me. You just wanted to own me. That's partly why it didn't work. You were so possessive I couldn't breathe. And finally I made a decision about my sexuality that you couldn't live with."

His soft words seemed to calm her down and she turned and glared at him. She knew he was right but she wouldn't admit it. That was simply Valensia.

"You're wrong. I did love you, in my own way." Her voice was flat.

He sighed. "Fine, have it your way. We're getting nowhere with this." He stayed on his feet as he waited for her to speak.

"Would you give up your man to get this book?" Her voice was silky. "If you had to choose between them, would you have him…or the book? If I remember correctly, you would have done anything for the Consortium. In fact, from what I recall, you did do 'anything.' I remember the Honour Whitebrook killings like they were yesterday."

Whatever you do, do not let her continue with that story. That memory will weaken you. Taliesin's warning vice echoed inside and Quinn's vision blurred at her gloating words and the satisfaction in her tone. He took a deep breath, trying to quell the sense of violence that welled inside him, the need he had suddenly to flash burn this woman through to her spine.

"You're dabbling in murky waters now," he said edgily. "I'd suggest you focus on the task in hand and not try and dredge up the past. I think it only fair to warn you I won't take anymore comments like that lightly."

"And what would you do, burn me? Hit me? I'd rather like that actually. I've found my tastes lately running to something just a little bit darker to get me going."

She moved over to him. "I asked you a question. Would you give up your Sprite to get the book? If you say yes, I'll see the old Quinn, the one who thought the end justified the means even if it meant getting a family of witches murdered in the process to protect your precious Daniel. Then I'll give you the book."

He just looked at her. Valensia took an instinctive step back as he moved toward her with the speed of a cat, gripping her left wrist so tightly she winced in pain. He concentrated his energy and she grimaced as the heat from his body transmitted itself into her skin. Quinn smelled her skin roasting.

Valensia cried out in pain and disbelief. He stopped his energy flow and released her wrist. She stepped back with a wide-eyed look, holding her singed wrist in her hands. He was surprised when she didn't respond with any counterattack of her own.

Well done. I have long wanted to do that. Taliesin's voice was satisfied.

"You're a real bitch," Quinn took a deep, shuddering breath, aware that his headache had suddenly sprung up from nowhere and that meant the nosebleeds weren't too far off. "You have no fucking heart. You're a complete narcissist and there's no bloody room in your life for anyone else. It's why you don't have anybody. It's why they all leave you in the end."

There was a slow tickle under his nose and he raised his hand to wipe away the blood, eyeing out the streak of crimson on his hand with a detached air.

Valensia watched him, her eyes narrowed.

"In answer to your question—no, I'd never give Cade up. He's the best thing that ever happened to me and if I have to make a choice it would be him every time. He's warm, passionate and he makes me laugh. And he really loves me. He doesn't simply want to mount me like a trophy on his wall—or just mount me, full stop."

Quinn's voice was deadly quiet. "So you can keep your fucking book." He laughed nastily. "I was a fool to think we could have a reasonable conversation with both of our kinds' best interests at heart. You haven't changed, Valensia. But I have."

He turned and strode angrily to the door, opening it and taking the stairs two at a time. The receptionist smiled at him as he left and he ignored her, pulling the wide glass door open with all his strength, feeling very disappointed when it didn't slam because of the runners on the door that softly closed it.

Well spoken. We will find another way. His Withinner's voice was resigned.

Quinn stood outside in the sunlight, wiping away more blood that dribbled into his mouth. He swore loudly and hunted for a handkerchief in his pocket. Someone came up behind him and he turned swiftly, his sudden aggression draining away when he saw who stood behind him. Valensia silently handed him a tissue and he nodded his thanks as he held it to his nose.

"Why are you having those nosebleeds?" she asked quietly, and he swore he saw concern in her eyes.

He shrugged. "It's a leftover of a Withinner Unity, a witch hex and a Warlock battle. Unfortunately it's left my brain a little scrambled. What do you want?"

She held out her hand and handed him a book covered in plastic. His eyes narrowed and he regarded her in suspicion but made no move to take the book. "Is that what I think it is? And if it is, why are you giving it to me? What's the catch?"

"It's the book you fucking wanted, so take it before I change my mind!" She spat fiercely. "Study it then let me have it back. There's no catch. Just promise to keep me informed of what you find. That's all I ask."

She thrust it into his hand and spun around, marching toward the building.

Quinn called out after her. "Valensia?"

She stopped and hesitated, not wanting to turn around. But finally she did so, slowly.

"I was wrong. You have changed. Thank you."

She is more now than the woman we knew, Quinn.

Taliesin's voice sounded regretful, even slightly sad. Quinn wondered what his Withinner had gotten into with this woman. Valensia nodded curtly and disappeared back into the building. Quinn stood there for a moment then went down to the car park for the drive home.

Chapter 8

When he got home, he smiled as he saw the blind at the front window twitch. The front door opened and a lean, tall frame lounged lazily against the door frame watching Quinn walk up the path. Cade laughed as Quinn bowed low.

"Home safe, my Queen. I promised, didn't I?"

Cade smiled at him, eyes amused, then drew closer, his eyes narrowed in anger. "What did that she-devil do to your face? Did she scratch you?"

Quinn kissed Cade, his lover's concern and love for him like a welcome-home present sitting on the hearth. "Valensia got a little irate at something I said but she calmed down and I got out in one piece, *virgo intacta*." He grinned wickedly. "I didn't have to hump anyone but I got the book!" He pulled it out of his jacket pocket with a triumphant flourish.

Cade gawped at him. "She just gave it to you? What did you have to promise her to get it?" He frowned. "No, don't tell me. I'll probably get all upset and then we'll argue and everything will just go to pot."

Quinn shrugged, knowing his silence would drive Cade crazy, and went into the house with his boyfriend hot on his heels. He took off his jacket, and as much as he wanted to go upstairs and study the book, he knew he still had a little bit of conversation with Cade to complete. Best get it over with.

"I didn't have to promise anything. It appears Valensia has mellowed somewhat with me since our last encounter. Prickly on the outside but surprisingly a little more relaxed beneath. So apart from a scratched face, now I have the book and I'm praying all the hopes we're pinning on it to find the man we're looking for won't let us down." He looked longingly across at the stairs down to the basement. "So I thought I'd go to the library and see what I can find out."

Cade shook his head in resignation. "You'll be impossible to talk to until you get this out of your system. Fine, off you go. Dinner will be a while." He glanced at him slyly. "I have a few things of my own I need to sort out anyway. I had another text from Cooper. That man is becoming quite a stalker."

Quinn frowned. "Cooper? Who's Cooper?"

Cade sighed. "I've told you about him. He's this rather forward young man at work who keeps me asking me out. Unfortunately he has my mobile number and insists on texting me rather sweet anecdotes now and then."

Quinn shook his head darkly. "Does he know you have me at home? Is he becoming a bit too much?"

Cade laughed. "Yes, he's well aware of you. And I can manage Cooper, I promise. It's rather flattering having a young man pursuing me so ardently."

Quinn was a little put out at Cade's obvious enjoyment of having another suitor. "Exactly how old are we talking about? And I can't have Valensia, but you can have Cooper?"

Cade scowled at his laconic retort and Quinn smiled at him.

"Cooper didn't have me imprisoned in a bedroom so he could screw me every time he felt like it. You know it's not the same. And Cooper is twenty-eight." Cade smirked.

"Wow, a whole seven years younger than you. He sees you as his sugar daddy then?"

Cade stared at him in exasperation. "I doubt that. He's just one helluva flirt." Quinn gazed at Cade innocently, and Cade heaved an exasperated sigh. "This is going nowhere, is it? Off you go then, down to your poxy basement. I suppose I'll see you at midnight."

Quinn grinned, needing no second urging. He was soon seated at his desk in the basement, the book in front of him, staring at it with a mixture of apprehension and expectation. "Right, let's see what we have here."

He reached out and gently took a sharp, thin knife from his custom-made toolkit, very slowly slitting open the plastic sheath. "I can't believe they've just wrapped it in bloody plastic!" he exclaimed to himself angrily. "A rare seventeenth-century book treated as if it's the latest paperback off the shelf. It's just as well I've got it now. It'll be taken care of properly."

Quinn had no intention of ever giving the book back. It was part of his collection now and he'd fight to the death to keep it that way. He slid the plastic carefully off the book and as it came free from its wrapping, his nostrils flared and he felt his Withinner's unease as well. The book reeked of death. It smelt of mildew, sweat, fear and blood and was overwhelming to one such as Quinn, whose senses were more refined than anyone else's. He took a deep breath, trying to rid himself of the feeling of abject horror that had claimed his mind and his heart.

I do not like this book. Taliesin sounded very uneasy. *It has a stench like an old abattoir, desperate and with a sense of total futility. Whoever's book this was, they suffered greatly and they knew they would never survive whatever it was they were facing. Their fear is the blackness that killed that poor young witch.*

"I agree, old friend." Quinn said thoughtfully as he looked at the book, not really wanting to touch it but knowing he had to. He could wear gloves to protect himself but that would defeat the object. Most of the book's secrets resided in its owner's thoughts and emotions and he had to get past those first before he could properly research what was in the book. He took a deep breath and laid his hand on the cover. Taliesin's disgust manifested at the same time as his own, a pervading feeling of sickness that invaded his body like icy fog. It got into each pore, worming its way into his muscles, his bloodstream, his bones. Overwhelmed, Quinn retched, acid bile rising in his throat. He turned and was sick in the wastepaper basket at the side of his desk. He waited for the nausea to subside before he touched the book again, getting the same sensation but less than before. He gritted his teeth and continued his exploration.

The book was small and leather bound and there were definite stains on the front. Quinn thought they were too dark to be water. He opened the front cover gingerly and saw it was just as Misty had described it. A wheel with eight segments, along with two symbols like an M and a V of slanted lines together. He picked up his mobile and took a shot of the cover and the first page.

He picked up the desk phone and dialled a number, tucking it into the crook of his neck as it rang. He rapidly compiled a message on his mobile to go with the photo then clicked Send.

Quinn spoke as Percy answered. "Quinn here. I got the book."

"She gave it to you? " Percy's voice was disbelieving.

"Yes, it was relatively easy, not as bad as I thought. I'm taking a look at it now and I've just sent you some pictures. I want someone in the Reponosium to look through everything we've got down there and try and find a connection to the symbols on the first page and anything regarding seventeenth-century witch trials. Specifically tell them to keep an eye out for witches that were tried and killed by the Witchfinder, but let them know any other connection is possible." He laid his mobile phone down on the table.

"I've got it. I'll put someone on it right away."

"Thanks. Let me know the minute you find anything."

Quinn disconnected the call and browsed through the book. He recognised some of the spells and chants. As Valensia had said, they appeared run of the mill, spells for wealth, health and love. But there were a few that were different, added to the very back of the book, ones that were darker and infinitely more dangerous unless you knew what you were doing. The one that Misty had chanted to restore the dead geranium and the one that had killed Melody were at the forefront of this new section. He frowned. To his eyes, it looked like someone had probably put the innocent spells at the front and tried to hide the more intricate ones at the back in the hope that no one would really find them. It wasn't a particularly clever plan.

Quinn. This book is covered in blood. Real blood. I can smell it.

"You mean the stains on the front?" Quinn stroked his chin thoughtfully. "I tend to agree with you. It has that—metallic—scent to it." Quinn's senses were on high alert. "It would be interesting to find out whose blood, though. Perhaps the guys at the Reponosium will find something."

He spent another hour perusing the book but came up with nothing more. He felt a glut of emotions as he turned the pages—some good, mostly bad. Finally he was exhausted by the mental and emotional drain the book levied on him and he closed it with a sigh. He stored the book safely in his air tight repository, cleaned out his waste bin then went upstairs to find Cade.

He was sitting in the lounge, curled up on the couch reading a book, a glass of wine at his side. The smile he turned in Quinn's direction as he entered still made Quinn's heart beat faster and warmth suffuse his body. Cade grinned at him.

"I didn't expect to see you yet. Dinner's ready in about half an hour." He patted the seat beside him. "Come sit down here. You look knackered."

Quinn sat down with a sigh and Cade leaned over and stroked his forehead as Quinn leaned his head back against the sofa, closing his eyes, relishing Cade's spicy scent of male and sandalwood aftershave.

"Did you send a text back to your ardent suitor Cooper and tell him how possessive I am and how much bigger I am than him?" Quinn chuckled. "In all the ways that matter?"

Cade laughed softly. "Yes, I told him you were a seven-foot warrior with a really mean streak and he'd better stop pestering me or you'd turn him into a toad."

Quinn groaned in pleasure as Cade rubbed his shoulders. "Did you find what you were looking for?"

Quinn nodded, the tension in his body dissipating at Cade's soothing massage.

"Some. Percy's got people working on finding out whose book it might be. The secret is getting that information so we can perhaps use the book to find the Witchfinder. If we can find out how the book worked to do what Percy thinks it did—releasing Matthew Hopkins's spirit—then using the book might be the only way of reversing the spell."

Cade leaned forward and kissed his mouth gently, Quinn relishing the taste of his lips with their sweet wine flavour.

"My hero, braving the big, bad witch to save the world." Cade whispered as he moved half on top of him, running his hands over Quinn's chest and slipping a warm rough hand into his shirt, through buttons which had suddenly become undone. Quinn's heart quickened at Cade's touch, and he marvelled at the fact that even after nearly a year together, the man still made him feel so horny. The aftershave he wore reminded him of their first meeting on Hampstead Heath. Quinn grinned at the memory.

Cade frowned. "Here I am trying to bloody seduce you and you find something funny? What gives?"

"I was remembering the first time we met, the time you were hiding behind a tree and you rushed at me like some kind of Amazon warrior and ended up flat on your face." Quinn chuckled at the thought as Cade's face darkened and he squeezed Quinn's groin tightly, causing him to wince.

"I wasn't hiding, and if it hadn't been for the fact that you had your Withinner reflexes, you'd still be bloody singing soprano." Cade tightened his grip.

Quinn took a deep breath as he fidgeted to get free of his lover's rather demanding grasp. "If you plan on using that anytime soon, you might like to let go. It's feeling decidedly threatened with that mean grip you have."

Cade regarded him with sultry eyes but didn't let go. He chuckled softly, making Quinn's skin tingle with the sheer sexiness of the sound. The fact that Cade's tongue was now trailing itself down the side of Quinn's throat certainly helped the sensation intensify.

"Did your big, bad witch do this?" Cade whispered as his hands released their grip and now softly stroked the front of Quinn's pants, causing him to groan softly. "Or this?"

There was a rasp as Quinn's zip was pulled down and he gasped as Cade reached in, stroking him with teasing fingers. Instinctively his hips curved up toward the source of his pleasure. Cade laughed softly and stood up, removing his clothes with a sleight of hand Quinn thought might make him a magician too. He stood before Quinn, all lean male lines and strong limbs, and Quinn thought he'd never seen anything so blatantly sexy.

He hungered for Cade, wanted his body so close to him that they melded into one. "Big, bad witch be damned," he whispered. "There's only you, only ever you."

Cade smiled as he proceeded to strip Quinn of both his clothes and all rational sense. Making love with Cade was always a journey, one that involved every body part, every slick, wet, heated movement the man could conjure up, every flick of a greedy tongue that assailed Quinn's skin and most intimate places and left him gasping for breath and what remained of his sanity. If Quinn was a lion, tawny and majestic, Cade was a panther—lithe, limber and more than a little dangerous. Finally Quinn was spent and lay back against the couch as Cade smiled down from above him, still impaled on Quinn's spent and tender, raw cock, both men sticky with their fluids.

"Christ!" Quinn gasped. "I still don't believe it feels this way every time we make love. It's always such bloody fun."

Cade laughed quietly as he moved off Quinn's body, reaching for his tee shirt and cleaning them both up as best he could. "It must be that Warlock-Fey attraction." He murmured as he gently cleaned the semen from their bodies. "No matter what you tell me about the feelings getting less every time we do it, it still sometimes feels like the first time we made love. Rather, when you seduced me." He grinned and tossed the rather sticky tee shirt to the floor as he curled, naked and cat-like next to Quinn on the couch.

"You'll never let me forget that, will you?" Quinn drawled as he lay on his side, looking across at his lover. "I'll always be the big, bad ravager of men to you, won't I? Even though you wanted to do me just as badly from the first time you saw me."

Quinn yelped in pain as Cade tweaked his chest hair fiercely. "Get over yourself. You had an unfair advantage. You know exactly why my insides turned to mush when I met you. Me, I just thought I was a total man whore."

Quinn mock frowned as he reached over and trailed his fingers down Cade's arm. "You are *exactly* that. I don't have a moment's peace with your rabid addiction to having sex with me. Not that I'm complaining."

He forestalled Cade's indignant response by claiming his mouth with his, pulling his warm body over on top of him, his soft hair falling across Quinn's face, tickling his nose. For a while there was silence, broken only by the sound of a cat's soft purr in the corner of the room.

Chapter 9

Jeremy Payton stood on the vast expanse of a flat Essex marshland in the village of Mistley. Shivers wracked his stocky frame and he pulled his grey duffel coat tighter around his body. The dwindling twilight made everything look colder. In the distance, boats anchored in mud stood stark against the skyline, looking like splintered skeletons, unloved and uncared for. Rowan Kirkpatrick, Jeremy's companion, had permitted himself a quiet chuckle when he'd seen the boat wreck nearest to where they were standing, so aptly called "Magic."

The swans sat immersed in the marsh whilst the seagulls and terns made raucous sounds and scrabbled for food.

The teenager muttered to himself as he stood stomping his feet to keep him warm. "It's a fucking joke, that's what it is." Jeremy scowled fiercely at the older man standing next to him. "He's got us out here at the arse end of the world just to perform a ceremony that could have bloody been done somewhere a fucking lot warmer! Just because he doesn't feel the bloody cold, he thinks it means we don't either."

Rowan regarded the boy without pity, his cold grey eyes flat. "Jeremy, firstly, don't talk so disparagingly about the man you sustain. Remember what happened last time. Secondly, this particular place had great significance to Matthew when he was mortal. This part of Manningtree on the River Stour was where he had his base of operations. Some people believe his earthly body is buried around here." He grinned nastily. "But we know better, don't we? So please do me the kindness of stopping your whining and let Matthew tell you what he wants you to do next."

Rowan Kirkpatrick regarded the young man with a sense of distaste. How the mighty Witchfinder General had ever had the bad luck to reside in this short, obtuse excuse for a young man was a mystery to him. He knew the boy was blood, but it was certainly an unfortunate circumstance that had led Matthew to where he currently resided.

Rowan was a self-professed expert on the works of the infamous Witchfinder General. He had a master's in Religion in Contemporary Society from King's College in London and had gone on to study further to the point where he certainly thought his studies and expertise allowed him to make such a claim. He'd been studying his subject matter for more than ten years. He was now thirty-five years old and wanting to move onto the next level. He'd never expected, however, to be contacted by this adolescent boy with an attitude and asked whether he wanted to be the new vessel for the reincarnated spirit of Matthew Hopkins himself. Rowan had to admit in his wildest dreams he'd never seen that coming. But after his initial scepticism that he was being trifled with, and a few very convincing displays of magyck and power, Rowan had accepted the honour with alacrity. He had few friends, little family and none that he really cared about, and his teachings were his passion.

Jeremy had been extremely aggressive at their first meeting, resenting the fact that his extra powers were going to be taken from him. But Hopkins had far greater ambitions that living inside a teenage body with all the angst and strife associated with it, blood descendant or not. He'd appeared to make that quite clear when he'd caused Jeremy's ears to bleed and afflicted the youngster with such severe muscle cramps that he'd almost been bent backwards.

After that little show of power, Jeremy had toed the party line with more grace.

Rowan had apparently been chosen because of his in-depth knowledge of the man himself and the fact he was "the right human vessel." He didn't really care how he'd got to this point, only that he had. Rowan was content to commit himself to the rituals Hopkins wanted to purify his body and prepare the vessel that was Rowan Kirkpatrick.

Since the beginning of October, nearly five months ago, Rowan Kirkpatrick had been leading a life of chastity, abstinence and, in his opinion, downright boredom. He'd been expected to abstain from sex, excesses of alcohol, smoking—all right, he wasn't a smoker, but if he had been, he'd have had to give it up— and he had to make sure he was eating the right diet. Hopkins had been quite specific about the amount of red meat he had to eat—a lot—coupled with what in Rowan's opinion was a really unhealthy obsession with cucumbers and quinces, both of which he heartily disliked. He'd also been given instructions to drink daily tinctures of the herb elecampane and eringus roots.

Rowan had been sick when he tasted them for the first time. He'd looked up their properties on the internet and stifled an expletive when he saw what they were used for in the seventeenth century. Eringus root was something used to prevent scurvy, which Rowan knew he didn't and never intended to have. It was also a mild laxative and sometimes used as an aphrodisiac, which given his current state of celibacy was not a good idea. Elecampane was an overall tonic and stimulant that appeared only to be used in veterinary practices now. All in all, between running to the toilet half the day to relieve himself in all aspects, and having a case of blue balls due to the lack of sex—exacerbated, in Rowan's opinion, by the Eringus herb—he'd lost weight. He also had a permanent heavy feeling in his groin which no amount of careful and intimate attention to his genitals when he was alone could permanently cure. He was looking forward to the day soon when he'd be able to put this all behind him and absorb the Witchfinder into his new bodily temple and perhaps get back to normal.

He stood now, watching Jeremy in his silent communion, feeling a prickle of fear for the first time. The special Mannacrux incantation they were about to recite on this day, the twentieth of March, had to be done just right for the start of his transition to begin.

Jeremy turned to him with the usual scowl on his face. "Right, Ichabod. He says to stand in front of me whilst I repeat the words he tells me. It has to be exactly seven p.m. when the chant starts." He looked up at the sky. "Everything is in place."

Rowan hated the nickname the teenage had given him, in his view an insult to his tall, crooked, spare frame, which, in Jeremy's opinion, resembling the unfortunate Ichabod Crane of *Sleepy Hollow* fame.

"What exactly does this chant do?" Rowan asked, ignoring the sneer in Jeremy's voice.

"It prepares the body you've been nourishing for the eventual psychic take-on of his spirit. That will only be done exactly forty-nine days from now, seven times seven, a very powerful number for the Witchfinder."

Rowan narrowed his eyes suspiciously. "For a being that professes to hate witches and everything they stand for, there seems to be an incredible Wiccan significance to what we're doing."

Today was Ostara, Lady Day, the day of rebirth. Rowan still didn't quite know why the Witchfinder General had planned this for a despised Wiccan sabbat, a sacred day for the very people he'd pledged to destroy, but he'd been assured that the magyck of the day was needed to make it work, to work against the witches. Hopkins had called it symbolic.

Jeremy glared at him. "The number seven is a powerful number in the Bible too. God created the world in seven days, remember? The seven deadly sins. The seven contrary virtues. The seven sacraments. The list of biblical references is endless. And anyway, March 20 is the feast day for various saints. Matthew knows what he's doing. So don't be all po-faced, Rowan. We're doing this with reference to *our* beliefs, not those dirty witches' ones."

It was probably the most educated and impassioned speech Rowan had ever heard from the young teenager, and he looked at him in surprise. Jeremy stared back impassively.

Rowan shrugged. "Well said. I apologise for doubting you or Matthew." He looked at his watch. "We have ten minutes before seven o'clock. Are we ready for this then?" He regarded Jeremy carefully. "What can I expect when this chant starts? Will it hurt, will I need to say anything myself?"

Jeremy nodded, a glint of satisfaction in his eyes. "It will hurt. But you need to stay silent through the chant. He says to stay calm, accept whatever happens and keep your mouth shut." He grinned wolfishly. "Matthew says you can open your mouth to scream if the pain gets too much but he'd prefer it if you didn't."

Rowan's heart beat faster. This wasn't something he was looking forward to. He took a deep breath as he readied himself for what lay ahead.

"Stand before me." Jeremy commanded. "Close your eyes and hold out your hands."

Rowan stood, towering over the younger man. Jeremy laid his hands on the other man's and waited patiently for seven p.m. They stood in silence until finally Rowan's hands tingled as Jeremy started the incantation. His voice was low, making no sense and

Rowan didn't recognise the words or the language. The tingle intensified, spreading up his arms, into his chest, making it tight as he struggled to breathe. His jaw ached as if he'd been hit hard. But the worst pain of all was in his head. He envisaged it like a thousand nanobots so often seen in the movies, invading his brain, circling aimlessly inside, their sharpened teeth bared to shred his brain to pieces.

He wanted to scream but the pain was too intense to even do that. All he could do was stand there like a marionette being pulled by invisible strings, his head jerking and his hands shaking. Jeremy kept up his chant, his words growing louder and more guttural.

Rowan knew he couldn't stand much more of this. Dimly, he heard the younger man's tones soften and finally fade away and then there was nothing more than a blinding whiteness, searing his eyeballs like looking into a nuclear explosion. Then there was blessed darkness and the pain disappeared; his chest opened up and he was finally able to breathe.

"It's finished." Jeremy's curt words cut into the silence of the marsh, overshadowed by the cries of seagulls as they flew above. Rowan opened his eyes and immediately wished he hadn't. They were terribly sensitive, prickling like pins and needles, and he saw nothing but darkness. He reached up a hand to touch them to find them wet with something. He gave a strangled cry, and reached out blindly to Jeremy.

Jeremy grasped his hands. "Relax. Your vision will come back. Give it a while." Rowan nodded, gasping with anxiety and Jeremy let go of his hands and reached up to his face. The teenager used what a handkerchief to wipe the wetness from his eyes.

"It's blood," Jeremy said disinterestedly. "It looks like you're crying tears of the stuff. Matthew says it will get better. He says you need a different perspective on things, to see what he sees, in order to be him. So he's changed your eyes a little. They won't look the same anymore."

"What the hell has he done to them?" Rowan whispered, squinting his eyes against the glare even though it was night.

"You'll see. I wish I had them." Jeremy sounded envious. "They look pretty cool, like one of those vampire people with totally black eyes. The ladies will love you."

He laughed softly and Rowan finally managed to open his eyes without too much pain. He blinked a few times as his eyes adjusted to the darkness. He could focus now and he saw the young Witchfinder in front of him, his silhouette emitting a strange orange glow, almost like an aura. Rowan gazed in wonder around him, seeing light where he'd never seen light before, noting the light around the trees, on the grass, on his own hands. He felt a sense of awe.

Jeremy turned and strode off toward the car. "Come on. I want to get home and you're the driver." He looked a little worried. "I hadn't thought of that. Can you still see to drive back to London?"

Rowan nodded. "I think so. It all looks very different but I can still see."

The two men got into the blue Rover and drove away, leaving a trail of exhaust fumes behind them.

Chapter 10

Quinn turned off the water in the shower, stepping out of the wet room and wrapping a towel around his waist. He frowned as he heard his mobile ringing downstairs.

It's Sunday. They can leave a message.

He finished dressing into comfortable chinos and an open-neck grey shirt, pulled on his loafers and went downstairs to wait for Cade to get back from his daily swim. Cade had been practicing holding his breath underwater and seemed to be pleased at the fact he could now reach almost seven minutes without coming up for air. Quinn had even found Cade disconcertingly immersed in his bathwater once or twice while he did the same thing, his hair floating around his face as he grinned up at him. He'd smirked and said he was getting his Sprite on. He hadn't been contacted again in the pond by any fellow Sprites and was a little disappointed.

Quinn switched on the coffee machine and sat down to check his mobile. The missed call had been from Percy. He knew he wouldn't have called this early unless it had been urgent, so he called his Marshall back. Percy answered almost immediately.

"Morning, sorry to call so early, but I have some good news to give you. We get so little of that nowadays, I thought you'd want to know."

"You got that right. What's up?" Quinn stood watching over the heath to see if he could spot Cade returning.

"I think those clever lads and lasses in the Reponosium have figured out whose Book of Shadows you have."

Quinn was all ears and he turned away from the window in anticipation. "That *is* good news. Tell me."

"Do you remember a witch named Elizabeth Clarke?"

Quinn nodded as he paced lion like around the living room. "Yes. She was the poor one-legged woman accused of being a witch by Matthew Hopkins and hanged at Chelmsford Crown Court in 1645." He frowned. "Are you telling me we have possession of *her* book?"

"I am," Percy said grimly. "She *was* a witch, a fairly powerful one from what we've found in the old texts. Matthew Hopkins set his cap at her for doing something bad to a tailor in the town. After that, there was no escaping the man. Elizabeth Clarke was taken to the cells, tortured and held prisoner until finally she confessed to anything that the Witchfinder General wanted."

Quinn frowned. "Is that what the initials are on the book then? I thought they were an M and a strange triangular symbol. How does that equate to E.C.?"

Percy chuckled down the line. "I had no idea either until the clever clogs at the research arm told me that they thought the symbols were old Elder Futhark runes, an ancient Germanic text. The M apparently symbolises the letter E and the smaller symbol is a K, which was also used for the letter C. So, the initials E and C. It fits in with the rest of the book contents, as there are various runes of the same language scattered throughout the book."

Quinn was impressed. "They're sure about this?"

Percy laughed. "Quinn, even you wouldn't want to go down and challenge Stephen Moreson on his interpretation of the hidden language of the book. Stephen's really passionate about his knowledge and his research and he's one of the world's experts on ancient languages. He's a really brilliant man and even *you* wouldn't be able to scare him."

Quinn grinned. "I might have to put that to the test sometime. So what else did they find out then?"

"This is the best news. If it's true, it's a real breakthrough and God knows we could use of one of those. There's apparently a story in the texts about Elizabeth Clarke damaging the Witchfinder General. She had very long fingernails, apparently, and as the man tried to get her Book of Shadows away from her, she dug her fingernails into his arm, slicing his arm badly and drawing blood, which spilled all over the book." Percy's voice was excited at the news and Quinn could see why. So could Taliesin. His Withinner sounded excited.

This is good news. We can track him down like we did Cade if the blood is indeed his.

"That means the stains on the front of the book could belong to Matthew Hopkins. That's a really powerful tool for us to use to track him down. I already have people on the lookout for any magyckal activity in Manningtree. Mistley actually, which was supposedly the place he was buried. Hopkins has roots there so it makes sense that Jeremy might go back there. We've had nothing yet but I'd imagine he's masking himself well. We might just need a stroke of luck to pin down exactly where he is."

A glimmer of hope surged through Quinn's body. Blood was always a powerful way of finding magyck practitioners and their arts and if that was true, it was a welcome bit of news. Percy continued his story, his voice fairly matter-of-fact.

"I know you won't like this request, but the research team have asked for the book to be sent over to them so they can do some testing on the stain and verify it is blood, see how old it is and what else they can find in the book. I know you sent over a replica but they really want the real thing. Now, I know how you feel about the book and you've probably married it by now and had a honeymoon, you may even have babies on the way, but—"

Quinn sighed heavily. "Enough already, you idiot, I know what I'm like and it's not a bad request. They deserve to see the real thing and if they can find out more about it than I can, they should have it. I'll get it sent over ASAP."

His Withinner commented silkily.

This is indeed an unexpected reaction. Normally you would have combusted at that idea like a chestnut in an open fire.

Quinn scowled.

Well, perhaps I'm learning a little bit of restraint, you poxy sorcerer. Now get out of my head and leave me be.

Taliesin shook in mirth.

"Wow, I must say I expected a lot more resistance to that idea than I got," Percy said, gob smacked. "You really are mellowing in your old age, aren't you?"

Quinn snorted. "Don't overstep the friendship line, Marshall." But his voice held laughter. The news had definitely made his mood better. He glanced out of the window and his heart leapt as he saw Cade's tall figure making his way across the heath.

"Once they have the book, let me know the minute they have any results on the tests. If it is blood, we can then convene a Withinner's Circle and between them, they can try and track down where Jeremy Payton is. Wherever he is, we'll find Matthew Hopkins. This has been great news. I'll come down to the Reponosium and personally thanks all those researchers for doing such a great job."

"They'll appreciate that, even though Stephen will probably ignore you and hurry back to his books. Don't be offended if he does; he's a strange bird."

Quinn chuckled. "I'll remember that. Anything else?"

"Nope, that was it for now. I'll be in touch as soon as I have anything new. Speak to you soon."

Chapter 11

Cade leaned back in his dining chair at the restaurant and patted his stomach. He grinned at Quinn, who sat opposite him, wincing at the amount of food he'd just eaten. He'd put away more food in one sitting than Cade had ever seen him eat.

"I am now officially stuffed. That was one of the best meals I've ever eaten." Cade gazed around admiringly at the dimly lit restaurant with its sophisticated ambience and quiet atmosphere. "I think all I want now is coffee and then home."

Quinn nodded. "Me too—except I think might have an Irish coffee instead." He beckoned to a passing waiter and placed their order then sat back in his chair with a satisfied sigh.

"This was a good idea, an anniversary dinner." He smiled at Cade. "I can't believe we've been together a year. It actually seems much longer. In a good way of course," he hastened to say.

"Not just been together," Cade chided him. "Today is the day you ravished me at that charity event. That was really our first date, hence the anniversary dinner tonight."

Quinn shook his head in amusement. "I'll never live that down, will I?"

He reached over and took Cade's hands in his, stroking his palm idly with his thumb. No one paid any attention to them. "I don't regret a single thing. Meeting you on the heath that evening was my saving grace."

Cade smirked in the candlelight. "Yeah right. I'm sure if I hadn't been there you'd have met some other sexy Fey who would have jumped your bones without the hassle I gave you." He picked up Quinn's hand and kissed it softly. "But I'm glad it was me."

The waiter arrived with their coffees and they sipped quietly.

"So, you said you didn't want an anniversary present." Quinn looked at Cade curiously. "Instead you said you had something else in mind that you wanted." He leered at him. "What could that be, I wonder?"

Cade chuckled. "Not what you have in mind, although that may come later." He hesitated. "You have to promise me you won't get upset when I tell you what I want. It's very important to me. I need to know you won't go all prima donna on me like last time."

Quinn's eyes narrowed. "I don't like the sound of this. Exactly what is it you want from me?"

Cade took a deep breath. "To talk. Really talk. At home there's always someone to interrupt us, or you can't wait to get to the basement to your books, or there's some life threatening event that you have to prevent. It's so difficult to actually have a conversation with you because you get distracted."

Quinn was still, his eyes wary. "Okay. What do you want to talk about?"

Cade drew a deep breath. "I want to talk about your childhood. I want to know what you did, how you grew up, what you were like as a young boy, a teenager. I know you went to the prom, but did you ever fancy a girl or a boy who didn't like you, did you get spots on your face—I want to get to know a bit about that part of your life."

Quinn was still as he toyed with the silver candlestick on the table. The candle had long burnt down. Cade waited to see what his response was.

Finally Quinn looked up and sighed. "I promised you I'd open up and try and tell you more about me. So it's not an unreasonable request as anniversary presents go. As long as you realise once you open my Pandora's box, there's no going back." He smiled grimly. "It's been a pretty eventful childhood so I hope you can stomach some of it. I'm no angel, I promise you."

"Nothing you could do would make me think less of you." Cade's hands covered his on the table. "I know this may be painful, but I'd really like to know a little about your parents."

Quinn looked down at the table. "They were pretty good, from what I remember." he said softly. "I only had them in my life for six years. My father's name was Christopher, my mother was Angela. My dad was the Grand Master of the Consortium and it was his full-time job. The Fairmont family has always had plenty of money so he didn't need to work at another job." He grinned slightly. "It's only overachievers like me that want to hold down a day job like a normal person."

Cade smiled at his comment, nodding his head in agreement.

"My mother was a witch. She fell madly in love with my father when they met at some convention when she was eighteen and it was love at first sight. They had me quite young. My dad was twenty-one, my mum a year younger."

He sipped his Irish coffee as Cade drank his coffee. Quinn's fondness for his parents reflected on his face as he talked about them.

"It was obviously a strange childhood. Where other kids were attending play dates with their pals and going to birthday parties, I was learning about magyck and spells and learning how to be physically strong. When you take on your Withinner at age seven, it's a really intense and physical ritual and they wanted me to ready for it. So I learned how to fight, how to deal with pain, how to be strong."

Cade squeezed his hands and Quinn smiled.

"It was a tough existence but it was rewarding and my parents did what they could to prepare me for what came later. I couldn't have had a better grounding. Of course, from birth I was being groomed to be the next Grand Master. But we didn't expect it would be so soon, that they would die so early."

His voice trailed off slightly.

"I didn't want to dredge up your parent's death," Cade said quickly. "I don't want you feeling uncomfortable. Tell me what happened when you were a teenager."

Quinn shook his head firmly. "You need to know everything I want to tell you. You can't take part of my life out because you don't want to hear it."

Cade stayed silent, watching him, knowing he was getting what he'd asked for. His lover's eyes were distant.

"We had a house in St. James, a large penthouse. I remember sitting in the lounge, playing with an aeroplane I'd been given for my birthday, when it got really cold. I thought the door had opened; it was the middle of winter and the hallway outside could get quite chilly. I remember getting up to go see what was going on and then…nothing. It's as if it just all got blanked out."

Quinn's face was tight. "The next thing I remember was seeing both of my parents on the floor." His voice was grim and he held onto Cade's hands tightly. "They were both dead already, I could see that. Their bodies were contorted and my father had been sick on the floor."

"Please don't carry on." Cade's voice was agonised. "This isn't what I wanted." He wished he'd never started this conversation.

Quinn smiled, his mouth twisted in pain. "I told you before, I don't have many happy-ever-after stories. Let me finish. It might be good for me to talk about this to you as well. That can be my anniversary present from you." He heaved a shuddering sigh. "The next thing I knew, someone picked me up and barrelled out of there so fast it was a bit like a dream. A Warlock friend of my father's had come over to see my folks, seen what had happened and got me out of there. His name was Edward Mistral."

Quinn's eyes closed briefly and an expression of pain crossed his face. Cade wondered what darker connection this Warlock had to him.

"Edward saved my life. Apparently I would have been next if he hadn't gotten to me when he did. He said there were Witchhunters in the apartment. I don't know how they got in or how no one sensed them. Edward destroyed them both and got me out of there. He called Daniel and his wife Moira, who as you know was my aunt and they came to fetch me. From that time on, I lived with them. Daniel was my surrogate father and Moira was, to all intents and purposes, my mother."

His voice went quiet. "Moira was killed four years ago by the Witchhunters Alliance. Daniel was devastated as was I. We both threw ourselves into work and fighting the Alliance and until I met you, that was basically all I did."

He caressed Cade's fingers gently with his. "Now I have you, and despite everything that's happened, I'm happy. It *is* our anniversary, Cade, so enough tales now of people dying."

Cade swallowed uncomfortably. "I'm sorry. I didn't mean to pry."

Quinn smiled gently. "Yes you did, you sexy little liar. It actually feels good to tell you about it. I haven't ever had someone I can do that with. It's been a good thing, I promise. I could get used to this baring of my soul." He chuckled softly. "And yes, I did have a crush on a boy when I was twelve who didn't return the favour and it broke my heart. I didn't have spots. I enjoyed looking down girl's blouses and checking out boy's crotches and was nearly expelled from school for being found smoking. Although it wasn't a cigarette; it was some herbal thing my aunt gave me to cure a sore throat but the teachers were having none of it. Typical adolescent behaviour, perhaps a little more strange than normal, but still just teenage angst."

Quinn's face was mischievous. "I went to my senior prom with a girl called Victoria, and I didn't get leg over like you did with Lurch. I was a perfect gentleman. And of course, you already know about my first sexual encounter so we won't go into that again."

Cade chuckled, glad to see Quinn joking again.

"No, we'll leave that one alone." He looked around the restaurant. "It's looking very empty, I think they might be waiting for us to leave. Perhaps we should get home and I can give you your other anniversary present."

Quinn looked at him with smoky eyes. "I hope that means what I think it means or you're going to have one very disappointed man on your hands." He stood up. "I'll go settle up the bill. You get your jacket and I'll see you at the desk."

He leaned down and kissed the top of Cade's head gently before disappearing to the counter to pay. Later that night they lay in bed together after Quinn had been given his anniversary present. Cade thought drowsily that he'd seemed very pleased with his bondage session and had certainly entered into the spirit of things.

"Are you awake?" Cade nudged his arm gently.

Quinn sighed. "I am now. I *was* just falling asleep."

Cade pressed into Quinn's warm body. "Thank you for talking about yourself. It was the best present I could have."

"It's a pleasure," Quinn said sleepily. "I'm trying to be a good boy and keep my promises."

Cade chuckled throatily. "You're always such a good boy. I love you—you know that, right?"

Quinn pressed lips to Cade's hair where it was tucked into the crook of his arm. "I love you too. Now will you please go to sleep? I have to be up early in the morning."

Cade wrapped an arm across Quinn's stomach and closed his eyes.

Chapter 12

Quinn stood up from his desk and stretched. He'd been busy in his library most of the morning. Daniel and Percy were coming around to give him an update on the research being done at the Reponosium. He locked up and made his way up to the living room. Cade was sitting in the armchair, a *Men's Health* magazine open in front of him. He grinned up at Quinn.

"Wow, the Kraken comes out of its den. It's a Saturday morning and you've been in your library for the past four hours." He looked at his watch. "Daniel and Percy will be here any minute. They said they'd be here about midday."

Quinn nodded as he took an ice-cold beer out of the bar fridge and drank it straight from the bottle thirstily. He wiped his mouth and plonked himself down on the couch, lying with his legs stretched out along the length of the sofa.

"I don't like meeting Daniel here at the house but I think we managed to make sure things are secure from outside eyes. But I won't make a habit of it. Percy said he had some more good news and needed Dan here." He grimaced. "Hell knows we can use something positive. I'm hoping he's found a way to track down Jeremy Payton. I'm getting a bit twitchy about the fact that he's been so quiet. At least on the Warlock side. I understand the witches have had a couple of strange deaths and Valensia has her teams on high alert."

He frowned. "I suppose we should count ourselves lucky there haven't been any Warlock deaths." The doorbell rang and Quinn got up to answer it. When he opened the door, Daniel and Percy stood there.

"Come on in." Quinn waved them into the living room. Quinn handed them both a beer as they sat down and settled himself down again on the couch. "It's good to see you, Daniel," he said quietly. "It's been a little while. How are things at the Alliance and RAW? Is everything still running smoothly?"

Daniel nodded, his sinewy frame getting comfortable in the chair.

"I'm still shuffling roles." He smiled tiredly and Quinn saw the strain in his mouth and in his eyes.

"Dan, if it's getting too much, you need to pull out. I know we agreed you could do this but I don't need you taking any risks. There's been enough tragedy already. We'll find another way."

Daniel shook his head. "I'm fine, honestly, I can do this some more. Believe me, I'll tell you when my double-agent status gets too much."

He grinned at Quinn but the Warlock wasn't quite sure he believed his uncle's words. He nodded dubiously. "Don't take chances." Quinn looked over at Percy. "So, you look as if you're dying to tell us all your news. Shoot, I'm ready."

He took another slug of his beer and got comfortable on the couch.

Percy leaned forward in excitement. "Those researchers at the Reponosium are worth their weight in gold and they really appreciated you visiting them to thank them personally. It went down well."

Quinn smiled. "I saw what you meant about that Stephen Moreson. He was a really strange bird. He didn't even seem to know I was there, just kept nodding at whatever I said but looked like he'd rather be anywhere else."

Percy chuckled. "It's genius, that's what it is. The man is so clever he has no idea how to interact with actual people. Anyway, the good news is that the stains on the book are definitely blood. They did some radio carbon dating on it and they are in agreement; it definitely could date back to the seventeenth century. We can't definitively say it's Hopkins's, of course, but given the stories, the book, the carbon dating and the fact it's blood, it all points to a pretty conclusive proof."

The little group was silent as they digested Percy's words. A surge of positivity radiated through Quinn's body. This was indeed very good news.

"And that's not all they found." Percy continued his tale with a distinct air of satisfaction. "There's a text in the Reponosium archives affiliated to the Witchfinder General that actually gives a way to destroy him. It's not gospel, it was thought of more as urban legend, but given what we know now, I think it's right."

Quinn leaned forward, his nostrils flaring and his eyes narrowing, like a fox in a hen house surveying his dinner. "How do we do that?"

"It's a little complicated so bear with me." Percy swallowed a gulp of beer as the others watched him intently. Cade shifted in his chair and Daniel grinned at him.

"Are you all right with all this? We're not boring you?"

Cade waved his beer bottle. "No, I think it's fascinating watching you guys piece all these obscure bits together to make sense of it. It's what I do as an anthropologist, just in a different way."

Quinn leaned forward, eager to hear the rest of Percy's story. "Go on, tell us the rest."

Cade rolled his eyes at Quinn's impatience as Percy continued his story.

"The documents we found relating to Montague Druitt—you remember he was the man who was thought to have had Matthew Hopkins channelled into him in the nineteenth century? Again, this was said to have happened as a result of a Book of Shadows being found and the spells being performed. For all we know it could be the same book that Quinn now has back in his collection. The chances are very good that this was indeed the case. Well, at the time there was this banishing spell in circulation, to send Hopkins back to his everlasting hell, wherever that was."

Percy rummaged around in his pocket and pulled out a piece of paper. "Apparently there's also a way that Hopkins, once he was in this world, could find himself a more suitable human vessel and actually reincarnate himself physically."

Quinn gave a hiss of displeasure at these words. "You mean he actually could do that?"

Percy nodded. "If he prepared the 'human vessel,' as it was called, using certain herbs and rituals, he could pass into that body. The purification ceremony had to happen on the twentieth of March and exactly forty-nine days later, seven by seven because of the auspiciousness of the number, he could perform the ritual that lets him be reincarnated permanently in a human body. In case you're all frantically working the math, that's on May seven." He looked at the group of people hanging onto his every word. "That's in just over two weeks' time," he said grimly.

Taliesin spoke sharply.

Hellfire, Quinn that leaves us very little time to plan anything. We will have to make haste if we want to defeat this Witchfinder from completing his plan. But I think Percy is right in his findings.

Quinn jumped up and paced around the living room, running his hands through his hair in agitation. "As Taliesin says, that doesn't leave us much time to stop the bastard! You said we could stop him. How?"

Percy shifted uncomfortably. "This is the part that's a little unknown, as we can't find any record of it ever being done. It was all conjecture. Perhaps it happened but it wasn't documented. But the texts say it is feasible. On the seventh of May, there's a solar eclipse. We won't see it here in the Northern Hemisphere, but that doesn't mean it isn't happening. There's a ritual chant that needs to be performed at the time the eclipse is at its maximum which is one twenty-three in the morning. Ideally, for maximum effect, it should be performed in close proximity to all three of them, which could be an additional problem for us. According to the texts, this was done in the nineteenth century to banish Hopkins back to where he came from and is the reason Montague Druitt was found floating in the river. The Consortium at the time then tidied up any loose ends and made it look like a random witch killing. If it was done, it had to have worked, because he wasn't around any longer until that coven in Suffolk messed with what we think is the same book and opened the door again for him." He stopped to take a breath and take another drink of his now lukewarm beer. He gulped it down and carried on.

"The only problem is we need something from the prepared human vessel to work with the chant. That, together with the destruction of whatever we get, basically makes the host untenable for Hopkins, forcing him back to where he came from."

The small party regarded him gloomily.

That is not an insurmountable problem. Taliesin sounded excited. *We could convene a Withinner's Circle perhaps?*

Quinn nodded in agreement with the voice in his head as he continued his pacing. "Christ, I thought we might be able to do this with just the chant and have nothing more to do with any of those poxy Witchfinders," he growled. "But that would just be too fucking easy, wouldn't it? So now we have to find this human receptacle and get something from him to perform the ritual." He frowned. "Taliesin has said we could convene a Withinner's Circle, with four of us, then use the book and the blood traces to try to track down exactly where Jeremy Payton is. If he's currently storing Hopkins, we should be able to find them both and maybe that will lead us to this human"—he waved his hands in frustration—"*container,* and then we can take it from there. We can use Taliesin, Nicholas, Attilius and Rupert. They should make a very strong circle."

Cade spoke curiously. "I know Nicholas, that's your Withinner, isn't it Percy? But who are the other two?"

"Attilius is Magnus's Withinner, and Rupert is with a man called Justin Leichner. He's an old friend of mine whom I can trust."

Quinn turned to Percy. "Do you think you can get hold of Magnus and I'll call Justin? He'll be glad to help, if I can track him down. The last time I heard of him he was in the Himalayas somewhere. If we can arrange for them to convene as soon as possible, we can perhaps stop this thing before it happens. We have no other choices, it looks like."

Percy nodded. "I'll let Magnus know to be on call and once you've found Justin, we can set it up." He leaned back with a sigh of relief, glad that his tale was over.

Quinn looked at Percy. "If you have a moment, there's something in the library I'd like you to see." He waved a hand at the others and made his way to the basement, turning to see whether Percy was behind him. Quinn heard Cade give a deep sigh of resignation and he smiled at his lover's reaction before entering his man lair.

*****

"Well, that'll be the last we see of him until midnight." Cade remarked drily, looking over at Daniel. "It looks like it's just me and you. Would you like coffee or something?"

Daniel shook his head. "No thanks, Cade. I'm good."

There was a companionable silence and Cade glanced at the older man. He'd met him before at Quinn's bedside when he was injured but that had been such a whirlwind of activity they'd had little time to get to know each other. Cade guessed Daniel to be in his early fifties, looking younger than his years despite his obvious stress, and he had a calm, thoughtful face.

"Quinn told me all about his parents' deaths the other night," Cade said softly. "It was a terrible thing for a six-year-old to go through. I'm glad you were there for him. I went through something similar with my step-mum, but I was a lot older than he was. I was able to cope better, I expect."

Daniel leaned forward. "I heard about your tragedy from Quinn. I'm sorry you had to face that. It must have been a very traumatic time. "

Cade nodded. "It was. But nothing like what Quinn had to face at such a young age."

Daniel nodded. "It was a tough time for him. He was a difficult boy and definitely a bit of a hellion in his younger years. He needed a father figure. He's not an easy man to control, as I'm sure you've found out."

Cade chuckled. "No one controls Quinn, least of all me. I'm just lucky he's finally started sharing his past with me. He has so many secrets, he's like a maze. You think you get to the end and see the exit and then you face yet another hedge that you can't get through."

"That's a very apt description of him," Daniel said approvingly. "Quinn's had to grow up terribly fast, and becoming Grand Master at the young age of twenty-one was an incredible achievement. No Grand Master has ever achieved the title that young before."

His voice was proud.

Cade looked at him. "What exactly does one have to do to earn that title? Is it some sort of ritual he goes through? Are there levels you achieve, like in the Masons?"

Daniel looked at him uncomfortably. "It's really just a case of making decisions, showing how strong you are and working the inevitable power game. Quinn is a master at it. There were people who thought he'd never get where he was but he proved them wrong. It became a challenge for him, and being Quinn, he had to win."

"What kind of decisions?" Cade asked quietly. "Quinn told me that at the age of twelve he had to make a decision to kill a man. I couldn't believe it. Are those the kind of decisions you're talking about?"

Daniel snorted. "You don't want to know all the gory details, trust me. You know how tormented Quinn is by some of his past? The less you know in this case, the better. I believe that with all my heart. I don't want you to get the wrong impression of him by telling you the kind of things he's had to do to get where he is."

"The end justifies the means. Quinn's mantra," Cade murmured.

Daniel nodded. "He has the weight of the Warlock race on his shoulders and he'll do anything to protect them. It's what he's sworn to do and he does it very well. There has been less trouble in Quinn's tenure than with any other Grand Master before him, including his father, who was one of the best. Christopher hated the fact that Quinn had to become it. He wanted Quinn not to have that responsibility because it's a burden, but he knew he couldn't stop it. And he knew Quinn would want it. It's who he is, who he was born to be."

Daniel fell silent, watching Cade's face.

Cade smiled at him. "He's very complicated, isn't he?" He heard the wistfulness in his voice. "Sometimes I have no idea who he is." He lowered his eyes to his hands. "Sometimes he scares me. He can be so damned implacable."

Daniel shook his head fiercely. "That man worships you. You're his world; never forget that. You're the only thing he'd put above the Consortium and his mantra and that knowledge scares him. He's never had that happen to him before. He thinks it makes him weak. You and I know it just makes him human. You need to bear with him. If he's opening up to you now, that's a good sign. You just keep chipping away at my boy. And never fear him. He'd never do anything to hurt you." He grinned. "Not intentionally anyway. He can be a bit of an arrogant, bad-tempered bastard, I know. "

The two men sat in silence and Cade was truly surprised when Quinn and Percy came back into the room. He'd expected Quinn to be longer, as was his way when he went into his study. Quinn looked at Daniel, then at Cade. He frowned.

Cade knew that look. Quinn was wondering if they'd been talking about him.

"I managed to track down Justin," Quinn said quietly. "He's somewhere in Tibet at the moment with his oil company but he'll join us for the circle at ten tomorrow morning and so will Magnus. Then perhaps we can find Hopkins. We don't have a lot of time so I hope this bloody works."

He scowled fiercely and looked at Daniel with a raised eyebrow. To Cade's amusement, Daniel ignored Quinn's apparent curiosity at what he and Cade had been discussing and stood up.

"Well, if that's it, I'm getting off. I have a dinner date with a very willing lady and as it's been a while since I saw any action, I'm raring to go."

Quinn shook his head in amusement. "You're assuming she's willing. I hope she likes short, skinny blokes with attitude. Then you should be all right."

Daniel laughed and came over to hug Quinn. Cade watched as Quinn hugged him back, marvelling at his easy acceptance of this man's affection. He'd never seen him do that with anyone else before, not even Percy.

"I'm going to get off too," Percy announced. "I might be able to salvage that late afternoon game of golf after all."

The two men departed, leaving Cade and Quinn standing by the front door as they waved goodbye. Quinn shut the door with a thankful sigh.

"It's been quite an eventful afternoon," he mused, looking at Cade. "Have you anything planned now that you want to do?"

"Nothing in particular. I do have some notes for a dissertation to finish for Ambrose so I suppose I'd better do that." Cade wrinkled his nose in distaste.

"I have a better idea," murmured Quinn as his mouth swooped down, parting Cade's lips and kissing him greedily. Cade surrendered to his embrace and decided it was definitely a better plan.

Chapter 13

Four men stood in a circle in Quinn's library basement the following morning, their faces expectant yet composed. It was a rare sight to see so many influential and powerful Warlocks in one place at the same time. Quinn looked around at the gathering of his close friends and confidantes and regarded each one of them in turn. Magnus, Percy and Justin gazed back with the same scrutiny. Justin's face, tanned from the Tibetan sun, seemed at odds with the paler faces of everyone else. He was a tall man, about Quinn's age and height, with a stocky frame and chiselled face.

Quinn smiled slightly. "Look at us. A meaner bunch of reprobates I've yet to see." The others grinned back. "Are we ready for this? Everyone knows what we need to do?"

They all nodded and Quinn nodded too in satisfaction. "Right, let's invoke those Withinners and get this party started."

All four men chanted their invoking words quietly and within seconds, the circle of human warlocks had changed to a circle of magyckal beings, all distinctly different. Taliesin was in his usual garb: breeches, jerkin and his long, swirling cloak. Draigh, Taliesin's familiar, buzzed impatiently around the room.

Nicholas, Percy's Withinner, was attired in a long, green robe with black trimming and astronomical symbols across the fabric. Attilius was dressed in a deep red, flowing garment that wrapped around his body, held in a place by a white sash across his waist. He had a long chain of Roman medallions around his neck, reaching down to his breastbone. It was Rupert, being the most modern of the current Withinners in the room that looked most out of place amongst the circle. He was casually clad in a pair of deep blue trousers, brown leather sandals and a white, billowing shirt, fastened at the neck by a small brooch.

Taliesin, as usual, took charge. "It is good to see you all again," he murmured. "Rupert, I swear you look more foppish each time we meet. "

The other Withinners grinned at the banter. It was a standing feud between Taliesin and Rupert to insult each other's dress sense.

"And I see you still wear the same clothes you had on when we met last time, Taliesin." Rupert twitched his nose in distaste. "It certainly smells like it."

Attilius chuckled, a deep belly laugh that shook his rotund frame and jiggled the jowls of his fat chins. Nicholas smiled quietly as Taliesin chuckled.

"Now we have the pleasantries out of the way, shall we begin? Time is short and there is a lot depending on us. Where is the Book of Shadows?"

Nicholas motioned to Quinn's desk. "I believe it is that one. It reeks of death even from here." He frowned. "Whoever owned that book suffered greatly."

Taliesin nodded. "If we all place our hands on it, and concentrate our energies, we may be able to get a sense of where this poxy Witchfinder is. Nay, we *have* to get a sense of where he is. We have only until the solar eclipse to try and destroy him so we must make haste and succeed in our endeavour."

The four men moved over to the book, each placing their left hand on a part of it, and grimacing at the feelings the book invoked.

"The blood trail is faint, but it is there," Attilius said quietly. "I see some images but it will take all of us to enhance this blood trail. Can I suggest we begin?"

The Withinners closed their eyes and each chanted their own words to amplify the images, sights and sounds they were receiving from Matthew Hopkins' blood. Their faces underwent transformations of emotions as they tapped into the spiritual essence overlaying the book. The air around them hazed up like heat rising off a scorching pavement. The men remained firm, their stances upright, and their murmuring grew louder. The book shimmered and rose slightly, but still the group kept hold of it. A red mist slowly rose from the front of the book, swirling around like pink fog and covering the Withinner's hands.

Nicholas gave a sigh of satisfaction. "I see something," he said quietly. "I see a church, a grey brick church, in a graveyard. The sign is faint but there are words on the sign outside the entrance."

"I see it too," murmured Taliesin. "It is called the Church of St. Mary and St. Michael. The words on the sign say it is the parish church of a place called Mistley, as expected. Can anyone see the people we are seeking?"

"I see a stone cottage, out in nowhere, behind trees and set far into the woods." muttered Rupert. "It is cloaked with magyck but not strong enough to hide from this exalted circle. I feel a bad presence in its midst. Something is rotten inside. Can we concentrate on this place? I feel it in my bones that the people we seek are inside. The stench is odorous."

All the Withinners focused on where Rupert had pointed them and finally Taliesin nodded in satisfaction.

"I see them. The cottage is buried deep in the woods, on a dirt road. I see a broken signpost saying 'Weathers.' I'm not sure if that is the name of the place or the area. I also see a copse of seven broad trees—they look like sentries, they stand so firm." He squinted, his brow furrowing. "There are two people in it," he frowned, "three of them including Hopkins himself. A boy, a tall, thin man and the Witchfinder essence. They are all together in this house. I think the boy is this Jeremy Payton that Quinn is seeking. The other man, he feels different, but he is not a Fey. He is still human but there is something strange about him."

"He will be the human vessel," said Rupert quietly. "The one the Witchfinder intends possessing on the forty-ninth day. The process of cleansing him has already begun. That is why he seems different."

Taliesin nodded as did the others. "The young man is calling him Rowan. He is spindly indeed. I had not thought to see a strange specimen of human so tall and thin. He looks like some sort of strange insect you would find in the woods, hiding under foliage."

The others chuckled grimly at Taliesin's words.

"This is good," muttered Nicholas. "We have found them. Our Warlocks will be very pleased."

The red mist around their hands slowly drifted down back into the book and when it was finally gone, the Withinners looked around the circle at each other and nodded their heads in deference to each other.

"We did well." Taliesin sounded smug. "I think our reward should be to stay in this place a little longer before being revoked. I could do with time away from my own home."

Attilius spluttered in laughter. "The last time that happened, you ended up very much in the disgraced favours of your Warlock for putting your manhood where it didn't belong!"

The others sniggered as Taliesin regarded his colleagues angrily.

"Will I ever be rid of that cursed story?" he snarled as the others chuckled loudly at his discomfort. "I did not know that everyone knew about that indiscretion. Quinn has been rather indiscreet it would seem."

"Quinn didn't tell us." Nicholas smiled. "Percy knew, so I found out and told the rest of them. I knew one day we could embarrass you with that story."

"Except for me." Rupert bowed slightly. "But I am now aware of the story and have yet another thing to vex you with when next we meet." He cocked his head and sighed. "I am being revoked. I had better get back to my own time and let Justin back in his. Farewell friends, until we meet again."

One by one the Withinners were revoked by their Warlocks, and soon Quinn, Percy, Magnus and Justin stood together again in the library.

Quinn regarded everyone with a broad smile. "I have to say that was a great success. Thank you all. We have a place to find these men now. Those seven trees sound distinctive and the name 'Weathers' gives us a clue. I am sure with our resources we can find this secret cottage in the woods. When we find the place, I'd suggest Daniel goes to get the bits we need. That way we don't jeopardise any surprise advantage we have by alerting him to magyckal activity in the area. I'll tell Daniel to find this Rowan person and get something personal, hair or blood, from him to do the ritual. Percy, you start working on the ritual we need to defeat this bastard."

Percy nodded. "Sounds like a good plan."

Quinn nodded. "Also have someone keep eyes on them. I want to know where they are at all times. Then when we're ready to perform the ritual, we can get closer to them. I have a feeling they'll stay close to home, waiting for their turn to shine. But we'll get to them first."

He frowned. "And have a word with that Withinner of yours will you, and tell him to zip it about my personal life. I know they like to needle Taliesin but I don't quite fancy that story about he and Cade getting it on being spread everywhere!"

Percy chuckled, as Magnus grinned beside him. "I'll tell him that. Sorry about that. Nicholas is a bit of a gossip."

He nodded at the other Warlocks and disappeared upstairs on his mission.

Justin nodded at his friend. "I'm glad I could help. If you need any more help to get these bastards, you make sure and let me know." He smiled. "I need to get back to Tibet. There's a lady waiting for me there and I don't want to disappoint her."

"Thanks Justin. Let's not make it so long next time. When you're about next, let me know. We can have a few tequilas together like last time."

Justin chuckled. "God, last time, that nearly killed me! But I appreciate the sentiment, old friend. I'll be in touch."

He invoked his Withinner and in minutes, Rupert had taken him back to his woman.

Quinn was left standing alone in his basement. He sat down at his desk and regarded the Book of Shadows curiously. It had certainly been a worthwhile trip to Valensia to obtain the book, which had proven a rich source of material to get them the success they'd had so far. He picked it up idly, turning it in his hands. As he did so, the red mist slowly lifted off the book, coating his hands with the cold and damp substance. He frowned as he lifted his hand, seeing the slight speckles of red on his skin. He laid the book down and went over to the basement bathroom to wash his hands. The residue, probably blood, had been left behind by the Withinner's activities, he guessed. He put the book back in its cabinet and locked it and went upstairs to find Cade. His lover sat outside on the patio, a glass of wine on the wrought-iron table beside him, jotting down notes in his study papers. The late April sun shone down on his dark hair and Quinn smiled at the sight.

Cade looked up as Quinn kissed his warm, sun-drenched hair. "Are you all Warlocked out, then, Quinn?" Cade smiled. "Has everyone gone home? Did you have any success finding who you were looking for?"

"I am, they have and we did. Percy is on his way there as we speak to see if he can find the human that intended taking on Hopkins. Once he does, he'll try and get something from him that we can use to hopefully stop this Witchfinder crap for good."

He sat down next to Cade on the sun lounger, stretching his legs comfortably in front of him as he leaned back and turned his face to the sun.

Cade reached over and ran his hands through his hair. "I love it when you have sunlight on your hair," he murmured. "It goes all golden and shiny. "

Quinn chuckled. "I'm glad you like it. I live to please you."

Quinn closed his eyes, enjoying the warmth on his face then started when a pair of warm lips came down on his, kissing him fiercely. He reached up, pulling Cade down onto his lap as Cade wrapped his arms around his neck. Cade's mouth tasted of wine and sunshine and for a while Quinn lost himself in his kisses. When he finally let him go, Quinn watched as Cade stood up and with a cheeky grin, he reached up and pulled his tee shirt off to reveal strong shoulders and abs. Then he slipped out of his trousers and stood naked before Quinn. Quinn lost his breath at the sight of his lover's taut, firm body and the evidence of his horniness jutting out from the curls at his groin. Cade regarded him with one eyebrow raised.

When Quinn found his voice it was husky. "Well, you *are* quite the man slut. What have I done to deserve this kind of attention?" He was extremely uncomfortable in his jeans, his cock ready to give something a pounding. He took a quick look around the garden to make sure it was private. Thanks to the high walls and tress, it looked fairly secluded. He hadn't actually done it in his back garden yet so this would hopefully be a first. Cade chuckled softly as he leaned down and unzipped Quinn's jeans, reaching in and grasping him. Quinn leaned his head back against the lounger, closing his eyes in pleasure.

"I figured you needed a little relaxation after a hard day Warlocking," Cade whispered as he stroked him gently. "I hope this lounger takes both our weight," he murmured as he proceeded to climb on top of Quinn, straddling him as he gasped in delight. "I'm just never sure whether the quality control sticker on these things actually means what it should—"

His words were cut off as Quinn's greedy tongue slipped wetly into his lover's mouth, and both men forgot all about the quality control of loungers as they moved together. Cade lowered himself onto Quinn, taking him inside. Quinn groaned loudly, the slick heat of being inside Cade causing incredible sensations in his groin.

Quinn's hands gripped Cade's hips as he rode him, causing unbearable friction and making him gasp. The warm sun shone down on his bare legs and his chest and he found it extremely erotic being so free, naked and bared to the mercy of the elements.

Quinn opened his eyes to find Cade staring down at him with such an expression of lust in his silver eyes that Quinn almost came there and then. Bright sunlight directly above pierced Quinn's eyes with flashes of colour and pain and he closed his eyes again. Quinn's hips thrust upward to meet Cade's movements, and for a while it was as if time was forgotten and the only sounds were deep sighs and grunts of satisfaction as two men made love in the sunshine.

Quinn's hand was around Cade's cock and he moved it in tandem with their hip movements, slow, enticing strokes that made Cade moan loudly. Finally Cade sighed deeply and Quinn knew his lover was on the verge of coming. He felt it in the swelling of Cade's cock, the subtle shift of the velvet muscles that held his own cock tight and in the deep breaths Cade took as he gave way to his orgasm. Quinn wasn't far away himself and he tried valiantly to hold off until after Cade had climaxed. The feeling of contracting and clenched muscles rippling around Quinn's cock would make it all the more worthwhile.

The warmth of the sun, the sheer eroticism of the moment out here in the air with Cade's scent in his nostrils—Quinn revelled in the sensations, the act of sex and love playing out on a garden chair between two people who were each other's universe. Quinn felt the most alive when he was inside Cade, the act of intimacy and trust reaching into his heart and warming it.

Cade's mouth opened in a moaning cry as Quinn's hands played their final, teasing symphony. Cade arched back as streams of come shot over Quinn's stomach and groin, wetting his hand with sticky warmth. Quinn's groin flooded with extreme prickling heat and he too gave a loud shout as he gave way to his own intense release, clutching Cade's hips tightly. Cade leaned down, his mouth finding Quinn's as he shuddered beneath him.

They lay coupled together in the sunlight, a slightly chill wind blowing now and making both of their skins tingle with goose bumps.

"I have to say, I really enjoy making love outside. We should do it more often." Quinn said lazily.

Cade kissed him. "You're welcome. It does make a change from the kitchen, the bathroom, the lounge, the bedroom, the entrance hall…" He grinned. "Is there anywhere in this house we haven't made love now? Apart from your 'sacred' place?"

Cade was referring to his basement library.

Quinn chuckled. "I think we've christened every room in the house, including the laundry room, if you recall. That poor washing machine will never be the same again."

Cade burst into laughter, obviously recalling the rather acrobatic session on the washing machine which had been in its fast spinning cycle at the time, adding a level of sheer decadence to their session. Quinn grinned, loving the sight of this man sitting on top of him, butt naked. He had never loved anyone like he did Cade. Not even Adam. Cade shivered as the chilly wind softly caressed his skin and he swung his legs over Quinn, standing up and reaching down to pick up his clothes off the ground. Quinn lazily pinched his backside as he bent down and Cade jumped up.

"God, that hurt! Don't be such a damn bully. I'm going inside; it's getting too cold out here."

Quinn watched languidly as Cade strode inside. He didn't really feel like moving but he supposed he'd better. He stood up with a sigh, feeling a sudden rush of blood to his head, making him dizzy. Frowning, he held onto the back of the lounger while his balance steadied. He felt the familiar tickle beneath his nose and cursed as he saw a drop of blood drip onto the white plastic of the sun lounger. Quinn reached up a hand and wiped it away with a muttered expletive.

What the hell had brought that on? He hadn't had a nosebleed for some time. Please don't say he was going to get one of these every time he exerted himself having sex. If that was the case, he'd almost have a permanent trickle.

He grinned at that thought and gathered up his jeans and disappeared inside to find Cade.

Chapter 14

Cade sat bolt upright in the bed as Quinn screamed loudly beside him, thrashing about the bed in a paroxysm of limbs and blankets. He reached over to him, his heart thumping as he tried to catch hold of Quinn's arm and calm him down.

"Quinn, for God's sake wake up."

Quinn was muttering names over and over again, the name of Honour Whitebrook, the little girl who'd been killed by the Witchhunters Alliance together with her family and another familiar name.

"Edward, God, Edward! Don't ask. Don't ask me to do that."

Cade switched on his bedside light then reached out firmly and shook Quinn violently, seeing his eyes open. A chill traversed his spine. His boyfriend's eyes had gone totally black again, face twisted in a vicious snarl that made him hardly recognisable as the man he loved. Quinn's arm reached out, grabbing his and gripping it so fiercely that he cried out in pain. Sweat glistened on Quinn's body and he sat up, his breath coming in deep, wrenching gasps. Cade pulled his arm free, leaning over to clasp Quinn's face in firm hands to make him look at him.

"Quinn! Calm down and look at me. Look at me!"

His commanding tone seemed to get through and his lover's eyes finally focused on him, even through their inky blackness. Quinn leaned back against the headboard, heaving a shuddering sigh as he passed a hand over his face.

"Cade? What happened?" Quinn looked disoriented and confused. Cade reached out a tender hand and caressed his face, feeling it slick with sweat.

"You were having a nightmare again." He watched Quinn helplessly as he sat back, his face drawn and pale, his nose already starting to trickle blood.

Cade reached over to his bedside table and picked up a tissue, gently holding it under his nose. "This is crazy. What's brought on this nightmare? You haven't had one for a while. And your eyes have gone all antichrist again."

Quinn shook his head dazedly. "I don't know, I can't remember much about it. It's just a blur. It might be because of that stuff from the book that I got on my hands earlier."

Cade stroked Quinn's cheek. "You were calling names out again. That little girl, Honour, and another one I vaguely remember from somewhere. Edward?"

Quinn's body shuddered in disgust.

Cade sighed. "Until you tell someone about why these people give you nightmares, you'll never be free of them. You obviously bottle it all up inside. I want to know who they are. You told me you'd tell me about Honour one day. Well, I want to know now."

Quinn shook his head in despair. "I can't. Please don't ask me to." He closed his eyes. Then he muttered. "I know, Taliesin. Easier said than done."

Cade ignored the conversation Quinn was having with his Withinner. He was used to them by now. But he was relentless. "You promised me you'd let me in, Quinn. I want to know why these names make you feel so guilty. Because that's what it is that torments you: guilt. But I don't know why. I can't help you unless I know the whole story." He waited for Quinn to breathe evenly then reached out and took his hands, holding them against his chest. "Whatever it is, I will still love you."

Quinn shook his head. "No, you won't. You'll think I'm a monster. And then I'll lose you." His voice was taut with fear and Cade's heart broke at the look of sheer desolation in his lover's eyes. He wasn't used to seeing this level of vulnerability from Quinn.

"I promise you that no matter what you have done or will do, I will always love you. Nothing will ever take that away."

Quinn studied his face quietly then leaned back against the headboard, propping his pillows up behind him. He took a deep breath as he readied himself to tell his story.

"You know that Daniel leads a double life as the leader of RAW as well as being the front man in a lot of instances for the Witchhunters Alliance—the ones who hunt us down and kill us. Having him inside gives us valuable intelligence on what they're doing and we've been able to stop a lot of witch and Warlock killings that way."

Cade nodded. He knew RAW was the Resistance against Witchhunters and that as a human, Daniel played a pivotal role in leading that organisation against the WA.

Quinn sighed raggedly. "One day he was asked in one of the WA meetings to sanction a killing of an entire family of witches living in Sudbury, in Suffolk. He asked me what he should do. I told him to sanction it to give credence to his position in the WA and we'd stop it before it happened somehow. I had no intention of letting anyone die."

His voice became flat. "But due to unforeseen circumstances, we couldn't stop it in time. Honour, her mother, her father and her little brother were massacred by the WA. Four people, Cade. Dying in agony because I gave an order to Daniel to sanction it."

Cade's heart tore in half at the self loathing in his voice. "You said there were unforeseen circumstances. Surely you couldn't help it?"

Quinn was silent as Cade waited for him to speak.

"*I* was the unforeseen circumstance. I got wind that someone in the WA suspected Daniel might not be who he said he was, and it would have meant his position in the WA would have been compromised. I couldn't have that. Daniel was too valuable where he was. So I convinced them to postpone the rescue of the family, whilst I waited to see what evidence this person had. I finally got the evidence and was able to destroy it and the person holding it, to protect Daniel. But the delay was too much of a reach and we just missed being able to save Honour and the others, even though we tried so hard. But I had to have the evidence in my hands or all our plans would have been scuppered. Years of work getting Daniel where he was; it would have been for nothing."

Cade swallowed. "So the killings went ahead." He felt bile rise up in his throat but tried not to show Quinn how disturbed he was at this story. Quinn needed him not to judge.

Quinn nodded. "Yes. And in doing that, it strengthened Daniel's position in the WA more than we could ever hope for. But at the cost of four witches' lives, including two children." His voice faltered. "What if subconsciously I did it on purpose? Let it happen and told myself I couldn't have stopped it anyway. *That's* the question I have to live with."

Cade had no idea how to react.

Quinn's face darkened at Cade's silence. "You're judging me," he said finally, his voice harsh.

Cade shook his head. "No, I'm *not* doing that. I just don't know what to say. It's a terrible story but I wasn't there. I didn't have to make the decision. You did."

They were quiet and Cade finally looked at Quinn. "Who was Edward? I remember the name from somewhere."

Quinn closed his eyes in pain. "Edward was the Warlock who picked me up and got me out of my parent's apartment when they were killed. Edward Mistral."

"Why would you feel guilt about him?" Cade asked quietly. "What did he do?"

Quinn laughed harshly. "It's not what he did, it's what I did. About five years ago, I was with Edward on the Isles of Scilly. He'd gone there to check out a book collection someone had. It was a sixth-century collection, something I'm familiar with because of Taliesin, and he asked me to go with them to verify the progeny of the books. It turned out to be a trap. There was another Warlock there lying in wait for Edward. Antoine had always been bitterly jealous of Edward's success and the fact that he was a well-respected collector himself. I got the feeling there was more to their relationship than simply business. I think they'd been lovers at some time."

His voice tailed off as he recalled the events that tormented him.

"We invoked our Withinners at one stage as we needed to get somewhere quickly. When we arrived there, I revoked Taliesin but Edward was always slow to do that. He tended to let Adelphi, his Withinner, stay a little longer in his place. It was an agreement they had. Antoine attacked Adelphi with a dragon claw containing dragon's blood. Adelphi died in front of me."

His voice was hoarse from talking. "I've never seen a Withinner die before. It was a horrible thing to witness and I couldn't do a fucking thing. Not as Taliesin or myself. All I could do was watch Adelphi die. And when he died, he just disappeared and Edward was left behind. I don't know if I've told you what happens when a Warlock's Withinner dies. The psychic shock after so long of having someone else inside you, being you, it's beyond compare. Edward was suffering there on the shore of the sea, in complete agony and being driven out of his mind."

Cade reached over and wiped away more blood trails from under Quinn's nose.

"He begged me to kill him. I told him I couldn't. He said he deserved to die after what he'd done and I had the right to kill him. I never quite knew what he was talking about. I put it down to the loss of his mind."

Quinn closed his eyes as he leaned forward in the bed, his hands over his face.

"He was suffering, so I killed him. I channelled an energy burst at him and I stopped his heart. I tried not to burn him; I couldn't have faced that. He died in my arms. He was the man who saved my life when I was a boy and I had to be the one to kill him."

His voice was anguished at the memory.

Cade sat there, feeling both horror and compassion at his stories. "What happened to the other Warlock—Antoine? Did you kill him too?"

Quinn shook his head. "No. Taliesin killed Antoine. He was so incensed at Adelphi's death, he wanted to kill Antoine himself. So I invoked him and he destroyed Antoine." Quinn smiled tiredly. "At least that was one death I don't have on my conscience." He leaned back and closed his eyes, exhausted.

Cade reached out and touched Quinn's face gently. "Come here. Lie here with me." Quinn came to Cade gladly as he pulled his shattered lover closer. Quinn laid his head on Cade's stomach as Cade stroked his hair.

"You've seen so much death and I don't know how you do it, keep going like you do. But I can tell you one thing. The man I love wouldn't have needlessly killed people just to justify the ends. I know it's your mantra but I happen to believe there are limits to what you'll do. I don't believe you let those people die purposely. You have to believe that too."

"It eats me up inside," Quinn whispered. "I thought I was a monster." He trailed his fingers across Cade's stomach lightly.

"You have to let it go, Quinn. Accept it happened and don't blame yourself, like Daniel says. You're no monster," Cade said softly. "I couldn't love a monster. And I love you dearly."

Quinn sat up, pulling Cade into his arms, burying his face in his neck. "I love you too. You're my rock, you know that? I don't know what I'd do without you."

Cade kissed him gently. "Go to sleep. I'll be here when you wake up. Try not to have any more nightmares."

Quinn nodded sleepily as he snuggled in to Cade's side. Cade lay stroking his forehead until he fell asleep then stayed awake himself for a while before falling into an uneasy slumber.

Chapter 15

Quinn stood in front of the bedroom mirror, scowling as he tried to fix his bow tie. He normally managed to do them up just fine but tonight for some reason he was struggling to get it straight. Tonight was Cade's annual ball at the Institute of Anthropological Studies, something he'd been looking forward to for the past week. Not for the dancing, he'd been quick to say, but because it was a great opportunity to let his hair down and get Cade to dress in a tuxedo. He looked very alluring in formal wear.

Quinn turned as Cade came in and he did a double take. "God, you look as sexy as hell. You clean up nicely."

Cade grinned as he performed a mock twirl and checked out his reflection in the full length mirror. "Yep, I thought I looked pretty good. My arse definitely suits these trousers."

Quinn agreed. His boyfriend might be more used to jeans, tee shirts and polo shirts, but in a suit, his lean, broad-shouldered frame was show cased with sophistication and sheer sexiness.

Cade saw him smile and looked at him quizzically. "I'm glad you like it. What's with the smile?"

"I was thinking about the first time I saw you, the night I 'ravaged' you," Quinn said drily. "I was wondering why the bloody Mirrabar blood wasn't working as all I wanted to do was bury my face in your crotch. It was a wonderful but rather alarming desire. I had visions of myself being arrested."

Cade chuckled. "All I could think about was ripping that white shirt you had on off your shoulders and biting them. It was fairly overwhelming as well."

They grinned at each other in shared memories.

"You do look amazing," Quinn said quietly. "I'm a very lucky man."

Cade kissed his cheek softly. "You look as sexy as hell too. I love a man in a tux. Especially this man."

He reached down and cupped his crotch teasingly and Quinn shook his head warningly. "God, don't start. Or we'll never make it to the party." He smiled slyly. "And I'll never get to meet Cooper."

Cade pulled away and regarded him with narrowed eyes. "You promised me you'd behave and not give poor Cooper a hard time."

Quinn shrugged. "I have no intention of giving anyone a hard time. Except you perhaps, when we go to bed."

"Honestly, is that all you think of?" Cade shook his head. "Come here and let me fix that bow tie. It's all askew."

Quinn moved over to him, his nostrils flaring at Cade's distinct woodsy scent as he expertly fixed the tie. Not for the first time, Quinn's senses tingled when Cade was close to him, his boyfriend's body heat sending signals to his brain and nether regions.

Quinn took a deep breath to suppress the urges that surged. Tonight, they couldn't be late, and doing what he wanted to do would definitely make them tardy. Tonight he wanted everything to be perfect. He had great plans for the evening, plans that made him feel very nervous indeed.

Finally Cade stood back and regarded him in satisfaction. "All done, so I suppose we should get off now or we'll be late. Come on, handsome. Our carriage awaits."

They arrived at the luxury hotel of the Wyndham Grand London in Chelsea Harbour about an hour and a half later, the taxi having been expertly manoeuvred through the busy London traffic. The couple got out and walked into the glittering entrance of the luxury hotel. The grand ballroom in the hotel was a magnificent venue and the Institute had definitely done itself proud. Quinn thought wryly that some of his grant money had probably gone into paying for all this extravagance tonight. He took their small overnight bag and put it behind the reception desk with a charming smile at the receptionist, who blushed.

A short, thin man in John Lennon glasses hurried over to them as they arrived. Professor Ambrose Tickler Brown smiled at them both as he clasped Cade's hands tightly and inclined his head at Quinn.

"Cade! You look very smart. Quinn, it's good to see you again. It's been a while."

Quinn grinned. "It has indeed, Ambrose. You're looking well. I'm glad to see the grant money has been put to good use."

Ambrose looked slightly embarrassed. "You know what it's like. You have to keep the facade up and the investors happy. It takes money to make money unfortunately."

He looked around the room. "I suppose I'd better get in and mingle, keep everyone happy. Cade, my boy, enjoy tonight. Have a great time, both of you."

He disappeared to mix with his guests.

Quinn looked around for the bar, and spotting it against the far side of the room, he pulled Cade over to it as they negotiated the throng of people in the room.

"I need a stiff drink," he muttered. "I think Ambrose has me giving some speech tonight as one of the patrons so I need a little bit of Dutch courage." He needed it for what he intending doing later on tonight as well.

"You didn't tell me you were speaking tonight. I'm so proud of you." Cade squeezed his hand as he ordered a glass of white wine and a large whisky on the rocks.

"It must have slipped my mind. I don't intend talking for long. I can't abide people who rabbit on about their good causes, it's so bloody boring. Short and sweet is what I like."

Quinn sipped his whisky as he looked around at the crowd. "It's a damn good turnout. There must be at least four hundred people here."

"Did you bring your glasses?" Cade asked anxiously. "You may need them to read your speech."

Quinn nodded and patted his chest. "In my pocket. But I won't need them because I haven't written anything down. It's all in here," he said loftily, tapping his head. "I don't need bits of paper."

"You're such a smart arse." Cade chuckled. "You might need them when we get to the room though. I have a yen tonight for the professor to make his debut. I feel like being his naughty college student who wants to jump his bones, so be prepared."

Quinn looked down at him, his eyes darkened with the promise of tonight. "I look forward to it."

"Cade! God, you look absolutely gorgeous. Come here and give me a hug."

A tall, stocky man with pitch-black hair and bright green eyes reached out with arms that looked like thick tree branches and pulled Cade into his arms, enveloping him in a hug that almost swallowed him whole. Eager lips pecked at Cade's, who leaned back, fending the man off with a low laugh. Quinn raised an eyebrow at the action but made no comment. Eventually the man released him and Cade shook his head, looking breathless.

"Cooper! For God's sake, how many times have I told you not to suffocate me?"

Quinn's eyebrows furrowed at the indication that this wasn't the first hug Cade had had from this man. He felt a tingle of both suspicion and annoyance at the man's impudence. *Turning you into a toad, Cooper, is beginning to look more and more like an option.*

"Coop, I'd like you to meet my boyfriend, Quinn Fairmont."

Coop? That is a little too familiar for my liking.

Quinn shook hands with the man, who smiled at him openly and seemed genuinely pleased to meet him. "Quinn. It's good to meet you at last. I've heard so much about you from Cade."

"Likewise." Quinn remarked laconically. "It's good to put a face to a name."

A younger, handsome and masculine face, one I am sure men go gaga for, even though I don't care for it much myself.

Cooper turned to Cade. "I need to speak to you at some stage about the dissertation I'm working on. I need some advice on Kenneth MacAlpin and I know you're the chap to give it to me."

Quinn hoped that was simply a figure of speech.

Cade smiled. "If it's Pict history you're looking to pick my brains on, you've come to the right place. We can chat about later when we're sat down for dinner. I think we're at the same table."

Quinn sighed. *Wonderful. Now I have to have the chap in close proximity all night.*

He wasn't sure why he had this irrational dislike of the man who seemed pleasant enough and he was a little nonplussed by it.

Taliesin interjected slyly.

I feel your jealousy, Quinn. Your man has an admirer, one who seems quite 'touchy feely,' as you would say.

Quinn tried not to let the green-eyed monster take root in his head as Cade turned to him. "Cooper is writing his thesis on early Pict settlements and history, and as you know, it's one of my specialities. There's a possible research programme in the works to go to Scotland for a month to do some studies up there. I've put my name down for it if it ever comes to fruition. It will be an incredible opportunity."

Quinn's ears pricked up at Cade's words. He hadn't been aware of this plan.

"Scotland? Any idea when it might be planned for?"

Cade shook his head. "Not yet. It depends on funding and some other circumstances. Ambrose is working on it with Cooper."

So Cooper would be going too? Quinn definitely didn't like the sound of that plan. He wondered if he'd be asked to provide the funding. He'd have to think about that if so. He wasn't paying for Cade to go on a nice long weekend with Cooper and no Quinn.

Are you going to stand for this young upstart to spirit your Cade away to a place of privacy, Quinn?

Taliesin's sly words were not helping Quinn feel comfortable about the rather effusive Cooper.

"Cade is a wonderful teacher," Cooper enthused. "He has a lot of patience and his knowledge is incredible. You should be very proud of him."

"Oh, I am." Quinn said silkily, drawing Cade closer to him possessively. "Extremely proud. I can safely say he's taught me a lot."

And he's mine, you arsehole, so back off!

Cade poked him hard in the ribs and Quinn smiled at him innocently. "It looks like everyone is making their way to the tables. I suppose we'd better find ours." He looked at Cade who nodded.

"Nice meeting you, *Coop*," Quinn said lazily.

Cade glared at him. "We'll go sit down for dinner. Cooper, we'll see you there."

Quinn took Cade's elbow and steered him away toward the bar.

Cade shook his head. "You said you'd behave!"

"I *did* behave. I didn't do anything untoward, did I?" Quinn grinned. "The man is still human and hasn't been turned into a chicken or lost his hair. I did think about making him bald."

Cade sighed in exasperation. "I know you. You have this way of charmingly brushing people off and making them feel that they should be glad they even had a minute to spend with you. You can insult people without them even knowing you've done it."

"I can't help my charm, it's who I am. I was just born this way." He ducked adroitly out of the way of Cade's fierce punch to his ribcage and chuckled at the swear word he heard.

"Hell, you're supposed to be a gentleman. Gentlemen don't say rude words like that." He leaned in and whispered in Cade's ear. "Not unless they're in the bedroom."

"God, you can be such an arrogant tosser." But Cade was smiling and Quinn knew he'd won him over.

They found their table and sat down whilst Quinn ordered more drinks. He was pleased that the crowd at the table were quite talkative and the time seemed to pass fairly quickly. Even Cooper had his moments of interest. Dinner was served, the drinks flowed and the conversation became animated. Quinn looked at his watch and nudged Cade on the shoulder.

"I'd better make my way to the front. Ambrose wanted me there at ten."

Cade nodded as Quinn picked up his jacket and disappeared toward the stage at the front of the room. The gong sounded and the ballroom drew quiet. The stage lit up as the ballroom lights dimmed and Ambrose Tickler Brown appeared with a microphone.

"Ladies and gentlemen, your attention please. Firstly, can I say how pleased I am that everyone is here enjoying themselves? I am very gratified at such a huge turnout, and I must thank you all for coming, especially as I know you may have much better things to do on a Saturday night." He cleared his throat.

"As you all know, the Institute for Anthropological Studies in Golders Green does a myriad of things. It teaches, it researches, it promotes studies of the subject to local youth groups and schools, and it tries to get the subject of our past across to people who might otherwise never have the opportunity to hear of what life used to be like before Blackberries, smartphones and the internet. Not to mention social networking."

There was low laughter throughout the room.

"But we cannot do what we do without the benefit of organisations who graciously fund us, giving us the money to create such programmes and get our message over to the public. Grants allow us to send our researchers to find out more about our past, the people and cultures that inhabited it and put together undergraduate and graduate programmes for people to study and propagate the research. The company that helps us with our funding is generous to a fault and has been supporting us for over fifty years. QuinnCo was started by a man called Christopher Fairmont all that time ago, and today we are very privileged in having his son and the current patron of the Institute, Mr. Quinn Fairmont, with us to say a few words. Quinn, we're very glad to have you with us tonight."

Cade's heart swelled with pride as Quinn appeared on the stage, the stage lights glinting on his tawny blond hair, looking very handsome in his tux. He saw more than a few avaricious stares at his man as he stood there, from men and women alike.

Eat your heart out, you lot, he's all mine.

Quinn took the microphone as the room grew quiet. "Ladies and gentleman, it's a pleasure to be here with you tonight. I promise I'll keep it short as I know you're all anxious to continue drinking that wonderful wine that's on the table. Plus luckily for you all I'm not given to long-winded speech like I know Ambrose is prone to."

There was a low buzz of laughter. Ambrose's predilection to rambling discourses on occasion was well known.

"My father took over this company when his father died and like me, he believed in what it was trying to accomplish. By learning about our past and the cultures that came before us, we learn more about ourselves and where we came from. QuinnCo promotes racial and cultural tolerance through its work with organisations like the London Project, an outreach for gang members and various what we call 'A-religious' groups which seek to promote understanding of each other's religions and beliefs, with an aim to accepting that whatever anyone believes in, there should be no stigma attached to it. We've even worked with Wiccan and other Neo-Pagan groups, as well as creationist and evolutionary organisations to try and promote cultural understanding."

He looked around the room. "I know there are some here tonight that disagree with what we do, just as I know there are others who are totally devoted to it and want to make it work. Anthropology gives us the insight of our origins and allows us to look back at the mistakes we made in hopes we don't repeat them. My father believed in this, as do I and this is why this Institute is so important to my company. It makes a difference and it's what each and every one of us should try to do. Thank you for listening to me and I hope you enjoy the rest of your evening."

He smiled and handed the microphone back to Ambrose amidst loud applause. Cade was so proud of him and his confidence and passion. Cooper, seeing he was a little emotional, smiled and leaned over and laid a hand on his.

"He's really good up there, isn't he? He really believes in what he says."

"You have no idea, Cooper. No idea." Cade murmured, wishing for one crazy moment that everyone in the room could know who Quinn was and what he actually stood for. Knew even who and what Cade was and the strange, wonderful world they lived in together. In a million years, Cade had never dreamt of anything such as what he had now. He still pinched himself. He could only imagine how other people, non-magyck, would see it. He and Quinn would probably both end up in the loony bin.

Quinn appeared at Cade's side with a smile that faded slowly as he saw Cooper's hands covering his. Cade hastily moved them away and picked up his wine glass, toasting Quinn.

"You were wonderful up there, babe. To say you did that all from your head, you did well."

Quinn smiled. "I'm glad." He sat down and pulled Cade's hand toward him as he kissed it possessively, glaring at a grinning Cooper. "It wasn't too long, was it?"

Cade shook his head. "No, it was just right. You speak with such conviction and it's really heartfelt." He lowered his voice to murmur into Quinn's ear. "I was just thinking that sometimes it would be nice for people to know exactly who you are, and why you can say you believe so much in what you do. With what you've experienced, people would have to believe you really know what you're talking about."

"Sometimes, I feel the same." Quinn's tone was wistful. "Sometimes I just want to invoke Taliesin and let him tell everyone about the death and destruction he's seen in the name of religion and cultural differences. But I can't. It would wreak complete and utter havoc. So we have to stay hidden away to do what we do."

It was almost midnight when Quinn and Cade said their farewells and went up to bed. Quinn watched carefully as Cooper hugged Cade, not missing his sly, seemingly accidental caress of Cade's arse. Words of magyck sprung into his mind, words he tried manfully to suppress. Fusing a man's fingers together was not something one could get away with at an event like this. Cade also looked quite tipsy and in the lift, Quinn smiled at him in amusement as he regarded the flushed face.

"Had a little too much there? You have that rather dreamy look on your face that always tells me you might have over-imbibed."

"Listen, handsome, I'm in a very happy place at the moment. It was a good evening, with great company, you by my side and from what I remember, you promised to be the naughty professor when we get upstairs, so this man has a lot to look to look forward to." Cade yawned sleepily. "I'll try and find my second wind by then, I promise."

"Hmm. That Cooper is a little more forward than I'd like. He seems to have no boundaries."

Cade waved an airy hand. "Coop is fine, just a little excitable. He's not a threat, Quinn, honestly. No man can measure up to you."

Quinn stayed quiet and Cade looked at him. "Is everything all right? Normally you'd have some witty repartee for me by now about the length of your dick or something."

"I'm fine," Quinn murmured, feeling a little distracted by what he had planned. They reached the room and he slid the key card into the lock and opened the door, motioning Cade inside. Cade entered the room and gasped at what he saw. The room was decked out with some very ornate and very large red rose bouquets, scattered around the room, in front of which stood a magnum of champagne and two glasses. Cade turned and gazed at Quinn, his eyes wide.

"Wow. This is quite a display. Did the hotel do this for us then? Or the Institute perhaps?" He leaned over and smelled the roses, breathing in their delicate scent.

"No, Cade, I did." Quinn reached over and pulled Cade closer to him, his hands encircling his waist as he looked deeply into silver—albeit slightly glazed—eyes. "I'm really not very good at this sort of thing, so bear with me." He took a deep breath, feeling like the first night at his prom when he wanted to kiss a special girl and wasn't sure how she'd respond.

"Cade, you know I love you. You're the best thing that ever happened to me, and meeting you on the heath that day was just meant to happen. I know that. But I don't think I tell you enough just how much I love you. You're my world."

Cade looked up at him with eyes that drank him in, and Quinn swallowed.

"I love coming home to you and seeing you curled up in your chair with the cat, and your books, just looking as if you belong there. There's no other sight I'd rather see. So I thought it was about time I made an honest man of you."

Cade's eyes widened and he swallowed, his full lips parting and Quinn wanted to kiss him so badly he had to look away. He reached behind the one bouquet of flowers and picked up the small box he'd hidden there earlier.

"Cade Mairston, will you marry me?" He took a deep breath and opened the box to reveal the ring he'd picked out of the safe earlier that evening.

Cade looked at him and Quinn saw the glint of tears in his eyes as he looked down at the ring. It was an eighteen-carat yellow gold wedding band, with three small diamond chips embedded on the top, simple but very elegant, like the man himself.

"It was my father's ring," Quinn said softly. "My father said the three diamonds symbolised the past, the present and the future, which is very apt considering who we are and where we've both come from. It's been in the safe since Daniel gave it to me when I was eighteen." He grinned slightly. "Dan said one day I'd put it to good use if some man was stupid enough to say yes, so I hope that'll be you."

Quinn watched Cade's face anxiously, looking for his answer and found it when Cade reached up to him, eyes glinting with unshed tears and kissed him with a tenderness that made Quinn's body ache with need.

"God, of course I'll marry you," Cade whispered. "I love you more than life itself, you know that. I don't need or want anything else other than you."

Cade's lips found Quinn's again and he melted into him, feeling Cade's hard body against his, feeling the heat in his own body rising with the embrace. Finally they pulled apart reluctantly and Quinn took the ring out of the hardwood box and took his left hand, gently placing the ring on his finger. It fitted perfectly. Cade looked at it in awe and then looked back up at him with such adoration that Quinn's chest surged with emotion.

"It's the most beautiful ring ever. I love it, and the fact it was your dad's makes it even more special." Cade frowned. "I guess that means I need to get you one, then? Something special because I don't have any family heirlooms to give you, unless there's a safety deposit box I don't know about somewhere and if there is, I haven't found it yet—"

"Cade," Quinn whispered with a wide smile, "You're blathering, sweetheart. I need to shut you up."

He reached over and cupped Cade's face, kissing him deeply and Cade moaned and pressed himself against Quinn with a ferocity he hadn't felt before.

"I should propose to you more often," Quinn murmured as Cade's hungry mouth travelled down his neck. "It seems to bring out the beast in you and definitely makes you ready for action."

Cade's tongue finished licking Quinn's skin and with a sly smile, he knelt down before Quinn, pushing him back against the wall. Quinn lost his breath. Cade on his knees was a real treat. He cleared his throat as Cade's fingers unzipped him and pulled his trousers down to his thighs. His very needy cock sprung up, and

Cade nuzzled his cheek against it. Quinn nearly blew just from that alone.

"Christ, Cade," he groaned. "You are such a fucking bad boy. For God's sake, either do it or get on the bed so I can make love to you properly."

Cade tutted and flicked the tip of Quinn's penis with a warm finger, causing him to hiss in sheer delight. "Stop your whining. I'm setting the mood. It's not every day a man gets a marriage proposal." His tongue snaked out and licked Quinn's tip and Quinn thought he might explode.

"Cade, I'm warning you," he grunted between clenched teeth. "Either suck it or get on the damn bed."

His fiancé—*God, I love the sound of that*—sighed heavily and wrapped his mouth around Quinn's cock, causing him to levitate onto his toes as a hot, wet tongue and greedy lips took control of that most sensitive part of his anatomy. Quinn's hands clutched Cade's hair in a grip so tight Cade felt like he was getting a facelift.

"Oh...my...God," Quinn moaned, thinking hazily that Cade's assault on his throbbing and needy erection made him eligible for a cock-sucking award of some sort. "Hell, you are so good at this." His voice trailed off to a moan as his dick was clasped in rough hands and pumped with the sort of vigour he'd only seen in porn. Quinn's knees threatened to give way, and he swore Cade was laughing, the rumble of his laughter reverberating against Quinn's extremely pressured cock. There was no way in hell Quinn was going to survive much longer. His balls were scrunching up, his arse tingling with his imminent orgasm and the heat in his groin unbearable.

He let out an unmanly warble as he blasted his way into Cade's mouth like a rocket launcher lifting off. His body shook, and he'd never realised he had the capacity to produce so much come. All the time Cade milked him dry, swallowing everything he was given. Finally, Quinn was spent and he lifted his hands from Cade's hair, splayed them out against the wall for support and looked down at the silver-grey eyes observing him wickedly. Cade stood up, licking his lips salaciously and, from the large wet patch on the front of his trousers and dreamy eyes, already satisfied. He licked his fingers one by one as he watched Quinn's face.

"That was so fucking hot," Cade murmured. "And you made me come in my pants. What the hell was that noise you made at the end? It sounded like a damn bird of some sort." He shivered in pleasure. "It was damn sexy whatever it was." He stopped the erotic sucking of his fingers and looked down at his groin in steady contemplation. "I guess we both need a shower now."

Quinn took a deep breath. "You bastard. That mouth of yours is pretty talented."

Cade shrugged. "I have my moments." He gazed over at the table, at the bottle of champagne. His eyes grew stormy. "Before we even think of getting clean, I'd like to get dirty again. I think we need to open that champagne and toast ourselves," he murmured softly as his hands caressed Quinn's jawline with fingers that smelled of sex. Quinn closed his eyes at the sensation. "In fact, I think you should pour it all over me and drink it off. I think I'd like that. Then I can return the favour."

He leaned in and ran his tongue across Quinn's bottom lip. Quinn's heart stopped at the thought of drinking champagne from Cade's body. Just when he thought the man couldn't surprise him any more…

"I think I'd like that, my dirty fiancé," Quinn murmured and Cade chuckled in satisfaction.

"Then stop talking, get undressed and open the bottle. I think this is going to get very messy." With a wicked grin and a swing of his hips, Cade sauntered over to the bed and turned, beckoning

Quinn over with one finger. Quinn was out of his depth with this rather bossy yet uber-sexy Cade but he had no intention of refusing anything the man wanted.

After all, it wasn't every day a man agreed to be your husband.

Chapter 16

Cade awoke the next morning feeling both sticky and sore from the activity the previous night. The drinking of champagne from each other's bodies had certainly been memorable but he didn't think the hotel cleaning staff would appreciate the mess they'd made. He smiled when he saw Quinn snoring lightly still, his arms flung out above his head, his chest hair matted with sticky champagne. He raised his hand and looked at his ring, still unbelieving of the fact he was now Quinn's fiancé. Cade felt a surge of happiness as he clambered out of the bed and made his way to the shower. Twenty minutes later he was towel-drying his hair when Quinn stirred and yawned, stretching his arms and his legs. He sat up, the sheet draped loosely across his waist and smiled at him widely.

"Morning. You're up bright and early."

"I was all sticky and I really needed a shower." He grinned. "You were very edible last night. We'll definitely have to do that again."

Quinn chuckled as he swung his legs out of bed and padded naked into the bathroom. "I have to say it was quite an experience. I had no idea champagne could get drunk out of so many places in the human body."

Cade flushed slightly at remembering exactly where Quinn had drunk his fill from. He heard the shower start and Quinn's whistling as he got into the water. His mobile bleeped as Quinn came back into the room, a towel around his waist, towelling his hair dry. Cade glanced at his phone then put it down.

Quinn raised an enquiring eyebrow. "Is that your friend Cooper again? What does he want now?"

Cade nodded. "He stayed over in the hotel too. He was wondering whether we're coming down for breakfast."

Quinn frowned. "He's quite a tenacious little bastard, isn't he? What's he going to say when he hears you've gotten engaged? I hope it cools his ardour a little."

"He's harmless," Cade said with a sigh. "He knows full well I'm attached."

"Hmm. He certainly seems to be a little *hands-on,* from what I saw last night. The man was all over you like a leech. That toad spell was starting to look pretty attractive to me."

Cade stood up, moving over to Quinn, leaning in and enjoying the fresh, soapy smell of him as he hugged him.

"You can't go around turning people into toads and frogs. You know you're the only one for me. Cooper's just a little showy, that's all." Cade kissed Quinn softly. "Once I show him this," he waved his engagement ring, "he'll get the message."

Quinn grunted. "He'd better. Right, shall we go down and get breakfast? I have to confess I'm starving after all last night's activity."

He picked up the room key as Cade followed him out. "Perhaps I should tell young Coop exactly what we got up to last night," he said slyly as he locked the door. "That would give him something to think about."

Cade shook his head fiercely. "Don't you dare embarrass me. I know you. You'll drop little sly innuendos just to make a point."

Quinn grinned. "You do know how to spoil my fun."

The lift pinged and as they stepped inside, Cade hoped he'd behave himself. Quinn could sometimes be too mischievous for his own good.

*****

The next week passed far too quickly as the date of the seventh of May and the eclipse drew nearer. Quinn and his team had managed to find the hidden cottage where Jeremy and Rowan were staying, thanks to some local knowledge. A helpful land conveyancer in the local council office and a rather eccentric botanist who knew the flora of the area backwards were able to identify the seven trees.

Quinn, Percy and Magnus put their plans in place to gather at the Mistley Flats to perform the ceremony to banish Matthew Hopkins.

Daniel, who'd been given the task of getting something personal from Rowan Kirkpatrick, had to get creative in his efforts so as not to draw attention to himself. He finally managed to achieve his objective one cold morning as he waited in line behind the stork-like man at the local coffee shop. Daniel was not a coffee drinker but it looked as if Rowan and his friend Jeremy Payton were. The man ordered two cappuccinos and two flat whites along with a variety of muffins and what looked like large, round biscuits. The two men definitely had a sweet tooth.

Daniel stood behind the tall, gangly man as the human vessel dithered with the change in his hand, deciding what coins to count out into the patient barista's outstretched hand. Daniel shifted behind him slightly, seeing a few stray hairs on the man's rather soiled coat shoulder. He made as if to lift his hand and swat something, and quickly made his action into something else, plucking the hairs off the man's shoulder and clutching them tightly in his hand. The man went still and then slowly turned around. Daniel had noticed the large sunglasses the man wore and wondered why in hell's name he needed them on a cold, grey Essex morning. He smiled as Rowan's gaze met his eyes. Daniel felt the stare even through the dark mirrored glasses.

Daniel nodded at him congenially. "Morning. Bloody cold out there, isn't it? I can see why a good cup of coffee might go down a treat."

The man simply stared at him. Daniel kept the smile on his face and Rowan turned back to the still waiting but now getting slightly impatient shop assistant as the young man cleared his throat.

"I still need twenty pence," he said politely. Rowan nodded as he fumbled in his pocket. As he hunted deep down in his jacket, a rather dirty handkerchief slipped out onto the shop floor. Daniel held his breath, hoping the man wouldn't notice, or some helpful but interfering soul wouldn't point out to the man that he'd lost his hanky. He might be human but his late wife and nephew were both well versed in magyck and he'd learnt a lot. He knew a used handkerchief would make a perfect totem or talisman for Percy's spell. He breathed a sigh of relief when no one seemed to bother and Rowan handed over a coin and turned swiftly to walk away with his coffee and pastries. Daniel leaned down quickly, trying to be as unobtrusive as possible, and picked up the grey hanky, putting the stolen hairs neatly inside and slipping it into his pocket as he stood up. Thankfully the people in the queue were fairly apathetic and no one challenged why he was picking up another man's dirty handkerchief.

He smiled at the shop assistant. "A plain filter coffee please, black." The barista nodded and turned to do his bidding. A few minutes later, armed with a cup of coffee he had no intention of drinking, Daniel left the shop and tipped the still-full cup into a waiting rubbish bin, checked his pocket for his prize once again, and returned to his Lexus to drive to meet Percy so he could start his preparations for the ritual to destroy the Witchfinder General and his human host.

Chapter 17

Quinn, Percy and Magnus sat shivering on the outskirts of the cold Mistley marsh flats as they waited for the right time to perform their ritual. The eclipse was on its way and all they could do was wait. They'd been there for two hours now and it was half past midnight with just under an hour to go. Then they could perform the ritual that would hopefully destroy both Jeremy Payton and Matthew Hopkins. They knew that gradually the moon would have covered the sun and with less than an hour to go, they waited patiently for the maximum time decreed in the texts that Percy and his researchers had discovered. As the eclipse wasn't visible in the Northern Hemisphere, all they had to go on was the time.

Percy hadn't been sure whether the ritual would adversely affect Rowan Kirkpatrick, aside from sullying him so that the spirit of Hopkins could no longer use his body. They knew Jeremy Payton might end up very badly off though and were prepared for that. The hairs Daniel had plucked from Rowan's shoulder when he'd got close to him would do the trick for that, together with the soiled handkerchief with its extra treasure of snot. The two men were still in the cottage and had not moved since the Warlocks had gotten there.

"We need to get as close as we can to the cottage when we do the ritual," Quinn muttered. "The closer we are the better the result. It will have to be timed just right so they don't sense us. We can't afford Payton dissipating like he did on the yacht."

Percy nodded. "Once the ritual is started, Hopkins won't be able to use his power. It will prevent him from doing so if the texts are correct. The ritual itself is fairly short. We chant the words exactly on time, burn the hair and the handkerchief with an energy burst together, and supposedly Payton and Matthew Hopkins should separate somehow. They could disintegrate, burn or just disappear. We honestly don't have a clue what to expect."

Quinn looked at the other two Warlocks in apprehension, a sinking feeling in his stomach. "*If* the tests are correct? Do we have a contingency plan in case this ritual is a load of bollocks?" he muttered quietly. "I didn't really want to have to consider an alternative, but under the circumstances, being so close to a progeny of Hopkins and Hopkins himself, that could be bad for us all if things go wrong."

Magnus chuckled softly. "That is a valid point, Mr. Quinn. I'd suggest we simply invoke our Withinners and let them take us away. Failing that, we can always try fighting our way out of any situation." He grinned widely, his teeth gleaming in the dim light.

"I promised Cade I'd try not to die again on this one," Quinn smiled wolfishly. "He made me promise before I left. So I don't really fancy going home to my fiancé in any other state that what I am now. He'll kill me."

Percy chuckled. "Well put. I wouldn't like to face him either if anything happened to you. So we have to hope that the bloody ritual works."

It was precisely one-fifteen a.m. when the three Warlocks made their way surreptitiously up to the stone cottage. Thirty feet away, lights flared from the small mullioned windows through slight cracks in the curtains. The clearing was shrouded in trees and the seven oak trees in particular looked like broad-shouldered giants. Quinn, Magnus and Percy waited in anticipation for the exact time. All of them had synchronised their watches to make sure they got the chant started at the right second. They'd memorised the chant, and the handkerchief and the hair were ready on the ground between them for the burn.

Quinn started as one of the lights in the cottage went out. He looked at his watch. One twenty-two a.m. "Nearly time, chaps," he whispered. "Get ready." He glanced at Percy. "We don't have to hold hands or something, do we?" He grinned at them as he tried to relieve the tension he felt in the air. "Because then I'd feel like I'm in a bloody boy band."

Percy shook his head, his eyes amused. "No, no hand holding." His face became set as his wrist watch vibrated against his arm. They had sixty seconds to do this.

"It's time, let's start the chant. I'll tell you when we need to burn the totems."

The three Warlocks closed their eyes and began the ritual chanting, repeating the words they'd memorized over and over again. They heard a strange humming that seemed to echo through the air, like the high-pitched tone of a violin string. The hairs on Quinn's body stood up, his whole being prickling with electricity. Taliesin was repeating the chant with him in a low, husky voice, his power adding to the spell.

The group looked up as the front door to the cottage was flung open and the stocky form of Jeremy Payton appeared in the doorway. The young man took one look at them and his face tightened as he realised they were not there to deliver Girl Scout cookies.

"What the fuck do you think you're doing, you bunch of wankers?" he shouted, the spittle flying from his mouth in silvery drops. "Matthew said he could feel someone trying to hurt him. Do you really think you can defeat him?"

He scowled viciously as he recognised Quinn. "You! Me and Rowan have been watching you and your fancy man at that posh place of yours." He grinned nastily. "I'm looking forward to having a little one-on-one time with him. I have a few ideas as to how to entertain myself. I know a few magyck tricks now that could make him scream."

Quinn's anger surged inside him and heard Taliesin's quiet voice.

Concentrate, Quinn, Do not let him distract you. It is what he wants.

Quinn gritted his teeth as the teenager moved purposefully toward them. The Warlocks kept up the momentum of their chant. They knew to lose it now would not be a loss they could take. Quinn hoped fervently that Percy's assumption of the Witchfinder General's magyck not working due to their spell was right or they'd be in real trouble. The teenager shimmered in the air as he walked toward them, similar to the shine Quinn had seen when he'd watched Jeremy board Andrew de Vere's yacht all those months ago.

Rowan Kirkpatrick appeared at the door, his tall, gangly frame watching the events with consternation. He wore sunglasses and Quinn wondered inconsequentially why that would be. As they continued their ritual, a faint mist rose from Jeremy, a haze that appeared vaguely human in outline. Even as they watched, it rose and sank again back into Jeremy. It seemed to be unable to leave his body and Quinn sensed the frustration in the presence as it struggled to get free. Over and over it rose and over and over it was forced back in. Jeremy stopped, his eyes widening as he struggled to understand what was happening to him.

He glared at Quinn fiercely. "What are you doing to me, you bastard? What's this all about?" He turned and tried to clutch at the mist rising from his body.

"Nearly time, chaps," gasped Percy, in between his chant. "Stay focused."

Rowan Kirkpatrick was at Jeremy's side, his face anxious as he too flailed at the mist rising from the boy as if trying to grab and hold onto it. Quinn saw a face form in the haze, a man's face, with a moustache and a full, long beard, his eyes observing them in sheer fury, his lips twisted and snarling at them in anger. Even from here Quinn could feel the power of Mathew Hopkins, the Witchfinder General of Essex.

The Warlocks continued their chanting, watching as the two men fought against what was happening. Rowan Kirkpatrick stared at Quinn and the Warlock felt the intense hate emanating from him from behind the sunglasses. His mouth was twisted in a snarl.

Percy stopped chanting and panted, "Burn the totems, now!"

Like a synchronised group, the three Warlocks raised their palms and blue bursts of energy flashed down toward the ground, instantly incinerating the handkerchief and the hair of Rowan Kirkpatrick. There was a loud and frightful scream from Jeremy, whose face was now frantic with fear and pain, his hands flailing wildly at his chest. The haze struggling to release itself was sucked back into him like dust into a vacuum cleaner.

"Get it out!" Jeremy screamed. "Get the fucking thing out of me! It hurts!"

The teenager ripped his shirt apart with his bare hands and beat at his chest, which was pulsing madly. Quinn was reminded of the scene from *Alien* where the monster broke its way through a man's chest in a burst of blood and tissue.

Jeremy's chest was bulging in and out, his breath coming in tortured gasps as he tried frantically to stop whatever was happening to him. Their work done, the Warlocks watched with widened eyes seeing the young man thrashing about in sheer terror.

He saw the trio watching still and shrieked dementedly at Quinn. "You dirty Warlock, Fairmont! You're doing this to me. You fucking arsehole, stop it now! You're killing me!"

Quinn couldn't quite tell the youngster that this had always been a possible outcome. Jeremy Payton finally gave an excruciated howl and spun around like a dervish. The Warlocks watched in complete horror as his chest exploded in a fury of flesh and blood, spraying Rowan Kirkpatrick and covering him with a paste of bodily fluids and tissue.

Well, that was an unexpected ending.

Taliesin's startled words echoed what Quinn felt. They'd known Jeremy may not survive but this whole blood-and-guts explosion seemed very extreme indeed.

Kirkpatrick screeched at being covered with the remains of Jeremy Payton, who now lay broken and ripped on the grass at their feet. The dark haze that was Matthew Hopkins shimmered in the air, becoming fainter and fainter.

Quinn heard a voice crying out in rage and fury at being thwarted. Finally the black mist dissipated completely and the air was clear.

"What have you done, you bastards!" Rowan was sobbing now, his hands reaching out blindly to the circle of Warlocks. "You've ruined everything! This was my chance to be someone and you've taken it away from me!"

Quinn stepped forward, his hands already raised to direct a fatal burst at the now useless human vessel, but Percy placed a firm hand on his arm.

"Don't kill him," he said softly. "That man has no more magyck in him. He's just an ordinary man, who'll go back to an ordinary life and be miserable for the rest of his days. Isn't that punishment enough? We can't destroy him like that. You don't want another human death on your conscience."

Quinn stopped and lowered his hand. Percy regarded him quietly as Magnus watched the interchange between the men in silence.

Quinn sighed. "Fine. If you're sure the man has no powers." Although it went against every instinct he had to destroy this man for good.

"I'm sure, as are you. You can't sense anything in him either. And the Witchfinder is dead. I can't sense him anywhere."

Quinn nodded. "Yes, I think he's gone for good now. I think we've just stopped the Witchfinder line from breeding any more of them. That's an achievement indeed. I never thought I'd see the day that happened." An incredible sensation of peace filled his body. Taliesin seemed to feel it too.

He has gone, Quinn. I cannot sense him either. This was a good plan.

Quinn smiled. *It was indeed, old friend. A good plan.*

Rowan was now kneeling by the dead form of Jeremy Payton, no doubt sobbing at trying to make sense of what had just happened to his beautiful dream of being a powerful Witchfinder General. He took off his sunglasses and the Warlocks gasped at the sight of his pure black eyes.

Quinn looked at Percy in exasperation. "That doesn't look like a man who has no magyck in him, Percy!" In truth, Quinn was a little scared at the sight of his own blackened eyes staring back at him. Rowan's looked exactly the same as Quinn's when he went into what Cade called his Antichrist mode.

Percy shook his head. "It's a side effect of the preparation to cleanse the human vessel. It's not magyck, more of a physical change to the eyes so they can see auras. The Witchfinder General apparently had the power to see them too so he needed to prepare the same in this man. It's more to do with certain herb mixtures and infusions that he would have drunk."

Quinn wasn't convinced. "If you say so." He wondered if that had anything to do with what happened to him when his eyes changed. He'd have to read it up on it again later. He walked over to the still-sobbing Rowan and stood over him.

"I'd suggest you forget about what you've seen here and get back to a normal life instead of hanging out with a couple of psychotic murderers," Quinn said bitterly. "You're lucky my friend here cared enough to spare your life. I'm not feeling as charitable so I suggest you disappear and we never see you again. I'll do you a favour and clean this mess up for you or I'm sure someone will think you did it. You have been living together, after all. Who knows what the neighbours might think."

He finally got to use his full energy burst on Payton's ruined body, reducing it to nothing but grey ashes within minutes. Rowan's black eyes glared at Quinn and he shivered. Now he knew why Cade had been a little scared the first time he'd seen Quinn's eyes do the same. Rowan said nothing, just gazed from Jeremy to Quinn then back again. His body seemed to have shrunk back into itself. He appeared defeated, cowed.

Quinn scowled and turned away from Rowan. "We're done here. Let's get home. I, for one, have a man waiting for me."

The Warlocks left Rowan by the pile of ashes that had been Jeremy Payton, invoked their Withinners and within minutes of the magyckal drama on a cold April night in Mistley, Quinn found himself instead in his bedroom on Hampstead Heath, listening to Cade's soft breathing as he slept. Quinn took off his clothes, left them lying in a heap on the floor and crawled into bed, bone tired. He lay back on his pillow, luxuriating in the feel of warm blankets.

Cade stirred and turned over. His eyes opened and widened in pleasure at seeing him. "You're home. Did everything go as you planned? You're not hurt, are you? I'm sorry; I didn't mean to fall asleep. I wanted to wait up for you." He moved over to him, exclaiming at the coolness of Quinn's body.

"God, you're frozen. I need to warm you up." Cade threw his warm arms across Quinn's middle, getting as close to him as he could. His lover's warmth seeped through to Quinn's chilled bones.

"I'm fine, everything went well. We got rid of the bastard, so I think it's all over."

"You came home without a scratch," Cade muttered. "That's a first."

Quinn chuckled tiredly. "I didn't want to risk upsetting you." He yawned widely. "Now will you let me go to sleep? I'll tell you all about it in the morning."

His fiancé nodded sleepily. "Okay. I'm glad you're home safe and sound."

"So am I," he replied softly. "Sleep tight."

Chapter 18

The following morning Cade woke up and gazed over at the sleeping form of Quinn beside him. His face looked properly relaxed for the first time in a long time. Gently he brushed a strand of hair from his forehead, smiling as Quinn muttered in his sleep. Cade got out of bed, pulling on his robe and went downstairs to make an early morning cup of coffee. He was sitting in the kitchen, looking quietly out of the window sipping his coffee, when Quinn came in behind him and nuzzled his neck, then wandered over to make himself a cup.

Cade grinned in appreciation as he regarded Quinn's topless chest and loose jogging bottoms around his hips. "Morning. I have to say I love the fact you're still in one delectable piece after your excitement last night, and I'm not visiting you at the hospital again."

Quinn chuckled. "You and me both. Actually it went very well considering we were flying by the seat of our pants." Quinn sat down, propping his feet up on the kitchen table as he drank his coffee.

Cade looked at him enquiringly. "So, what happened last night?"

"We performed the ritual at the right time and the young man, Jeremy Payton, came barrelling out of the house as if all the hounds of hell were at his heels. He threatened us but he wasn't able to make his magyck work, thank God." Quinn's nose wrinkled in distaste. "At the end, his chest looked like something was trying to burst out of it."

He frowned. "I'm not sure why we got such an intense reaction; there was nothing like that mentioned in the other case with the Druitt fellow. Percy seemed to think that it might have something to do with the fact that he was both Hopkins's progeny and had the actual spirit of Hopkins inside him, so it was a little bit of overkill. Basically the guy's chest just exploded and there was blood and guts everywhere." Quinn nodded in satisfaction. "And then there were none. We all agreed we couldn't sense Hopkins anymore, even the Withinners thought so, so we think it's all over."

Cade watched him with an open mouth, horrified. "What about the other guy—Rowan?"

Quinn's face darkened. "Percy asked me not to kill the bugger. He was a nasty little twat, but he certainly didn't seem too threatening when we left him crying over his dead Witchfinder." Quinn shrugged. "I did the humanitarian thing and left him alive. Percy was very proud of me."

Cade shook his head. "Will I ever get used to you saying someone's proud of you because you didn't kill anybody? Is this the barometer by which you're judged nowadays?" He felt a twinge of concern at the question he posed, even though his tone was joking.

Quinn grinned at him. "I'd certainly hope there are other more pleasurable ways to judge me." He leered at Cade. "Talking of which, perhaps we should go back to bed and you can do just that."

Cade thought he seemed in an inordinately good mood. He supposed defeating an ancient scourge that had terrorised his people and those of the witches for centuries was reason enough.

I suppose I should be glad he's happy and relaxed, he mused. *Be thankful for small mercies. Perhaps the nightmares will stop now.*

He stood up and beckoned Quinn to follow him. Quinn needed no further urging as they went back upstairs to the bedroom.

They were both nearly asleep again later on that morning when the doorbell rang. Cade groaned as he looked over at Quinn. He appeared fast asleep but Cade had the distinct feeling that he was simply pretending so he didn't have to get out of bed.

God, who the hell can be at the door at this time of a Saturday morning?

Cade pulled on his robe and went downstairs to see who the early morning visitor was. He opened the door to see the most beautiful woman he'd ever seen standing in front of him, her tall, regal form haughty and elegant. She regarded Cade with slightly raised eyebrows, her blue eyes looking at him with a scrutiny that seemed to say Cade was definitely lacking in interest. The woman reached up a long, white hand with scarlet-painted nails and brushed jet-black hair impatiently away from her face as the wind blew.

"Good morning. Is Quinn here? I'm Valensia."

Cade's mouth dropped open at the knowledge that this exquisite creature was the witch who had held part of his Warlock's heart and had held him captive to abuse his body for days.

He swallowed, feeling very much at a loss. "Erm, he's still in bed, I'm afraid, Valensia. If you'd like to come in, I'll go wake him up."

"No need, I'm up." Quinn's quiet voice behind startled him and Cade turned to see him clad in only his jogging bottoms, looking at Valensia with an expression he couldn't quite fathom.

"Valensia, what are you doing here?"

The witch looked at him, her eyes lingering on Quinn's torso and then moving down to his groin. Cade wanted to smack her beautiful face.

"What kind of greeting is that? Are you not even going to invite me in?" Her voice was mocking.

Quinn gestured for her to come in. "Sorry, I forgot my manners for a moment. Please, come in." His tone was slightly sarcastic.

Valensia swept past Cade and into the house. Cade looked at Quinn, who shrugged his shoulders.

"What exactly are you doing here, Valensia?" Quinn asked. "This is an unusual circumstance, even for you, coming to my house."

Valensia regarded him. "I heard about your victory against the Witchfinder last night. I wanted to come over personally and offer you my thanks. What you and your team did was incredibly brave and noble and I always give credit where it's due." She smiled slyly. "You should know that." She glanced at Cade. "I'm sorry I appeared unsolicited on your doorstep, but I have a business proposition to discuss with Quinn. Would you mind if I took him away from you for a while?"

"I'm not going anywhere with you," Quinn said quietly. "If you want to talk, we can do it upstairs, in my study. Follow me and I'll take you up there. But you'll have to excuse me whilst I get dressed. I'm not entirely suitable for company."

"Don't get dressed on my account," Valensia said languidly as she glided up the stairs, leaving Cade open mouthed at the bottom. "I think you look quite fetching just as you are."

Quinn looked at Cade and shook his head in exasperation as he walked up the stairs behind the witch. "I'll not be too long," he said quietly. "But I need to see what she wants."

Cade watched as he disappeared upstairs.

*****

Quinn changed quickly into jeans and a tee shirt then went into his study where Valensia was wandering around, picking up various articles and then putting them down again.

"What is this business proposition you want to talk about?" he said impatiently. "I assume it must be fairly important for you to disturb my weekend."

"God, you've become so parochial since settling down with one man." Valensia laughed softly. "Since when did the mighty Grand Master worry about his personal weekend time? If I recall, I used to have to literally drag you away to get you to myself."

"Since I found a man to settle down with whose company I really enjoy," he retorted, seeing her slight flinch at his cruel words. "So, enough of the personality analysis, thanks. Tell me why you're here."

She scowled and turned around to look at him "Fine. Let's get down to business."

He regarded her flatly. She frowned at his look.

"I really did want to thank you for destroying the Witchfinder. I still can't believe you did it and he's gone. Centuries of persecution gone just like that." She snapped her fingers. "It's truly remarkable. The whole Praetorium is talking about him. You've become somewhat even more of a legend than you were before."

"I'm pleased you're pleased, Valensia. It suits both of our people to have him out of the way. You contributed to that result by giving me that Book of Shadows. So you played your part in the success. As did many others."

Quinn had already spoken to Misty Ravenbrook and thanked her for her part in ridding the world of the Witchfinder General. He and Misty had communicated a lot since their last meeting, and had even lunched together a few times. Quinn found her quiet humour and intelligence very welcome and the two of them were fast becoming friends.

Valensia inclined her head at his words. "I heard it was one helluva sight, seeing him explode like that. He deserved it, the bastard. One of his kind killed my sister many years ago. At least now that's over until someone else comes along to take up the mantle."

"There'll be no more Witchfinders," Quinn said quietly. He knew about her sister Vanessa's death nearly seven years ago, together with her husband.

"Perhaps not, Quinn, but there'll always be someone looking to kill us. You know that as well as I do. You cut the head off the Medusa snake and another one grows in its place." Her voice was sad. "It will just be a matter of time before someone else comes along."

Quinn stood up and touched Valensia sympathetically on the shoulder, noticing that the usual tingle he'd have felt was missing. She saw it in his face and smiled softly.

"I'm not trying anything anymore. You've made it quite clear how you feel about Cade." She picked up a paperweight idly from his desk. "By the way, was that an engagement ring I saw on his finger? He's a lucky man; I hope he realises that."

"We got engaged a week ago. *I'm* the lucky man, I can assure you."

Valensia sat down and put her boot-clad feet on his desk. "The reason I'm here is because I think it's time for the Praetorium and the Consortium to join forces again."

Quinn regarded her with narrowed eyes. "An alliance? That's a fairly radical suggestion from you, considering how you felt about it all those years ago."

A spark of hope rose in Quinn with her words, knowing a partnership between them would make a lot of sense. Taliesin agreed.

Quinn, this could indeed be a coup for you if it happens. Not even your father could get that right in his lifetime. And he tried.

Valensia nodded ruefully. "I know the bad blood between our two kinds goes back to before we were even born and it just gets to be a self fulfilling prophecy. But your actions last night have made a lot of people sit up and take notice."

She grinned at him and he saw the trace of the Valensia he'd known all those years ago when she was twenty-one. "You're a hero. They'll be singing ballads about you one of these days."

He shook his head at his words. "Don't be ridiculous." But he smiled. "I wasn't alone. I had Percy and Magnus with me—and of course all the Withinners. Believe me, it wasn't just me."

"Perhaps, but you're the figurehead. People see what they want to see. The Council asked me to come and see if there were synergies between us we could exploit. I said I would see what I could do." Valensia stood up and walked over to him, her eyes bright. "We could do a lot together. I know you've always wanted an alliance. Well, here's your chance."

Quinn nodded. "Let me speak to the Consortium. I'm sure I can convince them to see it our way."

"Does that mean you're interested?" Valensia moved around to behind his chair and laid her hands on his shoulders. "It means we'll be seeing more of each other. Can you stand that? Will Cade understand?"

Quinn stood up too, standing just taller than Valensia, and looked down at her. "It will be purely professional, for the good of both the Consortium and the Praetorium. Can *you* manage to remember that?"

She laughed softly. "I'll give it a whirl. So I'll tell them you're intrigued by the idea then. Let me know once you've spoken to your people. I'm sure if anyone can convince them what they need to do, it will be you."

Quinn nodded even as he felt a thrill of expectation in his blood. An alliance like the one proposed would be an incredible achievement. "I have a question for you. It's a pretty personal one, and you don't have to answer, but seeing as how you're in a giving mood…"

She regarded him curiously. "Go ahead. I can't promise I'll tell you the truth if I don't like it."

"What the hell happened between you and Taliesin?" Quinn's Withinner moved in anger at his probing.

Quinn! That is none of your business!

Quinn ignored his Withinner's heated outburst. "He won't let me in to find out."

Valensia regarded him carefully. "Does that not tell you that he doesn't want to talk about it?"

Quinn grinned. "It does. But I'm still curious."

She laughed softly. "Back when we were an item, you invoked Taliesin for some mission you were carrying out. Needless to say, the attraction was fairly intense between us and we had quite a lot of fun together. Three days of full-on, mind-blowing sex, in fact. It was amazing, even better than you and I."

Quinn's eyes narrowed at that admission. "I don't remember spending three days away in a freezing Welsh cottage, whilst Taliesin got his rocks off," he said silkily, slightly irked at Valensia's last comment.

Valensia grinned. "That's because he cloaked it from you, with my help and a lot of my witchy magyck. We were having such a good time we decided you could stay where you were for a while. Taliesin had some sort of incantation he could use only once and he used it then." She looked at him sideways. "He seems to have a few of those kinds of spells. It was just after I did my imprisoning thing with you, the one that you got all upset about. I wasn't quite ready to give up the wonderful time I'd been having, once you broke the enchantment, so I made a plan."

Quinn was flabbergasted. "That conniving bastard! I can't believe he'd do that to me. And you bloody helped him! You just swapped one sex slave for another, from the sounds of it."

She giggled, a sound he seldom heard from Valensia. "Taliesin was very willing though, more than you. He was quite an animal. I became very fond of him."

"So why is he so upset with you now?"

Quinn! For mercy's sake, keep your own counsel. I implore you to be quiet.

Valensia looked nonplussed. "He's mad with me? Why on earth would he be upset with me? We had a great time and then you revoked him and he went back. I wouldn't have minded him staying. So why—"

Her voice broke off and to Quinn's total amazement, he saw her face flush with pink. "Fuck, he must have seen me with Armand."

Quinn hadn't expected such an in-depth conversation about his Withinner's sex life with his own ex-lover. "Who the hell was Armand?"

Valensia looked uncomfortable. "Armand was someone I had a relationship with. He dropped by to see me, one thing led to another when Taliesin was out doing what he does and," she shrugged, "we had quite a lusty shag session, then Armand went home."

Quinn shook his head in sheer disbelief. "You're something else. One man after another, even whilst you're still seeing another. You know there's a name for a woman like you." He was still slightly irritated with her comment about Taliesin being better than him.

Valensia scowled fiercely. "Hell, don't mince your words, will you? I can't help that I have a high sex drive." She turned around and made her way to the door. As she went out she turned back. "Tell him I'm sorry if I upset him. I didn't know he'd seen. But he hid it well enough. He still stayed another day after that and shagged me senseless."

Quinn followed her down the staircase.

"Sometimes this all seems very surreal," he muttered. "The conversations I get involved in are sometimes mind boggling."

If you had kept your mouth shut, this conversation would never have happened. Are you happy, now, Warlock? You know my innermost secret.

Taliesin, I'm sorry if I distressed you. I had no idea. You felt more for this woman that you claimed.

That is none of your business. She shamed me and I cannot forgive her that.

Quinn sighed in resignation at Taliesin's words. His Withinner was an extremely proud man and he would not have taken kindly to being cuckolded. He reached the bottom of the stairs and saw Cade reading in the lounge.

He looked up and smiled, getting up to say goodbye to Valensia. "You two have been a while. Did you manage to get it all sorted out? Your business, I mean?"

Valensia nodded her head, a slight smile on her face. "I think Quinn and I have come to sort of agreement. And by the way—congratulations on your engagement. I hope you will both be very happy with one another."

Cade nodded. "Thank you, Valensia."

Quinn opened the door. "I'll be in touch soon about what we discussed. I don't think it will be too long. I have a Consortium meeting in a few days' time. I'll talk to them all then."

"Until we talk again, then. I'll see you around."

Valensia walked down the garden path and Quinn shut the door behind her and turned to look at Cade, who raised an eyebrow at him.

"What business is this you have to talk to the Consortium about?"

"The witches want a formal alliance with the Warlocks. That hasn't happened in the last century, ever since they fell out. This is quite a step forward. I promised Valensia I'd talk to the council members at the next meeting."

Cade regarded him thoughtfully and Quinn sighed. "Cade, she has no ulterior motive, I promise." Privately he hoped that was true. "An alliance could be a very big accomplishment for me as Grand Master. I can't miss the opportunity."

"That would mean you'd be working with her fairly closely then?" Cade's face wasn't happy.

"Perhaps a little more than before, but it would be purely professional, I assure you. I made that very clear to her." He moved over and took Cade in his arms. "You have nothing to worry about. No more than I have to worry about Cooper. I trust you with him. You need to do the same with Valensia."

Cade shook his head as he laid his head on Quinn's shoulder. "I don't have a history with Cooper. I do trust you, but I can't help feeling a little concerned. What if she does some Fey-witchy thing again?"

Quinn waved his hands in frustration. "It's not going to happen. Trust me."

Cade nodded his head, not looking convinced. "Fine then. But if I find out she's made one move towards you, I'll scratch her eyes out, witch or no witch."

He glared at him.

Quinn laughed softly. "Okay, I'm sure she'll quiver in her boots when she hears that. I know I would. Especially with that fierce and scary look on your face. God, I love you, you feisty, impossible man."

Quinn pressed his mouth on Cade's warm, welcoming lips. He kissed him back, burrowing his hands possessively inside Quinn's tee shirt.

"You're mine," Cade whispered. "Don't ever forget that."

Chapter 19

Quinn sat quietly at the table in the Consortium boardroom watching the interplay between several members of the Council. He'd arrived that morning to a rousing cheer of "well done" for his part in the recent Witchfinder General episode and it appeared that the general consensus was that it had been a great success and a moment that would go down in Consortium history. However, when he'd told them about Valensia's visit and her suggestion about an alliance between the Warlocks of the Consortium and the witches of the Praetorium, the room had exploded in a sudden outbreak of sheer madness. There were some who supported the idea, like Justin Leichner, who'd recently returned from his travels to Tibet. It went without saying that Percy and Quinn were in favour too. But others, like the bluff James Barton Sinclair and his fawning prodigy, Troy Cavanaugh, were instilling a sense of rebellion in the other Council members with their one-sided—and Quinn thought dangerous—point of view.

Since the Council was a democracy, he needed to let it play out and see where it took him. He was conscious of Percy beside him, holding himself back in difficulty as Barton Sinclair provided his view with his usual loud-mouthed diatribe of what Percy termed "utter bullshit."

"You need to let him fizzle out," Quinn murmured quietly. "Let's hear what he has to say and then we're forewarned. He has some powerful allies in this room and we need to see exactly who they are."

Percy scowled, his chubby face furious. "You have allies too; more than that jackass. He's such a fucking blowhard."

"That's as may be but let's just play this by ear. Barton Sinclair is a bloody menace, but he has influence." He watched with a frown as Barton Sinclair held forth on the dangers of collaborating with the witches. His words were inflammatory at best.

"For centuries they've not wanted our help or our resources. They've believed they can do it all on their own. Well, now we've finally rid them of the one bane *they* couldn't get rid of and now they want to come back into the fold and create an 'alliance.' Well, I say fuck them. We've managed so far by ourselves." Barton Sinclair scowled fiercely.

Troy Cavanaugh nodded, his long face serious as he toyed with a lock of hair by his ear. He was an ethereal-looking man, with dark brown curls wafting around his face and a tight-lipped mouth that hardly ever smiled in a face that was almost white in its pallor.

"Well put, James. I say let those poxy witches get along by themselves. We don't need them."

James nodded sagely. "Everyone knows you can't trust bloody witches. They're liars, cheats and more trouble than they're worth."

Percy's hands clenched as he cast a furious look in James's direction. Anger flared in Quinn's chest, burning its way through his shirt. He was ready to erupt in a flash of sudden action and launch himself at Barton Sinclair to smack the self-satisfied smile off his face.

"James!" Quinn's strident voice echoed over the noise of the current tableau, causing everyone to stop talking and look at him in surprise as he stood up, his hands flat on the table. "I think perhaps you forget that there are a few people in this room who are descended from witches, myself included, and hearing you vilify them like you are does nothing for your supposed sense of decency and temperance."

Quinn's voice was harsh, barely concealing its fury, and some of the others in the room looked around at each other in concern. Justin was watching the heated exchange with a fierce frown.

"Perhaps if you could cease your fucking drivel long enough to actually say something that makes better sense, people might take you more seriously." Justin spat at Barton Sinclair.

Quinn knew he was making an even worse enemy of James but he was beyond caring. "Can everyone please sit down, shut up and we can outline the differing views and perhaps have an adult conversation instead of going off half cocked like a bunch of teenage boys in a locker room debating the latest merits of the football team."

He rose to his full height and glared around the room, causing people to sit down quietly, toying with their pencils, waiting to see what happened next. Some of them were smiling, nodding in satisfaction at Quinn's approach and inclining their heads slightly at him in support. Others, like Cavanaugh, were regarding him with barely concealed hostility.

James Barton Sinclair sat down slowly, never taking his eyes off Quinn's.

"Well, it appears our Grand Master has spoken in no uncertain terms. Is this what happens when someone says something you don't like? You use your formal decree and *tell* everyone what to do?"

Quinn knew just then that war had just been formally declared between him and James Barton Sinclair. He recognised the call to battle in the smug look in the other man's eyes. "If that's what I have to do to get both some civility and some structure to this meeting, then yes, that's what I'll do. Whilst I hold this 'formal decree' as you so eloquently put it, I'll use it to best advantage."

He looked around the room. "You've all heard the request from the Praetorium. They wish to work together going forward to help make both of our people safer and protected against any external or internal forces that seek to destroy it. You all know already I'm in favour of it. We might have defeated the Witchfinder General and taken that danger away, but there are others just like them that threaten us, some of them even within our own ranks. You remember the Warlock killings in Scotland last June. That was one of our own."

He looked at the faces seated around the table. "Despite what anyone may think, the truth is that the Praetorium is a powerful organisation. With the right alliance, it could make us stronger and give us a much wider network to draw on in terms of our intelligence network. Not to mention Valensia has access to people in high places whom we've been unable to reach."

"Does this council know about your past with the Regina? The fact you had a love affair with her many years ago?" Barton Sinclair murmured silkily. "In the interests of full disclosure, I think it prudent to mention that now." He chuckled drily. "Valensia's propensity for finding men in high places to get on her side is well known and no doubt some of these men are the ones Quinn has just referred to. Including Quinn himself."

Quinn's eyes regarded the other man with sheer dislike. "If they didn't know, they do now. I have nothing to hide. This is nothing personal. This is a business decision and should be made rationally and without emotion."

He didn't miss Barton Sinclair's disbelieving expression and raised eyebrow in his direction. Quinn wanted to choke the man until there was no more breath in his body.

He looked around the room. "You all have your ballots. On your way out, drop them in the box. They'll be counted up by the ballot team and the results will be announced this evening. Thank you all for coming."

He turned to Percy, who was regarding him with a worried expression.

"Fuck it," Percy muttered as everyone started to file out, dropping their ballot papers in the box as they left. "That man has openly declared war on you. You're going to have to watch him even closer than before."

Quinn sighed. "I know. I shouldn't have got so riled. But the man is a fucking idiot." He rubbed his eyes. "I just hope we get enough votes to make an alliance. I really want this."

"You could always do it regardless," Percy said gently. "The ballot result wouldn't stop you doing what you wanted anyway. You'd just have to do it on the sly."

"That's true enough, I suppose." Quinn smiled tiredly. "But it would be good to have the Consortium's support on this one."

Justin Leichner sauntered up to his childhood friend. He had a huge grin on his face. "I'm glad to see you put that wanker in his place, Quinn. He was really starting to piss me off."

Quinn sighed. "I know. I probably shouldn't have. But it's done now and I'll need to manage the fallout." He looked at his friend with a fond glance. "Anyway, I had you there to back me up. If things had gotten nastier we could have teamed up and given him a wedgie like we did to poor Ronald Gracie back in sixth form."

Justin chortled with laughter. "God, I remember that. Poor Ronald couldn't walk for a week, his balls were so sore. Not our finest hour, Quinn, but funny all the same." He clapped his friend on the shoulder. "I have somewhere I need to be. I haven't forgotten we still need to catch up on that drink. I promise I'll be in touch as soon as I can sort out these bloody terrorists sabotaging my pipelines. It's becoming a bit of issue and I need to teach them a lesson."

Justin owned an oil company and currently he was having trouble with eco-terrorists damaging his oil fields and exploration sites. Quinn thought they'd be lucky not to be turned into maggots if Justin finally caught up with them. He nodded.

"I'll hold you to that, old friend. Go well. Stay safe."

Justin nodded and left the room. Quinn turned to Percy with a yawn. "Let me know when the ballot results are in. I'm getting off home for a shower and a whisky. It's been a long day."

Quinn went into the small library on the side of the boardroom to fetch his jacket. He shrugged his shoulders into it, sensing someone behind him as he did so. Troy Cavanaugh stood there, a sneer on his face.

"Troy. Is there something I can do for you?" Quinn picked up his scarf and tied it loosely around his neck as he regarded the other man.

"I just wanted to tell you that I think James would make a far better Grand Master than you. He has vision and isn't so emotionally bound to the likes of witches and especially the Regina in particular. I think you're going soft."

He stood in front of the door, blocking Quinn's exit.

Quinn snarled. "Well, partial as I am to hearing Council members' points of view, I think I have to say, get the fuck out of my way. I don't give a rat's arse what you think, in fairness. You're so far up Barton Sinclair's backside, you two should be a couple."

He chuckled nastily. "For all I know, you are. Stay out of my way, Troy."

Troy paled at Quinn's words, such a look of clear hatred crossing his face that for a minute, Quinn wondered if he'd struck a nerve. He left the room without a backward glance, feeling

Troy's eyes burning into his back. Five minutes later, having invoked his Withinner, Quinn was back in the entrance hall of his home, feeling a little ill but glad to be home. It was dim, the only light a fire flickering in the hearth, casting shadows on the wall and filling the room with warmth and the fragrance of pine cones. He took off his jacket and his scarf, hanging them on the coat rack and went over to pour himself a drink. It was only nine p.m. He wondered if Cade was still awake. That question was answered when he saw him descending the stairs in his sweatpants and tee shirt with a warm smile on his face.

"You're back. How did it go?"

Quinn shook his head tiredly. "Not particularly well. Barton Sinclair was his usual charming self, and now he has a bloody acolyte, Troy Cavanaugh, which doesn't help matters. Tossers, both of them." He drank the whisky in his glass and poured another one and took a large slug.

Cade came over and grimaced in sympathy. "It must have been rough the way you're knocking that back. Did the council members cast their ballots?"

Quinn nodded. "Yes. Percy will let me know the minute they're in and counted." He smiled at him. "What were you doing upstairs then? Reading in bed?"

Cade shook his head. "I was on the computer. Cooper sent over the trip itinerary for the Scotland research project and I was just taking a look at it to see if I could make the dates."

Quinn frowned as he moved away to stare out of the window, sipping his whisky. "When are the dates, then?"

"August twentieth, through to the nineteenth of September. I think Ambrose will be happy for me to go."

"And what about me? Would you be asking me if I'm happy for you to go, or were you just going to tell me you were?" Quinn knew he was being unreasonable but he couldn't help himself. The pressures of the day still swirled beneath, his emotions tenuous.

Cade gazed at him with amazement. "I told you about this a while ago. You knew it was on the cards. This is my work. I also have a job, just like you do."

The hurt in Cade's voice cut Quinn to the core and he closed his eyes in shame. "I know that, I'm sorry. I just don't like the idea of you being gone for a month and with that fellow Cooper."

Cade came up behind him and wrapped his arms around his waist. Quinn put his drink down and leaned back into his lover, closing his eyes.

"Stop being so insecure about Cooper," Cade whispered. "He's just a friend and a colleague, and no man can hold a candle to you anyway, believe me. But I really want to finish this latest dissertation I'm busy with and the research project will help me do that."

Cade came around and stood in front of him, his hands cupping Quinn's face. "Do you really think I'd want to spend a month away from you if I didn't need to? God, I'll go crazy having no Quinn time for that length of time. We'll have to make a plan for you to travel up via that Withinner of yours—if decorum allows. We wouldn't want anyone seeing you suddenly appear."

His mouth found Quinn's greedily, forcing his lips apart as his tongue crept inside his mouth. Quinn moved his hands down to Cade's arse, loving the feel of his body through the soft pants he wore as he pulled their hips closer together. Quinn's erection pressed eagerly against the flat planes of Cade's stomach. "You have far too many clothes on," he whispered. "Take them off."

Cade gave a slow smile and moved away from him, leaving Quinn feeling bereft. Cade lifted his shirt over his head, tossing it on the couch then reached down and slid his pants to the floor. Quinn took a deep breath at seeing Cade standing nude before him, the lean lines of his body outlined in the orange glow. Cade moved over to the large Flokati rug in the middle of the lounge and lay down on it. Quinn lost his breath at the decadent sight of naked male perfection splayed out wantonly like some sort of celestial Greek gift.

"You are magnificent," he breathed in appreciation as he divested himself of his own clothes and moved over to where his lover lay. "I can't get enough of you, Fey attraction or not." He lay down beside Cade, taking his hands and placing them above his head, holding them there with one hand. Cade laughed softly, his silver eyes shining in the firelight.

"Then show me," he whispered as his body writhed sensuously among the soft white strands of the rug. "Show me how much you want me, Quinn. You have carte blanche to do anything you like to me, so do it. Drive me crazy, make me yours." He leaned forward and licked Quinn's ear. "Own me."

Quinn growled, already rock hard and ready. That was an invitation he relished, one that he couldn't resist even if he wanted to. This man before him made him insane with want and the need to possess him. The lithe lines of his lover's body made him want to bite, suck and taste everything he had to offer. From the heated look in Cade's eyes, the cock that stood proudly from his dark curls and the deep, rhythmic pants emanating from his mouth, the feeling was mutual.

Quinn grinned. "Oh, you have no idea of the things I can do to you. You haven't seen them all yet, so I suggest you lie back and prepare to be ravished." He moved on top of Cade, pressing cock against cock, loving the moan that Cade gave at feeling their mixed silk and heat. "I think I might still have a little magyck in me that you haven't seen."

Cade chuckled as he languidly stroked himself. "I can't wait to see it," he murmured, his eyes glinting in the firelight. "Bring it on."

Chapter 20

A couple of weeks later Quinn was lying in bed reading his book when his mobile rang. He frowned as he looked at the number, not recognising it. He thought about ignoring it altogether but then sighed. He'd better see who it was. He was surprised to hear the voice on the other end of the phone.

"Valensia? It's a little late for you to be calling, isn't it? It's eleven."

At the mention of the witch's name Cade frowned, looking up from the textbook he was flicking through.

Valensia's voice was amused. "Honestly? The Warlock Grand Master is worried about his bedtime? My, how the mighty have fallen."

"Did you just call to insult me or was there something I could help you with?"

She laughed softly. "Sorry, I've been with a bunch of idiots all day and as you know, they tend to bring out the worst in me." Her voice became more businesslike. "I wanted to talk you about the summit next week. I know that both of us have enemies within our own organisations who are opposed to this alliance and I wanted to be sure you and I agreed on our approach."

Quinn leaned back against the headboard, drawing the covers up over his hips. He was aware of Cade idly perusing his book but Quinn knew he was hanging onto every word.

"We both agreed we need the union of Warlocks and witches. The Council agreed too—you know the results of the ballot vote I initiated were in our favour. Now we just have to keep the peace."

"I had to deal with a real problem today." Valensia's voice was hard. "I found a witch plotting to disrupt next week's meeting with a fairly extreme plan to kill as many of us as he could. Luckily for us I managed to convince someone to tell me all about it." She laughed nastily. "Needless to say he's no longer with us, but it doesn't appear he was working with anyone."

Quinn sat up in bed, his knees drawn up, his face fierce. "Are you sure about that? The last thing we fucking need now is some sort of witchy terrorist attack and more of us getting killed."

Cade laid his book down and regarded him worriedly.

Valensia snorted. "I'm pretty sure he was alone, that he was a lone wolf. With what I put him through, I'm fairly sure he was telling the truth."

"Good. I think we need to organise a little extra security anyway. It won't hurt." He frowned. "Next week's first summit is important; we both know that. I've got Percy with all ears and eyes to the ground looking for similar insurgents. If I find any you have my word they'll be taken care of with the same efficiency you dealt yours. I'm not taking any prisoners this side and I'm glad you're not either."

"Well, it sounds like you're very satisfied with what I'm doing this side." The witch's voice grew throaty. "Imagine what a powerful union we'd be if we were still together. Are you sure you still want your Fey man? I can think of another union we could try that would bring so much more pleasure, just like it used to."

"I'm not having that conversation with you." Quinn glanced at Cade, wondering whether he'd heard Valensia's words. "Keep your mind on business."

As he said the phrase he groaned inwardly, knowing Cade would pick up on it, even as his fiancé stiffened and his eyes narrowed.

Valensia chuckled softly. "I take it your man is sitting beside you? Is he upset that I'm calling you so late?"

"Was there anything else you wanted to talk about?" Quinn asked curtly.

She sighed loudly. "You're not as much fun as you used to be; it's quite sad. Yes, I did have something else to ask you. I need the assistance of some of your research team to decipher an old parchment that's come into my possession. And before you ask, no, you can't have it." Her voice was wry. "I'm still waiting for that Book of Shadows to be returned. Will that be anytime soon?"

He smiled slightly. "You can use the researchers if you like, if you trust me not to steal it away from you. As for the book, well, I thought I deserved a little present for myself after all the work my team and I did on getting Matthew Hopkins out of the way. Are you going to begrudge me my reward?"

"I had another sort of reward in mind for you, one that involved me, you and a rather interesting bondage spell. But I suppose that's out of the question?"

"Hell, give it a rest!" Quinn shook his head in impatience. "Let me know when you want that parchment looked at and I'll sort it out for you. Was there anything else?"

"There was but you'll only shout at me again." The witch laughed softly. "Other than the thought of you spread across my bed again in nothing but skin and some silk ties, there's nothing else."

Quinn remembered a similar situation he'd been in with her in a previous life and he his face tightened. "Good. Then I guess I'll be seeing you next week at the summit. Good night."

Quinn disconnected the call and looked across at Cade, whose face was a picture.

"Did she realise that I could hear everything she said?" Cade said angrily.

Quinn looked at her in surprise. "Really?" His heart sank as Cade nodded violently.

"Yes. My hearing seems to have become a lot more acute of late. I guess it's my inner Fey working. Hell, Quinn, that woman is a menace. How dare she think she can proposition you like that? And as for that bit about being"—he huffed fiercely—"being tied down on her bed, that was just pure bloody mindedness. She knew I was fucking listening."

Quinn sighed. "Cade, she likes to rock the boat. Don't take anything she says seriously."

"You have to spend two days with that woman next week at your summit. How am I supposed to feel knowing she wants to tie you down on her bed and screw you senseless?"

Quinn chuckled at the aggrieved look on his fiancé's face. "That's not going to happen. You have my word." Privately he felt a little bit of apprehension at Valensia's renewed pursuit of him. He thought they'd had an agreement to let the past be just that.

"Well, I'm not happy. Valensia is really pushing the envelope."

Quinn sighed at Cade's mutinous expression. *Why couldn't that bloody witch have kept her mouth shut?!*

He reached out and pulled Cade over to him, sliding his hands down to his hips. "You are the only one I want tying me up and ravaging my body," he whispered, as his mouth kissed the softly pulsing skin at Cade's throat. "In fact, it sounds like a pretty good idea right now. Perhaps you could show me how that's done. The whole skin and silk tie bit and me spread-eagled on the bed."

He was feeling fairly horny himself with his own words, and when Cade reached over with darkened eyes and took the red ties out of his bedside drawer, Quinn knew he was in for a rough ride.

Chapter 21

It was a dark June night and Quinn and Daniel sat by the riverbank watching Cade swim tirelessly across the heath pond. His strong arms cut through the water as he propelled himself toward the opposite side of the bank.

Quinn thought Cade was certainly faster, stronger and more self-confident in the water than he'd been. Quinn couldn't say exactly what the full extent of Cade's powers were. All he had was the Sprite lore in his head and books. But they were learning more about the Sprite race together each day.

Now that Cade had more knowledge he was no longer worried about the ones in the pond dragging him under, and had in fact been a little disappointed that they hadn't tried to make contact with him again.

In addition to Cade's underwater breathing exercises in the bathtub, Quinn had even found Cade in a yoga position trying to "tap into his Spriteness" as he called it. Cade had been disappointed when the position of downward-facing dog had done nothing to help him find himself, but his practice of the position had done everything for Quinn's cock. Seeing Cade's pert arse tight and round before his eyes had definitely done things for Quinn's libido. Finding out his boyfriend had done yoga in his past had fuelled Quinn's sexual fantasies beyond the pale.

Quinn grinned now at the conversation they'd had one night while sitting around the dining table.

"Don't they want to Sprite with me?" Cade had muttered peevishly. "Now I fancy getting to know them, they're nowhere to be found."

Quinn knew he desperately wanted to find out more about his potential healing abilities. Cade had tried to tap into them when he'd caught his finger in a door and cut it open, but unfortunately, the good old practice of spray plaster and disinfectant had been the sum total of his healing prowess. The fierce concentration on Cade's face as he'd tried to think himself better had Quinn smirking behind his back. Cade had refused to let Quinn heal him either, saying peevishly that if he couldn't do it, it would have to heal naturally, like a human. Cade was stubborn that way.

Quinn had chuckled. "They're probably wary, given how you shouted at them the time they tried to make contact," he'd remarked dryly. "I have no doubt they will soon, though. Your prowess in finding out a little more about yourself is making you more comfortable with who you are. They'll soon pick up on that." He'd licked his lips. "Now I, on the other hand, would love to Sprite with you."

Cade had chuckled and ruffled Quinn's hair which had led to bedroom calisthenics. Cade creatively demonstrated his ability to attain various yoga positions Quinn hadn't even known were possible. Cade put his Kama Sutra book to shame.

Quinn had also reflected grimly that it was only a matter of time before Cade demanded even more information and he'd resigned himself to that fact. It was time to tap into Taliesin, who had been a complete and utter pain in the arse about his demand to help. Perhaps between them they could teach Cade some of the old Spritean language so he could make contact with them himself. Quinn felt a sense of dread at that thought.

"He's an impressive sight to watch in the water, isn't he?" Daniel muttered, drawing his old bomber jacket tighter around his shoulders. The cool night air was chilly and wrapped itself around the body like a blanket. "I can't believe he has the stamina to get into that bloody water and swim like he does."

Quinn chuckled. "Cade is probably more at home in the water than he is on dry land. If he doesn't get his swim every day he gets tetchy and I can't have that."

"Is that why you magycked open the gate in the middle of the night and we snuck in here like a couple of teenagers skinny dipping?" Daniel remarked drily. "Gates are meant to keep people out. You can't go opening them at whim and sneaking onto other people's property. Did I teach you nothing when you were a boy?"

Quinn laughed, his eyes twinkling. "A tetchy Cade is more than I can bear. I'd rather face the wrath of a constable patrolling the park. Them I can enchant, make them forget they've seen us. But that man of mine in a bad mood does not bode well for my sex life."

He grinned as Daniel shook his head in amusement.

Quinn eyed Daniel mischievously. "And it's not the middle of the night, old man, although it's probably past your bedtime. It's only nine."

Daniel reached out and punched Quinn hard on his arm, the force of his solid frame behind the blow making Quinn exclaim loudly.

"Enough of the cheek, you disrespectful bastard." Daniel scowled. "Did I teach you no manners?"

The two men grinned at each other fondly. Not for the first time Quinn wondered what he would have ever done without this man in his life to turn to when things got dark.

"I was very proud of you when I heard the result of the Union Summit," Daniel said quietly as Quinn watched Cade swim. "Not only did it go off without a hitch, you made history, you and

Valensia together. Your father would have been very proud of you."

Quinn felt warmth inside at his uncle's praise. "I was pleased with the result too.

It took a lot to get us to this stage but I think we've finally got a real ally we can work with." His voice was dry. "Even though Valensia is not my idea of the perfect partner in this enterprise, she's good at what she does and we have the same views on most things. And I know she can control her witches, so that makes things a lot easier."

He smiled. "And I have a great ally in Misty Ravenbrook, the witch that used the original book in her spells and started this whole thing off. We see each other occasionally and she's even coming over for dinner in a couple of weeks. We've become good friends. I want her to meet Cade." His voice faltered. "I have an idea I want to swing by him before she does though, something pretty mind blowing and it will need both Misty and Cade to get comfortable with each other."

Daniel looked at him curiously. "That sounds intriguing. Care to share?"

Quinn looked down at the ground, uncomfortable with how to broach with his uncle the subject he'd had brewing in his head for a while now. "Uhmm, not just yet. It's too early. I really need to speak to Cade about it before I tell anyone else."

"Wow. I've never seen you so ill at ease talking about something. This is a first. Fine, I'll let my curiosity rest. For now." Daniel grinned. "Are you sure it's a good idea having another witch meet Cade? Your track record with them hasn't been so good to date—Mary-Sophie, Valensia..." He chuckled at the expression on Quinn's face. "Come on, don't look so stricken. I'm joking." He grinned slyly. "Of course, Cade still has a bug up his arse about Valensia and you working together. I mean, she does seem to have a real yen for you still. Cade isn't happy, I can tell you." Daniel's voice was amused.

Quinn shrugged. "Cade knows the history we have, but I can promise you, Cade is more than enough for me." He watched as Cade started his swim back and he closed his eyes, lying back on the grass, appreciating the solitude of the pond. The night birds called loudly in the trees above and in the distance he could hear what he thought was a badger snorting. Daniel did the same, lying back with his hands behind his head and looking up into the clear night sky.

Quinn felt a strange sense of peace flood his body. He hadn't wanted to tell Daniel about his reason for inviting Misty over. In one of their lunch conversations, Misty had quietly asked him how the Fairmont line was to be continued if Quinn wasn't going to marry a woman and let her bear his children. To be honest, it had always been a concern in Quinn's mind but nothing that he believed he could solve easily. He'd been completely floored when Misty had said quietly that if he and Cade wanted, she was quite happy to be a surrogate for him and carry his child. The blood had rushed to Quinn's head and he had gaped at the witch. It was an offer beyond his wildest expectations—to have a renowned witch and someone he liked and trusted be the mother of any future children. He'd stammered and stuttered his thanks and appreciation at Misty's offer and she'd laughed gently, saying she knew it was early days but he and Cade must remember she was there if they needed her. Of course it was something Quinn needed to talk to his future husband about. He knew Cade loved kids but this offer was something else altogether.

They were both dozing when there was the sound of someone coming out of the water. He heard a sudden gasp, almost a deep sigh and he sat up, opening his eyes. He reached for Cade's towel, ready to take it to him. It was dim and as Quinn's eyes focused on the scene in front of him, his animal instincts kicked in and he leapt to his feet. Rowan Kirkpatrick stood over Cade, who was hunched on the ground near the steel steps, holding his hands to his chest.

Quinn rushed towards him, his heart beating wildly with fear. "Cade! Are you all right?"

Daniel sat up in alarm and scrambled to his feet. Quinn reached Rowan in seconds. He was trying to run away but had somehow got tangled up in Cade's swimming bag, the handle of which had snaked around his foot. Rowan cursed as he tried to free himself, but he was too slow. Quinn's palm connected flat against the other man's chest in a burst of energy that threw Kirkpatrick almost twenty feet away. He landed in a heap on the grass, where he lay still, his sunglasses broken beside him.

Quinn knelt down beside Cade, his face grey as he tried to see what had happened. Cade sat on the grass, hands clutching the left side of his chest. Blood gushed out of a wound that yawned open at least two inches. Quinn could see the white tissue and slowly pulsing blood as it oozed from Cade's body. It was reminiscent of the last one he'd seen on his Cade's body when Andrew de Vere had sliced him open. But this wound went much deeper, mortally so, he feared. Quinn laid Cade down on the grass, his heart pounding. Daniel stood over him in horror.

"Hang on, Cade. I'm going to try and heal that. Just hold on for me." His whole being went cold with dread. There was a terrible sense of déjà vu as he held his hands over Cade's body, his mind already chanting the words to heal him. Cade gazed up at him with pain-filled eyes and reached out a blood-covered hand to his.

"Quinn?" he whispered. His face was white, lips already paling.

Quinn clasped Cade's hand to his chest as he closed his eyes and desperately summoned the energy he needed into Cade's body, his Withinner adding to the power. When Quinn opened his eyes, the wound was just as bad as it had been. His heart froze as he closed his eyes and chanted again, laying his hands on the open wound. Cade's eyes were closed and Quinn could hardly sense his heartbeat.

"Dan, it's not working!" Quinn whispered agonisingly. "Why isn't he healing? Cade, open your eyes. Please, honey, open your eyes."

Daniel knelt down beside Cade, his face grave. He leaned in and listened to his breath, his face turning white as he realised Cade was hardly breathing.

"Quinn, I can hardly hear anything," he said falteringly. "Can you sense any heartbeat at all?"

Quinn shook his head, his eyes dazed. "My magyck isn't working, I can't heal him. We need to call 999."

His Withinner's voice echoed urgently in his ears.

Quinn, Cade will never make it. He is grievously injured. The wound has gone deep and he is bleeding inside. You have to lay him in the water. Let the Sprites take him.

"I'm not putting him in the fucking water to be taken!" Quinn spat out in agony. "He needs a hospital." He reached into his jacket pocket and took out his phone with trembling hands.

Daniel laid a cold hand on his and spoke softly. "If Taliesin is telling you to put Cade in the water, do it, son. An ambulance will never get here in time. Your Withinner knows what he's doing. Trust him."

Quinn's eyes flashed violently at his uncle. "I am not fucking losing him to the depths of a bloody Hampstead Heath pond."

He knelt down beside Cade again, closing his eyes as he tried once more to heal, but the wound just kept seeping blood, now at a much slower rate than before. Cade's face was ash white, his dark hair standing out starkly against the deathly pallor of his face.

Quinn. Your Cade is nearly gone. You have to put him in the water now before it is too late. There is no time for your modern medicine. He will not survive unless you do it now. The Water Sprites will take him and heal him as long as there is still a spark of life left in him.

"I can't. Don't ask me to do that. I can't." Quinn's voice was strangled as he struggled to compose himself. His body was cold, his mind sluggish and he had never felt so desperate.

Daniel strode forward and despite his small and wiry frame, he picked Cade up in his arms. He looked at Quinn, his voice resolute. "He's dying. This may be the only way to save him."

Quinn growled and reached out with a hand to hold him back. Daniel sidestepped him and looked at him with a resolute expression. "You can hurt me if you want but it won't help Cade. This is all we have left to try before he dies."

Quinn's hand still gripped him tightly and the older man winced.

"If anyone is going to do this, it's going to be me." Quinn's voice cracked and he held out his arms. Wordlessly, Daniel placed Cade in Quinn's outstretched arms and Quinn pulled his lover closer to his body. He walked down to the water's edge and waded in as Daniel watched helplessly from the bank, his face stark. Quinn gently laid Cade down in the water. He seemed to float for a while, hair spreading about in the water like black smoke. His face was still, eyes closed as Quinn held tightly onto his cold hand, rubbing his thumb over the engagement ring. Quinn's vision blurred as tears filled his eyes.

You need to let Cade go. Let him join his kind below the water. Trust me.

Taliesin's voice was soft, compassionate. Quinn heaved a shuddering sigh as Daniel joined him in the water, laying a comforting arm on his.

"I can't—" Quinn shook his head in grief, his heart breaking.

His uncle took hold of his shoulders, firmly holding him back. "There's no other way, son. Let him go."

Quinn relinquished his grip on Cade's hand, standing there as he heard a soft splash and saw the water rippling around them. As they watched, two sets of pale hands emerged out of the water, and slowly, lovingly, Cade was dragged gently beneath the dark waters of the pond. Quinn saw the hand with his ring on it slowly disappear under the water. It was the last glimpse he had of the man he loved.

His heart wrenched inside him, the pain impossible to bear. His life blood was being sucked from him and it hurt so much. His eyes flooded with tears and he blinked them back furiously. The water flattened as the two men stood in complete silence looking at the pond where Cade had been, its smooth surface belying what had just taken place.

Daniel reached out to Quinn. "Son, we have to have faith he'll find his way back."

Quinn shook his head, unable to speak. He looked down at the water again, hoping to see Cade suddenly appear. When he finally realised he was definitely gone, he turned and waded out of the water, toward the now-moving figure of Rowan Kirkpatrick.

Daniel shouted behind him. "Quinn. Don't do anything stupid. Remember he's human, not Fey."

"Too fucking late." Quinn muttered between clenched teeth. "I don't give a monkey's ass what he is, he's going to die right here, right now."

His vision was blurred with both tears and fury and the shifting lights of the auras of everything around him. He knew his eyes had turned black again. He reached the fallen man and violently yanked him to his feet then let him go. Rowan Kirkpatrick was unsteady on his feet, his body badly burnt, his shirt charred and sticking to his skin. His black eyes were full of pain but as he saw Quinn, his mouth formed a grotesque, blood-stained smile.

"I told you I'd get my own back," he gasped. "You took away my chance for greatness, now I've taken away everything you loved, you Warlock bastard."

Quinn's face was relentless, his pupils dilating, his eyes as black as onyx. Rowan watched in terrified triumph.

"What did you stab him with?" Quinn's voice was soft, dangerous. "Why didn't the healing work? Why didn't I hear or feel you near him?" He already knew the answer deep in his soul. Dragon's blood. It had to be dragon's blood.

Rowan gasped out words with an agonised breath as he held his hands to his stomach. "You stupid witch! I injected myself with dragon's blood. That cloaks your senses, doesn't it? I didn't need much but it did the job."

Quinn took a stride forward, his jaw clenched. "You laced that athame with dragon's blood too? That's why I couldn't heal him."

Rowan gave a strangled laugh as blood dribbled from his mouth. "Maybe. Whatever I did, it worked. Your fancy man is gone."

He grinned through blood-spattered teeth. Quinn had no doubt he was bleeding inside from the energy blow he'd delivered. The man's insides were probably mush by now.

Rowan spat blood onto the grass beside him. "Jeremy gave that blood to me a long time ago in case I ever encountered one of you. I'm glad it came in handy to kill *your darling lover*." His words were mocking and Quinn felt another surge of grief.

"You fucking bastard." Quinn surged forward and heard a satisfying thwack as his fist connected with Rowan's chin. Rowan staggered and fell onto his back. Quinn relished the physical contact and readied himself for a violent kick to Rowan's side.

Rowan lay on his back, then his arms lifted to the skies as if entreating someone. He was in obvious pain but he cackled loudly.

"I wanted you to suffer, to see your lover die in front of you. I bided my time because I wanted to make this perfect. The perfect judgment for what you did to me." He laughed, sounding like a loon. "You thought it was over but I showed you it wasn't."

Quinn growled loudly and reached down to fist Rowan's scorched shirt and pull him to standing. With superhuman strength, Quinn drew the man up and against a nearby tree, until Rowan's legs were dangling a foot from the ground.

Daniel stepped up to Quinn's side now and was watching the unfolding events with trepidation. "Don't kill him. Maybe we can get more information. Let the Consortium decide what to do with him. You have enough blood on your hands. He's dying anyway from the looks of it."

Quinn shook his head as he regarded Rowan, his face twisted into a snarl. "Fat chance of that. This stupid bastard's mine."

He leaned his face in toward Rowan's and the man flailed wildly, seeing the violence in Quinn's face. "You got too clever, you fucking retard. You should have come for me first and made sure I was dead. You're going to join your precious Jeremy and Matthew in whatever hell they went to, so I hope you're ready. Taliesin, help me. I want to fry this bastard."

I am here, Quinn. I am ready.

Quinn dropped Rowan to the ground and the man lay groaning on the cold grass. He raised his hands, ready to send a burning blast of energy into the man, just as he'd once done to Adam.

Daniel grabbed hold of his arm.

Quinn turned to him, his face vicious as he violently pushed Daniel's hands away.

"Leave me be and stay the hell out of this. This is personal."

"You don't want to do this, son. Not again."

Daniel's voice was full of pain but Quinn didn't care. He wanted Rowan Kirkpatrick in a smouldering heap on the ground. The man had taken Cade away from him and that was something Quinn could never condone.

Rowan looked at Quinn, his face gloating. "I may be a stupid bastard, but I still killed your little bitch."

Taliesin surged, his Withinner's anger at the man's words combining with Quinn's. When Quinn was finally able to see through the red mist of hatred in his eyes, he summoned all the strength he and Taliesin had. The energy from their combined power leapt out of his hands and shot into the man lying on the ground.

Rowan screamed in agony as he became engulfed in blue flames. Quinn watched expressionlessly, his eyes sensitive to the burning light, as the man scrabbled on the ground, his body jerking and spasming as the flames took hold. The smell of roasting flesh was vile. Daniel watched in horror, holding his hands over his nose, trying to block out the smell. Quinn himself felt nothing for the man's death. No guilt, no anger, no emotion at all. All he felt was sense of purpose that he'd killed the man who'd taken Cade and an overwhelming sense of grief for the loss of the man he'd loved more than life itself.

He watched through hardened eyes as Rowan Kirkpatrick died in agony, the heat of the blue flames reducing him gradually to nothing but charred bits of bone. It took a long time but finally the flames abated, having nothing more to burn. All that was left of a once living man was a pile of grey ash. Everything that had been Rowan Kirkpatrick was gone.

Quinn regarded the pile of ash thoughtfully and then moved forward purposefully and kicked it, displacing the ash into the grass, and into the air, kicking and grinding it into the ground until there was virtually no sign of anything ever being there. He wanted no reminder of this man left for anyone to see.

Daniel watched him in despair, his face gaunt and pale.

Quinn shook his head vehemently. "He deserved it. The man was a monster."

He turned to look at Daniel, who stepped back slightly at both the sight of Quinn's black eyes and the ferocious expression on his face.

"I'm going to get Cade's things and then I'm going home," Quinn said tightly. "Tell everyone to leave me alone. I don't want to see or speak to anyone for a while. Especially Percy. If he hadn't talked me out of killing this bastard when I wanted to, none of this would have happened."

Quinn went back to the bank and picked up Cade's bag, his towel and clothes, and walked back toward home. He didn't look back. His eyes were too full of tears to see anything. The auras of everything around him swirled and ebbed as he walked. He held Cade's shirt, still smelling of his aftershave, close to his chest. The raw ache in his throat and chest threatened to cripple him and drive him to his knees to howl at the sky. He had no idea what would happen now. He wasn't even sure if he cared about anything anymore.

He will come back. They will take good care of him. You put him in the water just in time.

Taliesin's voice was sad, an emotion Quinn had never felt from his Withinner before.

"He'd better, Taliesin. He was the best part of me and now he's gone." Quinn's voice choked. "I can't do this on my own, I just don't have the strength anymore. I'm so bloody tired of it all."

He stumbled as he walked, his tears blurring his vision.

We will get through this. My heart is heavy too. Cade was very special. Remember I am here. I have always been here for you. You are not alone.

Quinn got back to the dark and empty house and let himself in. He needed a drink, needed enough of it to blot out the events of the night and help him forget Cade wasn't at home. He poured himself a full tumbler of whisky and took it and the bottle over to the chair by the lounge window, the one that looked out over the heath.

The lithe form of Marco Polo wound itself around his ankles and it brought home with even more clarity that Cade was gone. Quinn sank into the armchair, his hands covering his face and his body shuddering with sobs as he wept.

Chapter 22

Daniel Wickman passed a hand over his eyes and yawned. He stretched as he stood up from the armchair in Quinn's lounge. The shadow of a cat moved along the dimly lit picture window and Daniel moved over to the window to let him in. Marco Polo glided softly into the room, his tail held erect as he meowed and jumped down from the windowsill. Daniel sighed heavily. The cat had been at odds with itself ever since the night three weeks ago when Cade had been taken by Sprites. At least the cat was still out and about, which was more than could be said for its current owner.

His phone trilled quietly in his pocket and Daniel answered it.

"Percy. How are things?" He kept his voice low not wanting to disturb Quinn. He'd hardly been sleeping and had fallen asleep on the couch only about an hour ago.

"Not good. What with Quinn refusing to attend the Consortium meetings, that bastard Barton Sinclair is on a right rampage, stirring things up. The whole 'unfit for duty' crap all over again. I need Quinn."

Daniel sighed heavily. "He's a bloody mess, Percy. He hardly leaves the house, is drinking far too much, he's lost weight because he won't eat and even Jomo can't bring him around. I think that poor man has given up trying to make Quinn see sense. Jomo is also singlehandedly looking after QuinnCo."

There was silence on the other end of the phone. "He won't speak to me either." Percy's voice was filled with pain. "He faults me for what happens and I can't really blame him."

"You tried to save a man's life, Percy, and get Quinn to do the right thing. None of us had any idea that Kirkpatrick was so bloody unstable."

"Still. Cade has gone and Quinn is falling apart. I've never seen him like this."

"He's never been in love before like he is with Cade," Daniel commented quietly. "I know how he feels."

Percy cleared his throat. "I've told everyone he's taking some bereavement leave. But he needs to get back before it all goes to hell."

Daniel gazed with unseeing eyes into the dark night. "He's having nightmares, Percy. I have a key to his place so I can stay over some nights. The man screams like a bloody banshee and nothing I can do is helping him. I just need to be here for him." His voice grew hopeful. "Cade will come back, won't he?"

Percy drew a deep breath. "I don't know for sure, Daniel. I hope so."

Daniel heard a noise behind him. "I'd better go, Percy. I think he's awake. If he finds me talking to you, he'll be pissed and think we're all going to try have an intervention or whatever it's called. I'll speak to you later."

"No problem. Just try telling him we're thinking of him this side. And please try get him to talk to me." Percy rang off.

He put his phone in his pocket and turned as Quinn came into the room behind him, dressed in just a pair of jeans, no top and a cup of coffee in his hand. His face was pale and the three week's worth of blond stubble on his face was starting to look more like a beard. Daniel wondered worriedly whether the coffee was laced with whisky. It wouldn't have been the first time.

"You're up. You should have tried more sleep."

Quinn shook his head. "I'm fine. You should stop worrying and go home. I don't need a damn babysitter." He moved over to the couch, sitting down with his coffee in his hand as he gazed at the cat with blank eyes.

Daniel sighed, knowing he was probably going to get a bollocking but thought he'd try anyway. "The Consortium Council is worried about you. I heard that smarmy bastard Barton Sinclair is still trying to get a motion signed to have you declared unfit for office due to your 'personal tragedy' and has very kindly offered to take up the mantle of Grand Master in your place if the motion goes ahead."

Quinn shrugged. "So what? Let them do it. Maybe that's the right thing to do." He sipped his coffee in apparent disregard.

Daniel felt the slow burn of anger in his chest. "For God's sake, that's no bloody answer! You've only just got the witch-Warlock Alliance going and you're going to throw away all your hard work? Valensia is worried about you too. She's been trying to get hold of you. As has Misty. Neither of them wants to see all your hard work together going to pieces. And Jomo is carrying QuinnCo on his own. You're lucky to have a friend like that. But he can't do it indefinitely. He needs you. God, man, you worked your arse off to get where you are and you're going to let some tosser like Barton Sinclair take that away from you?"

Quinn finally showed a spark of emotion in his eyes and voice when he replied. "Yes, look where it got me. Dead parents, a dead fiancé, who everyone outside of the Consortium thinks has left me and is off on an anthropological study in the south of France, no family but you to speak of, multiple near-death experiences, a lot of pain and deaths on my conscience that keep me awake at night. I'm truly a lucky man." His voice was bitter. "God knows what I'll tell people if he never comes back."

"Cade is not dead," said Daniel quietly.

Quinn snorted and looked at him with unbelieving eyes. "And you know this how? I don't. Shouldn't he be back by now if his

Sprite friends healed him? I let the man I love sink into a fucking pond and for all I know he's fish food at the bottom of the water by now."

Daniel swallowed at the anguish in Quinn's voice, feeling a lump in his throat at the man's obvious distress. "You must know that's not true. You better than anyone know the legends and we both saw those hands take him down. You have to believe he'll come back, son."

"I don't believe in anything anymore," Quinn's voice was dead. "It does no good."

Daniel exploded then with a rare fury. "Stop feeling so fucking sorry for yourself. I've never seen you this pathetic." He didn't miss the sudden spark of anger in his foster son's eyes at his words. "You mooch around this bloody house like some sort of recluse, refuse to deliver on your responsibilities, look like some sort of hobo, don't give a damn about anyone else that cares for you and did I mention, you're not the only person ever to lose someone you love. You need to get a goddamn grip. Percy needs you too; you need to bloody talk to him. The Consortium is going to hell in a hand basket."

Quinn regarded Daniel flatly. "Are you finished now? Because I have nowhere I need to be but I'm sure you do." He stood up and walked out of the lounge.

Daniel ran a hand through his cropped hair in frustration. Quinn had to be the most exasperating man he'd ever known. His shell was so hard it would have taken a bulldozer to crack it. He left the house, slamming the door and feeling a slight sense of satisfaction. Let the bastard stew in his own juice. He'd tried and failed and if Quinn didn't want to be helped, nothing would change his mind. All Daniel could hope for was some sort of breakthrough and that Quinn would come to his senses before it was too late.

Chapter 23

Quinn watched the angry form of Daniel stride down the garden path away from the house and heaved a juddering sigh. As much as he loved the man, he was in no mood for his speeches about honour and duty. He'd had his fill of that. It had cost him everything and had contributed to what he'd become. He went down to the basement and was soon in his library. He'd been researching everything he could about Sprite healing powers and the time it took, but there was nothing definitive about any of it. He had over five thousand books in his collection yet not one of them told him what he wanted to know: how he could get Cade back. Despite his words to Daniel upstairs, Quinn did harbour a desperate faint hope that he'd return. If he didn't believe that, he'd never make it through the next day.

He read through his old texts and his gilt-edged and leather-bound books until his eyes hurt. Still he could find nothing that told him what he could do to bring his lover back. Quinn wasn't a patient man and the waiting was eating away at him. He glanced at the gold ring on his left ring finger, the one Cade had bought for him recently. They'd visited a jeweller in the town of Glastonbury when they'd gone for a weekend away. Quinn had chosen his own engagement ring, a Celtic whorl of eighteen carat gold, simple but classic. Seeing it now made his heart ache even more.

He was putting an old book back on one of the higher shelves when a sudden surge of sheer frustration and anger washed over his body. He swore angrily and violently swept the row of books on the shelf onto the floor, knocking the ones that still remained one by one until he was surrounded by a ménage of open manuscripts and books, all huddled around his feet. He sank down against the wall in despair, laying his head back against the coolness of the wall and closing his eyes.

Quinn, your temper will do you no good. The nosebleeds will begin again.

"I don't give a damn," he said, tiredly rubbing his eyes. "Let them start."

Your self-pity is also saddening. Where is the man I once knew, the one who could take on anything and get through it?

"Fuck you, Withinner!" Quinn spat in fury. "Just let me be. Between you and Daniel, it's like having two nagging wives."

Taliesin was relentless.

You know Daniel was right. Your position as Grand Master is under threat. Will you do nothing to secure it? The old Quinn would have been fighting for his very survival had he been threatened thus.

"Taliesin, shut the fuck up, you bastard. Leave me the hell alone."

Quinn stood up and began picking up the books he'd swept onto the floor.

Cade would despair if he saw you like this. It would not be what he wanted.

"Cade isn't here." Quinn's voice was dead. "And don't presume to know what he would or wouldn't have wanted. He was mine, not yours."

I will leave you in peace for a while, to drown in your mire of self-loathing and pity. I hope you come to your senses soon. I cannot bear more of this.

Quinn scowled at Taliesin's words as he picked up a large red leather book and opened it to find a hollowed-out centre and what looked like a stash of letters tucked inside. The bundle was bound with a silver tasselled cord. He frowned as he pulled the letters out of their hiding place and turned them over in his hand. He didn't recognise the writing.

He sat down at his desk and slowly pulled the silver cord holding the bunch of letters together, freeing them. The paper was a pale blue colour, quite thick and creamy, with distinct gilt edging on the outside. It looked like very expensive writing paper and had a small symbol of an eagle with outstretched wings in the top right corner. Quinn slowly unfolded the top letter and looked at the date. Eighteenth July 1981. A slow chill crept up his spine. Just two months before his parents had been killed. They had died in September of the same year, the month after his sixth birthday. The writer's handwriting was florid and it looked as if there had been a lot of emotion in their words as they wrote, so deep was the ink etched into the paper.

Darling Angela,

Quinn frowned. These were letters to his mother.

You have still not given me an answer and I'm afraid I need to insist. I can wait no longer. I have told you how I feel about and I have every expectation that you should do the same. Christopher will never know about us, I will make sure of that. He is so busy with his Consortium work that he will scarcely know you are gone. Quinn is more than able to look after himself—he is a bright boy and has Rolly to care for him.

Rolly had been a nursemaid that Quinn had been very fond of when he was a child. She'd been let go when his parents were killed and Quinn had moved in under the guardianship of Daniel and Moira. He couldn't believe the words he was seeing. His mother had had an affair? The next words put his mind at ease.

```
    I know you have told me that you love
Christopher and would do nothing to
hurt him. But he does not deserve one
as lovely and as warm as you and I love
you deeply, Angela. I understand your
reluctance to accept my affections but
would ask that you reconsider.
    Your loving suitor
    Edward Mistral.
```

The world spun around him. Edward Mistral had been in love with his mother? That was something he would never have suspected or even considered. He laid that letter to one side and opened the next one, which was dated 31 July 1981, a couple of weeks later.

```
My dearest Angela
    I confess I find myself quite out of
sorts at your reply. I understand your
fears about leaving your husband,
although I confess I cannot see the
reason you would choose to stay with
someone who treats you so badly. How
many times have you seen him in this
past week? Perhaps a few hours? I would
always be there for you, and you would
be the most important thing in my life.
    Please reconsider your answer.
    Warm wishes
    Edward
```

Quinn shook his head in amazement at the gall of the man who was pursuing his mother so ardently. He'd no issue with someone showing their passion for another but reading between the lines, these letters almost bordered on stalking and obsession. He picked up the next one, the third of the four he had. Twenty-second August 1981. Three days after his birthday.

```
Angela
   I   am   most   displeased   with   your
attitude.   I   fail   to   see   your   reasoning
and   feel   that   I   must   insist   on   seeing
you   in   person.   Christopher   is   a
buffoon,   a   man   who   cares   nothing   for
you   or   the   boy   but   thinks   only   of   the
Consortium   and   his   work.   How   can   you
love   a   man   such   as   that?   I   must   insist
that   you   see   me   immediately   so   I   can
talk   some   sense   into   you.
   Edward.
```

Quinn remembered his father as a warm, loving man that had always made time for his family, regardless of his commitments to his title of Grand Master and Head of the Fairmont family. Christopher had always had time for him, despite his unusual upbringing.

Quinn could remember his last birthday party quite clearly. His father had refused to attend a Consortium meeting to be there for his son. He still remembered the birthday present he'd received—a construction kit containing what would eventually be a shiny blue Meccano aeroplane. As a boy, Quinn had a passion for aircraft and construction kits. His father had spent tedious hours with him helping him put it together and it was a memory Quinn held dear. He had no idea who the man was that Edward Mistral was ranting about, but it certainly hadn't been his father.

He opened the last letter and his face paled when he saw the date. The fifth of September 1981. The day before his parents had been killed.

Angela.

I am hurt at your action to involve your husband in our affairs. Christopher has been to see me and advised me in no uncertain terms to stay away from you and never to contact you again. I am devastated at your betrayal. You have my promise that I cannot let this lie. My integrity and affection for you has been questioned and I will not condone that from either you or Christopher. You shall pay for your indiscretion, both of you.

I imagine I will be seeing you both soon to resolve the situation.

Edward.

Quinn put the letter down, noticing his hands trembling slightly.

God! Edward Mistral sounded like a crazy man. Obsessive and sounding as if he had a screw loose. I knew him for a long time after my parent's death and I never saw that side of him.

A slow trickle of fear tickled from his stomach to his throat. Edward Mistral's last words about deserving to die and Quinn having the right to kill him echoed in his mind with a much more sinister tone that before given what he'd just read. He stood up, pacing around the library with an agitated stride.

"Taliesin?"

His Withinner was silent and Quinn had the feeling he was being ignored.

"Taliesin. Answer me, you sulky bastard."

What is it you want?

He sounded irritated but Quinn didn't care. "Remember I've always asked you to use your powers to unlock my memories of when my parents died? And you wouldn't because the risk was too great and I'd probably die?"

I remember.

"Well, I'm happy to take the risk. I want you to do a mind probe and take me back to that time."

I cannot. The danger to you would be too great.

Quinn scowled as he paced around the room, running his hands through his hair in frustration. "I've just found out something that may unlock the key to my parent's murder. I need you to do this. I have to know the truth."

You know I cannot. The probe could destroy your memories and whatever is left in your brain.

His Withinner's sarcastic tone irked Quinn and he slammed his fist down on his desk.

"I can take whatever it is you need to do. Besides, we've had a Unity. If I can withstand that, surely I can manage you squirreling around in my mind to get me some answers?"

Taliesin was silent and Quinn could feel he was onto a winning argument for his case. "With Unity we melded together at a much greater force than a mere probe—you know you can do this. I trust you."

He heard the pleading in his voice and hated himself for it, but he had to know.

"I'm begging you. Please let me get some answers about that time. I deserve that at least."

His Withinner was quiet then he sighed in resignation.

Fine. But again, it will hurt. I will try control it as much as I can. I would suggest you call someone to be with you in case you are left gibbering like a madman on the floor of your basement.

"Cheers, Taliesin." Quinn muttered as he took out his mobile phone. "That's a bloody comforting outlook, you miserable sod."

He dialled a number. Percy answered.

"Percy? It's Quinn."

Percy's voice was guarded. "Quinn. You're still around. I haven't heard from you in three weeks."

Quinn sat down in his chair, leaning back and closing his eyes as a sense of guilt overwhelmed him. "I know. I was dealing with it. I'm still dealing with it. I'm sorry I've been incommunicado but I needed to be alone."

"For three weeks?" Percy's voice was quiet. "Neglecting all your duties and avoiding me like the plague? Forgive me if I sound a little bitter. I thought we were friends."

"We *are* friends." Quinn heaved a shuddering sigh. "Look, I'm sorry. I imagine I've been a bit of a prick."

"A bit? Try total."

Quinn chuckled, despite himself. "Fine, I've been a total prick. I need your help. I know I don't deserve it but I do. If you could get over to my place now, to the library, I'd appreciate it. Then we can talk about my level of prick-ness and you can give me a telling off, like everyone else is doing."

Percy was quiet. Quinn waited. Finally Percy spoke. "I'll be there in a few moments."

The call was disconnected. Quinn walked up and down impatiently and finally saw Nicholas materialise before him. The Withinner looked at Quinn out of eyes that weren't particularly friendly.

"Quinn, before I am revoked, let me tell you how displeased I am at you for your bad treatment of Percy. He has been a miserable soul and it has not been easy for me either."

Quinn flung up his hand in exasperation as Percy appeared. "Fuck me, it's not enough having my own Withinner telling me what an arsehole I've been, now I have yours doing the same thing!"

Percy shrugged. "If the shoe fits..."

Quinn walked over and laid a hand on Percy's shoulder. "I've been a tosser not talking to you. It's been difficult for me, losing Cade like that."

"You blamed me, but do you know the worst thing? I blamed myself. If I hadn't convinced you to spare that man's life, Cade would still be with us. So I can't blame you for thinking the same. But I just wanted to speak to you to tell you how sorry I was for that and you losing Cade. That's all."

Percy's voice choked up and Quinn saw the man's grief alongside his. He reached out and hugged his friend tightly.

"I know, I'm a bastard and I'm sorry. Shit, I've never said that bloody phrase as often as I have tonight. But I mean it."

Percy pulled away and looked around the room. "So what am I here for? What do you need?"

Percy wasn't totally forgiving him but Quinn thought at least it was a start.

"I found some letters on the top shelf that Edward Mistral wrote to my mother a few weeks before my folks were killed. The tone of the letters suggests Edward had an axe to grind with them both. You can read them if you like."

He passed the letters to Percy who scanned them quickly, pursing his lips at the contents in consternation.

"Taliesin's going to open my mind and see if he can bring back the memories of the night my parents died. He's refused to do it before but I've managed to convince him. He's the only one with the power to unlock my memories and I'm hoping I might find out a bit more."

"That could kill you!" Percy exclaimed. "Or destroy your mind altogether."

Quinn nodded. "And that's why you're here. If I do become a drooling idiot, or die in the process, at least you'll be able to take care of the mess." He smiled slightly. "You are my Executor after all and you have my Power of Attorney." He hadn't gotten around to changing it over to Cade yet. He made a mental note to do so the minute Cade came back. He had to believe that would happen, that Cade would return.

Percy looked at him in horror. "That's as may be, Quinn, but I never thought I might get to use it!"

Quinn shrugged. "I've been through a Unity with Taliesin. Unlocking my memories after that experience should be a piece of cake for him. At least that's my hope. Are you ready?"

Percy shook his head. "No. But I won't be able to stop you if you've made your mind up."

"Taliesin, I'm ready," Quinn said quietly.

I will see what I can find, but be warned this will hurt. Those memories are deep and may even be enchanted to make you forget if your suspicion of Edward Mistral is correct. You do believe he killed your parents, don't you?

"I beginning to think that's a possibility, yes," Quinn said grimly.

Remember the last time we tried to undo an enchantment? It nearly cost you your life.

"Just do it." Quinn gritted his teeth as Taliesin began to search his memories, his magyck boring deep down into Quinn's subconscious. He held a clump of tissues in his hands for the nosebleeds that he knew would come. Percy watched anxiously.

Quinn started, his eyes closing as the pain grew worse. Taliesin was an invasive presence in his mind, and the Withinner's careful probing caused sharp currents of agonising pain to radiate across his temples and the back of his head. He saw flashes of the past, like a film reel running in slow motion. Blood dripped from his nose and Quinn hissed in pain as Taliesin dug deeper, seeing fragments of his past life laid bare like photographic negatives.

I think I have reached them. Are you ready?

"Just show me." Quinn hissed as he struggled to speak with the pain he was feeling. There was a sudden flash of light in his head and he fell to the floor, his legs unable to sustain him. He sensed Percy move across to him in concern.

Quinn saw his six-year-old self playing with a small, red tin plane in the lounge of their apartment in Chelsea. It was as if he was watching an old movie, slightly faded but still visible. His magyck book was spread out beside him, but the young boy that was him was paying no attention to it, being more interested in flying the little plane in the air, watching as it swooped up and down toward the ground, guided by his hand. Quinn heard his mother's soft laughter, and his father's amused voice at something she was saying. Suddenly the boy turned as if startled and a dark figure come flying past him, through the door, the man's long pea coat flicking against him as he sat with his toy plane.

There was the sound of shouting and the boy stood up, moving toward the lounge where the noise was coming from. The child reached the door and stood looking into the room. Quinn watched in horror as the tableau in the lounge played itself out. His father stood protectively in front of his mother, who was shouting, her eyes filled with tears, her hands holding his father back. The dark-coated figure moved forward, raising his hand. He had a curved dark object between his index and middle fingers and brought it down in a long sweeping motion that left a deep-bloodied scratch on his father's neck. His father reeled away to land a few feet away from his mother. His mother screamed and lunged forward at the figure, her face white but determined, and the figure swung his hand again, slicing a deep red cut across her cheek and then stepping back as she collapsed beside his father.

The figure turned and Quinn saw the twisted face of Edward Mistral standing there.

He'd killed his parents with a dragon's claw dipped in dragon's blood.

Mistral noticed the boy and made a move toward him.

Quinn saw the child move forward and launch himself at the tall figure's legs, his small hands flailing in anger at the man who was harming his parents. Edward Mistral violently hit the boy against the head with a fist, knocking him down to lay dazed and bleeding. Quinn lay there, not far from his mother and father, watching as they jerked and gasped in their final death throes, as Edward Mistral stood beside the boy and watched his parents die.

When it was over, the Warlock bent down over the prone form of the child, laying his hand on the boy's head and muttering some words. The boy cried out in pain then lay still, quiet and submissive, until Edward Mistral picked him up in his arms and disappeared out of the apartment. Everything went grey and the scene faded to nothingness.

Quinn's body was heaving the exertion of what he'd just seen. Coming back to the present, he saw Percy's feet standing before his face, as he lay on the floor, his body shivering with the pain he now felt, hearing Percy's voice as if from far away.

It is over. You saw what you needed to see.

Quinn struggled up with Percy's help, getting to his feet and staggering to the side of his desk, where he grabbed a pile of tissue to mop up the blood streaming from his nose. The pain in his head slowly receded and he turned and was violently sick on the floor. It was mostly bile, as he hadn't been eating, but it scalded his throat with acid and made him gag.

"Hell, Quinn, you need to sit down." Percy guided him to the chair and Quinn collapsed thankfully into it. His hands were shaking so badly, he could barely hold the tissue where he wanted it to go.

"I saw him. I saw that bastard Edward Mistral kill my parents."

Percy's face was white with shock. "God, I don't care what you bloody saw! That was a terrible thing to watch. I thought you were dying with all that blood. Here, let me hold that. Yours hands are bloody useless in their current state."

Percy grabbed another wad of tissue and held it under Quinn's nose. Quinn closed his eyes, his chest tight as he struggled to breathe.

"Mistral killed your parents? Because of those letters?"

Quinn nodded. "It was a crime of passion. Edward Mistral was in love with my mother and wanted my father out the way. But in the end he killed her too. They trusted him and he got close to them and murdered them both. They had no reason to think he would harm them like that. They were bloody friends, for God's sake." His voice was anguished.

Quinn. Are you all right?

The worried voice of his Withinner echoed in his pounding head. Quinn nodded tiredly. "I'm alive. Feeling like shit but alive. Thank you, my friend. Thank you for that."

You are welcome. I am glad you survived. I was not looking forward to finding myself another Warlock.

Quinn chuckled tiredly. "Nobody else would put up with you, you reprobate. I'm afraid you're stuck with me."

That pleases me. Even if you have been a complete horse's arse of late.

Quinn smiled and leaned back in his chair, exhausted by the events.

Percy laid a soft hand on his shoulder. "Is that it? Have you finally found closure on this part of your life?"

Quinn nodded. "The words Edward said to me when he died make perfect sense to me now." His voice hardened. "I lived a lie my whole life thinking he'd saved me. I'm glad he's dead and I'm glad I got to kill him. I just wish now it had been a more difficult death for him. Not only did he kill my parents, he killed all of Taliesin's memories of my dad, memories I could have shared in."

Percy sat down in the opposite chair and looked at his friend. "I know this is not the best time, but the Consortium needs you. That bastard Barton Sinclair is causing all manner of uprisings in the ranks. You need to pick up the mantle again and get back to work. We can't do it without you."

Quinn nodded his head. "I know I fell to pieces when Cade . . ." his voice faltered, "When Cade went. Daniel's been telling me the same thing, believe me."

He passed a trembling hand across his eyes. "Convene a meeting, Percy," he said quietly. "I'll be there."

Percy nodded. "I'll do that; it'll keep your mind off Cade until he comes back. Because he will come back. You have to believe that."

"I hope so, Percy. Because life will never be right without him."

Chapter 24

The next night Quinn dreamt he heard Cade's voice, calling to him. He smiled, looking around to see where he was. He found himself on the heath, in the forest, with the sun glinting through the trees and casting a dappled light on the forest floor. In his hand he held a black jacket, vaguely recognisable as one Cade had. He was walking around the quiet forest, peering behind bushes and looking up at the trees to find the source of his voice.

"Cade? Where are you?" he called out as he walked. "I can't find you. Come on out. I have your jacket. You must be cold in that water."

Cade's voice disappeared and Quinn panicked that he was no longer there. He walked faster, his eyes scanning everywhere he could, feeling more anxious as he broke the foliage and swung back the branches to get deeper into the woods. He heard his lover's voice again, clearer this time, and sensed his presence. He smiled as he turned, expecting to see him, and took a step back in horror at the apparition that stood before him. It was Cade but not Cade, some vague form of his man covered in green slime and fronds, his eyes black and flat, reaching out a skeletal hand to him with a smile from a mouth that had sunken into his face.

Quinn cried out loudly in disgust, trying to get away from him, even as he backed into a tree with branches that clutched at him, embracing him in its tight grip. He held up the jacket as if warding away the terrible sight that he faced and cried out again loudly as something shook him violently, gripping his shoulder.

"Quinn, wake up. For God's sake please wake up!"

He awakened with a gasp, his heart pounding and his vision blurred with stinging sweat running from his forehead. The room was dark and he was drenched, liquid pooling in drops on his body, causing his flesh to feel slick and clammy.

"Quinn, it's me. It's Cade."

Quinn cried out, remembering the dream and raised his hands in front of him. A pair of warm ones took his own firmly and lowered them, murmuring quiet words of reassurance.

"It was just a dream, I'm real. It's really me. I'm back. Ease up."

Quinn gazed in wonder at the form that sat beside him on the bed. He breathed in Cade's scent, sensed his unique presence and felt him as if he was part of him, but still he didn't believe it.

"Cade?" he murmured in disbelief.

Cade leaned forward, his beloved face inches away, and Quinn felt the warmth of his breath. This was no demon covered in pond slime. This was his Cade. Quinn cried out, heaving a shuddering breath as he reached over and pulled Cade to him, feeling his warmth and his solidness, and he held him so close it was as if he was pulling him into the core of him. Cade laid his face against his, his hands wrapping themselves around his neck.

"God, Cade," Quinn whispered brokenly. "I missed you so much. You were gone so long; I thought you were never coming back. Is it really you? I'm not dreaming, am I?"

Cade leaned back and regarded him with the smile he'd missed so much. "No, you're not dreaming. It's me. The new, reinvented me, but me." He frowned. "What the hell have you been doing to yourself? You're so thin, you look like you haven't eaten properly in the three weeks I've been gone. And what the hell is this beard? Couldn't you be bothered to shave whilst I've been gone?"

Quinn laughed loudly, a sound he hadn't heard in over three weeks, as he pulled his lover to him again and rubbed his beard against his cheek. "Now I know it's really you. Only you could give me a bollocking about something like that after coming back from the dead after so long. I missed you so much."

He reached over and switched on the bedside light but didn't dare let Cade go. Quinn was giddy with sheer joy and it was all he could do to restrain himself from jumping out of bed and cartwheeling around the room. The light flooded the room and he saw Cade clearer now, looking just the same as he had before. Pale, drawn and exhausted, but his Cade.

His grey eyes looked at Quinn in both love and exasperation. He wore a pair of jeans and a blue tee shirt. "You look like shit and I see those nightmares still haven't left you. Perhaps now I'm back, we can work on that."

Quinn reached over and claimed Cade's mouth in a kiss that encompassed weeks of grief and loss in one single action. Cade's arms wrapped around his neck and tears of relief fell from Quinn's eyes at the fact his waiting was finally over. For a moment there was nothing else in the room but Cade's mouth beneath his and finally he pulled away and cupped his face in his hands.

"Cade, what happened? How did they heal you? What did they do with you for such a long time? Why the hell did it take so long for you to come back to me?"

"Whoa, tiger." Cade chuckled softly. "One question at a time, but not right now. I just want to feel your body next to mine and be with you. I'll try and suppress my increased Fey instinct to ravage you, because honestly, I just want to hold you. I can't believe I'm home. I'm so bloody tired."

He sounded near exhaustion and Quinn resolved to let Cade find his own pace and tell his story. It was enough for now that he was home.

Cade crawled into bed fully clothed and into Quinn's arms, facing him. Quinn drew him closer, wrapping his arms about Cade in a possessive embrace that left no doubt for wondering what he might do to anyone who tried to take him away from Quinn. They lay together quietly like that for some time, as Quinn marvelled at the fact he'd come back. He heard Cade's gentle breathing as he lay there and felt the touch of his hands on his hips as he settled against him. He didn't want to interrupt the magyck of the moment so he stayed silent. Cade would speak when he was ready. But for now, he revelled in the moment, content that he was home with him.

Your Cade is back. I am glad for you.

So am I, Withinner. So am I. Thank you. You saved him and I will never forget that.

*****

Quinn opened his eyes to an empty side of the bed and for one moment he had a terrible feeling that he'd been dreaming and Cade wasn't really home. For a moment it seemed his heart stopped and he wanted to throw up but that was soon remedied by the sight of Cade walking into the room with a cup of something hot in his hands, sitting down beside him on the bed.

Cade held out the cup of coffee. "I'm still here. It wasn't a dream." He reached over and caressed Quinn's cheek tenderly. His hands brushed over the thick stubble on his cheeks and chin. "It looks pretty dashing, like you're some sort of eighteenth-century pirate. I suppose I could get used to it if you really wanted to grow it."

"The only reason I haven't shaved is because I didn't see the point." Quinn sat up, leaning against the headboard, holding the coffee in his hands. "I haven't really been out much and with you not being here, I couldn't really be bothered." He shrugged guiltily.

"And you losing so much weight? I suppose you didn't see the point in eating either?" Cade's voice was sad.

Quinn looked at him guilelessly. "No, I didn't. I thought if I didn't eat, nature would take its course sooner or later and devour me from the inside. I didn't really care."

Cade's eyes narrowed in pain. "God, I'm so sorry you had to go through all this. The waiting and not knowing must have driven you crazy."

Quinn shook his head. "It wasn't your fault. You had no choice in the matter. You were virtually dead by the time I finally found the courage to lay you in the water."

Cade reached up and clasped Quinn's face gently. "I can't even imagine how that must have felt. God knows what you went through that night. I don't remember much after that bastard stabbing me, it was all such a blur." He held tightly onto his hand and Quinn rejoiced at seeing Cade still had his engagement ring on his finger. "At least tell me you killed him, the man that put us through this bloody ordeal."

Quinn had never heard such a tone of hatred in Cade's voice before, not even for Mary-Sophie or de Vere. Quinn nodded quietly. "Yes, I killed him."

His lover nodded in satisfaction. "Good."

An unpleasant frisson of cold traversed Quinn's spine. Cade saw the look on his face and he sighed. "I know, that doesn't sound like me. But I'm a little different now to who I was when I left you that night."

"What exactly happened to you when they took you away from me?" Quinn asked quietly.

Cade regarded him thoughtfully and sat back on the bed, his head against the wall, jeaned legs stretched out in front of him. "I don't remember anyone putting me in the water. The last vision I have is of your face leaning over me, just after I was stabbed. You looked so anguished and I don't want to remember that bit. The next thing I knew, I woke up in some room somewhere, a very cool, tranquil room, like one of those places you'd go when you go on a spa day? There was a woman there, a very tall woman. Her name was Nydra and she was a Sprite of the Pond on the Heath. She said I'd been ill for a while and explained what had happened but that I was better now and she had a lot to tell me. And they did far more than that, Quinn."

Cade stood up and in one swift movement, he removed his shirt. He lifted his arms and turned around for Quinn to see. Quinn gazed at Cade in wonder, not just because he was seeing him half naked after a period of abstinence, but because the livid scar on his back from Andrew's savage cutting and the other one on the chest that Quinn healed—even the final cut delivered by Rowan—was gone. Cade's body was pristine, as if nothing had ever happened. Quinn moved swiftly out of bed, dressed in his pyjama bottoms and examined Cade with an air of disbelief. He was pleased to see Cade's nipple ring sill remained.

"All the scars have disappeared! That's incredible." He ran his fingers down where the scars had been, and Cade shivered at his touch. Quinn felt an intense surge of desire himself and took a deep breath.

Cade smiled. "They healed me. They told me I was just like them and they wanted to show me who I was." His voice sounded far away as Quinn sat down on the bed and drew Cade down next to him as he continued his story.

"Nydra showed me around what they call the Presusa, which is the place they all live. I still don't really know where it was, if it was under the water, in some parallel universe or what. I asked and she laughed and said it didn't matter. It was wherever there were Sprites. I told her I wanted to come home. I knew you'd be out of your mind with worry but she wouldn't let me. She said I had to learn first about myself before I came back to you."

Cade looked guilty. "I tried to sneak out one time to see if I could find my way home but I ended up going around in circles, the same place over and over again, and finally I gave up."

Quinn stroked his cheek gently. "That doesn't sound like my Cade."

Cade chuckled. "You try having a Groundhog Day and see how far you get. It was the most frustrating thing I've ever been through. So I had to learn some patience and Nydra taught me a lot about my great-great ancestors, Hester included. She told me the memories of my Sprite line died out after my mother died. Mum had been the one holding it all together, keeping the family heritage going. When she went, the others apparently just drifted and after a while, they forgot who they were. Some of them, Nydra hasn't been able to trace. She says the desire to be a Sprite needs to be there for them to connect."

He sighed sadly. "There were other Sprites there too. I got to know them a little but it was Nydra who I was with the most. She was a Seer, with the ability to see the past and the future. She had some sort of light thingy, like a ball, that she could take out of herself, and she'd put it in me, and I could see some of my Sprite past." His voice choked. "I saw my mum when she was young, saw some of her life events and others who came before her. It was pretty amazing though. I felt I began to know her and my family at last." He smiled softly. "I have those at least in here now." He tapped his forehead. "Nydra wouldn't ever let me see the future. She said all I would look for was you and that would distract me." His voice caught. "All I could think about was you. How you were coping, what you were doing, how much I wanted to be home with you. I missed you so damned much."

Quinn reached up and brushed a strand of hair from Cade's face. It had gotten longer and he quite liked it.

"Nydra said this ball of light was the past energy and knowledge of the Sprite. By having it in me, I could absorb it too and find my power." Cade grinned mischievously. "I also found I could move things, anything composed of fluids or water and one day I actually managed to take all the water out of the Presusa pool in the complex and dump it on a group of people. They weren't too chuffed at that, but it was an accident."

Quinn chuckled loudly, hearing the self-satisfaction in Cade's voice. "I'll bet it was. I know you. It didn't just happen to land on anyone, did it?" At Cade's guilty glance, Quinn gave a large guffaw of mirth. "Hell, who did you dump it on?"

"There were some of them that were a little above themselves, all cocky and know-it-all. They got a little wet when the water drenched them, I'll admit. But they deserved it."

Cade stroked his hand. "They also taught me about the power I have to heal. Not to the extent you and Taliesin can, but it's still quite powerful apparently." Quinn was fascinated by Cade's story, the desire to hear more and his need to feel Cade close to him at war with each other. He saw no such indecision in Cade's expression. His lover's eyes glinted with lust as he licked his lips, wetting them, and Quinn though he could come just from that action alone. Cade reached over, taking Quinn's lips in a possessive kiss and Quinn was lost. He was pushed back on the bed as Cade's tongue flicked in his ear, causing him to gasp and close his eyes.

"I think I want to shag you first then finish talking." Cade deftly took hold of Quinn's pyjama bottoms and pulled them off his body. Quinn's cock leapt up as if commanded to stand to attention.

Cade growled, and the sound made Quinn's heart beat faster and his groin flame. In one fluid moment, Cade had mounted him, sitting on his thighs and pinning Quinn down with a look of predatory greed. Quinn watched, open mouthed, at the sight of this sensual and perfect man preparing to take what he wanted from him.

Cade's eyes gleamed with desire as he ran his hands down Quinn's chest, rubbing his sensitive nipples with some force, leaving Quinn breathless. His cock was already wet and throbbing, and Cade leaned down, his hands on Quinn's hips as he licked the tip and growled with pleasure. That sound alone was enough to make Quinn hyperventilate with lust. He relished the feel of Cade's tongue on his prick, the long, slow lapping up the underside. Cade's hair brushed Quinn's skin, turning it into multitudes of nerve endings that threatened sensory overload.

"Cade, please," Quinn panted, all rational though gone, and he didn't recognise the needy tone of his voice. "Please, I want you to take me. I need you inside me."

Cade's eyes darkened as he licked his lips and Quinn moaned at the sight of that wet, swollen mouth.

"It's been a while for you, Quinn, are you sure?" Cade's voice trailed off as Quinn thrust his hips up under Cade.

"Yes, damn you. Now get *off* me and get *inside* me. I need to feel you, need to know you're with me, that you're real. Please."

Cade shifted and moved off Quinn's legs to kneel beside him. He reached inside the bedside drawer for the packets of lube and tore the corner off. The sweet smell of berries rose in the air and he laughed softly.

"*Berry* nice, Quinn. I like your taste in lube. I haven't seen this one before."

"Shut the fuck up about the damn lube and put it on your dick. Then put your dick inside me. Can you manage that, Cade? I thought your talking took place *after* sex, not before?"

Cade's answer to Quinn's sexually frustrated tetchiness was to lean down and take his mouth in a kiss that sucked the snark from him and left him dizzy. He watched through hazy eyes as Cade lathered his dick in lube and then pushed Quinn's legs back as far they could go. Keeping his silver eyes focused on Quinn's, Cade slowly slid a slick finger inside him, coating him with sweet-smelling gel. Quinn gasped at the cold feel then the burn as Cade stuck another finger inside and moved his fingers around. Quinn moaned, his head pushing back against the pillow, as his eyes closed and he revelled in Cade's touch.

"Do you feel met?" Cade whispered as he opened Quinn up. "Do you believe I'm here and I'm real now?"

Quinn gulped and nodded. "No more prep. I need you."

Cade ran his hands up Quinn's arms and slowly, lovingly, he pushed into Quinn, filling him up inch by inch. Quinn's legs ached from the position he was in and he loved every minute of it.

"God, yes," Quinn's voice was husky. "All of you, Cade. Every bit of you in me."

Their ballet of lovemaking was an intimate dance of two men so in tune with each other's bodies and emotions that it played out like a soaring symphony and Quinn roared in ecstasy at the beauty of it.

Cade's body, his skin, his lips, his silver eyes and his sweat all took possession of Quinn and he closed his eyes and gave himself up to the miracle that was Cade Mairston. Finally, with a loud cry of pleasure, he let go and threw himself at the mercy of the man who had returned from the dead, just to be with him.

Chapter 25

With Cade satiated and Quinn still in a state of shock at both the aggression and possessiveness of his new man, they lay together, Cade spooning into his back with his hands draped across his stomach. Quinn's arse hurt, his cock was sore with the amount of manhandling it had been subject to, and from the look on his face, Cade was also feeling the after effects of their violent and passionate coming together.

"That was intense," he whispered hoarsely, his throat still sore from all the shouting and gasping he'd done. "Christ, we're going to die if that's how it going to be from now on. Not that I'm complaining, it's a great way to go, but fuck, Cade. That was just—" Words failed him and Cade laughed as his fingers caressed Quinn's sticky belly.

"I agree. I think we just made the bloody earth move."

They lay quietly together, comfortable in each other's arms.

"Are you going to tell me more about your experiences now seeing as how you've had your fill of me?" Quinn chuckled softly in the dark. His sense of well-being at having Cade lying beside him still hadn't disappeared.

"I wouldn't say I've had my fill of you. I've got some weeks of lust to catch up on. But for now I'm okay." Cade laughed softly as his tongue trailed its way across Quinn's shoulder. "I like getting my Fey on. My instincts to ravage you seem to have gotten more intense since being gone."

Quinn chuckled. "I can't say I'm not liking it—even though it's going to kill me."

Cade shifted next to him. "I don't remember where I stopped my story, though, so you'll have to remind me."

"You dumped a load of water on some of your fellow Sprites." Quinn's voice was wry.

"Oh yes. That. Nydra taught me how to breathe in water." Cade's voice was awed. "It was quite the most incredible experience I've ever had. Nydra told me what those words meant that I said in the water when that Sprite tried to pull me down. It was 'áse me na fýgo' which is Greek for 'let me go.' She said I dredged it up from my subconscious. So you're not the only one now who can speak another language."

Quinn chuckled at his lover's smug tone even as his insides churned with fear.

Cade is different now. I will have to tell him everything I know now about being Fey to keep him safe. He may be in danger with healing powers like his, being descended from someone like Hester Vickers. Not to mention the fact any Fey is fair game for a Collector to steal their powers away. But that can come later. Now I just want to be with him. This homecoming is all that counts right here and now.

Cade crept closer to him, his hands gently stroking Quinn's hip and his stomach down by his groin, arousing him again. "It was a truly unbelievable experience being shown all these things and having Nydra tell me about my past and who I was." He laid warm lips against Quinn's shoulder. "Yet every minute I was there, I was waiting to get back to you. I would have given it all up just to see you again. Who I was just didn't seem to be as important as who I wanted to be with. Nydra said I could use more time with them, but I made such a fuss about coming back to you, finally she relented and got me back."

"You're home now." Quinn looked at Cade fiercely. "You are home for good though, aren't you? They don't want you back? Because I can damn well tell you I won't let you go—"

Cade's mouth found his and smothered his words. "No, I'm back with you," he whispered into his mouth. "No one's taking me away again from you again. I promise."

Quinn groaned as Cade's hands found him again and he caressed him softly, sliding his fingers up the length of him. "You're pretty perky again. I think I can put that to good use. But this time you can ride me, cowboy. I'm all dun tuckered out from last time."

Cade's terrible attempt at a Western accent made Quinn chuckle softly even as he got back in the saddle.

Chapter 26

Quinn took a deep breath and straightened his tie in the bathroom mirror. He'd needed a few minutes on his own before going into the conference room next door and facing what he knew was going to be a tough audience. He took a long, critical look at himself. His beard was gone and he was back to just his normal faint gold stubble on his chin. Cade had been fattening him up over the past four days, making sure he ate three times a day and snacking in between to get him back to what his bossy fiancé called his usual "brawny" self. Quinn wasn't sure he'd been brawny to start with, but Cade had insisted and Quinn had decided not to argue. Besides with all the sexual activity Cade was subjecting him to, he'd needed to replenish his energy levels constantly.

Quinn had spent the last few days with Cade as he showed him what Nydra had taught him. The Warlock was impressed with the extent of the Sprite woman's teachings. She'd certainly shown Cade a lot of his past and how to manage his powers.

Percy had convened a meeting for today, the eighteenth of July, and Quinn had a lot of ground to cover and claim back. His absence over the last four weeks had cost him dearly. Whilst his council had understood his so-called "compassionate" leave, Barton Sinclair had been busy doing everything in his power to undermine him.

Now Quinn had to go in and face the people he knew he'd let down due to his personal circumstances and try and get them to have confidence in him once again.

Percy walked in to the bathroom, going over to the urinal. Quinn turned away and once again regarded himself in the mirror, looking deeply into his own eyes as if searching for something. Percy finished his pee and zipped himself up to come over and wash his hands, standing beside Quinn.

"I'm glad Cade's back. It's good to see you getting back to your old self." Percy looked at Quinn in the mirror. "I know it's going to be tough for you in there, but remember, you have more friends than enemies. Justin's in the room too, and you know he'll support you. Just stay focused. Be your usual charming and autocratic self and the meeting will go just fine." He grinned.

Quinn smiled slightly. "Thanks, I know I've got my work cut out for me in there and I wouldn't expect anything else after neglecting them all for nearly four weeks."

"They knew about Cade. They understood you were taking some personal time. So people would have expected a little less face time from you anyway."

Quinn turned away from the mirror and took another deep breath. "Right, let's do this."

You will be successful. I can feel it.

"Thanks for the vote of confidence, Taliesin." Quinn murmured softly. "At least one of us feels sure about the bloody thing."

He walked out of the bathroom and into the corridor, Percy following behind him. Quinn reached the boardroom door and opened it with a show of confidence he didn't feel. The room was noisy with chatter and as he stepped inside, it quietened and people looked around expectantly. Quinn took his place at the head of the table and remained standing up, waiting for the room to settle down.

"Gentlemen, please, sit down." Quinn motioned with his hands to everyone to seat themselves. "Once you're all comfortable, I have something I need to say to you."

Justin Leichner was seated, watching the room. His friend's narrowed eyes slowly assessed the people around the table. Then Justin smiled and nodded at him. Quinn nodded back. Finally everyone was quiet, watching Quinn carefully.

James Barton Sinclair and his partner in crime, Troy, sat at the far end of the boardroom table. James had a sneer on his face.

Quinn took a deep breath. "Gentlemen, thank you for attending this extraordinary Council meeting today. I appreciate the time you've all given up to be here." He sat down and leaned forward. "As most of you know, I had a family bereavement some weeks ago and I decided to take some personal time off. Unfortunately it turned out to be longer than I expected and I apologise for that."

He looked around the table at the faces staring back at him.

Here goes. They say honesty is the best policy.

"I need to be truthful with you all. My intention was never to stay away so long but events took me over. I ended up feeling far sorrier for myself than I should have been."

Percy glanced sideways at him, a faint smile on his face.

"Of course, by now you all know that my fiancé, Cade, has returned and things are slowly getting back to normal." He smiled slightly. "As normal as they can be having gone through what we've been through."

"I sympathise with your situation and I'm very glad your fiancé made it back." Barton Sinclair's words sounded sincere but the underlying tone was definitely one of challenge. "However, this Consortium needs people who can rise above such personal tragedies and continue to lead. I think there are some of us around this table who believe that perhaps your behaviour of the past few weeks has shown this not to be the case. I feel it would be remiss of me if I didn't point this out."

Good Lord, Quinn, this man is a moron. My offer of gutting him and throwing in the river still stands.

Quinn suppressed a smile at Taliesin's angry words as he regarded James quietly. "James, for once in my life I cannot refute what you say. If the tables had been turned I might have been saying the same thing about whoever sat in this chair."

"No, actually, you wouldn't have. You're far more compassionate than that." Justin Leichner remarked laconically, his fingers slowly tapping on the table. Quinn looked at him in surprise as Justin turned his head and looked around the sea of faces that turned to him, waiting to see what he said next.

"Quinn here saw the man he loved stabbed to the core and found out he couldn't heal him. He then had to put him in some bloody pond and wait to see if anything would happen. Then he disappeared under the water and Quinn didn't see him for over three weeks. He didn't know whether he was dead, rotting at the bottom of the water or alive and in the hands of some Fey race that no one's seen for tens of years."

Justin's words were curt and he tapped louder on the table. The people around the table were quiet, Quinn included. "That scenario is bad enough for a Warlock, even a Grand Master. I'd hazard a guess nothing like that has ever happened to anyone else around this table?"

Justin's tone was challenging as he looked around, inviting comment.

"No takers?" he murmured softly. "Then imagine what that must have felt like as a man. A normal human being with emotions. Because, gentleman, that's what everyone around this table is as well as being a Warlock. We're men. We feel, we grieve and we rejoice when good things happen. Sure, Quinn went off the rails a little." He grinned at Quinn who grinned back, breathing a little easier now.

"But I think any one of us would have done the same. And what Quinn did or did not do in the last few weeks in no way mitigates what he's done since he was twenty-one and took on the mantle his father had before him. I'm not going into detail on this because you all know how much he's achieved. Not the least, recently destroying the Witchfinder General and putting in place an alliance with the Praetorium for the first time in centuries. So I think this man should be remembered for what he's achieved. Not for what he didn't do during one of the darkest periods of his life."

Justin stopped tapping and sat back in his chair. Quinn felt a tremendous lump in his throat at his friend's words and all he could do was nod wordlessly at him across the table. Justin winked.

This man is a true friend. He is honourable and sincere, two qualities hard to find in anyone nowadays. Taliesin sounded almost choked up himself.

"What a lovely speech, Justin." Barton Sinclair was sarcastic. "Eloquent and touching. You should be a poet. Notwithstanding, of course, the fact that the two of you are friends. The fact remains—"

"Bite me, B.S.," Justin said curtly. "Is that eloquent enough for you?"

James glared at the younger man who met his gaze flatly. Quinn thought he'd better step in quickly before the two men came to blows. "Justin. Thanks for those—"

He was stopped from saying anything further by a loud clap from somewhere around the table. Then another. Before long, men were standing up and clapping loudly, drowning out anything Barton Sinclair was trying to say.

Quinn stood speechless as Percy grinned widely beside him and Justin smiled down at the table even as he clapped too. Some men remained seated, scowling fiercely, and Quinn guessed they were the Barton Sinclair supporters. Finally the clapping abated.

"Quinn, most of us around this table did not doubt you." A large, stocky man smiled warmly at Quinn. Frederick Mulbarton was a well-respected Warlock from the North. "We knew you had a personal tragedy. We also knew that when you were ready, you'd return. We counted on Percy to keep us to date, which he did admirably. I for one am glad your tragedy had a happier ending and I look forward to your continued presence as Grand Master around this table."

"I concur." Avery Smith-Barker smiled at Quinn. "Thank you for your honesty with us, Quinn. It makes a change from the usual bluster we hear spoken around this table."

Quinn suppressed a grin knowing Avery was referring to Barton Sinclair. There was no love lost between the two men.

"Gentlemen, thank you for your continued confidence in me. I promise you I will do everything possible to keep this Consortium on track. I do however owe a debt of thanks to Percy Ballantyne, my Marshall, for his support, his unswerving confidence in me and his friendship. Percy, my friend, I owe you one."

Percy inclined his head, graciously accepting Quinn's praise and his IOU. "And I'll collect, Quinn," he murmured. "Have no fear of that."

Quinn chuckled at the words as he moved over to Justin Leichner who was standing quietly in the corner of the room. "I can't thank you enough for what you said," Quinn said softly. "You saved my bacon today and I don't know how I can ever repay that."

Justin shook his head. "I meant every word. We all know you're the best person for this job. You've been proving it since we were at school together. No one is ever going to take that away from you whilst I'm around, least of all that bloody idiot."

He cast a scathing glance at James Barton Sinclair who was huddled deep in conversation at the boardroom table with Troy and two other men.

"Watch him, Quinn." Justin said quietly. "I've heard rumours about him planning on taking your seat and he's like a spider. He'll bide his time until he thinks he can eat you alive. Don't turn your back on him or his bloody sycophant Troy. If I didn't know better, I'd say they were more than just friends—more like butt buddies. Troy's so far up his arse."

Quinn shook his head in amusement, remembering he'd said almost the same thing to Troy. "Stop rumour mongering. That'll be all I need, accusations of sodomy in the ranks." He grew serious again. "If you ever need anything, you know where to find me. Anything, anytime. You know that."

Justin reached out and softly touched Quinn on the arm. "I know, Quinnster. And if I need you, I'll call."

Quinn chuckled. "I haven't been called that since I was at school with you. That brings back memories. Like the night we broke into the school kitchen and stole all the picnic baskets that had just been filled. We took them to the local girl's dorm, remember?"

Justin grinned. "I remember. I also remember taking the booze from the Headmaster's cabinet with us as well. I think that might have been my first hangover."

The two men smiled at each other in shared camaraderie.

Justin sighed. "I'd better be getting off. I need to be in Moscow as soon as possible. Some more pipelines to double check and my company have a bit of a rebel problem at the moment that I need to sort out. It's not an easy business, this oil game."

"Sounds just up your alley. Look after yourself and stay in touch."

Quinn watched as the other man disappeared. He stretched tiredly and looked around the room. Everyone had gone, including Percy. It was time to get home to Cade. The last few days had been euphoric, catching up together, and he'd had more sex than he knew what to do with. Cade was certainly making up for the weeks of abstinence. Quinn was aware he'd changed subtly, become more empowered and certainly more in touch with his Fey side, and despite the misgivings he still had about that, he certainly wasn't complaining.

Cade had also taken great pleasure in being able to drench Quinn with large waves from the pond just by focusing on the water, and was intent on creating water whirlpools, although that was taking some practice. He hadn't yet had the opportunity to try out his own healing power despite Quinn offering himself up as subject, exhorting Cade to cut him so he could try fixing him. Cade had scowled and told him in no uncertain terms that wasn't happening.

Quinn grinned. "I imagine you've been having a whale of a time too, Taliesin." he murmured. "It's been pretty intense, hasn't it?"

His Withinner's voice sounded slightly aggrieved when he replied.

I have not been present at all your lovemaking sessions. I have attempted to withdraw myself from the proceedings to give you and Cade privacy. After what you both went through, it was only fair.

"Thank you, old friend, I appreciate the sentiment." He frowned. "But now begins the difficult part. He needs to know about the dangers he faces now that he's more in tune with his powers. That's not going to go down well with him. I may need your help."

He is indeed going to attract many unsavoury characters who wish to use his healing powers for themselves. Cade will need to be very careful. If I can help in any way, you have only to ask.

"Thanks." Quinn picked up his scarf and wound it around his neck.

"Best get on home and have that conversation, then," he said gloomily. "He'll freak out and say he can look after himself and I'm going to have the devil of a job convincing him he can't."

It never fails to astound me how you can face down a whole Council of Warlocks and various nefarious characters who mean you harm but still quiver in your boots when you have to tell your man something he does not want to hear. It amuses me greatly.

Quinn scowled. "This isn't just a man, Withinner. This is bloody Cade. It's not the same thing."

Chapter 27

Cade sat in the back garden, his latest thesis and research papers spread before him in an untidy sprawl. The mid-afternoon July sun warmed his body as he wrote copious notes and reminders in the margins of the document he was working on.

Ambrose Tickler Brown had been very grateful seeing him back after Quinn's very inventive story about his lengthy disappearance. His fiancé's original cover tale had been that they'd both needed a break from one another after an altercation and one of the other major French universities had requested Cade's presence on a dig in the South of France. Quinn had said that they were willing to pay a lot of money to the Institute for his time and the two of them thought it would be a good idea to be apart for a while. Of course, QuinnCo (ergo Quinn) had put up the funds, but Ambrose had been only too happy to accept the very generous donation in return for Cade's absence once Quinn had sweet talked him into it. Ambrose had also expressed his fervent wish that he hoped they worked things out. Cade had actually been a little aggrieved at the fact that the professor had been happy to pimp him out and rearrange his classes with such alacrity in return for the huge donation. Quinn had shaken his head in amusement at Cade's reaction.

Cade had been researching the history of the Picts and the life of Kenneth MacAlpin as a favour to Cooper. The planned research trip to Crieff in Scotland with Cooper and the rest of the team from the Institute had been planned for late August, only a few weeks away. As keen as he'd been to go before getting almost fatally stabbed, Cade wasn't all that sure now that he wanted to leave Quinn for such an amount of time. Sitting there sucking his pen, he realised that his priorities had changed.

"I suppose that's what a near-death experience does to you, Marco," he murmured to the cat lying curled up on the tabletop in the sun, his paws spread over one of the research documents. Marco was used to their one-sided conversations and Cade loved the fact he never disagreed with anything he said.

"I missed him when he wasn't there with me. It was like a whole part of me was gone. I knew he'd be blaming himself for what happened to me, although I never thought he'd grow a beard like Sir Walter Raleigh and stop eating."

His voice quietened as the thought of Quinn's torment. "But I suppose if that hadn't happened he'd never have got in a temper in his study and he'd never have found those letters from Edward Mistral."

Cade sighed as he scratched Marco Polo behind the ears and the cat purred and stretched his legs. He heard a loud rustling noise at the bottom of the garden in front and he peered at the area curiously. It sounded like a fairly large animal. The cat had heard something too. He sat up, his ears flattened against his head and a slight hiss emanating from his dainty mouth. His blue eyes regarded the bushes with suspicion.

"There's nothing there. It was probably just a squirrel or another cat." Cade stood up and stretched. "I'm just going inside to get a glass of wine. If I'm going to carry on with this studying, I need a boost."

He disappeared into the house. When Cade came out a few minutes later, Marco Polo had gone. He looked around the garden, and not seeing him, shrugged and sat down to finish his research.

Quinn arrived back at home later that afternoon, looking tired but fairly elated that his position as Grand Master was still supported by the majority of his Council. He helped himself to a beer and sat with Cade outside in the garden.

"Justin was a real trooper. I didn't know he was so articulate." Quinn grinned as he remembered his friend's words to James Barton Sinclair. "But he warned me that James was plotting something. I'll need to be careful around him." He drank his beer in appreciation as he looked over at Cade. "How's the research going? Will you be ready for your trip to Scotland then?"

Cade knew from previous conversations that Quinn wasn't altogether convinced he was happy about him going but he was supporting it anyway. He nodded.

"I'll be ready in time. But I was telling Marco earlier, I wasn't sure I wanted to go anymore."

Quinn's face brightened at the admission. "Oh? Why not? I thought you were looking forward to it." He smiled. "What did Marco have to say about it anyway? Did he offer any words of advice?"

Cade chuckled. "No, he was very happy to let me have my say without interrupting. It's what I love about him." He frowned as he looked around the garden. "I wonder, where is he anyway? He's been gone ages. He's not normally this long when he disappears."

"Perhaps he's found a lady friend." Quinn leaned back in his chair and closed his eyes as he enjoyed the sun on his face.

Cade didn't look convinced. "Hmm. He'd better be back soon. I don't fancy looking for him when it gets dark." He stood up and walked over to Quinn, leaning down behind him and kissing his warm forehead softly as he draped his arms over his shoulders. "I was re-thinking going to Scotland because I didn't think I wanted to leave you again for a long time. I've only just come back and I don't really want to leave you alone again. You might stop eating and grow more facial hair."

Quinn chuckled. "I appreciate that, but I think I'd be okay." He sighed. "I don't want to be without you either for such a long time, especially seeing as how you'd be with dear old Coop, but I don't want to be selfish. If you need to do this, you should. I'll leave it to you to decide."

Cade ruffled the top of his warm head. "I'll see how it goes. It's still a way away so I have time to make a decision." He moved away. "I'm going to see if I can track down Marco. He heard something in the bushes over there earlier so he may be stuck there or something. Be back in a mo."

He crossed the garden toward the dense shrubbery that surrounded the back of the yard. The garden itself was generous by London standards, a large lawn leading down to a border of thick, overgrown bushes and overhanging trees.

The area Cade was heading for had a short path leading into shaded darkness. He'd often wondered whether in the past Quinn had ever ventured much out in the garden at all, as it all seemed very unloved and unkempt. Cade enjoyed gardening and vowed to get out and do a little as soon as he could. He stepped into the still, cool air of the shaded place and walked carefully across the uneven ground.

"Marco? Here, kitty. Are you in here?" He tripped over a root growing out from a huge oak tree and muttered a loud expletive as his ankle turned. "Shit! That's bloody sore. Marco, you stupid cat, I'm not coming in any further. If you're in here, you can bloody well stay here."

Cade turned to leave and as he did so, there was a faint "meow" from a bush to the side of him. Exasperated, he strode over to where he'd heard the sound. "Cat, you'd better have a good explanation for why I'm crawling around in these bloody bushes looking for you."

His voice tailed off when he saw that Marco had indeed got a very good explanation for why he hadn't been seen. The Persian lay on the earth, blood pooling around his legs. Cade gave a horrified exclamation at seeing the large gashes in his side that were still seeping red.

"What the hell happened to you?" He knelt down frantically beside the animal, which looked up at him pitifully, blue eyes shadowed in pain. The gashes looked as if they had been done with a small garden trowel, so deep and multiple were the wounds. As Cade touched Marco, his little body flinched with pain.

"Hold on, kitty, I'll take you to Quinn. He'll help you."

He reached for Marco and as he touched the blood-soaked fur, there was a strange tingling in his hands. He drew his fingers away sharply. Again he reached toward Marco to pick him up and again there was that strange prickling sensation in his finger tips. Cade heard a soft sigh in his head. It sounded like Nydra.

You can heal him too, Cade. Use your powers.

In his panic over finding his injured pet, he'd forgotten about his own power to heal.

Time to try out what Nydra taught me. Cade uncertainly held his hands over the cat's side, hovering just above his fur. The tingle increased. Cade took a deep breath, closing his eyes, visualising the skin closing up, the flesh that was currently torn and oozing becoming whole again. His hands warmed, the prickling sensation growing more intense.

Marco meowed feebly, but louder than before, then opened his eyes and struggled to his feet.

The deep gashes in his skin were gone and although his fur was matted with blood, Cade thought he looked a damned sight better than when he'd found him. Marco was standing now, regarding him with a basilisk stare that only a cat can give. Cade gazed at his hands in wonder then reached down to pick up the animal, who curled into his arms with little resistance. Cade walked quickly out of the garden, over the grass up to where Quinn still sat basking in the sun. Cade shouted, startling him, seeing him sit up sharply.

"Quinn! God, you should see what I just did! It was incredible."

Quinn strode toward him with urgency and as he reached him, Cade looked up at him. "I found him in the bushes. He'd been injured. He had these great bloody cuts in his side. I held my hands over him, Quinn and he healed up. It was the most incredible feeling—"

"Cade, I know you're excited but slow down."

Quinn's quiet voice made Cade stop suddenly and stare at him. His lover's face was set and he looked as if he smelled something extremely offensive. His nostrils flared and his eyes narrowed dangerously. "You say you healed Marco? What exactly was wrong with him?"

Cade looked at him in consternation. "He had these large gashes in his side, as if something had torn at him. He was just lying there—"

"Give him to me." Quinn's voice was quiet and he reached out and took the cat from him. The cat lay still, watching him with trusting eyes. Quinn bent down and sniffed him, his nose wrinkling in disgust. His eyes darted around the garden and he looked apprehensive.

"He was attacked by a Chaser. I can smell it, even now. The poison is still in Marco, but it's very faint. When you healed him, you also diluted the poison. Lucky you found him in time. It's pretty virulent and can be fatal."

"What in hell's name is a Chaser?" Cade looked at him in confusion.

Quinn regarded him carefully. "It's a pretty nasty little creature, the size of a—" he struggled to find a comparison—"the size of a large chimpanzee, for want of a better word. They look like goblins, if you're familiar with them."

Cade stared at him.

Quinn sighed. "Obviously you've never seen one, but they have very wide hands with large curved nails they use to transfer poison into whatever they claw. I think that's what happened to Marco based on the stench."

He set the cat down on the ground and it wound itself around his legs.

Cade was gobsmacked. "We have goblin-like creatures in the back garden? Really?"

Despite the situation, Quinn chuckled at his obvious disbelief. "There are far worse things you'll get to see if you stick with me. Now that you've had your Fey side enhanced, believe me, you'll start to recognise them too." He looked around at the dimming light in the garden. "Let's go inside. Bring Marco as well. I can't smell anything now but where there's one Chaser, there's normally another."

He turned and disappeared inside, leaving Cade feeling stunned by the sudden events. He followed Quinn into the dining room. Quinn waited for him and Marco to come in then closed the patio doors and locked them. He flicked a switch on the wall and the darkening room was suddenly flooded with soft light. Quinn walked into the lounge, sitting down on the couch and patting the seat next to him for Cade to sit down too. He did so, curling his legs beneath him as he looked at Quinn anxiously.

"What the hell's all the cloak-and-dagger stuff about?"

Quinn reached out and took his hand, covering it with his warm one.

"Right. Tell me exactly what happened, how you managed to heal Marco and anything else you remember."

Cade told him the story from start to finish and Quinn listened intently. When he'd finished he smiled despite the shadow in his eyes. "I'm glad those healing powers are working; that's incredible news. Maybe next time you can be the one healing me." He grinned. "I'm not sure how strong they are, though. I guess we'll have to find out."

"I doubt I'd have enough power to do anything with you," Cade muttered. "Not the state you get into."

Quinn laughed. "I don't intend getting into any more 'states' but I have been feeling a little out of sorts lately. I think something is going on with Taliesin." His voice grew serious. "I've been meaning to have this conversation with you, so this is the perfect time to do it."

Quinn reached over, taking both of Cade's hands in his as he regarded him seriously.

"With you having your new powers, there are a lot of people out there who'll want to use them for their own ends. Sprite healers are fairly sought after by Collectors for their ability and if they get wind of you, which they seem to have done, we'll need to be very careful."

"What do you mean, Collectors?"

"Just what it means." Quinn said grimly. He'd seen firsthand how destructive they could be. "They can be any variant of Fey but they have one thing in common. They hunt down other Fey and try to take their powers for their own. Most of them we know, and we keep tabs on them, but every now and then a new one comes along. They tend to use Chasers to scout out areas and clear the way for them to surprise a Fey and strip them of their powers."

"How do they do that?" Cade asked quietly.

"Some of them don't generally intend to harm the Fey they're tracking, and they're able to take the powers by only magyck spells and chants. Collectors tend to have no qualms about using anything they can to enhance their abilities to do that and of course, the more powers they steal, the stronger their own magyck. But they have to get very close to do that. There has to be physical contact. It's not something that be done remotely."

He was quiet. Cade reached over and touched his cheek softly. "And the others?"

Quinn looked at him with a flinty stare. "Others don't give a damn about the other Fey and in reality, the easiest way to gain their power is simply to kill them and then reach in and take it. I mean literally. I've seen many a Fey body that's been ripped to pieces by an unscrupulous Collector using a certain magyck spell that makes it much quicker. It takes less time than the other way and also gives them more satisfaction. There were a few of those about."

"God, do you think this is what happened today? Was there a Collector in the garden?"

Quinn shook his head. "No, I would have known. There's no Collector nearby at present. But a Chaser—that could be a sign that there's one coming."

"You said there *were* a few of those Collectors about—the ones who rip you open. Past tense. What happened to them? Does that mean there aren't any more?" Cade's voice was hopeful.

Quinn shifted in his seat, sitting back as he released his hands, regarding him broodingly.

"What did you do to them?" Cade asked softly.

Quinn scowled fiercely. "What needed to be done. We hunted them down and destroyed them. As another one rises, we do the same thing. I haven't heard of one for a while now. I made a few examples of the ones I killed. I'd hoped we'd put anyone else off."

Cade swallowed.

Quinn's face darkened. "And once again I scare you." He stood up, pacing around the room like a caged tiger. "I hate doing that. I see that expression on your face and it makes sick to my core that I can do that to you."

His hands clenched and unclenched at his side as he stood before the picture window looking out. Cade sighed and stood up, moving over to his lover's rigid body and wrapping his arms around his middle, laying his head on his shoulder. Quinn's body tensed as Cade spoke softly.

"Yes, I sometimes get a little afraid of you. Not because I think you'll do me harm or anything but because sometimes I remember just who you are and what you have to protect. I'm scared *for* you. You have this responsibility and you can be so bloody ruthless about it and I confess, sometimes it shocks me. But I know you do it because you have to, not because you want to."

Quinn stayed quiet, his body gradually relaxing as Cade's arms held him tight. "I know you, and you're not cruel or vindictive." Cade hesitated. "Well, maybe sometimes. Percy told me what you did to Rowan Kirkpatrick. But I understand that. I have no idea what I'd have done if that had been you that had been stabbed and put in the water. That man deserved to die."

Cade moved around in front of him, standing gazing into his eyes, cupping his face in his hands. "I love you, Quinn. Just as you are, every single last little bit of you, inside and out. And the not-so-little bits too." He grinned at him.

Quinn shook his head in amusement. "How the hell do you do that? I was being all tormented and angsty and you just say a few words and I'm putty in your hands."

Quinn pulled Cade to him, covering his mouth with his. Cade sank into him with a sigh, revelling in the feel of his man and feeling the heat in his body at his touch. When Quinn finally let his mouth go so he could breathe, he held him close.

"You mustn't underestimate the danger you might be in," Quinn said quietly. "If there's a new Collector in town, it could be a while before we find him. The Chaser leads me to believe there is. You have to be careful. I want Magnus to keep an eye on you until I find out what's going on and which kind of Collector might be coming after you."

Cade stepped away, his face set. "I appreciate the offer, but if I have these powers, I'm going to have to start looking after myself. You can't protect me all the time and neither can Magnus. You need to show me what I need to do to do that. You said these people had to get close to do what they do. Well, I'll just have to be careful about whom I let get close to me."

Quinn shook his head. "You're right and I know I have to let go at some time. But I can't lose you again. I—"

Cade held up a hand and placed it gently against Quinn's mouth as he spoke firmly. "This time there won't be any negotiation. You can teach me what to look for, how to feel them coming, even teach me a little more kung fu in case I need it. But I am not running scared from these bastards."

Quinn sighed loudly. "Fine, you win. I'll tell you what I can and perhaps help you develop some of the power you have inside you to make you more aware of other Feys." He smiled, a little tiredly. "I draw the line at teaching you kung fu, though, for the very good reason that I haven't got a clue. I'm no martial arts expert. I can get someone to do that for me though."

Cade touched his cheek gently. "And if I just happen to see a seven-foot Warlock lurking about because you've asked him to follow me anyway, I shall be very upset." The guilty expression on Quinn's face made Cade chuckle loudly.

"You bastard, you actually were going to have him watch me anyway, weren't you? You're so bloody sneaky. No wonder you're Grand Master. You just can't lose, can you? What the hell am I going to do with you and that arrogance?"

Quinn ignored his words completely, his eyes narrowing and his nostrils flaring, and he reached out, pulling his face toward his as he kissed Cade. Quinn's lips were greedy and demanding, his tongue sliding into his mouth. Cade tasted the faint flavour of the beer he'd drunk earlier. Quinn's hands moved down slowly to cup his arse and press him closer. Cade gasped as his lover's hardness pushed through the cotton shorts he wore, pressing into the hard swell of his own groin. Quinn was voracious, his hands sliding under Cade's tee shirt, stroking the soft, warm skin beneath. Cade groaned as Quinn's hands kneaded his backside and the kisses grew more urgent, his teeth biting Cade's bottom lip and making him hiss in both pain and pleasure.

"You taste so good," Quinn whispered as his mouth found Cade's ear and he darted his tongue inside. "I am so bloody horny suddenly I can hardly stand it. I think your increased Fey abilities from using your power have heightened my senses too. But we both have far too many clothes on. Undress me. Right here. Then you can undress for me."

Cade swallowed, his groin flooding with heat even as he reached out and stripped off Quinn's polo shirt, dropping it to the floor. Quinn watched, his breath uneven and deep, his eyes black.

"Quinn, you've gone all antichrist again." Cade's stomach fluttered madly and the ache between his legs intensified. He was so damned hard it hurt. "God, you look so fucking sexy."

He ran his hands over Quinn's chest, as he gasped in pleasure at the touch. Cade leaned in, trailing his tongue around his nipple as he unzipped him and then slowly pulled Quinn's trousers and boxers down his legs to land in a pile on the floor. Quinn stepped out of them, his cock flushed and ready. Cade's hands trailed up Quinn's bare arms, goose bumps forming on that skin.

"You are so bloody beautiful," Cade murmured as he touched Quinn's cock lightly, hearing his groan, loving the sense of power he had over him. "Like a proud lion."

Quinn reached over and stilled Cade's hands, his face watching his intently. "Your turn to undress. I want you naked. I really need to be inside you before I explode."

Those growled words made Cade's own cock jerk against inside his trousers, desperate to be free and feel Quinn on it. Cade reached down and teasingly lifted the tee shirt he wore over his head, making sure his arms flexed and his stomach contracted as he did so. Quinn watched his movements with avarice, drinking in every move he made. His hands moved toward him as if to touch him, then he stopped.

"Keep going," he murmured hoarsely. "Get those damn jeans off."

"God, you can be a real bossy bastard." Cade's own desire swelled, seeing Quinn's obvious arousal at his slow but inexpert striptease. Slowly, deliberately, he unzipped his jeans, taking his time. As the zip parted, Cade reached down and palmed his cock against the silk of his boxers. His own touch made him gasp, he was so turned on, and Quinn's black eyes narrowed in lust. He reached over and slapped Cade's hands away.

"You leave that be," he growled huskily. "That's mine to play with. You'll have your work cut out for you with mine."

Cade laughed. "Hell, there's that true alpha male making its appearance." But he moved his hands away from his eager cock and finished sliding the jeans and boxers down his legs. He stepped out of them, completely naked, and then slid his hand up and down his slick cock, with a sultry look at Quinn. "Is this what you want?"

Cade was unprepared for Quinn's reaction. He made a sound halfway between a loud growl and a roar and moved forward swiftly, propelling Cade back toward the couch. He pushed him onto the sofa roughly, his knee between his legs, pulling Cade's hands up behind him and then slowly sliding his hands down the inside of Cade's arms, causing shivers of expectation and body-prickling heat to course through his being. Quinn's black eyes bore into Cade's and he felt faint at the look of extreme lust on his lover's face. Cade himself wanted nothing more than to feel Quinn inside him, and bugger any preparations. He knew he was more than ready for whatever Quinn had to give. Cade gasped as Quinn moved between his legs, pulling his hips towards him, spreading him and drawing his legs almost to his chest. Quinn reached down and slicked his fingers with his own glistening fluids, sliding one finger inside Cade and scissoring his fingers roughly. Cade groaned loudly, his head arching back against the couch, eyes closing in bliss at feeling Quinn's desperate finger inside him.

"Oh God," he moaned. "Quinn, honest, I don't think you need to do that, amazing as it is. I need to feel you inside me. Please, Quinn. Now."

Quinn's black eyes bore into his, fathomless and obsidian, and Cade thought he had never seen anything sexier than this man at the peak of his desire with pupils resembling a vampire's. Quinn grinned wolfishly and nodded, his hot mouth finding Cade's eager lips as he pushed himself inside. Quinn filled Cade so completely and with such force that he cried out against his mouth. It seemed to incense Quinn further as he moved on top, snapping his hips against him and they moved together as only two people who knew each other's bodies intimately could do.

"God, you feel incredible," Cade whispered. "I shall have to get slutty more often."

Quinn's teeth gleamed whitely in the dimming light as he smiled then buried his face in Cade's neck. He moaned in his ear and Cade felt he was close to climaxing. In truth, he'd been ready to blow a while ago, but had been trying to make the incredible sensation in his cock and balls last longer. Heat rose in his lower body, the heavy sensation in his groin throbbing and pulsing with a life of its own. Cade finally came with a loud cry, his fingers digging into Quinn's broad shoulders. Quinn drew a deep breath in both pain and ecstasy as his body shuddered with the force of his orgasm.

There was a sticky heat between his arse cheeks and Quinn's post-climax spasms took hold as he collapsed on top of Cade, his hands entwined in his hair and his breath coming in loud, panting gasps of satisfaction.

"Hell, I think you scratched me to bits," Quinn panted, as he rolled off to lie beside Cade. "I'm pretty sure you drew blood. You must have half my skin under your fingernails. Cut your damn nails."

Cade chuckled. "You were such a bloody animal I got caught up in the moment. You were really horny, weren't you? I think this time might even have surpassed the very first time we made love when we first met."

Quinn snorted. "I was feeling fairly amorous, I have to say. Maybe it was the fact you used your healing powers for the first time, but I just wanted you so badly all of a sudden I could hardly wait."

"I'll have to use them more often then," Cade snuggled into his side as Quinn put his arm around him. "I like making you crazy. I get a lot out of it as well." They lay together in the darkening lounge as the sun dropped over the horizon.

"Perhaps we should go to bed," Cade said softly. "I know it's a little early, but it's been a rough day and we can always have another session later if you want."

Quinn chuckled in the darkness. "That sounds like a good idea. I need a shower first, though."

He swung his legs off the couch and stood up, padding through naked to the bedroom. Cade shook his head and sighed as he regarded the clothing left on the floor. He leaned down and picked it up.

"Honestly, I'm not your bloody housekeeper," he muttered under his breath. But he smiled as he wandered through to the bedroom. Quinn was already in the shower and Cade waited for his turn. Half an hour later they were wrapped up under the duvet together. Cade intended reading for a while but he could see Quinn was already half asleep.

"Sleep tight, Quinn. Try not to have any nightmares," he murmured. In truth, since his return, Quinn had had few nightmares and was definitely sleeping better.

"I'll try," came back the already sleepy voice.

Cade shook his head at the fact that sex seemed to send Quinn to sleep better than anything else. It tended to make Cade's need for post-coital conversation a little frustrating for him. He tried to concentrate on reading his book, but he kept seeing poor Marco lying torn and bloody on the ground. Cade *was* worried about the Collector and the Chasers. He knew he'd be stupid not to be. He'd even thought guiltily that perhaps he'd been a bit hasty in telling Quinn to let him look after himself without the comforting form of Magnus watching over him.

Oh well, I've made my bed now. Hopefully Quinn can teach me what to expect and I'll manage. I have to; the alternative is too terrible to contemplate.

Chapter 28

Quinn sat back with a sigh in his upstairs office and regarded his computer screen with sheer frustration.

"Thousands of people out looking for this bastard Collector and nothing," he muttered to himself. "Not a scent of anyone in over a week. Maybe I'm wrong. Maybe there is no bloody Collector." His voice was hopeful but his Withinner's words took away that hope.

He is out there; make no mistake about it. That Chaser was here for a reason.

Quinn took off his glasses and passed a hand over his tired eyes. "I suppose you're right, but if there is someone out there, why the hell haven't we found them yet? Something should have come to light by now."

He is hiding his tracks well. You will find him. You have to.

Quinn stood up and paced around the room as he thought. Percy had said he'd heard a rumour about a strange Fey woman asking questions about Cade and Quinn. Perhaps that might bring in some news. At least there had been no other incidents with Chasers or anything else strange which was a blessing. Quinn had managed to teach Cade to further develop his own Fey senses into a place where he could comfortably recognise others. In Quinn's opinion this was the most useful skill. It would stand his fiancé in good stead should a Fey come calling unexpectedly. It might not be the best defence mechanism but it was certainly a start to making him feel better about Cade's safety.

There was a click as the front door opened and he heard a faint murmuring as someone came into the house. Quinn sensed Cade and walked out of his office to stand on the upstairs landing. His fiancé looked up at him and smiled as the cat wound itself around his feet.

Quinn thought Cade looked a little tired. Quinn knew he hadn't been sleeping well since the incident with Marco. "You're back from the Institute a little earlier than usual. Is everything all right?"

Cade nodded as he set his briefcase down on the loveseat in the entrance and toed off his shoes. "Everything's fine. I finished all the research papers I was busy with for the trip, took my last class and decided to call it a day. I thought perhaps we might go out and get something to eat instead of cooking."

Quinn came down the staircase to give him a hug.

Cade kissed him hello. "What about you—how was your day? Did you manage to find this rogue Fey who you think is coming after me?"

Quinn shook his head as he released him and wandered into the lounge. "No. Nothing yet. Percy's on it and I'll know the minute he does if there's anything new. Do you want a glass of wine?"

Cade nodded and Quinn poured a cold glass of white wine from the bar fridge and handed him the glass. Cade took it gratefully and sat down on the couch with a contented sigh.

"God, I'm glad to be home. Today was absolutely bloody hectic and this trip in August is causing a lot of work for everyone." He grimaced. "There's just so much planning to do."

"You'll get there, I'm sure." Quinn watched Cade carefully as he sat down next to him. "You still intend going to Scotland then?"

He wasn't keen on him going away for a month to Scotland with Cooper for two reasons: one was Cooper, the other was the threat of the Collector hanging like a sword of Damocles over their heads.

Cade sighed in exasperation. "Yes, I'm still going. I told you I wasn't running scared from anyone and I really need to get this done despite my earlier reservations. Besides, if I get into trouble, you'll know anyway and you and your Withinner will be up there before the haggis has even run around the hill a second time."

One of the side effects of Cade's newly enhanced status as a Sprite was that Quinn had intensified feelings as to where Cade was and how he was feeling more than ever before. Quinn's senses were on full alert and he welcomed the change. Cade, however, saw it as an invasion of privacy and thought it was the magyck version of Big Brother watching him. Quinn personally thought it worked just fine this new way.

"Talking of Taliesin, he's been a little quiet lately," Quinn said, frowning. "You know we can feel each other's emotions and usually I tend to switch his off mentally or they'd drive me crazy because he's such a moody bastard, but I get the feeling lately something's different with him. His happy times are certainly no fewer—in fact they've been getting stronger—but he's been less vocal than usual. I've been feeling a little unsettled, as if something's not quite right."

"Maybe he has a girlfriend in his own time?" suggested Cade. "Maybe you're not the only one in his life any more. The bromance might be dying."

He grinned mischievously and Quinn chuckled. "That might be it. Although who'd be stupid enough to take on his moods and bad temper?"

His Withinner was silent where once Quinn would have expected some smart rejoinder. Quinn was definitely curious about his silence.

"So…you're going up to Scotland when?" He looked at Cade questioningly.

"The idea is to leave on the twentieth of August in a couple of weeks and the latest we'll be back is the nineteenth of September. That should give us time to do all the interviews, look at all the material the chaps up there have and compare some notes so we can finish this dissertation."

Quinn nodded but wasn't particularly thrilled with the news. Having Cade out of his life for a month wasn't a great prospect.

His fiancé saw his face and chuckled. "I've got one of the cottages on the Loch up there in Crieff all to myself. That's our base of operations to do the research. My idea was that you invoke that Withinner of yours and come and visit me *very* often for a booty call." He grinned. "I insisted on having my own place before I even agreed I'd go. It was one of the conditions."

Quinn's spirits lifted at Cade's words. "Really? You're sure you don't want to be left alone to do your thing without me interfering?"

Cade reached over and caressed his cheek gently. "Don't be daft. You being there isn't interfering. I'm going to miss you, make no mistake. I'm also going to get just as horny as you. We just have to make sure no one sees you, of course. That would take a bit of explaining." He scowled. "And as long as you can tell Taliesin to let you revoke him when you want to. If I thought he'd behave I'd love to pick his brains about what he knows about the Picts. I'm sure he could tell me a lot about them."

Cade looked at Quinn hopefully and he shook his head vehemently.

"I'm not sure there's any chance of that, Cade. I don't want another episode like the last one. And with your increased Fey attraction I'm not even willing to chance it." Quinn said grimly, hoping his Withinner was listening. Taliesin remained silent.

Cade shrugged. "Well, what with you being able to sense me all the time and the ability to appear in my bedroom basically whenever you fancy, I don't think I'll be giving Cooper a good time so you needn't worry about that."

He chuckled loudly at Quinn's black expression.

"Don't even joke about that," Quinn said silkily, pulling Cade to him possessively and holding him tightly in his arms. "I'm not likely to appreciate it and Cooper could find himself joining Nessie in the Loch."

"Nessie doesn't live in this particular loch. But I get your point."

Cade snuggled into Quinn's open arms and Quinn kissed him softly on his almond-scented hair.

"Do you feel better now?" Cade murmured as he nibbled his ear. "The fact you can visit me whenever you want to, within reason of course."

"Define 'within reason.'" Quinn closed his eyes, enjoying the feel of Cade's teeth slowly teasing his ear. He heard Cade's soft chuckle as his warm breath caressed his cheek.

"Oh, I don't know. Perhaps we should agree on Mondays, Wednesdays, Fridays and Sundays. Four nights a week should keep us going."

Quinn laughed. "I'll take that under advisement with the man downstairs. If he feels that's enough, well, we can do that. But if he gets a little tetchy I reserve the right to call ahead before I appear in your bedroom. Deal?"

"God, you are such a needy sod. Okay, it's a deal. Ditto my side if I feel I need a sudden shagging."

Quinn chuckled at Cade's words as he reached over and kissed him, feeling his warm lips against his, revelling in the fact that this man was all his. Cade tasted of wine and cherries for some reason, and as his tongue slid softly into his mouth, Quinn wanted for nothing more.

*****

A few days later Quinn got the break he was waiting for. His mobile rang in the early hours of Tuesday afternoon.

It was Percy. "I've got some news for you on that Collector."

Quinn was immediately alert. "Tell me. Have you found him?"

Percy's voice was grim. "Her. It's a woman. She's a witch, believe it or not. We managed to track her down a few days ago but I wanted to make sure she was the one we were looking for before I told you. She's been watching Cade for about two weeks now. There's photos of Cade all over her house in Richmond, along with other various magyck paraphernalia which doesn't look as it's meant to do good. What do you want me to do?"

Quinn wanted nothing better than to get down to wherever this Collector was and sort the problem out personally. But he had a partner now for this sort of thing. He sighed heavily.

"It's a witch. If I do anything, Valensia will kill me." He looked up as Cade walked into the room, raising his eyebrows at his last comment. "Send me what you've got and I'll ask her to sort it out. This is her bailiwick. She'll want to handle it herself."

"I'll get it all emailed over to you. Tell Valensia this is one of the nasty little buggers, the ones who don't give a damn about the Fey they take the powers from. It's been a long while since we saw one of these, so I imagine she'll want to make an example of this one." Percy's voice was grim.

Quinn nodded. "I'll let her know. She can be pretty...inventive...when she wants to be."

Quinn. I am glad you found the person who wished to hurt Cade.

Quinn thought his Withinner sounded tired.

"Where've you been, Taliesin?" he murmured as Cade watched him talk to himself. "You've been very quiet. I was actually worried about you."

I had a few things to resolve of my own. There has been some trouble this side. But I am unharmed and managed to keep you away from it all. You did not need the distraction.

Quinn frowned. "Withinner, that sounds a bit ominous. Is everything taken care of now?"

Everything is fine. Do not worry.

"Good, I'm glad you're all right. But you really need to talk to me if you need anything. Think about it." He put down his mobile and looked across at Cade. "We found that Collector we think was stalking you. I'm going to ask Valensia to deal with it as it's a witch involved and it's more than my life's worth to rain on Valensia's parade."

Cade looked at him with narrowed eyes. "Will it be over then? Once Valensia's 'handled' the situation?"

Quinn sighed. "For now, at least until another one rears its head. But to be honest, they aren't very prolific; it takes a lot of time to become a collector and we know about most of them anyway and watch them, the ones who don't maim their victims. So we'll just have to keep an eye on things."

He sat down at his computer and checked his email. Percy's message had come through so he forwarded it to Valensia's email address. He picked up his phone and dialled Valensia's number. It rang a few times then he heard her curt voice answer.

"Valensia? It's Quinn."

"Darling, to what do I owe the pleasure of you calling me for a change?"

Quinn rolled his eyes at Cade. "I have some information to share with you. I thought you'd rather manage it instead of me doing something about it. We've found the Collector—but she's a witch."

Valensia was silent on the other end of the phone. Quinn waited for her to respond. When she did he could hear the fierce determination in her voice. Knowing Valensia, he pitied the Collector.

"Have you got the evidence? Knowing you, I imagine you have empirical proof that this person is who you think she is. Can you send it to me and I'll take care of it?"

"I emailed it before I called. It should be in your inbox as we speak. Can you let me know when you've dealt with the situation so I can tell Cade for sure that there's no more danger?"

"I'll be in touch." The witch rang off.

Quinn looked at his fiancé. "Well, I think I can safely say that little problem will be resolved. You should feel a little safer now."

Cade nodded but Quinn saw the slight trepidation in his eyes. He reached over and took Cade's hands in his. "Relax. I won't let anything happen to you. Never again, I promise."

Cade nodded. "I trust you. It's just it seems to be one thing after another with us, doesn't it?"

Quinn grinned. "Life has certainly become more interesting for you since you met me."

Cade smiled. "I wouldn't have it any other way, but sometimes the nice quiet life seems very attractive." He turned and walked out of the study. "I have some swimming to do. I'm off to the pond."

"Be careful, please." Quinn still had hidden fears about Cade at the pond, that one day he might not come back after swimming if the Sprites decided they needed him more than he did, which to him was inconceivable.

"I will make sure my spidery senses are on full alert. I'll see you later."

Cade disappeared down the staircase. Quinn turned his attention to his computer. He had a catch-up with Jomo later by video conference and still had a lot to prepare.

Quinn. I have thought about it. May I speak with you?

Quinn frowned. Taliesin asking permission to speak was a new one.

"Of course." He leaned back in his chair and closed his eyes. "Is anything wrong? It's very unlike you to ask permission to talk rather than just putting your piece in."

There have been some happenings this side which have taken up a lot of my time lately. There was an uprising here in the villa— just a small, insignificant battle—and I needed to protect the community. You may have felt some strange feelings as I have been doing much magyck.

"I thought something was afoot. I've been feeling pretty strange this side. Is everything back to normal now? You weren't injured? I still seem to be in one piece." He grinned.

I am uninjured. Others were not. I had a lot of work to heal the wounded and we had many dead. Some good friends. I needed some solace time. I am sorry if I neglected you and Cade.

"Hell, you deserve any time you need. I'm sorry to hear about the troubles. Do you need anything from me in this time? Do you need medicines, herbs or anything from here? If you do, tell me and I'll invoke you."

Thank you. But I have no need of anything at the moment. Perhaps in a little time I will take you up on your offer.

"Anything you need, old friend. Just let me know." He frowned. "You heard we found the Collector?"

I heard. I believe Valensia will do justice to her promise to deal with the situation. But you know that when one is destroyed, another one takes it place. It may take time but it will happen.

"I know, Withinner. It's the story of our lives." Quinn sighed. "But we can only deal with them one at a time."

Cade is much stronger than you think. He is formidable. You are a very lucky man.

"Talking of getting lucky, you seem to have had your fair share." Quinn chuckled. "I try and blot it out but with the regularity you seem to be getting some, it's getting a little difficult. I woke up the other night feeling extremely horny and had to stop myself ravishing Cade whilst he slept. He wouldn't have appreciated that."

He frowned slightly. "At least I don't think he would." He thought he might pursue that avenue at a later stage. He quite liked the idea of starting something whilst Cade was asleep with a view to waking him up and carrying on with his warm and willing body.

I do seem to have found myself a lady friend. She is most...accommodating. And buxom. With long dark hair and legs that are more than willing to wrap themselves around me.

Taliesin's voice was satisfied and smug. Quinn laughed loudly.

"I am glad to hear you're getting your itch scratched often. I can see I'm going to have to concentrate a little harder keeping your urges at bay."

You are getting more than enough of your own that I can feel, came his Withinner's dry response.

I have been looking at the oddity of your eyes changing. I know it has happened since you were a boy but it is happening more often, especially when your emotions run deep. I believe it is simply something that has manifested itself more since the Unity we shared. It is a slight change in your body chemistry and will not harm you.

Quinn sighed. "Rowan Kirkpatrick's eyes changed in a similar fashion and Percy said it was because of some herbs he was taking." He smiled softly. "Cade likes it, anyway; it turns him on and that's good enough for me. I'm not really fussed about the why. It just makes things look different, that's all, like auras around everything, in different colours."

Then it is of no consequence.

Taliesin was quiet for a while then spoke suddenly.

I am being summoned by the lady. I shall no doubt be "getting lucky" again. You may want to block it out.

Quinn chuckled loudly at his Withinner's words. He was relieved that everything was all right. He had been a little worried.

And have no fear that, if you need to invoke me to see Cade when he is away, that I will do anything untoward. I give you my word that I will not do anything to disappoint you again.

"I appreciate that, old friend. Now go and get your leg over. It's rude to keep a lady waiting."

Quinn grinned to himself at the conversation with his Withinner.

"One day, mate, you'll get caught talking to yourself like this and the men in white coats will definitely arrive to take you away."

He sat down at his desk and about twenty minutes later the door bell rang. He frowned as he stood up to answer the door. He saw the broad figure of his friend even before he opened it.

"Jomo, since when do you ring the bell? Haven't you still got your key?" His words were teasing and Jomo grinned faintly.

"I was not sure whether I still had that privilege, old friend, after everything that has happened." He stepped inside and Quinn moved forward to clasp his friend's shoulder tightly.

"I know it's been a little crazy, but you are always welcome here, you know that. This door is always open to you. Come on in, let me make you some coffee and we can talk."

The two men went through to the kitchen and Jomo sat down on a bar stool at the island as Quinn made coffee in the machine. Once everything was bubbling and the strong smell of roasted coffee drifted through the air, Quinn sat himself down beside his friend and partner and regarded him thoughtfully.

"I didn't realise you were coming over today. But I'm very glad you did. I know we've talked and I've apologised to you about the state I got into when Cade left me." He felt very uncomfortable saying these words—one, because it was a lie, two, because it dented his pride a little telling people Cade had left him, even though he knew it was the only option, and three, Jomo's face looked as if he didn't believe a word of Quinn's story.

The other man smiled softly. "Ah, yes, the separation. You know, I never quite believed that story. Yet I would never pry because you are a true friend and I know you must have a very good reason for the distorting of the truth."

Quinn swallowed, looking down at the tabletop guiltily.

Jomo chuckled as he reached over a huge hand and covered Quinn's with his own. "No mind. You are here now, back together and things are as they should be. That is all that matters. Are you going to pour me a cup of that lovely coffee or is it just going to turn to tar in the pot?"

Quinn chuckled and stood up to pour the coffee into mugs, added milk and sugar for Jomo and brought the two mugs over to the kitchen top.

"How is Ulinda? I haven't seen her for a while. We need to get together for dinner. I'll speak to Cade and let the two ladies organise something soon."

Jomo nodded. "Ulinda is wonderful. I am still singing for her and keeping her happy."

Quinn laughed. "I'm glad to hear it. So what brings you over this way then? Are you thinking of coming back here full time to work?"

Jomo looked a little embarrassed. "I wasn't, but if you want me to—"

Quinn shook his head. "No, I was joking. I know you like working from home with Ulinda there and our Skype calls and conference facilities are more than enough for what we need to get done. I do miss your company though," he said wistfully. "But I guess that's what happens when we grow up. We get our own families to manage and things tend to drift apart."

"That will never happen," Jomo said quietly. "We see each other often and talk often and we are still friends. I am always there for you, you know that."

"And I for you." Quinn grinned and the two men sat back, the bromance moment behind them.

Jomo smiled shyly. "I wanted to stop by and tell you that I am thinking of asking Ulinda to marry me and when she says yes, I want to organise the wedding for about eight to twelve months' time, depending on what Ulinda wants. I want you to be my best man."

Quinn gaped at his friend. "Wow, that's great news and of course I'll be your best man. Who else would you choose?"

He stood up and pummelled his friend on the arm before continuing. "Honestly, take it from a man who's already there. It's great being engaged and knowing one day you'll get married. Then before you know it, babies will be on the way."

He felt a surge of envy at that thought. Dinner needed to be scheduled with Misty to introduce her to Cade. Quinn was a little nervous about the topic of discussion. Misty had told him chidingly she believed Cade would be fine with the idea of her carrying their child when they were ready.

Jomo grinned. "I hope to have Ulinda to myself for a little while before that happens. I cannot think of having a child just yet. I'm glad you have agreed to be best man. It means a lot to me."

"It would be an honour," Quinn said quietly. "After everything we've been through together, everything seems to be coming full circle, just like it should."

The two men chatted for a while about weddings, work and women and finally Jomo drained the dregs of his umpteenth coffee and stood up.

"I need to get off," he apologised. "Ulinda and I have dinner plans and if I'm late, she will kill me. And then you wouldn't get to be best man."

Quinn saw his friend off with the promise of getting in touch to arrange dinner plans and then closed the door behind him. He was pleased for Jomo and Ulinda and knew Cade too would be thrilled at the prospect.

Chapter 29

Daniel Wickman looked at his nephew across the Consortium table. The two men were seated together waiting for the rest of the Council members to arrive. Daniel was Quinn's invited guest, preparing to give feedback on the latest developments within RAW, the Resistance Against Witchhunting organisation, and his double life as a trusted confidante of the Witchunters Alliance.

Daniel was bone tired. His dual role was definitely starting to wear him down. Just that week he'd been asked to sanction yet another witch killing, one which had thankfully been stopped in time, but he was getting sick to the bone of narrowly averting tragedies.. Quinn had asked him to come along and give an update to the Council, along with the work he was doing with Quinn with the Praetorium and Valensia. For a human, Daniel thought wryly, he'd been drawn into the Fey world more than he'd ever thought possible. It was a side effect of having a witch for his late wife and a Warlock as a foster son. He sensed Quinn's eyes on him, probing as only his nephew could, with a stare that seemed to bore down deep into his soul.

"Daniel, are you ready for tonight?" Quinn's quiet tones harboured a distinct concern. "I know you're exhausted and I'm really glad you're here, but it might get a little tough around the table. Barton Sinclair and his little helper Cavanaugh have been doing the rounds the past week or so trying to drum up support for their bid to oust me as Grand Master. Whilst I don't think they've got much, it will still be a fairly fiery debate, I can promise you."

Daniel grunted tiredly. "I know, I've heard the scuttlebutt around the cauldron. The Praetorium is no fan of him, I can tell you." He smiled slightly. "In fact, there's a current little bit of fun going on in the organisation. Some of the members pick the animal they'd like to turn him into and the weapon of choice to dispatch him with. My personal favourite is a warthog as it comes with a bow and arrow. I fancy me a bit of crackling."

Quinn chuckled and Daniel smiled. "Barton Sinclair stands no chance and he must know it. He's just a big bag of wind who picks at a situation bit by bit in the hopes he can wear you down. He doesn't know you like I do, or he wouldn't even bother trying."

Quinn nodded. "Thanks for that vote of confidence."

Someone came into the room and Daniel's jaw dropped. The most exotic-looking woman he'd ever seen glided in, her deep, warm red jersey dress clinging to her curves like cling wrap and her deep blue eyes assessing Quinn with a definite predatory look. Daniel wished a woman, any woman, would look at him the way this woman was looking at his nephew. He was sure of one thing: Cade would want to scoop her eyes out with a spoon.

"Quinn, am I on time? I tried so hard to be fashionably late but it looks like I didn't try hard enough." She smiled and reached over to kiss Quinn on the cheek. Quinn nodded.

"Valensia, glad you made it. Let me introduce you to Daniel Wickman, my uncle, and the man we have to thank for a lot of the intelligence we get from inside the WA."

Daniel took the witch's hand and a tingle swept across his palm as she held it longer than normal.

"I am indeed indebted to you, Daniel." Valensia smiled as she regarded his face curiously. "You're nothing like I thought you would look. I thought you'd be…taller?" She grinned slightly.

Daniel's heart skipped a beat. *God, what was wrong with him, the woman must be nearly half his age! He was a fifty-two-year-*

old lecher and she could certainly be no more than thirty—or younger.

"Yes, well, you know the saying: small packages and all that malarkey." Daniel was well aware that his five-foot-seven frame and wiry build tended to make people underestimate him, mostly to their own detriment.

Valensia smiled. "That may be but I've always preferred to make up my own mind about what they say about smaller men. Size doesn't always matter as long as the man knows what to do with it." She chuckled softly.

Daniel's legs almost gave way. He gripped the back of the chair tightly.

Quinn grinned widely at Daniel's obvious discomfort.

"I've heard a lot about you and the work you do on our behalf is welcomed." She hesitated. "I was very sorry to hear about your wife. I knew Moira. She was a great woman."

Daniel nodded. "She was. Thank you."

Quinn stepped forward. "Right, now we have the introductions all sorted, I'd better let you know that no one's expecting you here tonight so it's going to be a bloody great surprise to all of them when they see you."

Valensia gazed at him in exasperation. "For God's sake, you didn't tell them I was coming? I wondered at all the cloak-and-dagger stuff when they brought me up here."

Quinn shook his head, his smile wolfish. "No, I thought it would have more impact this way and perhaps give that arsehole Barton Smith something to put in his pipe and smoke. I know you can handle them."

"Talk about putting Valensia on the back foot! That's typical you, putting the cat amongst the bloody pigeons to see what happens." Daniel was a little aggrieved at Quinn's manoeuvre.

Quinn raised his eyebrows at his uncle's apparent concern. "It looks like you have a champion, Valensia," he murmured as he went to the door to peer out and see if anyone else had arrived. "Be careful what you wish for, Dan. She can be quite a handful."

Daniel frowned at Quinn, his face fierce. "Fuck off."

Quinn's chuckled quietly and Valensia threw an enigmatic smile his way. Daniel felt very out of his depth.

"Never mind him," Valensia's soft tone whispered close to his ear. "He can be a real arrogant sod, I'm sure you know that better than most. And by the way, age really is all in the mind of the beholder."

Dan was still fairly taken aback by her age comment. *Had she been reading his mind? Could witches do that?*

Daniel nodded. "He's always been like that. Sometimes I've just wanted to lock him up in a bloody cage and watch him pace up and down like a captive lion whilst throwing pieces of raw meat at him. He has that effect on people."

There was the scent of jasmine in his nostrils as Valensia moved closer to him.

"Yet still you trust him and still you'd support him no matter what—as would I—so what does that say about us both? Are we both fools or is Quinn more manipulative than we both think?"

Her tone was slightly sad. Daniel looked up into her eyes and saw an emotion there he couldn't quite fathom. *Regret, perhaps?*

Daniel sighed. "It says he is who he is and we have to live with it."

He looked around at the room filling with people, most of them eying out Valensia in appreciation and some of them with downright lust. But she didn't seem to care that the whole room of men was staring at her with avarice.

Barton Sinclair's eyes were bugging out, his face almost pink with apoplexy, his hands beating a fierce tattoo on the conference table.

"It looks like Quinn's plan has worked," Valensia murmured quietly as she turned to smile at the men in the room. "There is a lot of stiffness and testosterone in this room tonight, something I'm sure he planned as a distraction at my expense. If it's any consolation, with regards to my earlier comment, I don't think either of us are fools."

She laid a soft hand on his arm then released it, moving off to work the room with her charm and beauty.

Daniel found he could breathe again. The woman definitely had an impact; he'd have to admit that. He knew about Quinn's relationship with her many years ago, and he was flabbergasted that Quinn would decide he preferred men to that specimen of womanhood. There was no accounting for sexual tastes obviously. He sat down at the table and waited for the meeting to begin.

Valensia came over and sat down next to him and there was a slight surge of satisfaction that she'd chosen to do that. He saw Quinn stand straight at the head of the table and stare around the room with an expression that made everyone fall quiet. Once everyone was settled, Quinn smiled briefly at the group and waved in Valensia's direction.

"Gentlemen. You may have noticed we have someone in the room who certainly isn't one of our usual members. I'd like to welcome Valensia to this meeting and ask you all to respect who she is and who she represents—the Praetorium of the Witches. I thought it might be useful to have her here to answer any questions about the union between our two organisations as I know some of you have some concerns."

He smiled but Daniel noticed the smile didn't quite reach his eyes. "I'll also have no gym locker talk in this meeting, so please can I ask you all to keep any ribald or sexist humour to yourselves until you get home, or to the mistress's home or wherever else takes your fancy."

There was a quiet round of chuckles at his words and then silence.

"We have someone else with us tonight who has contributed to a lot of what we have achieved: Daniel Wickman, head of RAW and also, as some of you may know, my uncle. Daniel has been working with RAW for many years and is also a key member in the Witchhunters Alliance, the people who try to kill us with regularity. I know the members of this council can be trusted. As you all know, Daniel's position is one of the biggest advantages we have. Whilst I know I shouldn't have to say it, I will, just for clarity. Daniel's position in the WA is of utmost secrecy and outside of this room, no one knows about him. It must stay that way."

His voice was vaguely threatening and Daniel had no illusions about what might happen to someone who broke Quinn's rule. His nephew could be an unforgiving soul.

"Daniel will answer any questions you have about either of the organisations that he represents. He'll also be working a little closer with the Praetorium going forward so we can begin to gain an insight as to how this union is benefitting us both."

Daniel looked at Quinn in surprise; this was news to him. He glanced over at Valensia and saw the quiet smile on her face and he just knew she had been aware of Quinn's intentions. He felt a little put out at being the last to know.

"Right, so we can call this meeting to order now we've all been introduced. I'll open the floor to questions for Valensia, I think. Ladies first."

Quinn sat down and loosened his tie, opening the top buttons of his shirt. He winked at Daniel.

Of course, true to expectations, Barton Sinclair was the first to address Valensia with a smarmy smile. "Valensia, it's good to finally meet you. I was beginning to think Quinn was keeping you all to himself. I can certainly see why, if that was the case."

"James." Quinn's voice was quiet but dangerous, any previous good humour dissipating like a puff of smoke in a breeze.

Barton Sinclair waved a hand in dismissal. "Don't get your panties in a bunch. I was merely complimenting the lady."

Valensia leaned forward, her long fingernails tapping impatiently on the table. "Do you have a question for me, James?" she drawled.

"I do. I merely want to know what the Praetorium is bringing to this relationship that we didn't already have. I have no problem with a union as long as it benefits us but frankly, I've never quite seen where Quinn sees this benefit to be."

Valensia sat back and regarded James thoughtfully. "The Consortium has definitely done a lot to benefit the witches. Your researchers figured out the Book of Shadows. Quinn and his Warlocks also got rid of the Witchfinder General and his new vessel. So we do owe you a debt of gratitude. But I confess I find your question a trifle naive. Do you own a company?"

Barton Sinclair looked a little taken aback by the sudden question. "I do. What has that to do with anything?"

"Have you heard of a little business tradition called networking?" Valensia tilted her head enquiringly.

"Of course I have. It's a common business practice," James blustered.

"You speak to people who provide you with information, sales leads, and intelligence and you make valuable allies in your quest to build your business. It's how you grow and become stronger as a business. Would you agree with that?"

Quinn was smiling and Daniel could see he knew where this was going, as did he.

"I suppose so." Barton Sinclair looked a little uncomfortable with some of the sly glances and chuckles around the room.

"Then I confess I'm a little confused as to why you wouldn't see the union between our two organisations being much the same. We share intelligence, we support each other, we make friends and allies and when things go wrong, together we find the solutions. Is that not a very useful alliance to have?"

Valensia reached down and picked up her large handbag sitting by her side. She plonked it loudly on the table and reached inside and took out a large plastic bag, inside which resided some strange-looking object.

"I'm sure you'll all recognise what this is." Valensia reached in and took out the object and there was a collective loud gasp of disgust around the table. It was a hand, cut off at the wrist and still covered in dry blood.

Daniel stared at her in awe. *The woman had a dismembered hand in her bloody handbag!*

"This belonged to a witch who planned to disrupt the last summit we had back in June. I've been keeping him on ice especially for a situation like this one. Had he made it through with his plan, many of you sitting around this table may well not be here now. My team got wind of this plot simply through their own vigilance. I dealt with this particular traitor personally. Now, I know a lot of you will say that if we hadn't had a union, we wouldn't have had a summit, and hence the problem wouldn't have occurred. That was what you going to say, wasn't it, James?"

She looked over at Barton Sinclair who was sitting looking at the lonely hand in fascination, his mouth open as if poised to speak.

Her voice hardened. "But you all know that if it hadn't been this summit, it could just as well have been another one of your Warlock conferences as this particular witch had a thing against the Consortium. He had a personal axe to grind. So I suppose you could say that I saved your bacon."

She looked over at Quinn and he acknowledged her words with a wide smile and a wink. "And that I think sums up quite nicely what I think we bring as a benefit to this union." She looked around the table. "Are there any more questions for me?"

The room remained silent. Valensia sat back, placed the hand back in the bag and sealed it. She took out a small container of antiseptic wipes from her bag and took one out, rubbing it over her hands. She waved at the baggie containing the severed hand. "Not very hygienic having one of those in your bag, but it serves its purpose."

She put it and the container back in her bag and sat back in her chair. Daniel had never seen such a display of complete confidence and sheer power. It was such a turn-on. He was entranced at the knowledge that if Quinn and Valensia had actually become a couple and had children, it would have indeed been a riveting union and an incredible family dynamic, one that would have definitely been out of this world.

"Gentleman, if there are no more questions for Valensia, I suggest we turn our attention to Daniel." Quinn's voice was tinged with amusement and he looked over at Daniel, who drew a deep breath.

Barton Sinclair was talking quietly to Troy, but when Quinn shot a fierce glance in his direction the two men fell quiet.

The door opened and a woman came in bearing a trolley filled with tea, coffee and biscuits. There were a few satisfied murmurs throughout the room.

Quinn chuckled. "Change of plan. Daniel, I know you've got a few stories to tell us. I suggest we all help ourselves to a drink then we can get back together in about ten minutes." He stood up and walked over to Valensia as the men in the room made their way toward the catering trolley.

"Well done," he murmured quietly as Daniel looked on. "That was unexpected but totally in character. I should have known you'd do something so totally out there."

He grinned at her with sheer affection and Daniel felt a little jealous, even thought he knew he was being totally unreasonable.

Quinn, my boy, you've got a bloody man of your own. You don't need to charm this woman as well! God, I hate getting older.

Valensia moved closer to Quinn, her hands lightly grasping his bicep, and Quinn's nostrils flared. She nodded at him in acknowledgement of the compliment. "I'm glad you enjoyed the show. I'm pleased I can still shock you just a little bit."

Her voice was husky. Quinn moved away from Valensia, a look of slight uncertainty on his face. That expression on his face wasn't one Daniel would have expected to see from Quinn.

Valensia turned to Daniel and laid a soft hand on his shoulder as she leaned into him. A sense of insignificance assailed him in the presence of this tall, powerful and extremely alluring woman.

"I'm looking forward to what you have to say, Daniel. I'm just parched, though. I need coffee." She moved over to join the rather willing men at the drinks cart.

Quinn looked at Daniel. "She's been up to her old tricks again," he said angrily. "Just as I think I can begin to trust her, she goes and messes it up."

Despite his perverse feeling of resentment towards his nephew, Daniel was curious about Quinn's words. "What are you talking about?" he asked, watching Valensia laughing with the group of men around the cart.

Quinn looked at him as if he'd said something he shouldn't. "Uhm, it's nothing. Don't worry about it."

"I saw your reaction when she touched you." Daniel said softly. "Something happened to you."

His nephew looked very ill at ease. "She has this annoying habit of enhancing her Fey side, being half witch, half Fey, and she knows it makes me feel bloody uncomfortable."

"Ah. I see, that wonderful Fey-Warlock sexual thing. I didn't realise she was half Fey. I can see that must be a little difficult for you."

"The woman just can't accept the fact I'm with Cade. She's a bloody menace but I need to work with her."

"Quinn, I heard that." Valensia's voice cut in like iced water as she came up behind Quinn. Daniel turned to see her pale face and clenched lips. She looked formidable.

"I have not done anything to attract you, I can assure you, you arrogant prat." She spoke the words between gritted teeth. "If you're having urges for me, they're your own, not due to anything I'm doing." She glanced down at Quinn's groin. "Perhaps you should be controlling yourself a little more, or perhaps you're not getting enough at home." The witch spat out the words.

Quinn's face was expressionless. Valensia turned to Daniel. "I think my part of this dog and pony show is over. I shall remain and listen, Quinn, but don't bloody talk to me. Daniel, it's been lovely meeting you, which is more than I can say for your imbecile of a nephew. Perhaps we could get together some time for a drink and you can fill me in personally on your work. I think I might like that."

She handed Daniel a small silver-embossed card. "My number. Call me."

Valensia moved to the far end of the boardroom table and sat down. Her body language was one that dared anyone to approach her. Daniel thought she might rip off people's heads and chew on them just for fun. He looked at the card in his hand then up at Quinn's white face.

"Erm, that didn't go too well for you. She was really pissed off."

Privately he was wondering whether there had been any double entendre in her words about "filling her in personally," or whether it was just perhaps his mind in the gutter. This woman seemed to have that effect on men. And for the first time in his life, Quinn seemed lost for words.

"I really thought—" Quinn shook his head as he cut off his own words. "I thought she was trying it on. Shit, she *was* pissed off with me, wasn't she?" He looked around to see if anyone else had noticed the heated exchange then glanced at Valensia who ignored him completely.

Quinn looked at the card in his hand. "Daniel—"

"Oh no, don't you dare get involved. I'm a big boy now. I'll make my own mind up about things." Daniel heard the steely determination in his voice. "I can look after myself."

Quinn shrugged his broad shoulders. "Okay. You do that. Don't say I didn't try and warn you."

He moved away to round up the men for the rest of the meeting. Soon they were seated again listening to Daniel tell them about the latest news from RAW and the latest plans to murder witches by the Witchhunters Alliance.

"They asked me to sanction two killings earlier this week. Witch and Warlock. I did, but it was a touch-and-go situation to try and save them both in time. It was almost like the Honour Whitebrook killings. Something happened to scupper our plans and we had to work twice as hard to get to them."

Quinn winced at the reminder of the Whitebrook incident.

"But I'm slowly feeling as if I'm running out of time. I think there have been too many last-minute rescues and I think they may be getting a little suspicious. Not of me, per se, but that something isn't quite right. So I need to be very careful and keep my head down." He looked around at the serious faces watching him speak. "If I was a real bastard, I'd say I need to let someone die so I build some more trust. But I'm afraid I'm not that man and I can't do that."

He was very aware of Quinn's utter stillness at the head of the conference table as some eyes glanced furtively in his direction. There were still some around the table who believed that Quinn's decision to delay the rescue of the Whitebrook family had been a stroke of genius and one that Quinn had planned all along to enforce the deaths of the family. But they didn't get to see the man who had nightmares and woke up soaked in sweat, his face white and his body trembling with grief.

James Barton Sinclair leaned forward in his chair. "Daniel, we are all very supportive of your role in the WA and it has been a key position of strategy for this Council for the past many years. We can certainly appreciate your position and the personal sacrifice you have made in getting where you are. It appears to me that we need an event that will further cement your position in this organisation, one that cannot be made with emotion and one that is made solely with the interests of the greater good. I confess there was a time when I believed Quinn to be of the same opinion but he appears to have grown a conscience, something which ultimately may lead us to a path down which we do not want to travel."

Quinn's fists clenched and unclenched on the table and Daniel sensed the imminent danger in the man's body language as he listened to James' dissertation. He knew Quinn was not upset at what was being said about him but rather about the direction that the conversation was taking.

Barton Sinclair looked around the table, obviously relishing the attention of the Council. "As Grand Master, there may be certain decisions that need to be made that are unpalatable and frankly, inhuman. But this position demands such decisions be made and one cannot ignore one's duty for the sake of humanity. Some lives need to be sacrificed for the many. There are others around this table that feel the same way." His lips curled in a sneer. "And as Justin Leichner is not here tonight to support Quinn as usual, we may be able to speak more freely on this issue."

"Are you saying you think Quinn should sanction these witch killings to secure my place in the WA?" Daniel's voice was conversational but inside he was burning with fury at what Barton Sinclair was trying to do. Valensia was regarding Barton Sinclair with eyes that were acid with dislike.

"You're *his* inside man, so *his* to do with as he sees fit." James voice hardened. "I know what I would do if my key man's position in the WA was threatened."

Quinn stood up slowly, his hands drawn into tight fists and his face black with fury. "I'd be interested to hear what Valensia has to say about that, James." He gestured in the witch's direction.

She watched Quinn, then James with flinty eyes. At the expression on her face Barton Sinclair blanched. Valensia regarded him with scorn as she rose to Quinn's challenge. "You'd like to tell me, the Regina of the Praetorium, that as well as Warlocks, you intend having some of my people killed to protect a man, a human, who is working with the Consortium of Warlocks?"

"That will never fucking happen," Daniel said hotly. "I would die rather than see others die for me. Barton Sinclair, you are a pompous, arrogant and dangerous arsehole." He turned to his nephew in frustration. "Quinn, how can you let him say these things—"

Quinn waved an imperious hand, cutting him off. "Daniel, calm down. I have no intention of letting James put any of his misguided ideas into play. Neither will Valensia, I assure you. It's not something either of us would condone for a millisecond."

"And you know her so well, you bedded her. You know her inside out," James said with a sneer. He looked around the room, pleased with his own wittiness.

A pulse throbbed in Quinn's throat and Daniel thought things were definitely going to get nasty. His own throat was choked with anger.

Valensia stood up, her gaze on James deadly, her fingers flexing.

Daniel wondered if she too could throw energy bolts like Quinn. He had visions of the whole room going up in flames with Barton Sinclair acting as the torch.

She and Quinn shared a fierce glance and then, slowly, she sat back down and stared at James with dislike. Her fingers tapped a secret tune on the table.

"I shall ignore that last comment and not rip your fucking jowly throat out." Quinn's voice was deadly. He looked around the room. "Are there any others in this room that feel we should protect Daniel's position by killing innocent people just to keep him in there?"

There were some glances around the room as the men looked at each other, then slowly, a few of them raised their hands, Barton Sinclair and his lapdog Troy Cavanaugh being two of the six currently with their hands in the air.

"By my reckoning, that's less than half of the current Council voting for this option."

Barton Sinclair looked around in confusion and Quinn imagined he thought he'd bullied more people into supporting him and that those people had now changed their minds, leaving him high and dry.

"Six out of a council of fourteen. I know what Justin Leichner and Frederick Mulbarton would say and it probably wouldn't be very complimentary to you, James. And you know what? You're right. Some time ago I might have given credence to such a notion. I doubt I would have done it but I would have thought about it. But I have changed for the better, I hope. And there is no way on this earth that I would fucking agree to killing innocent people so Daniel can retain his position. We have a union with the witches now, a powerful ally. We will either find some other way to keep Daniel in there, or else I will remove him and we will live with the consequences. I will not lose Daniel. If he feels threatened, he needs to leave immediately. I will not lose another family member or another good man to this war we fight, if I can help it."

Quinn's voice was fierce and Daniel's throat constricted at the emotion in Quinn's voice. "And I will not have men in this Council who think we should. Those of you who put up your hands can leave this room and not come back." The Grand Master's tone was harsh.

The men who had supported Barton Sinclair looked around in confusion, meeting the steely gazes of those who had not.

Valensia smiled and licked her lips as she watched Quinn. Daniel swallowed at that look. She might know she didn't have a chance with Quinn, but by God, she still wanted him. He wished a woman would look at him that way. Power and strength obviously turned her on. He'd have to remember that.

"I mean fucking *now*. Get up and leave." Quinn leaned forward on the table, his tone leaving no room for doubt what would happen if they didn't. The men slowly stood up, filing quietly out of the door

Barton Sinclair was the last to leave. His eyes were full of hate. "You can't do this, Fairmont," he snarled. "There are rules and regulations and you cannot simply throw us out because we disagree with you. You're a fucking dictator."

"I'm not asking you to leave because you disagree with me," Quinn said quietly. "I'm asking you to leave because you sicken me with your ideology. It has no place in this room. If that makes me a dictator, so be it. I can live with myself. But I couldn't live with the thought that I have men like you around this table who think that destroying lives is the answer to everything."

He stared flatly at the other man and Daniel noticed for the first time that Quinn's eyes were pure black. Barton Sinclair seemed to notice as well as he stepped back with an expression of fear on his face before he turned and strode out of the room. Quinn watched him go.

Daniel laid a hand on his arm. "Quinn, sit down. Take a breath."

"In a minute, Daniel. Let me finish this up." Quinn looked around the room at the other men still seated. "Some of you may not agree with what I've just done. But I can't afford to have men like that in positions of trust on this council."

He looked at Daniel. "Daniel, I want you out of the WA. If I know Barton Sinclair, this will piss him off to the point where he'll do anything to get back at me. He knows one way to do that will be to harm you. I want you out of there. We'll figure out how to do that without tipping the WA off."

He looked at the silent room full of expectant faces. "For those of you who are still on this Council, thank you for your support. I think it's late enough now to call it a night. I'll be in touch with each one of you in the next few days and let you know where we're going from here. Thank you, gentlemen. And lady."

The men stood up quietly, most of them shaking Quinn's hand as they left, others simply nodding at him in agreement. Valensia glided over to Quinn and observed him with keen eyes. Then she nodded haughtily and walked out of the room. Finally it was quiet and Quinn sat down, passing a trembling hand over his darkened eyes.

"Hell, that was intense. Not only did I piss the queen of the witches off, I pissed off six of some of the most influential Warlocks in the country. Never let it be said that I do things in halves."

Daniel chuckled quietly. "You've always had a tendency to do things in the most unorthodox way. It what makes you a great Grand Master and an even better leader."

Daniel reached down and grasped Quinn's shoulder tightly, feeling the tenseness in the younger man.

"Go on home; get to Cade. Let him take some of that tension out of your body, son. And what the hell is all that stuff with your eyes? It looks bloody scary." He grinned.

Quinn smiled back at him. "It's a stress thing but I'm getting used to it. And Taliesin has been extremely vocal tonight. He's driving me crazy. The things he wants to do to Barton Sinclair I can't even repeat. I wouldn't mind doing some of them to the bastard myself except I'll end up in jail." He groaned softly. "I need to make nice with Valensia as well, I suppose, on my faux pas. She's unforgiving and she'll make my life a bloody misery." He glanced at his uncle with a faint smirk. "If you intend taking on Valensia, you'll need big balls. Believe me, I know and I meant it when I said be careful what you wish for."

"I'm a grown man and my balls are big enough, I hope."

Quinn stood up and stretched. "Time to get home. We'll talk tomorrow and make a plan to get you out that keeps you safe. There must be a way."

Daniel nodded sombrely. "I can't say I'll be unhappy to leave, it's just how we do it that's the problem." He turned to leave the room then turned around. "You did well, tonight, I'm very proud of you. Your father would have loved to see you throw that jackass out on his ear."

He left Quinn in the room and made his way down to the lobby. He'd get a taxi home, bugger the trains. There was a definite sense of relief that he was getting out of the Witchunters Alliance. It would give him more time to devote to the resistance group, which was his main passion. Daniel knew things were going to get a little tougher over the coming weeks, not least of which was calling Valensia for that drink she'd promised. He'd play that one out, see how it went. After all, he was only human.

Chapter 30

Quinn got home just before eleven p.m. and tried to walk quietly into the bedroom so as not to disturb Cade. He undressed, leaving his clothes spread across the floor as he crept into bed.

His body felt as if he'd been in a boxing ring with a sumo wrestler, tense with knotted muscles. He turned over to sleep and started as a pair of warm hands slid up his back and made their way to his shoulders. He moaned as Cade kneaded them, his strong hands finding the knots and working them out.

He felt the heat of his lover's hands on his skin and groaned softly. "God, I need that."

"Bad meeting then?" Cade's mouth brushed his back and Quinn's groin surged at the breath on his skin and the touch of his tongue as he ran it across his shoulders.

"I've had better. I managed to really upset Valensia and had to get rid of six council members who now hate me and have no doubt vowed vengeance. So yes, not a particularly good evening."

"What did you say to Valensia to make her so mad?"

"It was a misunderstanding, a miscommunication. I'll call her tomorrow and apologise."

"*You* have to apologise? What the hell did you say to the woman?" Cade was sitting up in bed now and Quinn felt his eyes boring into the back of his head. He wished, once again, that he'd kept his mouth shut. This whole thing about relationship transparency was about to get him into trouble once again.

"I made an assumption about something I thought she was doing and she got royally pissed. It was a Consortium thing, and in hindsight, I was wrong, hence the apology."

He wasn't going to tell Cade the full story as that would invite far too much commentary and questions about why he'd gotten horny in the first place when she hadn't apparently even been trying. Quinn still wasn't sure himself what had happened. He imagined it was his heightened senses wreaking havoc since Cade's return. He'd have to watch that.

"I see. Was it Barton Sinclair you kicked off the Council?"

"Yes, he and five others. They supported an idea I couldn't in all honesty give credence to. They wanted me to sanction more actual witch killings to secure Daniel's position. Just let deaths happen for the greater good. I couldn't do that."

"You made the right decision. I'm really proud of you for getting rid of those smarmy bastards. Barton Sinclair is an absolute prick."

Quinn chuckled at Cade's words, closing his eyes in satisfaction as eager hands slowly slid down his side, caressing the scar on his hip and moving down over his backside, to the tops of his thighs.

"Cade?"

"Um-hm?"

"Are you going to take advantage of me? Because I'm pretty tense in one particular area and I really need it relaxed."

Cade laughed softly as he leaned over him, his hands sliding around to his erection and touching him teasingly. Cade's tongue teased Quinn's ear and he grew even harder. His groin flooded with heat and his breath quickened.

"I think I might manage to do something about it," Cade murmured, his voice sultry as he pushed Cade onto his back and stared down at him with hooded eyes. Quinn closed his eyes as his fiancé proceeded to take care of his tension problem.

*****

The following morning Quinn sat bare-chested in his jeans, looking out at the early morning mist rolling over the heath as he dialled the number he wanted.

Daniel answered, sounding quite put out. "Quinn, it's eight o'clock on a Saturday morning, for God's sake," the older man grumbled. "What's so important it couldn't wait until a more civilised hour?"

Quinn chuckled. "I was thinking about how we're going to get you out of the Witchhunters Alliance without raising suspicions about you. I was in the shower and I had an epiphany."

"Bully for you," Daniel grunted. "I hope it didn't hurt. You should be more careful."

Quinn shook his head in amusement. "I'm trying to be serious. Will you hear me out please?"

Daniel sighed loudly.

Quinn smiled. "Right, you grumpy bugger. Here's my suggestion. We turn the whole thing on its head and tell the Witchhunters Alliance that for the last two years, whilst you've been busy trying to infiltrate RAW for them, you've finally got them to really trust you. So you're moving on. You're going to leave the Alliance and get yourself ensconced in RAW and report back on them to the Alliance. We can feed them disinformation and the occasional genuine scrap to keep them happy. That way if that tosser Barton Sinclair decides to spill the beans on you—and he will, have no doubts about that—it looks like it all fits together."

His voice was grim with his next words. "James will have no compunction making you the sacrificial lamb so he can gain kudos with his followers and show everyone how tough he is. He'll do anything to get back at me, even if it means losing a valuable resource within the WA. The bastard will cut his nose off to spite his face; he's that kind of man. This is all about keeping you safe."

This is a good plan. I like it. Taliesin's tone was approving.

Daniel was quiet on the other end of the phone. When he spoke he sounded a little confused. "So, let me get this straight. These past few years I've been running RAW under the covers but was assigned to the WA as a 'double agent' to drip feed them false info on the resistance and the Consortium and any other bloody organisation they hated. I then reported back to RAW on what the WA is doing so we were forewarned. Now you're suggesting I tell them I've finally fully 'infiltrated' RAW and I need to be more visible there, hence me leaving the WA. To them, I'll be working in RAW knowingly and feeding them, the WA, bits of info from the inside."

"Eureka," Quinn said drily. "As Professor Higgins so eloquently said, 'By George, you've got it.'"

"Hell, you're bloody scary." Daniel's voice was impressed but Quinn could also hear a faint trace of something else—fear? "That must be the most Machiavellian bloody plan I've ever heard. And you came up with it in the shower?"

"It works. It means that if James lets slip you've been involved with RAW, then you can counteract it by saying, of course I bloody well was, and now I've finally got where I wanted to be. Full time inside RAW, in a pretty senior position. It is risky and it will take a really good acting performance from you to pull it off, to both discredit James and make the WA think he's got the wrong end of the stick, but you can do it. This way, you get back where you truly belong, the WA think they've got a prominent insider in the resistance and you can keep RAW going without the distraction of playing the double agent in their camp. Instead you're a treble agent in your own."

Daniel groaned. "I don't even want to go down figuring out how the treble agent thing works in your head. It was bad enough when I was a double."

Quinn laughed softly. "It sounded logical at the time, but I think even I'd have a job explaining it now. What do you think? Can you pull it off?"

"I can." Daniel's voice was firm. "If it gets me out of WA without too much suspicion and lets me fight them from within my own organisation, I'm all for it." He went quiet.

Quinn knew what he was thinking. "I'm hoping that with us feeding them what they think is much more valuable information on RAW directly and keeping them distracted, you won't get too involved too much anymore in sanctioning some of the killings the WA want to do. But you'll still have to have your finger on the pulse inside there for a little while. We have to know when these things are happening so we can protect the witches and Warlocks they're targeting.

"If we don't, Barton Sinclair will have won and the body count will be far more than just taking the decision to let one get killed every now and then. Valensia and I already had a plan to get someone else in there to replace you—another human. We've been working on it for a while. But whilst we knew we might have to replace you at some stage, I had no idea how to do it without them getting suspicious. Now I do." Quinn chuckled. "If you remember I said at the meeting I intended you working with the Praetorium a little more closely. And I didn't mean the fact she gave you her card and invited you for a drink."

Quinn, Daniel should be very careful. He does not know Valensia like you and I.

I know, Withinner. But he wants to do this own way. He can be as stubborn as I am.

"Enough already about that," Daniel said in exasperation. "So this other human—they'll take over what I was doing?"

"Yes. Valensia's pretty convinced they'll be able to do it, and to be honest, it takes the responsibility off my shoulders and puts it on hers. I can't say I'll miss it either. So it's all coming together."

He sighed heavily. "I had a feeling I'd need to get you out of there as soon as I could the way the Council meetings were going, with Barton Sinclair getting more aggressive. It was only a matter of time before I lost my rag and kicked him out. I knew when that happened you'd be in danger because James is a vindictive bastard. So I asked Valensia a while ago for her help in grooming a new candidate to take your place. One James wouldn't know anything about. I just didn't have the time to arrange it myself."

Daniel snorted. "I don't want to see inside your head. It must look like Spaghetti Junction in there with all these threads, plans and political plots. I don't envy you the job at all."

I can confirm that your head is not a good place to be, Taliesin chuckled.

Shut up, sorcerer. I wouldn't say yours is any better, you supercilious bastard.

"You definitely don't want to see inside my head." Quinn gazed across the heath, his eyes unfocused, his face bleak. "It's a pretty scary place to be, even for me."

He brought his attention back to the present. "I'll be calling Valensia later to eat humble pie and apologise for my misunderstanding yesterday. I'll let her know all this then. If she's still talking to me. I'll let you know how that one goes."

Daniel chuckled. "Good luck with that one. It was nice knowing you. I'll catch up with you later then. I may as well get up now, seeing as how some rude bastard woke me up."

The call disconnected and Quinn shook his head in amusement. He looked at his watch. Eight-thirty. Early enough to call Valensia, who would be up by now. Quinn heard Cade moving around in the bedroom and he went through to finish dressing.

Cade raised an eyebrow. "Warlock business done then? Are you ready for our morning walk on the heath? I might even get in a swim." He bustled around, filling his swim bag with clothing and his swimming trunks.

Quinn nodded. "Yes, just give me a minute. I need to go to my study and call Valensia. I have an apology to make so she'll talk to me again." His face grew serious. "I also have some plans to make in getting Daniel out from the Alliance. What with me giving Barton Sinclair the boot yesterday, life will become a lot more difficult for him, I'd bet on it." He heaved a sigh. "You carry on. I'll be down in a jiffy."

Fifteen minutes later Quinn rubbed his eyes tiredly.

Christ, at least that was over.

He wandered down to where an exasperated Cade stood, swim bag slung over shoulder, glaring at him impatiently. "Finally! I thought you were going to be all bloody day talking to that woman. How did it go anyway?"

Quinn sighed. "She was icy and scathing and I had to eat a lot of humble pie. I explained I thought that perhaps my senses were just heightened thanks to you. You do play havoc with them since you got your Fey on." Cade smirked and Quinn grinned at him. "She finally put it to rest and she seems to like the idea I had for Daniel to get out of the position he's in. So it all ended well enough."

The door bell rung and both men looked at it in surprise.

"Expecting anyone?" Quinn asked as Cade went to answer the door.

Cade shook his head as he opened the door. "Nope. I—Ooof!" A large figure barrelled into the entrance, clasping Cade in a firm embrace, knocking him backward.

"Cade, baby. I was in the neighbourhood and thought I'd pop in to talk about the plans for the Scotland trip."

The smiling face of Cooper Evans seared itself into Quinn's mind like an unwelcome disease. His hands unclenched from battle mode as Quinn realised the threat was not that extreme and he scowled as Cade stepped back and untangled himself from the younger man's clutching limbs.

"Fucks sake, Coop, how many times have I told you not to bloody do that? Remember we talked about boundaries at work?" Cade's voice was censuring but he grinned. "I was just on my way out with Quinn."

Cooper shrugged and brandished his leather satchel. "Cade, we leave in a week's time for Crieff and we still have things to sort out. And work is just too damn busy to actually get anything done. So I thought I'd surprise you."

"You've certainly surprised *me*," Quinn muttered drily.

Cade flicked a wary look at him. "Let me sort this out with Coop and then we can maybe take that walk. I'm sure this won't take too long." He cast an apologetic look at Quinn.

Quinn shrugged. "Fine with me. I'll take myself off to the study and catch up on some work. You boys have fun." He turned and walked up the stairs.

*****

Cade watched his fiancé ascend the staircase and sighed. Quinn was still a little twitchy about him going away to Scotland with Cooper. He turned to Cooper, who was looking at him unabashedly.

"Cooper, you just have to stop bloody tackling me like that. You'll make my life a misery with Quinn. You know what's he's like."

"Oh, phooey." The younger man's eyes twinkled. "It's just a bit of fun. Monogamy was never meant to be in the gay man's repertoire, Cade. I don't think I've ever been exclusive in my life. I'm still enjoying the fact that the menu out there offers a lot of choice. Just the other day, I went off with the leather daddy—"

"Cooper, I really don't need to hear that," Cade exclaimed. "Hell, you have no shame. Come on into the kitchen. We can sit there and you can tell me what was so important you had to swing by."

Half an hour later, sitting on stools at the kitchen island and drinking coffee, Cade finally managed to finalise most of Cooper's outstanding preparations for the trip. Cade was rather excited about the whole thing. Four weeks of research, digging, exploring and getting passionate about his subject of the Picts was manna from heaven. And while he knew he'd miss Quinn, the fact that he could travel up and see him at any time using his Withinner was a warm thought that meant really, they'd probably be apart very little. Quinn could be needy when it came to his regular routine of lusty sex and intimacy with Cade.

Thinking about that, Cade smiled and turned to face Cooper to let him know he'd overstayed his welcome. Instead, what he got was a pair of hard, moist, eager lips pressed against his, wet tongue seeking entrance and hands already creeping down to his crotch to palm him roughly. Cade was so taken aback he let the man's mouth plunder his longer than he normally would have allowed until finally coming to his senses and pushing away the hungry lips and hands assaulting his body.

He propelled himself off the stool to stand further away. "Jesus, Cooper, what the fuck are you playing at?"

Cooper laughed and flipped his hands in a *"comme ci, comme ça"* gesture. But it was the loud inhuman growl from the kitchen door that made Cade look up in trepidation.

Quinn's thunderous face glowered like a dark storm. The most disturbing sight, though, was the image of Quinn's fingertips with blue sparks spitting from them. Cade knew exactly what that meant and it was an indication of Quinn's fury. He was manifesting Warlock traits in front of a human. In desperation for the situation not to get any worse and end up with a work colleague fried on the kitchen floor, Cade stood between Quinn and Cooper, flapping his hand at Quinn behind his back to calm down.

He addressed his grinning friend. "Cooper, I think you need to leave. Those boundaries we spoke about before? You just bloody crossed them. I suggest you take that libido of yours and go and find another leather daddy to quench it."

Cooper shrugged as he stepped from the stool and picked up his satchel with a laconic gesture, stuffing the papers from the kitchen table back into it.

"Hey, Cade, you're damned irresistible, what can I say? And you really do taste good."

He turned his back to fasten his satchel now perched on the table and Cade took the opportunity to move to Quinn and grasp his hands. Quinn stared at him, his eyes like flint.

"Quinn, Coop is leaving. Can you stand aside so he can go? Please? This whole 'bastion of the door' thing is starting to freak me out."

"I'd suggest he leave quickly before I deck him one," Quinn's voice was deathly quiet. "And there is no fucking way you're going with him to bloody Scotland."

Cade's ire at being summarily commanded flared. "Quinn, we'll talk about this. Don't blow a stupid, opportunistic kiss out of proportion. Cooper was just being an arsehole. And he won't get the opportunity to do it again, I can assure you."

"No, because I'm going to seal his lips shut and do the same to his dick—"

Cade reached up and placed a hand over Quinn's mouth. "Cooper, can I suggest you leave the fuck now before my fiancé does something he'll regret? I'll see you Monday at work. And believe me, we will talk about this stupid stunt. I thought you understood my position."

Cooper picked up his satchel and threw it over his shoulder as he moved toward the door. "Fine, Cade. Jeez, I just bloody kissed you, it's not like we fucked or anything." He smiled wickedly at an ever-tensing Quinn as Cade pulled his lover out of the doorway to allow Cooper exit. "I'm sorry, Quinn. I agree I messed up. I won't do it again. It's just that Cade has these amazing lips—"

"Cooper, leave. Now. You can see yourself out." Cade's fierce words spurned Cooper to action, and with a chuckle he waved an airy goodbye as he departed for the front door.

"See you Monday, Cade. I hope you're still going to be able to make our play date. Daddy seems pretty uptight about the whole thing." He disappeared and Cade closed his eyes in despair at the parting words. Trust Cooper to add fuel to the fire calling Quinn "Daddy." The part of him that wasn't trying to stop a Warlock King frying one of his friends into a blazing flesh ball was quite amused at the whole thing. But Cooper's irreverent attitude was going to cause all kinds of hurt for them both, from the look on Quinn's face.

"Quinn, Cooper was just being an idiot. Hell, he's just a kid really. Cut him some slack."

"Has he kissed you before? Groped you like he was doing here, in my own house?" Quinn's snarl was low.

Cade's hackles rose. "No, he hasn't. And I thought this was 'our' house? You're overreacting to this, Quinn. Just let it go."

Quinn's face darkened. "Let it go? That's the man you're planning on spending four weeks with on an 'archaeological' trip." He snorted. "At least that's what you tell me. He seemed pretty familiar with your lips."

Cade stared at Quinn in disbelief. "Quinn, you do so *not* want to go there." Anger rose in him like a steady tide of darkness taking him over. "I'll let that slide. This time."

He turned away and began banging coffee cups into the dishwasher. The air was heavy with tension as Cade tried to keep his temper at Quinn's unfair words at bay.

Since when have I ever given him any reason to suspect I'd cheat on him? The arrogant bastard.

He'd just finished loading the machine, something that was usually Quinn's chore, when Quinn spoke.

"Cade?" His fiancé's voice was quiet, hesitant. Cade ignored it as he switched on the dishwasher. "I'm sorry." Warm hands brushed against the back of Cade's hair. "I was wrong to say that. I know you'd never do anything with Cooper. I was just angry, seeing him touch you like that. You're right. I overreacted."

Cade turned around to see Quinn's face shadowed, his tawny eyes dark.

He ran a hand through his hair in exasperation. "Uh-huh. Just a tad. Honestly, for a man in charge of a world of bloody Warlocks and witches, fighting magyckal battles and not afraid of anything, you're damn insecure when it comes to me."

Quinn acquiesced with a nod of his head and a faint smile. "I won't argue with that. You're my one weakness, my Kryptonite."

Cade heard the vulnerability in Quinn's voice and a warmth suffused his body that Quinn felt that way about him. He walked over to Quinn and wrapped his arms around his waist, kissing him softly on the side of the neck.

"Quinn, what's going on with you? You've been a little at odds for the last few days. Is there something you want to tell me?"

Quinn's hands cupped his arse and drew him nearer as he nuzzled his ear. "There was something I wanted to talk to you about but I just haven't known how to broach the subject yet."

Cade took Quinn's hand and led him into the lounge. He sat down on the couch and patted the seat next to him. "Spill it. Tell me what has you so damned stressed out that you can't talk to me about it."

Quinn sat down, rested his arms on his knees and leaned forward. "Cade, I know it's only been sixteen months. I know we've been through a lot together and I know I damned well love you more than I've ever loved anyone before."

Cade's heart swelled at those words and he reached over to brush a strand of wayward hair from Quinn's cheek. Quinn grasped his hand and held it against his chest. "So I've been thinking about us getting married. I want to be able to call you my husband."

Cade hitched a breath. They'd only been engaged just over three months and Quinn was talking getting married already? He had no issue with it; he just wasn't sure why Quinn wanted to move so quickly.

"Why on earth would that be so difficult for you to say?" Cade asked gently. "You know I've already said yes to you," he flourished the golden ring on his hand, "so of course, if you want to get married now I'm all for it. 'Husband' has a great ring to it." He grinned. "It's not as if either of us has any huge family to involve, so it's all friends and colleagues. A wedding should be a cinch to organise without interfering mothers-in-law and well-meaning sisters."

Quinn nodded. "That's not all." He sounded ill at ease and Cade's mouth dropped.

What else could there be other than getting married?

"Cade, I'm thirty-eight next week." Cade knew Quinn's birthday wasn't a big deal for him although they'd planned a quiet dinner together just before Cade left for Scotland. "And I'm not getting any younger. You remember I said once that if the chance arose, I'd need to think about propagating the Fairmont line, making sure I had an heir? Well, that's been on my mind too."

Cade's head spun. "Wait, Quinn, hold on. You've been thinking about having children?"

Quinn nodded, his eyes lighting up. "Yes. I know it's still early and we don't have to make any decisions just yet, but Misty—you remember her, the witch that started the whole Book of Spells thing that led to us destroying the Witchfinder? Well, she and I have become good friends, very good friends actually, and she's offered to be a surrogate for us. The chances are with the magyckal alliances, it would be a well-conceived pregnancy and our son would be something really special."

Cade was having trouble keeping up with the tumble of words that were falling from his lover's lips as his arms waved animatedly and his face sparkled. He knew that Misty and Quinn had formed a friendship and they had yet to all have that dinner that had been scheduled before he'd been stabbed and given over to the Sprite world. Cade felt a sense of wonder that Quinn was so into the thought of having a child. To be honest, the idea was one Cade had occasionally thought about idly, as he wouldn't mind having one either. But this was all so sudden. Marriage and children all in one conversation?

Quinn's face fell. "Christ, I've just scared the hell out of you, haven't I? I'm sorry, I'm messing this up—"

Cade reached over and placed a finger on Quinn's lips. "Shh. You're not scaring me; it's just that it's a bit sudden. I had no idea you were contemplating this." A tingle of excitement ran through his body. "I mean, I love the idea of getting married and having kids, don't get me wrong. It's just...wow." He frowned at something Quinn had said.

"You said 'our son.' How do you know it would be a boy?"

Quinn smiled widely. "Fairmonts always have boys. It's just the way things are."

"And you'd trust Misty to carry our child? Well, your child, really, as it would be your sperm so that the birthright was truly Fairmont and I don't think they've got the capacity to have two sperms fertilise an egg yet—" Cade was aware he was babbling but the idea was growing on him.

"Cade, baby." Quinn reached over, his eyes filled with love. "It might be my sperm but this would be *our* child. I couldn't even think of doing this with anyone other than you."

Cade nodded, speechless now, and Quinn leaned in and kissed him, warm, hungry lips parting his as they lost themselves in their passion. When they finally pulled apart, Quinn was smiling.

"So what do you think? Can I start make wedding plans so we can get married and think about becoming dads together sometime in the near future?"

Cade's eyes prickled with tears as he nodded. "Hell yes. I can't think of anything better. I think I'm going to bloody cry."

Quinn chuckled and pulled him closer, planting a soft kiss on the top of his head as Cade closed his eyes and listened to his man's heartbeat. "Well, while you're away I'll get someone at the office to start making some enquiries. I have no idea how long it takes to organise a decent wedding, but we can talk about it when you get back from Scotland. I'll arrange dinner with Misty too so you can meet her, get to know her like I do. And Cade, I do trust you. And I'm sorry I lost it. I love you."

"I love you too, Quinn. And you need not worry about Coop. You're the only man for me, you know that. In fact, I'm thinking it's about time you made it up to me with actions, not words." Cade stood up and extended a hand to Quinn who grinned and took it as he got to his feet.

"Why, Mr. Mairston, you little slut. I'd be happy to."

Chapter 31

The cold wind howled across the vast expanse of water in Crieff, in the highlands of Scotland, causing it to ripple as the surrounding conifers swayed fiercely. Cade sat by the roaring log fire in his cabin. The cabin he was staying in on the spectacular Loch Manzievaird was beautiful and luxurious but simply the high keening sound of the wind outside was enough to make him shiver. The past few weeks had been hectic to say the least, as the anthropological team he was part of put their research hats on and travelled the area anxious to pursue the history of the Picts, particularly the saga of the ninth-century Pict King Kenneth MacAlpin. It had been a fairly intensive project and Cade was glad it was coming to an end in two days. He'd be glad to get home.

Cooper had been warned in no uncertain terms that Cade was off limits and in fact, his original ardour seemed to have cooled somewhat. Cade had seen him making out with some young twink in a rowboat on the Loch only two days before.

Quinn of course was inordinately satisfied at this turn of events. "You can't trust these younger men," he'd murmured smugly the last time he'd appeared in Cade's cabin. "Fickle fellows, they are."

Cade waited now for Quinn to appear on what he called laughingly his "conjugal visit" and he smiled at the thought of seeing him again. The fire was burning, the logs stacked up to keep it burning, and the red wine was currently breathing on the table. There was the familiar disconcerting change in the air as Quinn's Withinner transported him up to the Highlands of Scotland from their cosy home in Hampstead Heath. Cade turned to see Taliesin standing behind him, his dark face smiling, his eyes warm.

"Taliesin, it's good to see you again." Cade moved over and they shook hands. The Fey urges the pair had originally experienced had disappeared altogether from their first rather raunchy meeting, although Cade's face still flushed in sheer embarrassment when he saw him. The Withinner looked pleased and bowed slightly.

"It is good to see you too, Cade. I asked Quinn for this time together so I could present you with something." He rummaged around in his cloak and pulled out a small item that looked like the muslin pods used to make mulled wine. He placed it in Cade's hand.

"This is a good luck charm for the marriage. It has been enchanted to wish you personally all my best wishes for the coming nuptials with Quinn." He grinned sardonically. "You are going to need it, probably more than one bag if truth be told."

Cade chuckled loudly. "Thank you, that's a lovely thought. I think you're right on the needing luck part."

The two men grinned at each other conspiratorially. Taliesin grinned. "You are looking well. I wish I could say the same for Quinn. He seems very moody the last few days with all his wedding plans."

Cade guffawed in amusement. "Really? My big bad Quinn is stressing over wedding favours and venues?" Quinn had been emailing Cade with suggestions put forward by his team of QuinnCo virtual employees serving as wedding planners so Cade could be involved from the start. Cade quite enjoyed all the preparation work and decision making.

The Withinner nodded. "He has been short tempered and rather testy." He grinned. "Quinn is impatient to get here. He revokes me. I wish you well and look forward to meeting you again."

The air changed slightly and as Cade watched, his future husband appeared in front of him. He had to admit Quinn looked a little haggard.

Quinn smiled at him. "God, it's good to be here again. I missed you."

He leaned forward to give Cade a bear hug.

Cade kissed him deeply, his hands wrapping around his waist. "It's only been three days," he said wryly.

Quinn chuckled. "I know. I had some business to take care of yesterday that took a while." He made his way over to the table lit up by the flickering flames of the fire and poured two glasses of red wine. He handed one to Cade.

"Is everything still on track for you to come home on Friday?" Quinn's voice was hopeful.

"Still the plan. Then I'll be able to help you more with the wedding plans. I understand from Taliesin that you may be showing some signs of stress?" Cade said slyly.

Quinn flushed. "It's no big deal," his fiancé growled as he sipped his wine and sat down on the sofa by the fire. "I'm perfectly capable of organising our wedding in your absence. It's my employees who are testing my patience with their endless questions. What about this colour, these flowers, these centrepieces. Perhaps we should get married in the registry office then swan off to some Caribbean island for an extended honeymoon…"

He looked at Cade hopefully. Cade ignored the entreaty. This was his first and —he hoped—only wedding and while it wasn't some huge celebrity bash worthy of appearing in *OK!* or *Now* magazine, the lure of having a Wiccan-Warlock ceremony with he and Quinn exchanging vows and the resulting festivities was too much for him to resist. Besides, he was getting the honeymoon anyway as a wedding present from Quinn.

Quinn scowled as he realised Cade wasn't falling for his plan. He took off his shoes and socks, chucking them carelessly at the side of the sofa as he settled back comfortably on the couch. He closed his eyes and Cade sat down next to him and caressed his hair. He'd always thought his man was a definite Leo the way he loved his hair stroked.

"How did your business meeting go?" he asked as his lips slowly nibbled Quinn's ear. "Was it all about Barton Sinclair again?"

Quinn nodded. "The stupid bastard has formed his own organisation and appointed himself as 'Worshipful Master.' What a crap bloody title. He has his little sycophant there, Troy Cavanaugh as well as a few other misguided tossers that don't know their arse from the elbow."

"But he does have a large following," Cade said quietly. "He could be trouble for you."

Quinn sighed as his eyes opened and he looked at him. "Yes, he could be trouble. But I'll have to deal with it seeing as how I'm the one who caused it in the first place. But I'm not going to worry about that until something actually happens. For now, let him build his little empire. Mine's bigger."

Cade shook his head at the satisfaction in Quinn's voice. "You are so bloody arrogant," he whispered, as his tongue delved into Quinn's ear, making him shiver. "I love it when you're so masterful."

"I'm glad you like it," Quinn murmured, his voice husky. "I've got a few plans to be just that later on." His eyes closed again and he sighed in content.

"How's Daniel?" Cade asked.

Quinn's eyes flicked open. "Daniel is finally safe in RAW and managing to play the spy even better than before now that he's on his own turf. Everything seems to have worked out for the best and

Valensia is doing her bit to help. She seems to have really taken to him."

He laughed softly. "But Daniel is playing with fire." He stretched his long frame, raising his arms above his head and yawning. "He's seeing Valensia despite my warnings and the man is going to come off second best. But he thinks he knows better. I think he plans on bringing on her to the wedding reception as his plus one. That'll be a hoot." He chuckled.

Cade slapped his shoulder with a frown. "The man's having some fun, for God's sake. What's wrong with that?"

"The man is almost twice her age. She's a witch, he's a human. She's a conniving and complicated woman and he's a decent man. You can't tell me that's not a recipe for disaster." Quinn scowled fiercely. "I just don't want him getting hurt."

"Daniel is a grown man. Let him make his own decisions and fate." Cade whispered seductively in his ear. "You're not perhaps a little jealous, are you? I mean, that she might want him for her sex slave now instead of you?"

Quinn opened his eyes and Cade shivered at the predatory look in them.

"Cade, my sexy Sprite," he said silkily as his arms pulled him closer, onto his lap, facing him. "You're *my* sex slave. I have no need of anyone else and I definitely mean to prove that later tonight. I even brought the ties with me." He reached into his jeans pocket and Cade gasped as Quinn pulled out the four red ribbons they'd used in a previous bondage session.

Quinn grinned. "That lovely wooden bed over there is not going to know what hit it," he whispered softly, as his tongue trailed down the side of Cade's throat and licked the pulse flickering in his throat. Cade moaned softly.

"Perhaps you should take your clothes off," Quinn murmured. "And I'll do the same."

Cade stood up and slipped his sweatpants and boxers off, leaving them in a pile on the floor. He tugged off his tee shirt and that too was thrown unceremoniously into the corner. Quinn stood up and unbuttoned his jeans, stepping out of them fluidly and reaching up to take off his blue sweatshirt in one quick, catlike movement.

He stood naked before Cade, his eyes assessing him, and then Quinn sat back down on the couch, legs spread, motioning with an imperious gesture for Cade to get on top of him. Cade noticed Quinn was definitely ready for the night's event. His lazy grin as he stroked himself idly made Cade's blood heat up and his throat dry. Cade loved it when his lover was like this. This was the one area in their relationship that he loved Quinn's arrogant, dominant side and his man played it so well.

Cade moved onto Quinn's lap, straddling him and reaching for the lube. He opened the tube, squeezing it onto his fingers and reached around to open himself up.

Quinn grinned. "Nuh-uh. Tonight I want you inside me."

Cade was always more than happy to make his slow languorous way inside Quinn's body, feeling his lover clench tight muscles around him and drive him crazy with lust. It happened often enough, although Cade's preference was having Quinn's cock thrusting into him with either slow, teasing moves or powerhouse drives that made him beg for more. Tonight though, from the look in Quinn's eyes, it was Cade's turn to be the pile driver.

Cade reached over and took Quinn's lips in a passionate kiss, as teeth clicked together and greedy tongues played a game of catch inside each other's mouths. Finally, panting, they drew apart and Cade moved off Quinn and pushed him onto his back.

"Just lie back and enjoy, lover boy," he murmured as his fingers slid their way inside his fiancé and Quinn's breath caught, face lighting up with pleasure. Soon there was only the slow, languid movements of two bodies so in tune with each other that it became an opus of passion and lust, heated bodies rubbing against one another until that sweet, intense climax when both of them exploded with their need and desire to be as one. It was this melding of minds and bodies that took Cade's breath away, that made his heart beat frantically in his sweaty chest and made his groin heat up in sheer abandon and release. The feeling of coming inside Quinn was primal, and Cade revelled in hearing his lover's cry as his head arched back and his hips thrust upward as he came. Finally, Cade lay spent against the stickiness of Quinn's stomach and chest hair, matted with come, as he watched his lover's face slowly relax and the eyes that only a moment ago had been black pools of desire turn soft with glances of love and possession.

Quinn looked at him from hooded eyes, in which flames from the firelight flickered. "Cade, do you think you could get off me? I'm bloody freezing and your skin has gone all goose bumpy. I think we should sneak in under the bed covers now and keep each other warm." Quinn grinned and Cade moved off him. Quinn stood up and threw more logs on the fire, causing it to hiss and spit as the flames reared up. He padded naked over to the bed and drew back the covers, looking at Cade wickedly. "Don't forget to bring those ribbons over here," he said huskily. "I've a definite need to do something with them later."

Cade chuckled as he watched Quinn crawl under the goose-down duvet and settle back with a sigh of contentment.

Could this get any better? He thought to himself. *Quinn in my bed, becoming my husband when I get home, a plan for a child underway and an evening of what looks to be fairly strenuous and exciting sex with the man of my dreams.*

Cade stood for a while, naked in the cabin with the log fire roaring and the wind howling outside and simply embraced what his life had become. He had never felt so complete.

"Are you coming to bed?" Quinn's eyes were dark as he watched him, and his gentle smile told Cade without words just how much he loved him.

"Yes, I'm coming to bed. I was just thinking how lucky I am."

Quinn spoke quietly. "Ralph Waldo Emerson said, 'Shallow men believe in luck or in circumstance. Strong men believe in cause and effect.' To me, nothing happens by chance. You and I were meant to be together. It was no accident meeting on the heath all that time ago."

Cade climbed into bed beside Quinn and burrowed into his shoulder as Quinn's arm went around him, stroking his hair softly. "I love you, Cade, heart and soul. You're the one I've been waiting for all my life. You've helped me banish a lot of demons and given me your unconditional love and for that, I will always be grateful. And now we're going to become fathers together and that's just a miracle I'd never really seen coming."

Cade reached up and touched Quinn's face tenderly. "I love *you* with everything I've got. You are my rock and my world and I could never think of having a life without you. And having a child is just going to make that love stronger. We're going to be a family, and I love the sound of that."

Quinn laughed softly. "I think we should use these words in our wedding vows. I still have to write something and until now I was struggling to find the right words."

"God, I'd forgotten about that. I've nothing either." Cade nestled closer against him, his hands running through the hair on Quinn's chest as his lips gently kissed his shoulder. The cabin was filled with the sounds of the night storm outside as it began to rain, the drops plopping down onto the roof and running down the windows in icy rivulets. Outside, the sounds of the tree branches rustling as they were battered in the wind was calming. There was a distant sound of thunder.

"I love it here but I'll be glad to get home," Cade murmured. "I'm looking forward to being your husband. Mr. Cade Mairston-Fairmont. It has a good sound to it. Almost royal."

Quinn moved his arm from behind and moved toward Cade as he half covered his body with his, the red silk ties he held in his hand teasingly trailing them across his stomach. Cade stared into his eyes, seeing them darken as Quinn's pupils grew wider and he shivered in anticipation for what he was promising.

"Time to put these to good use, Cade," he purred. "I've been looking forward to this all day. My turn to be inside you now."

Cade saw the desire in his eyes and as he reached out for him, he sighed and waited for Quinn to work his magyck.

The End

AUTHOR'S NOTES

The beautiful village of Mistley in Manningtree in Essex, the county I live in, features quite a bit in this series. It's a serene, coastal town where the Witchfinder General, Matthew Hopkins, is supposed to be buried. You can find out a bit more about it and Matthew here:

http://www.visit-manningtree.co.uk/places/mistley.html
http://en.wikipedia.org/wiki/Matthew_Hopkins

Taliesin was a great (and real-life) bard who lived in the sixth century. If you're interested in finding out a little more about this enigmatic man then is the place to go.

http://en.wikipedia.org/wiki/Taliesin

ABOUT THE AUTHOR

Sue Mac Nicol was born in Leeds, Yorkshire, in the United Kingdom. At the age of eight she moved with her family to Johannesburg, South Africa, where she stayed for nearly thirty years before arriving back in the UK in December 2000. The first year Sue was back in the UK, it snowed on her birthday, as it did the day she was born in 19—cough—and she swears this was England welcoming her back.

Sue's career has mostly been in the financial services area, and she specialises in what she calls "boring" compliance and regulatory work. That's why she escapes into the world of writing and fantasy where she chats to her characters ad nauseum and is overjoyed when they reply. It beats the monotony of legalese, contracts and legislation—and let's face it, writing hot scenes between men can only be rewarding.

Sue's M/M Romance books, *Stripped Bare*, *Saving Alexander*, *Worth Keeping* and *Waiting for Rain* have all hit various bestseller lists, a fact that continues to awe and humble her. Sue is a PAN member of Romance Writers of America and a member of the Romantic Novelists Association in the UK. She lives in the quaint village of Bocking in Essex, set in the countryside and not far from the sea should she get the yen to eat oysters.

Did you enjoy this book? Drop us a line and say so! We love to hear from readers, and so do our authors. To connect, visit www.boroughspublishinggroup.com online, send comments directly to info@boroughspublishinggroup.com, or friend us on Facebook and Twitter. And be sure to check back regularly for contests and new releases in your favorite subgenres of romance!

Are you an aspiring writer? Check out www.boroughspublishinggroup.com/submit and see if we can help you make your dreams come true.